Praise for the novels of Maisey Yates

"Yates brings her signature heat and vivid western details to another appealing story in the excellent Gold Valley series... Fans of Kate Pearce should enjoy this."
—*Booklist* on *Rodeo Christmas at Evergreen Ranch*

"[A] surefire winner not to be missed."
—*Publishers Weekly* on *Slow Burn Cowboy* (starred review)

"This fast-paced, sensual novel will leave readers believing in the healing power of love."
—*Publishers Weekly* on *Down Home Cowboy*

"Yates' new Gold Valley series begins with a sassy, romantic and sexy story about two characters whose chemistry is off the charts."
—*RT Book Reviews* on *Smooth-Talking Cowboy* (Top Pick)

"Multidimensional and genuine characters are the highlight of this alluring novel, and sensual love scenes complete it. Yates's fans...will savor this delectable story."
—*Publishers Weekly* on *Unbroken Cowboy* (starred review)

"Fast-paced and intensely emotional.... This is one of the most heartfelt installments in this series, and Yates's fans will love it."
—*Publishers Weekly* on *Cowboy to the Core* (starred review)

"Yates's outstanding eighth Gold Valley contemporary... will delight newcomers and fans alike.... This charming and very sensual contemporary is a must for fans of passion."
—*Publishers Weekly* on *Cowboy Christmas Redemption*

D0205148

Also by Maisey Yates

Confessions from the Quilting Circle
Secrets from a Happy Marriage
The Lost and Found Girl

Four Corners Ranch

Unbridled Cowboy
Merry Christmas Cowboy
Cowboy Wild

Gold Valley

Smooth-Talking Cowboy
Untamed Cowboy
Good Time Cowboy
A Tall, Dark Cowboy Christmas
Unbroken Cowboy
Cowboy to the Core
Lone Wolf Cowboy
Cowboy Christmas Redemption
The Bad Boy of Redemption Ranch
The Hero of Hope Springs
The Last Christmas Cowboy
The Heartbreaker of Echo Pass
Rodeo Christmas at Evergreen Ranch
The True Cowboy of Sunset Ridge

For more books by Maisey Yates,
visit www.maiseyyates.com.

MAISEY YATES

Cowboy Wild

HQN

HQN

ISBN-13: 978-1-335-60096-7

Recycling programs for this product may not exist in your area.

Cowboy Wild
Copyright © 2023 by Maisey Yates

Her Wayward Cowboy
Copyright © 2023 by Maisey Yates

This is a work of fiction. Names, characters, places and incidents are either the product of the author's imagination or are used fictitiously. Any resemblance to actual persons, living or dead, businesses, companies, events or locales is entirely coincidental.

For questions and comments about the quality of this book, please contact us at CustomerService@Harlequin.com.

HQN
22 Adelaide St. West, 41st Floor
Toronto, Ontario M5H 4E3, Canada
www.Harlequin.com

Printed and bound in Barcelona, Spain by CPI Black Print

CONTENTS

COWBOY WILD

CHAPTER ONE

ELSIE GARRETT HAD quite literally been born in a barn. And she felt like it was a metaphor for her entire life. She was comfortable with the outdoors. Comfortable with dirt, hard work and horses. She was less comfortable with the Friday night bar scene in Smokey's Tavern. Oh, she was comfortable enough with beer. With fried food and hanging out with her best friend. But she was a lot less comfortable with the male-female dynamic. More specifically the fact that everyone around her was clearly here to hook up. Well, everyone except her friend Alaina, who was also just here for the onion rings.

"He's the most beautiful man I've ever seen in my life."

Or maybe not.

Elsie looked at her best friend, whose tone had become that of a dreamy, lovelorn schoolgirl, and followed her gaze across the crowded bar. She grimaced when she saw exactly whom Alaina was staring at.

Six foot four of dark-haired, overly muscled, square-jawed cowboy.

Broad shouldered, in a tight black T-shirt—that was just tight for show because there was no earthly reason for him to buy them that small—blue jeans and a black hat.

"Honestly," Elsie said, wrinkling her nose. "I don't understand what head injury has induced this fascination with *Hunter* all of a sudden."

Hunter McCloud was infuriating.

And Elsie knew that better than most. He was her older brother Sawyer's best friend, and she had practically grown up with him in their house. She was beginning to work with him on an equestrian program at McCloud's Landing—the plot of land adjacent to Garrett's Watch, her family's parcel of land that made up a quarter of Four Corners Ranch. And she did not understand why Alaina—who knew him about half as well as Elsie, but still well enough—should suddenly find him so compelling.

Elsie thought he was *too much*. Too big, too broad. His jaw too rough-looking from stubble, his hands too rough from work. His energy too…intrusive. He rubbed her the wrong way and that was fine. She didn't hate him or anything. But she didn't see why her friend was obsessed.

"Maturity," Alaina said.

"Really? Is that what you call it?" She let her eyes linger on him and for some reason found it difficult to look away. "I mean, I'm not going to pretend that he isn't *handsome*." Because it would be churlish and an outright lie to deny it, but just saying it made a strange sort of prickling sensation line her throat. "But he's…"

He was currently across the room, chatting up a blonde girl in a pair of tight jeans. She was not from around here, and neither were her friends.

Elsie knew everyone who was from around here.

There weren't that many of them.

Blondie's friends were the kind of women her brothers would've been chatting up only a few months before. But not now. Because they were all settled. Which was the strangest thing. She had never thought that Sawyer or Wolf would ever end up domesticated.

She didn't think she ever would be. She just didn't see the point of it.

Good for Sawyer and Wolf, though. They were happier than she'd ever seen them. And she preferred them being at home with their wives to having to watch them pick up women in the bar she was in.

"What?" Alaina asked, taking a drink of her beer and keeping her eyes pinned to Hunter.

"Just like those men are," Elsie said, leaning back in her seat and crossing her arms. "Look at him. He's going to pick her up and take her back to his place. And he won't even remember her name tomorrow."

"No," Alaina agreed, looking down into her beer. "He won't. But I bet she'll have a good time."

Elsie shot her friend a look out of the corner of her eye. "What do you know about that kind of good time?"

"Nothing," Alaina said, sighing. "Absolutely nothing. But Hunter McCloud is the kind of guy that would be fun to learn from."

The idea of her best friend in the world learning about sex from Hunter—her best friend in the world's only intimate sex knowledge coming from *Hunter*—made her want to be dead.

Because Alaina would want to *tell* her about it and against her will Elsie would want to know.

Not because it was Hunter.

Because she knew *nothing*.

She'd never seen a naked man.

Well, she'd seen the blurred impression of naked men running down to the watering hole to jump in and skinny-dip on a hot summer day, but that wasn't the same thing.

Elsie would be curious and compelled to ask, and then she'd be forced to picture...

Ugh. And no.

"Not a good idea," Elsie said. "You have to see him all the time."

"So what?" Alaina asked. "It doesn't have to be a big deal."

"Oh, I agree," Elsie said. "I'm just not about to…throw my unfettered support behind you trying out sex on *Hunter McCloud*."

"Because you don't like him," Alaina pointed out.

Elsie frowned. "That's not true. I like him." She wouldn't be able to deal with him if she didn't like him. She liked him in that way that… He was more like family. She was stuck with him more than anything else.

"And your feelings on the new ranch hand at Garrett's Watch?" Alaina smiled sweetly.

Elsie waved her hand. "Different story altogether. First of all, he's probably a temporary addition to the ranch."

"You think?"

"Anyone that good-looking is not going to stay for very long. He's single. He's going to find the pool of women to be regrettably shallow."

"And?"

Elsie sharpened her gaze. "I'm going to make a move."

"Really?" Alaina looked skeptical.

"Yes. That's why coming to the bar is useful," she said, looking around the place. Pretty much everyone here was looking for a good time. And she figured there was definitely information to be gleaned from watching the proceedings.

Elsie herself was overly familiar with cowboys. She knew all about them. She'd grown up in a house filled with them. She worked with them, all day every day. She knew how to relate to them in the same way that she related to Alaina. She knew how to talk to them. What she didn't know was how to flirt with them.

She didn't know how to flirt at all.

Normally, that didn't bother her. But the notable changes in her family had made her pretty conscious of her...well, the lack of movement in her own life. She didn't care much about men, not in that way.

Until Travis Young had wandered onto the property.

He was the prettiest man she'd ever seen.

He had clear blue eyes like the sky, and thick blond hair. He was lean and just about an inch taller than she was.

He smiled easily, and laughed easily too.

He made her feel *fluttery*.

It was nice to feel that way. It was...fun.

And she had decided that she would really like to figure out that whole man-woman thing.

One thing she was smart enough to realize was that it wasn't as simple as gaining the trust of an animal. She couldn't just walk up to him, let him smell her hand and offer him a carrot. That might work with recalcitrant horses, but it wasn't going to be the way that she connected with a man. Which was a pity because she had a hell of a lot of carrots.

Hunter took the woman out on the crowded dance floor— which was really just a small section of the bar that had tables and chairs pushed away, with the jukebox in the corner—and pulled her against him.

The woman looked absolutely elated to be the center of his attention. Elsie frowned.

Hunter didn't have any particular skill set that she could see, other than looks. And women just... Women were ridiculous over him. Not even Alaina was immune. Which she found completely annoying.

Alaina was chewing her lip and watching Hunter and the blonde with irritation sparking in her eyes.

And what Elsie really hoped was that Alaina didn't do

anything embarrassing. One thing about Alaina that Elsie admired was that her friend was all-in on whatever feelings she was having in a given moment. And she was a fighter. When Alaina wanted something, she went for it with all the conviction in her body—and it was a lot of conviction.

Alaina was all passion.

But Elsie also worried about her friend getting hurt.

"I don't want a local guy," Elsie said. "They'll treat me like I'm a kid anyway. I've known them for too long."

"Well," Alaina said, "that is a hazard of living in a town this small, there's pretty much no way to avoid knowing everybody. And we all went to a one-room schoolhouse. Mystery is a little bit hard to come by."

"Agreed."

"That's why I like Hunter," Alaina said. "He's not part of our class, you know? He's older."

"As old as *my brother*," Elsie said, wrinkling her nose.

"Your brothers are both also hot, Els," Alaina said, grinning.

"Ew."

Alaina shrugged and ate a fry. "Facts are facts. Sexy is sexy."

"Whatever. I don't want to date a boy we grew up with either." As in, sat next to in that one-room schoolhouse they'd gone to. No, the very idea appalled her. "I want some mystery. It's rare."

The town of Pyrite Falls, Oregon, was tiny, and Four Corners ranch—four ranches operated in together by the Garrett, King, McCloud and Sullivan families—was even more insular.

They worked on the ranch, they lived on the ranch, they'd gone to school on the ranch.

As kids there had been a lot of workers' kids to play

with—but not many had stayed more than a couple of years. Only the four primary families were truly constant.

Four Corners was its own world, and Elsie loved it—but it had also kept her oddly sheltered. They'd had their share of hardships—Elsie's mother hadn't stuck around, her dad had died when she saw young, so in some ways she was an old soul. Much older than her actual twenty-four years.

In others…she felt much, much younger.

Only recently had it occurred to her that the steady rotation of ranch hands could be useful. They had a lot of young men come and go. And many of them had been handsome enough. And hadn't known her since she was an actual baby.

But Travis was the first one to really, truly catch her eye.

"True. But *you're* not exactly mysterious, Elsie," Alaina said.

"What you mean?"

"You say everything you think."

Elsie wrinkled her nose. "So?"

"I don't think men like that."

Elsie sighed. "No offense, Alaina, but you don't know what men like."

"Boobs," Alaina said pragmatically.

Elsie snorted. "So, do I just go up and flash him?" She thought back to her earlier ruminations on baiting horses and blinked rapidly. "Are boobs the carrot?"

"The carrot?"

"That's how you get horses."

Alaina looked at her like she was a tragedy. "You are a strange girl, Elsie Garrett."

"Well, we both know more about horses than we do about men." And generally, Elsie was okay with that. But right now… Less.

She looked back over at Hunter, who had his arms wrapped around the woman now, and he was kissing her. The blonde arched her whole body forward, her boobs crushed against Hunter's chest as she returned his kiss with reckless enthusiasm. And in spite of herself, Elsie found herself tilting her head slightly, as the woman did.

Heat prickled all over Elsie's skin. She did not want to see that. His large hands moved over the woman's body, and there was a curve to his lips, even as he kissed her.

A little bit wicked.

Mysterious.

No.

That shook her out of the weird trance she'd fallen into. "Okay," Elsie said, bringing her beer bottle down hard on the table. It was still half-full, but she and Alaina cared more about people watching than drinking. "I am done with bar time."

Alaina looked over at the dance floor too, and grimaced. "Me too. I'm okay with the fact that he's gonna hook up, but I don't actually need to *see* him with someone else."

"That is the state of Hunter McCloud, Alaina," Elsie said, because she knew Hunter. Because he wasn't mysterious at all. Because she was actually pretty expert on the guy. Hazard of him being her older brother's best friend, and him always being around. "There's always someone else. Don't take it too personally. And don't get too caught up in him."

"Too late for me," Alaina said, sounding mopey.

Good. Mopey Alaina was fine.

It was angry Alaina everyone had to fear.

They had driven separately, and Elsie waved Alaina off while she went to the bar to pay the tab. She looked back over at Hunter, and didn't see him at all. She wondered if he had gone off with her already.

She frowned. It was a lot like watching her brothers hook

up, really. That was why it irritated her. She didn't want to see that. Not ever.

The door opened, and she turned around as cool air whipped inside. And it was Travis. Her heart bumped against her sternum, her hands going shaky. And she paused. She felt a little bit guilty because she had told Alaina that she was leaving. But maybe she would stay. Maybe, she would stay.

She walked across the room, and he saw her, jerking his head upward and smiling. "Hey there, Elsie."

She fluttered.

Every bit of her.

"Hi," she said, squaring her shoulders and standing up straight and trying not to show that she was fluttering. "What brings you out tonight?"

His mouth quirked up into a half smile. "Same as everybody else, I expect."

Same as…

Oh my.

Was this it? Was this flirting? She didn't know how to tell the difference between flirting and talking.

Except her face felt red. So maybe that was it.

"Right. Me too."

"Good. I'm meeting someone, actually. I'll see you tomorrow." And he walked off, crossed the room and went right over to the compatriot of Hunter's friend. And she felt… singed.

The girl, a redhead with long, bouncy curls, leaned in and kissed Travis on the neck, and everything in Elsie went cold.

The girl swirled around and laughed, and was generally adorable, effortlessly capturing and maintaining Travis's attention.

And she really wished that she had left. In fact, she was going to.

"You're not leaving already are you, Elsie?"

SOMETHING HAD STOPPED Hunter McCloud from leaving with the particularly bubbly beauty he'd had on his arm earlier. She had been irritated at him, but he just hadn't been in the mood. He'd *thought* he was, but he wasn't.

Hunter wasn't one to think about his actions all that deeply. He did what he wanted. He didn't do what he didn't.

But now he knew why he'd stayed. Because Elsie Garrett was standing at the bar looking a whole lot like she'd been kicked in the stomach. And he didn't like that. If Elsie was going to be annoyed, he preferred to be the source of it. But the look on her face now… No, he didn't like that at all.

"Yeah," she said, "just going."

She didn't act surprised to see him. Or happy. Which meant she had realized he was there already. And hell, Elsie was never all that happy to see him. Or at least, she pretended not to be. She was a feisty little cat, was Elsie. He had a feeling that being a grumpy hellion was how she showed affection.

"The night is young," he said.

She huffed. "The night is sagging and halfway to toothless in my opinion," she said.

"Well, that's a bit harsh." She looked behind him, her eyes going sharp. And he followed her gaze.

He saw Travis, the new ranch hand, with that redhead—he thought her name might be Jessica, but sometimes when he couldn't remember a woman's name he just decided she was Jessica or Sarah and he had pretty good odds of being right depending on how old they were.

"Oh, I see," he said. "Ginger Barbie over there has your man?"

Her eyes widened, then narrowed. "Hunter," she said, scowling, her cheeks turning bright red.

Well, shit. "So she does," he said.

Her lip curled. "I don't give a damn about Travis," she said. "And I don't have a man."

It was clear she *did* in fact give several damns about Travis.

"You in the market for one?"

"Stop being such a pain in the butt," she said.

She turned away from the bar and started to head toward the door. He caught her arm. "Don't leave now," he said.

"Why?"

"Because. You're not going to let her chase you off. And you're not going to act bothered."

"But I'm bothered," she said.

Oh, bless her. Her eyebrows went down, her mouth going into a pout. She didn't help much, Elsie. But, when she did, it reminded him of when she was a kid. "I know you're bothered," he said. "But honey—" he reached out and tipped her chin up "—you have to act like you're not."

"How come?"

"Because you don't want to let him know that he affected you."

"He won't notice or care."

"Okay, sure. Maybe if you leave he won't notice or care. But if you hang out tonight, he might just look over and see you having fun. And look, she's real pretty, that woman he's with. Had I not been interested in a blonde tonight, I might have gone redhead. I can see the appeal. But I bet she can't run a barrel racing course in ten seconds flat. And I bet she's not one of the best horse wranglers around."

She reluctantly looked pleased. "You think I'm one of the best horse wranglers around?"

"If I didn't, you wouldn't be hired to the ranch work at McCloud's, would you?"

His family had a fine equine operation, breeding some of the finest animals in the state, with a view to expand to equine therapy—his brother Gus's idea. Bringing Elsie on was absolutely a testament to her skill.

She sniffed, a sad-sounding sniff. "To be quite honest, I thought you were doing my brother a favor."

"No. I don't like the son of a bitch *that* much."

"You don't?"

"I don't like anybody that much. I don't give pity work. Not when it comes to my ranch. Not when it comes to my horses. It's about the only thing on God's green earth I take seriously."

And that was the truth. Hunter didn't care much about anything. But he did take his work at McCloud's Landing seriously. And he most especially took work with his horses seriously.

"Come on," he said, split-second decision. "Let's dance."

"No," Elsie said, looking horrified.

"You dance at the town hall meetings all the time."

"Not here. Not with you."

"Is that any way to treat your savior?"

"Did your girlfriend reject you, Hunter?"

"Now, Elsie, you know that I don't have girlfriends."

Another truth.

She shot him a very narrow gaze, but ended up following him out to the makeshift dance floor. The music was upbeat, and he grabbed her hand and twirled her. She smiled, and he could tell that she didn't really want to smile. Elsie's hands weren't smooth. Not like the woman he'd been dancing with earlier.

But then, Elsie was a cowgirl.

Her work, her passion, was in those calluses on her hands. And when he wasn't giving her a hard time, he found her damned respectable. He hadn't been lying when he'd said that she was the best horse wrangler around. It was true. It was unorthodox for a member of one family to be working at the ranch of another.

Typically, they stuck to their own corners.

But Elsie was good enough that he wanted her there for the expansion of their equestrian facility.

Even Gus said she was that good. And it was a known truth that Angus McCloud was too cranky a bastard to compliment someone just for fun.

Elsie was great with the horses, and additionally, he felt like it would be beneficial to have a woman on hand. The McClouds were all men, and with the therapy program they'd be doing, a woman would likely be necessary. The music slowed and he pulled her closer, and she stumbled back.

"I'm hot," she said.

"All right," he said.

He walked back to the bar with her. "Beer?"

"Sprite," she said.

Her cheeks were red. She took hold of the Sprite and started to drink it quickly. And she looked furtively back over at Travis.

Hunter touched her chin, and diverted her focus back toward him. Her brows knit together. She looked at him, shock and something else in brown her eyes.

He dropped his hand back down to his side—quickly— and took a step away from her, rubbing his fingers together because they felt strange.

"Don't do that," he said. "Don't look at him for the rest of the night."

Elsie shifted. "Well then, how will I know if he saw me?"

"Believe me, you will. Eventually."

Frankly, Hunter thought that guy was not all that much to get worked up about. He'd interacted with him a couple times.

He seemed…young. Stupid.

Didn't have the kind of steady hand or fortitude with animals that Hunter liked to see. Not that he was a terrible cowboy or anything like that. Just a new one. Greenhorn. And Hunter had no real patience for greenhorns. But hell, if Elsie did, that was her business. He didn't particularly like the idea of his best friend's sister getting it on with some wet-behind-the-ears kid who probably didn't know readily how to find a woman's clit, but it wasn't his business. And nothing about Elsie's body was his concern at all.

"You're an expert, are you?"

"Elsie, I think you know I am."

"Master of the casual bar hookup?"

He shrugged a shoulder. "Never pretended I wasn't."

"Fine. So, you have pointers, then?"

"I'm giving them to you, you salty little wench."

She shot him a furious look. "I am not salty. And I'm not a wench."

"I'll let you argue with me about being a wench, but you are for sure salty."

"Fine. Then I want you to give me pointers and help me land him."

"You want me to give you pointers, and help you land him?"

"That's what I said." She glowered at him. "There is no need to repeat me."

"I had to make sure that I heard you right."

"I'm helping you with your new equine therapy endeavor," she pointed out.

"You were hired to do a job."

"But I'm helping. You need me, and you value my input, right?"

"Elsie, if I'm going to help you, then you have to value *my* input. And, also not tell Sawyer that I'm helping you hook up."

Sawyer would literally kill him, and under other circumstances…well, if Sawyer and Wolf weren't recently married off, Hunter wouldn't take up Elsie's cause.

But the fact was, her brothers were distracted. And Elsie wasn't just a loose cannon. She was a whole unwieldy battalion and when she set her mind to something the girl could cause chaos on an untold scale.

She needed some guidance and he'd give it. End of story.

He didn't want her doing something dumb, he didn't want her humiliating herself. And he…well, hell, he felt sorry for her.

No, it was more complicated than that. He felt like he was looking at a hurricane barely contained in the form of this woman he'd known for all her life. And if left to her own devices… Hurricane Elsie could be a whole problem.

He wanted to contain the hurricane.

He wanted to keep her…safe.

He didn't normally get involved or stick his nose into things, but when it came to Elsie, he'd make an exception.

Sawyer and Wolf would just go all overprotective brother and Elsie would respond by going category five, and that wouldn't help anyone or anything. Guidance was required here. And he was the only man for that job.

"That isn't his damned business," Elsie said. "He used to hook up all the time. What's wrong with me hooking up? And I'm the first to admit, I don't know anything about flirting. Or about how to be…that," she said, gesturing slightly over toward the redhead.

"Yeah, I'm aware."

"So, I need help figuring it out. Alaina is my best friend in the entire world, but she doesn't know anything about it either."

"Fine. You did good. Consider tonight your first lesson."

"Excellent," she said.

"But this cannot distract you from your work. No getting busy during the hours when I need you at the ranch."

She frowned. "I would not be…doing things like that during the day."

He internally groaned. "Right. Nobody does that."

"It's settled," she said. "We get to work on the camp, and you get to work on helping me flirt. And get Travis."

He was going to regret this. He just had a feeling.

She stuck out her hand, a grin on her face. She was fresh and far too enthusiastic. And he had no idea how Elsie had managed to make it through her particular childhood as optimistic and unspoiled as she was. A pain in the ass, sure, but generally unspoiled.

And he could only hope that he wasn't going to be complicit in spoiling her in some way. But the thing was, Elsie was going to do what she was going to do. And her brothers weren't going to help with this. No one would. The last thing he wanted was for her to get hurt. And, anyway, he didn't have time for her to mope around. He had a program to get up off the ground.

Rather than worrying too much about it—because it wasn't his way—he took her hand and shook it.

"All right, Elsie Garrett. You've got yourself a deal."

CHAPTER TWO

"YOU SHOULD HAVE stayed last night," Elsie said, maneuvering her horse up behind Alaina's.

"Why exactly?" Alaina asked without looking back at Elsie, her eyes firmly fixed on the trail ahead.

"I ended up talking to Hunter."

Scenes of the night played through her mind. Dancing with him till she was hot. Drinking a Sprite he'd bought for her.

The way he'd touched her chin.

And it was strange, but she had trouble getting a clear picture of her interactions with Travis.

"That's not weird," Alaina said. "You always talk to Hunter."

"At the bar. That means that you could have talked to him."

"I thought you were leaving," Alaina said, dodging a tree branch that was sticking out into the trail. They were each taking the afternoon off and enjoying the nice weather.

"I was going to. But Hunter said… Well, horrifically, he was aware that I was pouting because Travis was flirting with that other girl."

Alaina's shoulders shot up to her ears, her recoil visible from behind. "Well, that's terrible."

"I know."

She wasn't sure if she was ever going to be able to recover from that particular humiliation. She had been pretty certain that she wasn't all that obvious. But apparently her emotions were a whole lot easier to read than she thought. Not very fair considering she wasn't sure she had the best read on her emotions on a good day.

But Hunter seemed to know. And even though Hunter drove her nuts, the thing about Hunter was…he'd always told her the truth.

Sawyer and Wolf wanted to protect her. They'd been her real guardians most of her life and they'd done their best with her, but they wanted to shield her.

When she'd asked all the time as a little girl if her mom would come back, they'd dodged her questions. Hunter had sat down with her one day and said: *Hey, Sawyer's mom hasn't come back, has she?*

No.

Wolf's?

No.

Mine?

No.

They don't come back, Els.

It had hurt bitterly. And she'd hated him for it for a few days. But then at some point she'd realized the hopeful ache in her heart was gone. She missed it for a while. But then in its place came closure. A sense of finality and peace.

He didn't spare her feelings.

And he hadn't here either. Maybe that was why she wanted him to be the one to teach her to flirt. She knew he'd teach her right and true, and he wouldn't let her embarrass herself.

He wasn't blunt for the sake of it. He spoke plan, and then he offered solutions. Maybe she wasn't as nice to him as she could be.

But on a daily basis he got under her skin.

For big things, though, he was pretty good to have around.

"Did he leave with that girl?" Alaina asked.

Elsie shook her head. "No. Oh wait, do you mean Travis or Hunter?"

"Hunter," Alaina said. "Sorry. It does matter if Travis left with that other girl, I'm being... I'm being selfish."

"Hunter didn't. Travis did. But you know, it doesn't matter. You know how they are." It didn't matter for them. That was the thing. The men seemed to trade partners around like it was nothing.

"Cowboys," Alaina agreed.

"It's not fair," Elsie said. "If I acted the way that Sawyer and Wolf did before they got married they would have put a leash on me."

"I don't have brothers," Alaina said. "I'm free of that kind of nonsense."

"Sure," Elsie said.

She wasn't going to argue with her friend, but the real truth was that any guy from the other three families would happily play the part of overprotective older brother for Alaina if the moment presented itself.

The Sullivans were all girls. The McClouds were all boys. The Garretts and the Kings were mixed. But there was definitely a level of protectiveness that all the men put on the Sullivans.

Gus McCloud was acting patriarch of the McCloud clan, and it seemed to her that he had always been around to bail the Sullivans out when there was drama. In fact, she could recall him plucking Alaina out of the pond when she was five years old, like an angry kitten.

Elsie had also been five, and terrified that they were going to get in trouble for playing around the pond.

So, she had hid while Gus rescued Alaina.

One of her poorer showings as a friend, but Alaina hadn't been in danger, she'd just been soggy.

"And you don't think your sisters would have a thing or two to say?" Elsie asked.

"No," Alaina said. "I don't. Because we respect each other as women. Hotheaded women who are to be respected and feared."

That made Elsie laugh because that was definitely true. You didn't mess with a Sullivan unless you wanted to get it in the neck.

She and Alaina had been best friends their whole lives. And she had always been grateful for the Sullivan family, without which she would have had spare little exposure to femininity. Not that it had taken. But Elsie's mother had run off when Elsie was just a baby. And her dad had been… well, no good, really. There was a reason he had run off three baby mamas. There wasn't a full sibling to be had among the Garretts.

She'd had her grandmother up until she was six. The most steady, stable influence in her life. But then she'd died, and with it, she'd taken Elsie's deepest concept of affection and love.

And it had taught her that everything was fragile, so you couldn't afford to be.

She'd learned to shore herself up. To be strong.

And to hold on to the people she had.

"So, did he just make fun of you?" Alaina asked, shifting the conversation back to Hunter.

"No," Elsie said, frowning. "He didn't. He made me stay. He…he made me stay and danced with me."

Alaina's head whipped around, and her horse followed,

the paint broadside on the trail now, stopping Elsie's mare in her tracks. "He what?"

The jealousy apparent on her friend's face shocked her. Elsie had never done anything that could possibly make someone jealous in her whole life. And seeing Alaina all het up over her and Hunter was just… It was weird.

Her stomach felt tight.

"Oh, don't be like that. It's Hunter. He said that I looked like I was going off in an obvious sulk, and he thought that if I really wanted to attract Travis I should stick around."

"Really?"

"Yeah," she said, a little bit defiant. "That's what he said."

Alaina's dander started to lower. "That's probably advice I should take."

Elsie didn't want to say anything, but Alaina didn't have a chance with Hunter. With or without the advice.

Not because her friend wasn't beautiful, she was.

With her tangle of wild red hair and sea green eyes, she was *stunningly* beautiful. She was rambunctious, and precocious, but in spite of all that, she'd always seemed heaps more feminine than Elsie.

The essential problem for Alaina was just that there was a dearth of *new* men around these parts. Men who hadn't known them all their lives. Men who didn't see them as kids. But that was starting to change. They were getting older, and more and more of the single ranch hands that came for a summer were age appropriate for them.

But somebody like Hunter was not going to look at her and see anything other than a child. The King boys were even older. Gus McCloud was older than Hunter, Lachlan and Brody barely younger, but not enough to make them not *older*. It was just…not a thing.

But she wasn't going to *say* that. Because what was the harm in a little fantasy, after all?

It was just that it wasn't the same as her thing for Travis. First of all, she wasn't in love with Travis. She was just starting to think that she wanted to try to date somebody. It was time. The upbringing on Four Corners was unconventional. And it made traditional dating difficult. The way that they were all thrown together from the time they were kids made them more like family than anything else. The town of Pyrite Falls beyond Four Corners wasn't much bigger, and sure some of the kids there got bused into other schools, so they were a little more mysterious, but at the end of the day, most of the young people moved away. They didn't stay unless they had a family ranch.

It was just difficult. And unless Elsie wanted to leave, and she didn't, she was going to have to start picking up experiences *somewhere*. It was why she didn't really mind Travis going off with someone else. It bothered her, but it didn't devastate her.

She wasn't in love with him. She just thought he was hot.

"Anything else?" Alaina asked.

Yes. There had been a bit else. But Elsie wasn't sure that she wanted to share it. It was weird, the hesitation to share. But it was just that Alaina wouldn't understand. Hunter offering to teach her to flirt would sound… It would just sound kind of weird. Elsie knew that it wasn't. Because Hunter was Sawyer and Wolf's best friend. And she had known him all of her life. Like family. She had grown up much closer to her than he had Alaina. He wasn't just like a cousin or something. He was like another brother.

It was why they sniped at each other all the time. But at the same time, he *wasn't* her brother, so he was distant enough to… Well, she didn't really know why he had taken up her cause. But he had, and it was probably the least jackass thing that Hunter had ever done. So she was just going to keep it between the two of them. And keep it to herself. Even if it felt strange when she usually shared everything with Alaina.

"I'm just excited about the new horse program that Gus wants to get going. The therapy thing?" Elsie said, trying to get on a new subject.

"Right. That's what you've been working on," Alaina said.

"You know, we could probably use your help."

"I appreciate that," Alaina said. "Especially because I just think you're trying to help me get in proximity to Hunter. But my sister is going hard on the garden this year, and we have to get the farm stand running. We want to get a place set up so that we don't have to take everything down to the store. I mean, we still will, because if we take it off John's store he's going to get mad. But it'd be nice to be able to sell honey and nuts and all the fruit and veggies straight from somewhere on the property."

"But is that what you want?" Elsie asked.

She knew Alaina felt like she owed it to her sisters to work with them, to go along with what Fia wanted, but Elsie didn't like to see it. Wolf and Sawyer were fine with her working with the McClouds because the work suited her better. She thought Alaina should push to be where she wanted, not just try to make her sisters happy. They loved her. They would be happy with what made Alaina happy, Elsie was sure of that.

"I just have to be around to help with all that," Alaina said, stubborn and insistent as ever. "We have to see just how much increased production we can get. You know it's hard for us. We piece together our income leasing out our land and doing the gardens, and selling baked goods. We don't have men to help out. And we're strong women, Els, as you know, but have to work smarter or we'll just end up working harder for our reward."

"I get that." She did, but it didn't make her feel less sorry for Alaina. "But if you ever want to come and lend your horse expertise at McCloud's Landing, you know there's a place for you."

"And that is why you're my best friend," Alaina said.

Elsie smiled and tilted her face up toward the sun.

Last night in the dark bar, things had felt a little bit grim. But now it all felt fine. Just fine. She sometimes questioned the logistics of staying here. There was a limit to what she could do here, who she could be. Or at least, it had felt that way before Hunter had asked her to work on the equine therapy at McCloud's Landing.

The program Gus was working on was the kind of thing she would want to do *anywhere*. Horses had long been her greatest love. It was one of the things that bonded Alaina and her. And she had to think that in truth, she had been giving herself equine therapy from the time she could walk.

She had been an extremely lonely kid sometimes. With no mother that she could even remember. But now she had her best friend living right on the property with her. Her brothers. Her niece, and a nephew on the way. And there was even a real live actual guy in proximity that she was interested in…dating. Hooking up with. Whatever. Things felt like they were coming together. And that was a pretty damned good feeling.

"NOT HAVING DINNER with your *real* family tonight?"

Hunter looked across the table at his brother Lachlan. He could never decide how much weight was actually behind comments like that. If his brothers actually resented the amount of time he spent with the Garretts.

They weren't big on having heart-to-heart talks.

They preferred a nice physical brawl.

But right now, Hunter decided not to punch him. In the McCloud house, emotions were often expressed with fists. But at least among the brothers it wasn't with the intent to actually harm. More than could be said for their father.

Gus had just thrown a fifth pizza into the center of the table, a gourmet effort that had involved taking the pizzas out of the freezer, unwrapping them and sticking them in the oven.

And they wondered why he preferred to eat with Sawyer, who had acquired a wife that was an excellent cook. Hunter's sister-in-law Nelly was a decent enough cook, but Nelly was a quiet, bookish librarian and she and Tag only graced them with their presence for dinner a couple of times a week, which meant they didn't always get the benefit of her cooking.

"It isn't you," Hunter said to Lachlan. "It's that I have a strong preference for Evelyn Garrett's cooking.

"Ungrateful shit," Gus said, sitting down at the head of the table.

His oldest brother was a mean-looking son of a bitch. Scarred all to hell from something that had happened with their father when he was a kid. Something he never talked about. But Hunter wasn't dumb. He knew what burns looked like. What he didn't know was whether his father had actually been trying to kill Gus or not.

He wondered if *Gus* knew.

Hunter'd never asked.

McClouds didn't do heart-to-hearts or feelings.

They preferred guilt, bottled-up emotion and hard work. In that order.

"Not that I don't appreciate the effort involved in unwrapping these pizzas," Hunter said.

"Good," Gus said, putting his boots up on the table and taking a drink of beer.

"Cheese in the crust," Brody commented, taking the first slice and not bothering with a plate. "You spoil us."

"I'll clock you if you don't shut the hell up."

"Love you too," Brody said.

Gus, Lachlan, Brody, Tag and Hunter had been hell in cowboy boots all their lives. There was barely a year between each of them—only eleven months between Brody and Lach—and they'd spent most of their time running around outside avoiding their father growing up.

Making their own guns, slingshots, rabbit traps and shelters. It was a miracle they'd survived their childhood.

Not even so much because of the homemade weapons. It was their dad.

They'd grown up thick as thieves and caring for each other.

And it wasn't any different now.

They'd been feral and wild back then and...well.

The house was a mess. It was such a bachelor hellhole they should all be ashamed. Granted Gus made his home in the main house, like a bear in a den. Lach had his own cabin, and so did Tag, Brody and Hunter.

Tag's house was nice now, since he had a wife to impress. He made it plain he didn't have Nelly doing all the work. But now that he had someone else to live for, he treated his own life like it mattered just a bit more. And that included making a nicer home for them to enjoy.

"When are you going you get yourself a wife, Gus?" Hunter asked. "Sawyer revolutionized his place with one."

"Sawyer needed a mom for his kid," Gus said, talking around a mouthful of pizza. "None of us are stupid enough to end up with accidental babies."

It was true, the Garretts had had a rash of accidental babies lately. Sawyer had gotten a bar hookup pregnant and had ended up facing down the prospect of being a single father. Rather than have his child grow up motherless the way that he had, he had gotten himself a mail-order bride. Evelyn.

She had worked out better than anyone could've imagined.

Then there was Wolf, who had gone and gotten some pretty young thing from Copper Ridge knocked up, and had married her for good measure. Though, they seemed sickeningly in love at this point.

Wasn't Hunter's thing. He was happy for them. But it also meant that while they still did some work together, things were different. They weren't going out to the bar anymore. They talked about babies and how expensive colleges were—as if any of them had gone, but of course they figured their kids would—and dilation. Hunter did not want to talk about the dilating of anything.

Tag was married. That would solve the issue of "would anyone inherit McCloud's Landing someday?" Not that it was an issue any of them wasted too much time worrying about. When he was dead he wouldn't care who worked this piece of ground. He liked to think he'd be too busy to worry about shit like that.

But you know, in the abstract that had been a bit of a thing, and now Lach, Gus, Brody and he were free of that concern.

Big ups to Tag.

"Maybe not a wife, then," Lachlan said, "maybe you just need Snow White to show up."

"Too bad I'm not a tiny man," Gus said.

Brody hooted out a laugh and Lachlan snickered into his beer down at the end of the table.

"Well, once we're done pouring money into this start-up maybe you could consider a housekeeper," Hunter said.

"I don't go over to your place and criticize the cleanliness," Gus said.

"You also don't come over to our places," Hunter said. "Because we do everything here."

"Fine. If it bothers you so much, princess, maybe I will. Didn't realize my mess was a pea under your mattress. Once we get everything up and running with the new facility. Once we get new arenas and paddocks put in, we can focus on guest cabins. And maybe after that, I'll worry about the state of this place."

"Fair enough," Hunter said.

"The guest cabins are going to require a little bit of song and dance with the county. We have so many dwellings on this property just because we're grandfathered into previous laws. Getting new permits might be a pain in the ass."

"Yeah, it might be," Hunter agreed. "But it'll be worth it in the end. Because some people might need long-term therapy, particularly if they're coming from out of town... There's not enough lodging in Pyrite Falls to make it easy."

"Yep. Hey. Are you going to make that trip up to Vancouver to talk to the owner of Running Y about his horses he's off-loading?"

"Yeah. In the next week or so, I was thinking." He and Elsie were still working with the horses that they already had, making sure they were safe for any people they might be bringing in. The next step was to look at new horses. And he knew that Gus was feeling keen on the animals up north because the five that they were looking at had actually been used in therapy before, and could alleviate a lot of unknowns. It was a good start-up move, but they were very expensive. And it wasn't that they didn't have money, they did. But the way the finances worked at Four Corners meant that they needed to have buy-in from the others. While they operated autonomously from each other, they had a board of sorts. Unofficial, maybe, but they all had to live with each other, deal with each other, so they played by the unofficial rules. Making sure that everybody was happy with the direction things were going was extremely important.

Still, Hunter was kind of the…the face of this sort of thing. He knew most people would find it distasteful to make jokes about Gus's appearance, but gallows humor was another McCloud family virtue. It was just how they dealt with things.

Gus didn't have any issues or false ideas about what their father's rage had left behind. Hunter knew how to turn on the charm when he had to. And he didn't mind doing it in this case.

He might be the youngest, but in some cases he had to hold things together. That was just fine with him.

Anyway, it was the least he could do. All shitty things considered.

"Good," Gus said. "The sooner you can come back with all the information on that, the sooner we can present it at the town hall and finalize it."

"Why are you suddenly so into this?" Brody asked. "I mean, it's a good business move, but you've never been all that into the business aspect of things."

Gus shrugged. "Because I can't just sit on my ass."

"You're a rancher," Lach pointed out. "You don't sit on your ass. Unless it's on a horse. But we do it some twelve hours a day and it's damned hard work."

"You know what I mean. If we're not moving forward, then what the hell are we doing?"

"Certainly not cleaning the house," he said. "Or learning to cook better food."

"Same goes for you," Gus said. "I don't see you offering to put on an apron and bake some bread."

"Maybe Charity would cook for us," Brody said, directing that at Lach with a smirk.

"You can suggest it," Lachlan said. "But I suspect we'd all end up ingesting horse tranquilizer. She might look sweet, but she's got a backbone of steel."

Lachlan's best friend, Charity Wyatt, was the most unlikely creature Hunter could have ever imagined his brother forming a friendship with. But he'd met the elderly town vet's only daughter when they were thirteen and had formed a deep bond with her that nothing had ever come close to breaking.

Lachlan was a manwhore, a lot like Brody, but with some of Gus's intensity. And it was a mystery to Hunter why that sweet, caregiving Charity seemed stuck to him like glue.

Or why Lach was stuck to her.

Not that Hunter didn't *like* Charity. There was nothing to dislike about her. It was just his brother was one of the last people on earth he'd ever think could be just friends with a woman.

"I'll pass on the horse tranquilizers," Hunter said. He finished eating the questionable pizza, then tipped the rest of his beer back. "I've got to head out," he said. "It's an early morning."

"It's an early morning for all of us," Gus said. "Every day."

"Yeah, but you don't all wrangle Elsie Garrett daily."

Brody chuckled. "No. That is true."

He felt a little bit mean saying that. Particularly after yesterday. Yeah, Elsie was kind of a pain in the butt sometimes, but he supposed that was kind of like having a younger sister. Being the youngest, he didn't really have that experience. Though he wasn't sure that the McCloud brothers really followed birth order. They were all too close in age. They stepped all over each other all the time.

Sawyer and Wolf were good to Elsie, but they shielded her in a way Hunter didn't think did her any favors. Someone had to be honest with her, and he'd taken it upon himself to give her that honesty. He knew she didn't like it all the time, but he considered it a service.

He made a big show of taking his paper plate to the trash, and putting his beer bottle in the recycling bin, which was overflowing. Then he tipped his hat and walked out of the place, headed down the trail that led to his cabin. There were some wooden steps, embedded tightly into a hillside, that led down to the back of his cabin. It sat just above the river, with a great view and better fishing off the dock just below.

Yeah, their parents might've been a total loss, but the legacy of the McClouds had to be this land. They couldn't take credit for its creation, but one thing he could say was that mostly, over the generations, they had been good stewards of it. The houses that had been built here were sturdy, and they had done a good job utilizing the resources here. The pine trees that ran along the banks of the river were thick, different shades of dark green behind them, leaving the forest looking untamed and mysterious. If he was given to being poetic about the land, it pertained to its mysteries. He lived here all of his life, and still, standing there right next to his house, looking across the water and into the forest, he could imagine there were things there that he had never seen. That there were mysteries he would never know, because he was just a man, and nature was something else altogether. Wild and unknown, and all the better for it.

Hunter appreciated that. That even in all this sameness there could be something new.

The land provided a hell of a lot of fulfillment for him.

And maybe that was what Gus was looking for with this new move that he was making. An additional way to use it. To give back. To be something other than what their father had made them into.

Hunter, Gus, Brody and Lachlan had decent reputations about town. Yes, it was true, there were rumors that Gus had killed their father. But in truth, that didn't actually damage his reputation. For some people, it strengthened it.

Gus said that their father had up and left. After Gus had given him a beating. Hunter believed his brother. But honestly, if Gus was lying, Hunter wouldn't have judged him.

Which was maybe a little bit grim. But their lives had been grim.

Running a facility that offered therapy to people who had experienced trauma...he supposed they were full of trauma themselves.

Maybe that was the closest the McClouds could get to admitting they had trauma. Trying to help other people.

That made him pause for a moment, uncomfortable memories hovering around the edges of his mind.

Hell, you couldn't change the past.

As far as Hunter went? He would just keep on working the land. That was where he found his satisfaction.

Working the land. Working with horses.

People…

Hell, he had friends. He loved them. He loved his family. But as for deep connection…

He shrugged off the strange ghost of a feeling that overtook him.

Sometimes the river reminded him of his mother. Of nice afternoons spent fishing and the way she'd smiled when she looked out at the scene around them.

And he didn't like being reminded of her.

So he did what he always did in that situation. And it wasn't turn away from the water. Instead, he went for his fishing pole.

Because when he had a feeling he didn't like, he liked to stand in defiance of it.

It was just how he did things.

So he stood out there until well after dark, the floodlight from his cabin providing all the light he needed.

And when he went to bed, he fell asleep right away because he never let himself hit the mattress until he was too exhausted to think.

CHAPTER THREE

"So ARE WE going to start with the flirting lessons or what?"

Elsie looked up at Hunter, impatience rioting through her like a restless horse.

"No," he said, sounding so uninterested it made her want to punch hm. "There's work to be done, Elsie, I don't have time to indulge you on the clock."

"You're not *indulging* me," she said. "You said that you would *help* me. So I don't see why we don't incorporate it into the workday."

She scampered around to the side of the horse and mounted quickly. Chester was docile, and Elsie didn't have any further concerns about using him for therapy. He was incredibly responsive, and he could handle commands, and wasn't spooked by much of anything. Including a rider who might not know what they were doing.

But still, they were doing exactly what had been outlined in the handbook that they'd been provided for this sort of thing. Which meant that they would do the amount of testing required, regardless of her personal feelings.

"One thing at a time," he said.

Today they would be taking the horses out on some more challenging trails. Not because they were going to do it with their clients, but because it was good to get a read on how the horses reacted to new situations.

Hunter was on a more volatile animal, not one they

would be using for therapy, by design. To see how Chester would react in a more uncertain situation.

And to see if Hunter would be able to take control if necessary.

"You're such a pain in the butt," she said. "You offered to teach me."

"But not while I have work to do. Anyway, it could be argued that you're the pain, Elsie."

"Seems like a matter of perspective to me," she said.

Hunter swung himself up onto his mount with ease. He seemed to do everything with ease. Never out of his element. And while Elsie was not out of her element when it came to horses, she was decidedly out of her element at the bar. And she wondered if it was just a side effect of being so much younger than most of the other people that had always been at Four Corners.

She and Alaina were the youngests of the four primary families. And they had banded together because of that. But there was a whole bunch of them right in their thirties, and they had each other. For flirting and dating and all of that. For friendship and support and collecting information on experiences. It was just different for Alaina and Elsie. They had each other, but they couldn't learn a damned thing from each other.

"How did *you* learn to flirt?" she asked.

Hunter snorted and eased his horse forward. "Some things come natural."

"I'm serious. And why does it seem like there's an endless collection of women at the bar down in Pyrite Falls?"

"Because," he said, "they're buckle bunnies. And they come for the express purpose of hooking up with a cowboy, which they know they can find down at the bar."

"Isn't there some kind of cowgirl equivalent? Like… rhinestone chasers or something?"

He chuckled. "I'm sure there is," he said. "But you probably wouldn't like them. Because they'd probably just be city boys."

"I wouldn't care," Elsie said, tossing her braid back over her shoulder. "It would give me something to do."

"You don't feel like you have enough to do? Because if so, I'm not a very good boss."

"I didn't realize you were my boss, Hunter."

"Oh, I am," he said.

"Whatever," she responded. She shifted uneasily. They pushed through an open field, dotted with purple flowers, which gradually gave way to a worn-out path, which was easy at first, but began to narrow and climb the side of a hill.

Not really unlike where she and Alaina had chosen to ride yesterday. It was all easy stuff for Elsie.

"Why are you still here?"

"On this trail? Because you're my boss and this is where we said we were going to ride. Or did you forget what we just talked about? You might be getting geriatric, Hunter."

"I mean at Four Corners. You're upset about the whole situation. You know you could move to a bigger place. Where people don't know you. Where they don't know Sawyer and Wolf, probably even more to the point. You could meet new people, new men…"

"I don't want to leave," she said.

The idea made her heart feel fluttery. Panicky. She didn't like it particularly. It was like panic. And she didn't like to feel that way.

She liked to feel in control. And she supposed that was half of what always being at Four Corners offered her. Control. Because it was familiar. And she felt familiar in it. It was a blessing and a curse.

"Well, to be honest," she said, chewing her lip as she looked around at the scenery. There was a large ravine on the other side of the trail, and it looked out over an expansive piece of timber. Evergreen trees as far as she could see. "I thought about it. But... Then... You know, then Sawyer had June. And now Wolf and Violet are expecting. And we got started with this. And it feels like doing something. And I think maybe if I hadn't had anything to do with myself in terms of work... My heart just isn't in cattle ranching. It's never going to be. But I'm interested in what's happening at McCloud's Landing. And I love it. I'm excited about it." She shook her head. "I don't know, Hunter. I try to picture life away from here, and it's a big blank space. I know there are things out there, but I can't really imagine them. I don't know what life would be like away from everybody here. So it's easy for me to make up situations that might be better. But anyway, the ranch hands are finally my age."

"God help Sawyer," Hunter said, shaking his head.

"Well, it's true," she said, feeling insistent on driving her point home. "I was too young for them for a long time. Now I'm not. So it occurred to me, I should do something about it. That's one of the biggest problems with living in one place for a long time. You forget that you've changed. Because everything around you is kind of the same. You know?"

He shrugged his shoulder. "I guess."

"Well, I imagine when you started going to the bar there were suddenly all the...the bunnies."

"Fair," Hunter said.

"Anyway, I don't want to leave. I just need to figure

out what it means to take control of my life here. Which is what I'm doing. And try not to make an ass of myself while I do it."

She had to ruefully admit to herself she had been well on her way to doing that last night.

"Right." They came upon a small gully in the trail, and predictably, Hunter's horse balked. Kicked up a fuss. And she waited to see if Chester would react to that. To the other horse's nervous energy.

Thankfully, he stayed calm.

"I think that Chester is perfect. And he's going to work great for the kind of therapy we have. I don't think anyone is going to be able to rattle him."

"You really like that horse, don't you?" Hunter asked.

"I like every horse. Because unlike people they don't let you down."

Hunter paused and stared at her. There was something about that stare that made her insides itch. Something that she recognized, but couldn't quite place. "Yeah. True."

"That's the thing I like best about you," she said. "You understand horses."

"You know, that's the funniest thing about my dad," he said.

She felt like she had a little bit of whiplash at the mention of his father. Hunter rarely talked about his father. It was funny he was doing it now, and with her. It made her feel like the air, the moment, had closed in slightly around them.

She didn't really have many memories of Seamus Mc-Cloud. She'd never been allowed near McCloud's Landing when he was still around, and they hadn't had the town hall meetings yet, where all the ranching families got together.

The main families had been splintered back then, each of them distant and working almost independently. It was their generation that had brought them back together. That had started taking Four Corners back to its former glory, and even on to new glory.

"He tried to be a horseman. It's what the McClouds did. It's what we've always done. We came from Scotland with horses generations ago. But the horses always hated him. They always did. Because they can tell. They know when somebody's not a good person."

She nodded slowly. "It's true."

And she watched the ease with which Hunter handled his mount, and it made her wonder if sometimes she was a little bit too hard on him. But then, she thought he was irritating, she didn't think he was a bad person. She had never thought that.

"I guess I kind of think that working on this with you is going to help. Wolf and Sawyer are going to have to realize that I'm more than just a kid. And maybe other people will notice too."

"What exactly do you want, Elsie?"

"I feel like you guys are all able to have full lives here. And that's what I want."

They kept going for a while longer, and once they reached the end of the trail, turned and started to head back.

It was getting warm, and Elsie grabbed the top of her shirt and picked at it, using the fabric to fan herself. She hated that damp valley of sweat that formed between her boobs. They weren't even very big, and still, she ended up sweaty there. One of the great injustices of being female. Particularly when she hadn't reaped any of the benefits of being female.

"So when exactly are we going to do our lessons?"

"Tonight," Hunter said, maneuvering his horse around

hers. "Come over tonight. Wear whatever outfit you would wear to pick up a guy in a bar. And we'll go from there."

"Okay," she said.

And as annoying as Hunter was, one thing she could say was that at least now, in this, he was treating her like an equal. Like an equal who needed to learn some things, but he was…well, he was actually treating her sincerely. And that she could appreciate.

She took that short trip back to Garrett's Watch after her shift at McCloud's was over and went into her room. She opened up the closet and hunted around. She had her regular old tank top that she often wore to work, and she had some different T-shirts. Black jeans. Those were a little bit fancier. She had one pair of black jeans, and a black belt. Plus a gray T-shirt that was really comfortable. It might not be fancy, but she didn't really do fancy and, anyway, if she was comfortable, she was more likely to be natural, and surely that had to count for something?

She thought about all the women that Hunter typically associated with. She didn't think they were comfortable. But it wasn't like Travis had never seen her before. He had. He saw her all the time around the ranch. So it wasn't like he didn't know how she looked in a T-shirt and jeans. She wasn't a shape-shifter, after all.

It wasn't like she was going to fool him even if she did put on something a little bit flashier. Anyway. She didn't have anything flashy.

She grabbed the denim jacket and ran out the front door, taking the steps to the front porch two at a time. She was so focused on getting back to her truck that she nearly ran square into her brother Sawyer.

"Where are you headed?"

She frowned. "What are you doing here?"

"I came by to see if you were going to come for dinner."

"Oh, I might," she said, feeling caught and guilty and she shouldn't. "But later?"

"You going out?" he asked, frowning.

"Yeah," she said. "But I don't think I'm going to eat. I'll text you. Why didn't you text me?"

"I was driving by and I saw that your truck was in the driveway, so I thought I'd just pop in."

"Yeah. I have to go over to Hunter's place for a bit. We just have some work stuff to discuss."

It was sort of a lie. But she couldn't really talk to Sawyer about this. It was weird. And she supposed that was everything she needed said internally about Hunter and his status as a brother. He was, but not. Because they were at least able to talk about this.

But then, maybe it was because she had never really cared what Hunter thought about her.

She cared what Sawyer thought. Deeply.

Her older brother was the best man in all the world. And he had ended up doing half the raising of her after her mother had run off and their father had died.

She wanted him to be proud of her. She supposed that added a little bit of tension to everything all the time. Because she wanted to be her own person, but she also wanted to be someone that Sawyer approved of. Not that he was a prude or anything like that. It was just that anything new felt tenuous. She wanted to be established in it, sure of it, before she brought it to him.

"All right," Sawyer said. "He should feed you, though, if he's going to have you working late."

"I'm not worried about it," Elsie said.

"I am. I don't want him using you for cheap labor just because we're friends. You're an expert with horses, Elsie, and he's not doing you a favor by having you do work there. You're benefitting him."

Her brother's words warmed her. That he cared so much and thought she was good mattered so much. But she didn't want him thinking Hunter wasn't being good to her, when in reality he actually was helping her.

"He doesn't treat me like cheap labor, Sawyer. He's been more than fair. Actually, he's great to work with and he's really excellent with the horses."

"You're...defending Hunter?" Sawyer looked up at the sky.

"What?" Her gaze followed his.

"I'm just looking for a flying pig."

"*Hey*, he might be a pain in the ass, but he is actually a good boss." Though she nearly choked on the word *boss*. "And I swear to you, he's not taking advantage."

She felt bad because tonight wasn't about work at all, and technically Hunter was doing her a favor. But she didn't feel bad enough to tell Sawyer the truth.

"Like I said, I'll text you," she said.

She got into her truck and started the engine, waving at her brother as she pulled out of the driveway.

And a couple of minutes later she was at Hunter's cabin. And for some reason her stomach fluttered. Maybe because she hadn't really thought through the fact that he had asked her to dress the way that she would pick up men, which meant that he was going to be passing some kind of judgment on what she was wearing.

And she and Hunter had never had a discussion about what she was wearing ever. Not once.

It made her feel weird and exposed, and she didn't like it. Her pace slowed. And then she went to the door, taking a deep breath. This was ridiculous. She had just seen the man an hour ago.

She started to knock, and the door swung open. His dark gaze raked over her quickly, neutrally. Sort of to an upsetting degree.

"What?" she asked.

"That's what you'd wear?"

"Yeah," she said. She crossed her arms defensively. "Does a girl have to be caked in makeup and sparkly shit to get attention?"

"No," he said.

"Well, then, is there something wrong with this?"

"Come in," he said.

"All right, I'm in. Now explain." He said nothing, and it only made her mad. "Hunter, I'm counting on you to be straight with me. You're the one who told me I was tone deaf and should not sing in the Four Corners talent show, and I listened and did calf roping instead and I was better off for it. You told me why I couldn't pee standing up like my brothers when I was six. You told me my mom wasn't coming back. So don't go getting soft on me now. Give me honesty. I need it."

He still hesitated.

"Don't get the wrong idea," he said. "Your figure's cute. Which means whatever you wear is cute."

He said that so offhandedly, and it made her feel… It made her feel like he had dumped the room on its head. And somehow she was still standing there right side up. Her figure was cute? He thought her figure was cute.

"I…"

"Statement of fact," he said, moving past it quickly. "I guess the question is this. What exactly do you want from Travis?"

"I don't want to marry him," she said.

He sighed. "Well, do you just want to fuck him or...?"

Her face went hot. All over. "No! I didn't say that. I... I want to... I don't know, isn't there some middle ground in there?"

"Never personally walked upon it, but I hear tell."

"I want something normal. I want to feel like if I like a guy I can... I don't know. Hang out with him, kiss him, sleep with him without weird hang-ups. Isn't that fine?"

"I just want to know what you're after," he said, maddeningly unflappable in the face of her total embarrassment. "Because if the only aim is for you to hook up, I'm going to have to have some plausible deniability so Sawyer doesn't kick my ass."

"He can't possibly think I'm going to be a virgin for the rest of my life."

That right there made Hunter's face do something weird. His brows went flat, his mouth too, and his jaw looked tight. He didn't say anything.

What had he thought? That she wasn't a virgin? That she'd found someone to hook up with before this? She thought of the absolute dearth of men in her life who would have been both available to her before this and also appealing to her. There really wasn't any crossover. She'd thought that was obvious.

Apparently not.

"Whatever, don't think too hard about that," she sniped. "Just... I want to get where it's not a big deal and I feel normal and nobody treats me like a kid."

"And somehow you see this thing with Travis as a gateway to that?"

"You have to take the first step, right? Climb the first

mountain? Get on your first horse? There's always that first one and then after that it's no big deal."

He coughed, but she didn't think it was genuine. "Sure."

"What?"

"Sex isn't riding a horse, though, is the thing," he said.

"Which is too damn bad because if it was, I wouldn't need your help, would I?"

He huffed a laugh that sounded awfully like a cough. "So, what, you want to be able to talk to men?"

"Yeah and like…let them know I'm interested? Like, I count. I'm a woman. I'm here."

"You could always just walk up to him and offer to hop in the sack, he'd probably take you up on it."

She frowned. "I don't…"

"Okay, look, don't do that." He gestured to the small table in the dining area of the cabin. "Have a seat."

She followed his orders and pulled out the small green-and-red-painted chair, then sat. "Hey, what does it mean that I have a cute figure?" She immediately felt a surge of embarrassment that she'd said that.

"What?" he asked, like he'd forgotten he'd said it.

But he had. And she didn't think he'd forgotten it either.

"You said I had a cute figure. What does that mean? Like that's not…like it means I have small boobs?"

His throat worked, and for a moment, she thought she'd successful rendered Hunter McCloud speechless.

"It means you're cute, Elsie," he said, his voice hard, "but I haven't spent a ton of time thinking on that, okay?"

"Well, but you didn't say sexy or…"

She trailed off, suddenly feeling mortified. Why had she thought this was a good idea? She didn't know how to have this conversation with him. She didn't know how to have this conversation with anyone.

"My point is it's not like you need different clothes to look good," he said, taking a seat across from her. "It's just…you said it. Men here treat you like a kid. They look at you and see Sawyer and Wolf's sister. Those women that come in from out of town are dressed to draw attention, and if you changed up what you wore…well, people might look and see something different."

"That sounds like you're saying a woman's clothes can mean she's asking for it."

"Nope, didn't say that. What I'm saying is there's a pageantry to it, okay? You dress the part, just like the guys do when they go out. Stetsons and belt buckles and all that."

"Right. Got it. Like a flock of birds. Showing off."

"Sure. I guess so."

"I'll feel stupid."

"Well, I can't help you with that."

"I'll look like I'm trying too hard."

He leaned back in his chair. "Elsie, what… I… Did anyone ever talk to you about…"

"Sex?"

"*Relationships*. But yeah, sex too."

"When I was twelve I went out to the pasture with Sawyer and there was a stallion who mounted a mare and he told me that was where babies came from. And I didn't have the heart to tell him Alaina had snuck me one of her mom's romance novels a year earlier and I'd already read all about it." She'd never told anyone that. How she'd learned about sex from a book. She'd been horrified and fascinated all at once by the descriptions on the page and had howled about it to Alaina at their next sleepover.

Why would anyone ever let a man do that to them? Put his hand here? And put his mouth there?

Alaina had sighed. *Sounded nice to me…*

Elsie had cringed.

Then she'd read the book three more times before shoving it firmly under her mattress, where she'd kept it hidden for another two years.

"Right, well, that's not really all that helpful, is it?"

She shook her head. "Can't say that it was, but he tried."

All they'd been able to do was try their best. They'd had a bad hand. Their mothers leaving, their father kicking the bucket when he had. She'd never really gotten the chance to be attached to him.

Or maybe he'd never been attached to her.

Like her own mother, who was surely out there somewhere, knowing that her dad had been gone all this time—likely—and still not coming back to find her.

They don't come back.

Hunter had said it himself.

"So you're good on mechanics, then," Hunter said.

"Yep."

He dragged a hand over his face. "Thank God. So you don't need sex ed. It's the talking-to-a-man part you need help with?"

The idea of sex ed made her feel flushed and hot and she was starting to get twitchy.

"No. Hell no, I do not need sex ed. And yes, it's the talking. You know, the real problem is I haven't had to get to know too many people in general. Evelyn and Violet are the first new people to come into my life in a long time, and getting to know women who are mostly into your brothers is…different. I had an easy enough time talking with Evelyn, but I think I'm too honest. Is that a thing?"

He nodded. "It is. You've got to play your cards close to your chest. Be a little mysterious. And you want him to come to you."

"Is this more caveman stuff? Because I don't see why a man—"

"It's not about men and women. I like women to come to me. I can go to them. If I want. But I also know how to make them cross a room to meet me. You want to be in the power position."

"I do?"

"Yeah, you do. Travis Young thinks he's hot shit."

"In fairness, so do I or I wouldn't want to—"

"Sure, great," Hunter said, looking like he desperately didn't want to hear the rest of what she'd been about to say. "But like you said, there are plenty of ranch hands who come in that are in their early twenties. More and more fish in your particular sea. You don't need him. And if you keep that in mind, you're going to drive him crazy."

"Okay, so I do what?"

"You go into the bar, and you don't need to wear what those other women wear, just something a little different. Something to make them sit back and take some notice."

"Right," she said.

"Then you sit down. See who asks if you want a drink, someone will."

"And I take it? Even if I don't…"

"Yep. You know what men like? A woman who has another man's attention."

"This is all super childish."

He nodded. "It is. Men are basic. Women are basic. Humans—" he tapped the table "—are basic. We want food, we want drink, we want sex. And we don't act all that different when we want those things." He sighed. "You sure this is what you want? To be part of all that?"

"I want to be normal."

She felt stupid, and very sad when those words left her mouth.

"What's normal?"

"I don't know, just…someone who has an easy time going out, making friends, attracting men, having fun with them. Not a sad girl whose mom left her."

And Hunter knew her. All the parts of her life story. But somehow admitting this felt…exposing, and she was sorry she'd said it. Sorry that she always led with honesty instead of sitting with her words for a while and deciding if they needed to be said.

He might know her life story, but he didn't know how it made her feel.

No one did.

And now she'd gone and told him.

But then, to her relief, the corner of his mouth lifted into a smart-ass smile.

"Around these parts parental abandonment seems to be the most normal thing there is."

She was grateful. So very grateful that he'd made a joke. That he'd lightened the moment. Lightened the weight on her chest.

"Maybe I want to forget that part."

"You want to get married?" he asked. "Have a family?"

Just thinking about that struck terror into her heart. "No. I want a date. And we'll go from there."

"Okay."

She sighed. "I wish there was a place for me to buy clothes. I could borrow some from Alaina." Alaina's clothes wouldn't fit her right. Her friend was shorter and curvier.

"I have to go up to Vancouver. I'll be gone a couple days, but I'm headed up to Running Y Ranch to see some horses, and I was thinking about this anyway, but...you should come. We can stop by some actual stores."

"Really?"

She hadn't left Four Corners or the general Pyrite area in way too long. Months, maybe. And even then she'd only gone to Copper Ridge, not anywhere like Vancouver.

"Yeah. It's for work."

The unspoken part of that was: *tell Sawyer it's for work.*

She nodded. "Yeah. For work."

"It's settled, then. We leave on Friday."

"Okay."

She had a feeling that that concluded the evening, so she got up and took a step back. "Thanks," she said. "For tonight."

"No problem."

She left, and as she walked down the stairs she texted Sawyer and told him she'd be there for dinner in five minutes.

CHAPTER FOUR

Hunter hadn't worked with Elsie today, and he felt grateful for the break. He wasn't really sure why. Maybe it was because she was just so... She was like a dog with a bone when she got something in mind. And he wouldn't have been surprised if she had hopped off her horse today and demanded he give her an exhaustive list of...sexual positions or something. And he just wasn't in the space for that.

For some reason, his fingertips—the ones he'd used to grab her chin the other night—felt hot.

He'd thought he might have a whole day not dealing with her, but then Evelyn texted him and asked if he would like to come have dinner tonight. And he would. So he agreed to go over to the Garretts' house for dinner that night. That didn't mean Elsie would be there, but there was a high likelihood.

By the time he washed up and headed that direction, he had accepted the inevitability of it.

Sawyer's house was all lit up when he arrived. It was a nice place, modern, remodeled some years ago. But now it was different than it had been. Because now he had a wife. A kid.

It was the strangest thing. The way that he and Wolf had domesticated so suddenly and quickly.

He shook his head, got out of his truck and noticed that Elsie's was already here. He shook his head again. Well, he'd chosen this. A night in with his friends, their wives, their kid and a half, and their kid sister who acted like she wanted to take a chunk off him with her teeth, when she wasn't asking him for help with something.

He walked right in the front door without knocking and was greeted with an uproarious screech by June Bug, Sawyer's daughter, who was one now, and hell on two feet. She ran toward him, little toes slapping on the hardwood floor.

And he had no choice but to bend down and pick her up. Because nobody could deny a cute little creature like that. And if you did, you were something more than dead inside.

"Hey there, varmint," he said, putting his cowboy hat on her head, much to her delight. Even though it immediately fell down and covered her eyes.

She reached her chubby little hands up and tilted it, looking up at him with sky blue eyes.

"You're very popular around here, Uncle Hunter," Evelyn said.

"Women love me," he said, flashing her a grin.

"Not all of them," Elsie said, her toothy smile full of cheek.

"You should be nicer to me," he said, leaning in and bumping his elbow against her arm.

Her eyes went wide, and he knew that she was afraid he was going to give away her little flirting initiative. Good. She *should* worry.

"Because I sign your paychecks now," he added.

"Right," she said, snappish.

He carried June into the dining room, and everybody else went too. There was a beautiful dinner laid out. Roast chicken and gravy, potatoes, homemade bread. Evelyn really knew how to treat…well, *everybody*.

She made a case for any man having a wife. It had to be said.

He sat down, and Evelyn relieved him of June, putting her in the high chair. Wolf and Sawyer were already seated at the table.

"Glad you could make it," Sawyer said.

"Yeah," Hunter agreed.

Elsie ended up taking a seat beside him. She put a boot up on the table.

Evelyn smacked it. "I will not have you teaching June to be a little heathen."

"What's wrong with that?" Elsie said, reaching forward and grabbing a slice of bread, buttering it generously.

"I set a nice table, Elsie Garrett. And you live to lower the tone."

"In fairness," Hunter said, "it's usually me that lowers the tone." He didn't know why he felt compelled to defend her, even while he felt compelled to be a little bit of a dick to her. Par for the course, he supposed.

Just how they were.

"Well, you don't put your boots on the table."

"Most things I say are a 'philosophical boot on the table' at a dinner party, Evelyn. You can't really take me anywhere," he said.

Wolf's wife, Violet, leaned back in her chair, her hand on her swollen stomach. "Let's eat," she said. "I'm exhausted. And starving. Don't banter at the expense of serving food."

"I don't have to be asked twice," Wolf said, dishing a full plate of food for his wife, before passing the potatoes down the table.

"So," Sawyer said, "tell us about the progress you guys are making over there at McCloud's Landing."

"Oh, it's been really fun," Elsie said. "All equine work. So, I'm in heaven."

"She's great too," Hunter said.

She looked at him, surprise on her face. "Well, thank you, Hunter."

"You didn't let me finish my sentence. I was saying she's great…for a mean little weasel."

"I ought to bite you like a weasel." She wrinkled her nose and narrowed her brown eyes, and his first thought was that it was awfully cute.

He did not know where that came from.

He shook his head, and turned his focus to filling his plate.

"We're going to have to get some safety and board certifications to be approved for therapy," he said. "And Brody hired somebody. Elizabeth Colfax. She's a STRIDE mentor. I'm not entirely clear on the acronym. But she's going to oversee the program, and she's an approved teacher to help us get certified, and then she'll stay on as a lead."

"Wow."

"And Charity is going to pick up some extra work on medical for the horses. We've got some places for people to stay. Because the focus is going to be rehabilitation for people who are injured, neurodivergent clients and at risk youth. And sometimes there're going to be long-term programs in place."

"And Gus came up with this on his own?" Sawyer asked.

"I don't really know where Gus got the idea. But you know how he is. You can't get him to talk. Unless he wants to. And he doesn't often want to."

"Yeah," Sawyer said. "True."

Hunter trusted Gus with his life. Hell, he couldn't know for sure, but he suspected that Gus had saved his life on multiple occasions.

But his brother wasn't like the rest of them. He hadn't

come through their childhood with any kind of sense of humor intact. That was for sure.

Of course, Gus had taken the brunt of it. The absolute worst of their father's temper, again and again.

A temper that had only gotten worse once their mother had gone.

A temper Hunter knew he bore some responsibility for.

Pain he knew he bore responsibility for.

And when it wasn't Gus, it was Lachlan. Tag had taken his fair share, and so had Hunter. Brody... For some reason Brody had been the golden boy. The only one that Dad had ever been proud of. And the only one dad hadn't hit. He'd never laid a hand on Brody in anger once.

And Hunter knew that ate at Brody. In some ways, he imagined it was worse than being like them. Worse than having endured his father's fists. Because at least they were all in that together.

And they'd survived it anyway.

Though deep down, Hunter felt like maybe he was on the outside too. It was just his brothers didn't know his whole story.

No one did.

"He just doesn't seem like the outreach type," Sawyer said.

"He's not. But he's...the protector type."

"Are you going to get certification, Elsie?" Wolf asked.

"Well," Elsie said, "in very typical Hunter fashion, this is more information than he's given me before. So I don't know."

"If you want to," Hunter said.

"Of course I want it."

He looked at her, and his mouth twitched. And he

couldn't help poking at her a little bit. "You're really on a journey of self-improvement lately."

She sputtered on her mashed potatoes.

"Are you?" Violet asked keenly. "What other self-improvements are you doing?"

"I..."

"Elsie is very devoted to learning how to bake," Hunter said, grinning.

"Really?" Elsie asked.

"That's what you mentioned the other day. That you wished you could set a table the way that Evelyn and Violet do. Isn't that what you said?"

"Yes," she said, smiling sweetly, but the intensity of her grin drew the focus to her teeth. And he had a feeling she was thinking of fighting again.

"Well, you're in luck," Evelyn said. "We're doing the baked goods for Game Day. So there's going to be quite a lot of work to do."

"Fantastic," Elsie said, her grin turning crisp.

"It's nice to see you so devoted to your personal enrichment," Hunter said.

"I heard you were wanting to sharpen your castration skills," she said. "You know," she added, "when Sawyer and Wolf need extra help come that time."

"Thank you," Hunter said. "You know I value improving my neutering skills."

"I don't know what's going on here," Sawyer said, "but if the end result is me getting extra help come castration time, I am okay with it."

"If it's going to end with me getting extra help in the kitchen, I don't care either. Keep on sniping at each other," Evelyn said.

It was accepted that he and Elsie had their own language.

That they did things their own way. That they were mean to each other. But also often sat next to each other. They were…whatever they were.

But right now they had a secret. And it lent a strange sort of edge to the teasing.

"We're headed to Vancouver in a few days," he said.

"Really?" Sawyer said, his mouth turning down into a frown.

"Yeah. We have some horses to look at. I need Elsie's expertise."

"Thank you," Elsie said. "I like to think that I have a fair amount of expertise."

"She does," Sawyer said. "She's brilliant."

Elsie flustered a little bit under the compliment, and it was such a strange thing that he couldn't help but notice.

"We'll go after Game Day."

"You better," Sawyer said. "Because I don't want to miss the chance to destroy your family."

"Ha! We'll definitely be doing the destroying," Hunter said.

"Not likely," Elsie said. "Just remember. I owe you."

He knew that she meant it too. That she was going to make him pay for the baked goods that she was going to now have to prepare for the big event.

When the four ranches got together and competed in a ridiculous string of summer games, followed by eating. Potato sack races, three-legged races, basically any kind of race they could think of where their legs were hobbled. Tackle football. Mostly because it felt good to hit each other at least once a year.

And he had a feeling that she was going to hit him as many times as possible.

He welcomed it.

That, at least, was normal. In a long string of things that weren't. That, at least, was normal.

IT WAS GAME DAY, and Elsie was furious at having been roped into being baking help. Her arms were sore from kneading bread, and she had asked multiple times why in the world anybody needed to make bread when you could easily go to the store and buy it. And for cheap.

"I don't want your cut-rate white bread," Evelyn said.

"I like baking," Violet said. "It's satisfying to have made it yourself."

"I don't know," Elsie returned. "Don't you find the simple motion of undoing a twist tie to be satisfying?"

"I guess we all get our satisfaction different ways," Violet said, patting her hand.

"My throwing arm is going to be compromised for football," Elsie said.

"You're not going to play football with them, are you, Elsie?"

"Sure," she said to Violet. "All the girls play."

Evelyn grimaced. "Not all the girls."

"Well, clearly not me," Violet said, pointing at her stomach.

"All right, all the girls who want to. But plenty of us do." She shrugged. "The Sullivans do. But somebody has to always play for them. It isn't fair if they don't have any men on their team."

"I've always wondered what it's like for them," Evelyn said. "It must be such a different mood to the rest of the ranches."

"It is. I mean, you've been to the farmhouse."

"A feminist utopia complete with gingham everything," she said.

Elsie laughed. "I think utopia is an overstatement, but it's nice."

"And it gives you a little idea of how it is," Evelyn said. "It just must be very interesting to be at a ranch that isn't run by men at all."

"Well, Fia is a fierce taskmaster, and frankly, makes Sawyer look chill."

"That's terrifying," Evelyn said.

"But amazing," Elsie said by way of agreement.

When they finally finished, Elsie swung by her cabin and got her gear together. Some kneepads, because she didn't like to have to worry about how hard she might go down, either during football or the three-legged race.

Game Day was a huge deal for Four Corners. And everybody showed up with canopies at the lake and lawn chairs, blankets and copious amounts of food.

Sullivan Lake was an important part of the ranch. Sawyer and Evelyn had been married there last summer. And Elsie thought it was a very nice place to have a wedding.

Not that she ever intended to have one. But if she did, in a different life, a different time, it would be there.

The lake was so named because it was on Sullivan's Point, but all the other families had easements to use it. The families from Garrett's Watch, McCloud's Landing and King's Crest all made use of it at will.

But this was the most cheerful of days.

By the time Elsie got there, many of the canopies had already been set out, and the families had gathered, along with participating employees.

She saw Travis standing over with the Sullivans, and she wondered if he was the one who had been tapped to play for them this year. It suited her because it would give her an excuse to go and talk to him.

The idea invigorated her.

He said something to Alaina, and Alaina laughed uproariously, her red hair flying back on the wind, and Elsie frowned.

No. She wasn't going to go having weird feelings just because he had talked to Alaina. Alaina had every right to talk to him.

She took a sharp breath and then looked over at the McClouds. They were assembled beneath a canopy, just lounging on lawn chairs. Brody was standing just outside the canopy talking to a pretty girl Elsie didn't recognize. Probably a relative of one of the ranch staff members. She was laughing and holding a red Solo cup. And Brody did love to make people laugh.

Then there was Lachlan, reclining in the shade with his petite friend Charity sitting beside him. She was picking blades of grass and listening to him intently. Tag was leaning against a tree holding his wife, Nelly, up against him.

And she didn't see Hunter.

She craned her neck, looking around, and then turned around and nearly ran smack into him.

"Steady there," he said, grabbing her shoulders.

"There you are," she said. She belatedly realized she'd admitted she had been looking for him, and felt mildly embarrassed. Even though she didn't know why that should embarrass her.

"Yeah," he said.

"I was just… I saw your family."

"Yeah," he said. "Brody really needs to address his whole situation," Hunter said. "Because I think her dad will probably come looking for him with the shotgun."

"Sounds like a *him* problem," Elsie said.

"If we end up having to get in a fight, it's going to be an *all of us* problem," he said grimly.

"Good point," she said.

"Looking forward to absolutely wrecking you people in today's game," Hunter said.

"Oh, not as much as I am."

She looked back over at the Sullivans and saw that Travis was gone. And she had missed a chance to talk to Travis because of Hunter.

Well. Never mind. He would have seen her talking to Hunter. Maybe. And that might work in her favor.

Maybe.

They had food set out for everybody on big tables, and Elsie started to graze right before they got set up for the three-legged race. They agreed that she and Wolf would represent the Garretts.

It was Nelly and Charity who went in for the McClouds, with Rory and Fia going in for the Sullivans, and Arizona and Denver in for the Kings. Unsurprisingly, it was Rory and Fia who took an early lead. She had been hoping that Wolf's stride would help, but the two sisters being closer in size gave them a more coordinated advantage.

And at a certain point, Wolf just got irritated and pitched them both to the ground.

"Hey!" she said.

"We weren't winning anyway," he said, laughing.

"That didn't mean I wanted to be thrown on the ground."

"Chill out, squirt," he said, tugging on her braid.

Her face was beet red, and she hoped that Travis hadn't seen that. She really didn't need her brother treating her like a baby, not when she was trying to get him to recognize that she wasn't a baby anymore.

She huffed and rolled over onto her stomach, freeing herself from their three-legged prison.

She sulked off the field and went and got a plate full of food, determined to sit the remaining events out.

Evelyn got tapped for the potato sack race, and was dismal at it, which Elsie had expected. Her sister-in-law was great at a lot of things. Physical activity—when it wasn't dancing—was not one of them.

It was Nelly McCloud who triumphed in that event, and Tag picked her up and carried her around like she was the trophy, then ran them both into the lake, while she screeched at him.

And Elsie couldn't help but stare. At that relationship. Really, it was the same with her brothers. And their wives. It was like they'd transformed. They laughed now. They had fun. She had never really associated that with relationships, but it seemed to be a part of theirs.

And Tag and Nelly's too. Apparently.

She made sure to fuel up until it was time for football. And for this, they divided themselves in half.

The Garretts ended up with the Sullivans, and associated ringers. Which did include Travis, and that pleased her immensely. They would have an excuse to get in the huddle together. But that also meant that the McClouds were paired with the Kings. And frankly she thought it was an unforgivable advantage.

Her brothers were great. But they were the only men of any real size on the team. Travis was handsome, but he didn't have the height or muscle mass of any of the McClouds or Kings.

She really liked Travis. She also liked to win.

Denver, Justice, Daughtry and Landry King were terrifying. And Arizona might be small, but she was mean.

Penelope, usually called Penny, had lived at King's Crest—a ward of sorts of the Kings—for a number of years, but they were insular, and so as a result, she was too, and Elsie didn't even know her whole story in spite of the fact they were very close in age.

But at least she wasn't helping the McClouds. She was fluffy, and soft, and sitting under a tree with a small chicken beside her. So she wasn't going to be causing any drama with the game.

Then there were…the McClouds.

Getting hit by Gus was probably like being hit by an actual freight train. The others would be like all the rest of the cars rolling right over.

"What's the matter with you?" Sawyer asked, elbowing her as they took their place in the huddle.

She realized that Travis was in there too.

"Nothing," she said, gasping for air.

"Good. Get your head in the game, Garrett."

"I think we have to acknowledge we are a little bit outgunned," Fia said.

"Yeah," Wolf said. "But they aren't going to tackle *you*."

Fia looked back over her shoulder, and Elsie was fairly certain she was looking at Landry. "I would not be so sure."

"Play the small helpless female thing to your advantage," Sawyer said.

Alaina and Elsie snorted in unison. "We will not," Elsie said, feeling free to answer for the two of them.

"Come on," Travis said, elbowing her gently. "Pretend you sprained your ankle."

He winked.

He *winked at her.*

For a moment, everything seemed a lot brighter.

Her stomach did a funny little shiver.

But then she looked out of the huddle, and saw the opposing team lined up and ready to go. And saw Hunter. His eyes were focused. Intense.

She knew beyond a shadow of a doubt that he was coming straight for her.

And that made her stomach do something else entirely.

She took a breath. "I'm ready."

"Break," Sawyer said.

They got lined up, ready to hike the ball, with Sawyer and Gus head-to-head.

And when play started, it started hard.

It was a melee. There was no real refereeing in the situation, though people tried to call outplays and penalties from the sidelines. It was difficult to get anyone playing to pay attention.

The McClouds alternately had Charity and Nelly running around on their side, which made things feel a little bit more even. But then Wolf bumped Charity in an attempt to retrieve the ball, and that earned him a sack from Lachlan, even though he wasn't even supposed to be on the field.

Wolf was grumbling about his knee when play started again, and in the confusion, the ball went loose. Elsie scrambled for it, scooped it up into her arms and started to run like a jackrabbit as quickly as she could for a first down.

And that was when she found herself flying through the air. Taken completely off her feet. She landed roughly in the grass, with Hunter's arms around her. She clutched the ball to her chest, looking up at him with ferocity.

"You snake," she said.

"I don't think you got a first down."

"I *did*," she said.

"Didn't," he said, grinning.

And for some reason, the voices all around them went

fuzzy. And her heart started to beat a little bit harder. So she did what any reasonable person would do. She reared up and bit him on the forearm.

He cursed, jumping back and freeing her.

"You," he said.

"Deserved," she said.

"Break it up," Sawyer said, coming in and waving his arm. "This game is supposed to be civil."

"He *tackled me*," she said, pointing toward him. Then she realized her hand was shaking and she put it down.

"Tackle football, Elsie," Hunter said. "If you're too fragile to handle it…"

"I am not fragile," she said back.

And she was going to lie in wait.

Alaina managed to get the ball at one point and was making a run for the goal line when Gus scooped her up and threw her over his shoulder like she didn't weigh a thing.

Alaina's howl of fury echoed across the surrounding mountains.

"Carrying!" Sawyer shouted.

But Gus said nothing, he only ran the length of the field and crossed the goal line, with both the football and Alaina.

"That doesn't count," Wolf said.

"If you say so." And he almost smiled. Or at least, it was one of the closer things Elsie had ever seen to a smile on his face.

Play resumed and finally, Hunter got the ball, and she saw her opportunity. He wouldn't see her coming. He was on his guard for Wolf, Sawyer or even Travis. And she could see his attention focused there. She came around behind while he was running, and dove straight for his knees.

She shrieked in glory as he went down, and the two of them rolled in a violent ball of fury.

And landed so that she was sitting on his chest, staring down at him.

He was breathing hard, and she could feel his heart pounding against her.

Right against her...

Her eyes suddenly widened as she realized.

She was sitting on him. And she was just suddenly very aware of all the parts of her that were making contact with him. She had never...in her life thought of anything this way.

Especially not...

Their eyes met, clashed. That was the best way she could describe it because it was almost as if it made a *sound*. A crash. As if it had impact.

Her heart leaped up in her throat. And she scurried off of him. "That'll teach you," she said, trying to disguise how breathless she sounded.

"Yes," he said. "I feel very taught."

Everything was sideways after that.

The Garretts and the Sullivans got completely thrashed. And by the time Elsie limped off the field she realized she had spent the entire game obsessing over scoring points against Hunter, and not really paying attention to Travis being on her team.

And she didn't really know what to make of that in the end.

There was a small first aid effort made after the game, but Elsie bypassed it. Sawyer was wrapping a brace around his wrist, and Gus put a Band-Aid on Alaina's upper arm, in the back where she couldn't reach.

Elsie went straight for refreshments. And not coincidentally, Travis.

"Have a beer," Travis said as the sun went low, and they got a bonfire started down the beach.

Elsie blinked. "Thank you."

Alaina started to head their way, post bandaging.

"You can have one too," Travis said, holding a can out to Alaina.

"Sure," she said, walking over.

"Hunter never tackled me," she whispered. "Lucky."

"*He's* lucky," she said, looking back over at him, "that I didn't kill him."

"I think he always considers himself lucky that you don't do that," Alaina said, laughing.

"You all do this every year?" Travis asked.

And Elsie chose to focus on his easy manner. Because he was easy to talk to. He had such nice blue eyes, and he wasn't…intense or foreboding or anything like that.

"Yes," she said. "Though sometimes it feels a little more evenly balanced."

"It would be," Alaina said, "if Fia didn't refuse to be paired with the Kings. We could mix up into more combinations then."

"What is her deal?" Elsie asked.

"Love affair gone wrong?" Travis asked.

"Probably," Alaina said. "Though honestly, when you look around here, you would expect there to be more of those than there have been."

"Yeah, you would," Travis said. "Nobody else…"

"Oh, I think they do. Pretty often," Alaina said. "I just think mostly they keep it casual."

Travis grinned, and he directed it right at Elsie. "I like the sound of that."

Elsie took a sip of her beer. And she thought maybe they had almost flirted. But she hadn't done a very good job of that. She didn't know what to say back. So she smiled. And it seemed like it was good enough.

When the evening ended, Lena slipped her a small high five, and that made Elsie feel immensely satisfied.

And things were only going to improve. Because she and Hunter were going to Vancouver. He was going to teach her everything she needed to know, so that next time Travis talked to her, she could keep it going.

Hunter.

She thought back to that moment. That one that was so alarming she didn't even really want to reflect on it. Because of all the parts of her it had made her aware of.

That didn't matter. He was just Hunter. That was all. He irritated her. It was why she had gone after him like she had. Other people had tackled her during the game, but only Hunter had infuriated her.

But the payoff for that would be that he was going to teach her what she needed to know.

Everybody had their uses.

Even Hunter.

And she was not above exploiting him.

CHAPTER FIVE

"So today is Vancouver day?"

Hunter looked over at Sawyer, who was standing in front of the hay truck with bales he was delivering to McCloud's Landing.

"Yes, it is," he said, feeling a strange tightness in his chest.

"Condolences."

"Oh, Elsie's fine," he grunted.

"She's not still sore about her epic football defeat?"

Hunter didn't want to think about that day. He didn't want to think about the moment he'd realized he'd made a mistake in tackling Elsie. Right when he'd had her body beneath his he'd remembered what he'd said about her figure.

Commenting on her figure hadn't been anything he'd ever thought he'd do. *Thinking* about it was even lower on that list of Likely To Evers, and yet he had. And then when he'd been on top of her he'd been…

Unbearably conscious of it.

He hadn't really thought that through when he'd said that it was cute in the first place. Because she was Elsie. Because she was Elsie, and it hadn't seemed like it would be a problem to weigh in on her outfit choice or anything like that. It had just seemed like a natural offer. Then she'd shown up in her gray T-shirt and black jeans, looking like she always did. That was the thing. She looked like she al-

ways did. But by asking her to show up as a woman looking to pick up a guy, it forced him to look at her like a man
who might want to pick up a woman.

And he'd been forced to concede that, while she wouldn't
be the flashiest girl in the bar, men would notice. She had
a neat little figure. Small boobs, she'd said it herself, and
a lean waist that was strong from all the hours she spent
riding horses. Her hips were only gently flared. He hadn't
been lying when he told her that her body was cute.

It was.

He had just never particularly wanted to observe that.
And now he had.

Not that it was a big deal. He was a grown-ass man who
had all the opportunity in the world to hook up. He tended
to like a flashier sort. That was just his deal. Because it
was obvious, and he was a man who liked the obvious.
Except, verbalizing that about her had made him feel like
a shithead.

To tell her that there was something wrong with her outfit, when there wasn't. She looked nice. She didn't need to
slap makeup on, she didn't need to do anything that made
her feel uncomfortable. She was cute. *Pretty* even. And the
entire interaction had left him feeling like an absolute dick.

It was just that in order to do what she wanted, where
she wanted to do it, he had a feeling that she was going to
have to shake things up. Because all the men around here
didn't know her. And she was going to have to do something
to signal that she didn't want to be treated like Sawyer and
Wolf's younger sister. And the changing of her look was a
good way to do that. But then she basically called that out,
and made it sound as stupid as it was.

And that would have been okay, had it not been followed
up by the football game.

Where he'd felt her *small boobs* pressed up against him. And then…then she'd tackled him. And sat on his chest. And he'd looked up at her face and he'd sworn…

"Elsie's been good to work with," he said, feeling more defensive of her than usual because he was feeling like an ass. "And this is a work trip."

"Yeah. So what exactly are you doing?"

"There's a ranch up north that used to do equine therapy. They're shutting down, and they've got some animals for sale. But they're already trained, so they cost a ton of money. Gus wants me to go scope it out. I'm good with that. But Elsie's expertise is useful." It was. He wasn't lying. Not really. He was just leaving out the part where he had specifically asked her because of the whole flirting thing that he was keeping from his friend.

"I hope you appreciate that," Sawyer said. "She's great with horses."

"I know," Hunter said. "It's why I hired her. I don't need any lectures from you on that." He laughed. "Believe me. I didn't sign up to get hissed at all day by that little weasel to do anyone a favor."

Sawyer laughed. "Now, that sounds more like you and Elsie."

"Like I said, she's fine during work."

She was…well, she was Elsie. She was a little bit hotheaded. She was a little bit of a loose cannon, it had to be said. But nothing he couldn't handle.

He could certainly handle having looked at her boobs.

"Good. So how are… You know, how are things?"

"What the hell, Sawyer? Are you going to ask me about my feelings next?"

"No, it's just that because of the start-up over at Mc-Cloud's, you haven't been working over at Garrett's Watch anymore. That was your trade for stealing Elsie for all this. So things have changed and, you know, we don't really go out to the bar anymore."

"I'm sure your wife would let you out once in a while."

"She would," he said. "It's just that… I dunno, it just doesn't hold that much appeal. But you're coming by for dinner sometime after you get back from Vancouver."

"All right."

Sawyer shook his head. "I couldn't have imagined how much life would change in the last year. It's weird. You live in a place like this all your life and things don't really change. Until they do."

Hunter nodded. Except for him. Things hadn't really changed, at least not substantively. Yeah, the work that he was doing at McCloud's was a little bit different, he didn't have the drinking buddies he once had. But they were all still there. He didn't anticipate that changing anytime soon. Or ever. It was a strange thing, though, if he really thought about feelings—and he tried not to—how much things had shifted with Sawyer. They'd been thick as thieves all their lives. And now Sawyer was a father. He was married. He was definitely more into his wife than he was into anything else, and that was how it should be. At least, Hunter figured.

He didn't have that kind of future in front of him. And he knew that. He'd never been sad about it.

It was just that he and his brothers had been made to feel somewhat broken from birth. And the ways that they had dealt with that were not all the same, and not necessarily functional in the traditional sense either.

Tag had sorted things out, and he'd gotten married. But that was Tag. He'd always been lighter.

"Hey, it's all good," Hunter said. "I'm busy enough with

the horse stuff, and as far as I'm concerned, you and Wolf being off the market just opens things up for me."

"Yeah, maybe Gus could be your wingman sometime."

Hunter laughed. Genuinely laughed. "I can't even imagine. I don't want to scare women away. I'd say that to his face. Also, his face has nothing to do with it. When women like him, that's one of the things they like. But it's a particular kind of girl that's okay with…all of that."

"Yeah, that's why he's a good wingman. You don't attract the same girl, that's for sure."

"That is true. His personality is sometimes a barrier, though."

"Still, I hate to see you alone."

"Hey, you don't need to worry about me."

He knew Sawyer did, because Sawyer worried about everybody.

"I'm not worried about you, asshole. I just don't want to be the guy who bailed on his friend because he got married."

"I'm fine. We'll go fishing, we'll have dinner. But we don't need to talk about our feelings."

"But I do have a lot of new June Bug pictures."

"Yeah, I'm sure you do. No need. I'll come by and see the little mite in person."

"All right."

They unloaded the hay, and he said goodbye to Sawyer, then he headed down to the paddock to get one of the horses out. He rode in circles in the arena, doing quick changes in testing his responsiveness. And his mind kept on wandering back to Elsie.

To whether or not he should even be doing this at all.

Seriously, though, she's going to do what she's going to do, and without your intervention…

That was the thing. That was the thing that he hadn't fully understood until last night. Elsie Garrett wasn't a hurricane. She was a loaded pistol. And she had a lot more potential to get out there and cause damage than he had realized.

Targeted damage.

He had just been thinking of her as little Elsie Garrett. And that was the problem. That's what most men around here thought. But if they ever opened their eyes and looked...

Well, little Elsie Garrett wasn't little anymore. She was cute, and she was after something.

Well, hell.

Yeah. All for the better that he was involved in this. All for the better that he was going to offer some guidance.

Sawyer would actually thank him if he knew. Not that he was ever going to know. But Hunter would. Because sending her out there with no breaks was a bad idea.

He was just going to pump those breaks, send her out a little bit strategic. Send her out a little bit prepared.

That was all.

He wasn't going to be able to stop the storm, but he could provide an umbrella.

Hunter McCloud was usually a little more active in the cause of disasters than the prevention of them. But in this case, he would consider it his mission. To prevent an Elsie Garrett Level Disaster.

Luckily, this was his game.

And he was going to have no trouble taking her in hand.

THEY WERE HEADED off to Vancouver today, and Elsie was so excited she was having trouble focusing on her work. She wasn't supposed to go over to McCloud's until later, and she had promised that she would see to some chores at Garrett's Watch. But that put her in potential proximity of Travis, and she was already so wound up over the trip that she had a feeling if she did see him, she was going to have difficulty keeping any kind of cool.

It was a pretty long drive up to Vancouver. Which meant that it was going to be a lot of hours in the truck with Hunter. But that was fine. They could talk more about everything. Then out of the corner of her eye, she saw him. Travis. He wasn't wearing a hat, and his curly blond hair was visible, shining in the sunlight like a golden halo from his position on the back of the horse.

Her stomach did a little twist, and she spurred her horse forward, moving in the direction that he was in. She had valid work reasons for approaching him. "Hey, Travis," she said, trying to sound cool and casual.

"Elsie," he said, grinning. "What's going on?"

"I was wondering if there were still stragglers that needed moving down to the lower pasture. Sawyer wanted me to help with that before I headed out."

"Nah, we got them all," he said. "Thanks for checking. You're awfully good with horses," he added. She had taken quite a few compliments on her horsewomanship in the last few days, and she was deeply enjoying it. "Not so great with football, though."

"That was all Hunter's fault. He was a jerk."

"It's my impression Hunter kind of is a jerk," Travis said.

"He isn't," Elsie said, feeling defensive. "He was *being* a jerk, that's all. He's actualy great, he's…whatever. He's just him."

Travis looked at her speculatively. "Right. Hey, were you at the bar the other night?"

"I was," she said. "I—I didn't see you there." She was

lying. But she had a feeling that this was kind of what Hunter was talking about when he'd advised playing it cool. She was going to play it cool.

"Oh," he said, and she could tell that he was taken a little bit aback by that.

And she felt like she had won. Or at the very least scored some points. And she hadn't expected to score any points, not this early in the game.

"Yeah. I was just there to hang out with Alaina."

"You danced with Hunter," he said.

"Oh yeah," she said, waving a hand. She was tempted to add that Hunter was like a brother to her. But then she didn't. Let him wonder.

But Hunter is *like a brother to you.*

She swallowed hard, remembering when they had danced. It had been short and casual, but he was strong and solid. But they had danced together just teasingly at the bonfires and things before. There was nothing terribly groundbreaking about it. She remembered how rough and warm his hands had been.

And then there was the tackling.

And that time he'd touched her chin.

And she felt lit up like a beacon everywhere he'd touched. Like a roadmap of places Hunter McCloud had placed his hands had been imprinted on her body.

"Well, maybe next time I'll buy you a drink."

"Yeah," she said, her voice scratchy. "I'm going to be gone for a couple of days, though. Hunter and I are going up to Vancouver." She smiled, then she turned the horse around and rode back toward the stables. And she couldn't keep the grin from spreading wider and wider on her face.

For the first time in her life, Elsie Garrett felt like she might be a little bit mysterious. At least, to Travis. And she kind of liked it. She could barely contain her excitement about the interaction with Travis for the rest of the afternoon. She was still buzzing by the time she hefted her duffel bag into the back of Hunter's truck, and got into the passenger seat.

She hadn't ridden in his truck since he had gotten his new one. It was very nice.

She started fiddling with things on the dashboard, and then froze when he got in.

"Don't break anything," he said. "This thing is—"

"Fancy," she said. "I've never seen anything like it."

"Well, Sawyer could quit driving that beater if he wanted to."

"Sure." She wrinkled her nose. "So could I, I guess."

"Why don't you?"

"I don't go anywhere. My truck gets me from point A to point B. I don't need to be fancy about it."

"Don't you ever want to be fancy about it?"

She shrugged. "If I want to, I will."

He stared at her for a moment. "I suppose that's true."

"I talked to Travis today," she said.

He started the engine and pulled out of the driveway, and they began down the long dirt road that would carry them out to the main highway. "Did you?"

"Yes. He didn't mention this at Game Day, but he asked if I was at the bar the other night. I told him I didn't see him at the bar. But he saw me dancing with you." She left out the part where he'd called Hunter a jerk and she'd felt compelled to defend him.

His mouth curved up into a half smile. "See. There you go."

"Yeah," she said. "I did it. I'm mysterious."

"I don't know that you could ever be accused of being mysterious."

"Don't burst my bubble," she said.

"I'm not about to try to burst your bubble, sweetheart."

"Honestly," she said.

"No, that's good. You did exactly what I would've told you to do."

"He said maybe he'll see me at the bar again sometime. Which is perfect, because I'm going to get something so that I can be dressed up next time I go to the bar."

"Perfect," Hunter said.

She settled back into the truck seat. "Yeah. I'm just curious," she said, "why...why is it a game? I mean, I don't play around with you or Alaina, but it's like this thing... Like a dance that you have to know the steps to if you want to make sure somebody knows that you have a thing for them. I don't really get it."

"Protection," Hunter said.

"What, condoms? What does that have to do with anything?"

He laughed. One short, sharp crack. "That's not what I mean. I just mean... I don't know, I think people feel exposed when they let somebody know they want to sleep with them. It's a thing. So you pretty it up and put all these layers around it. Play cooler than you might otherwise."

She frowned. "Do you feel vulnerable?"

Hunter was like a mountain. Nice to look at, but forbidding, unforgiving and just as hard. She would never look at a mountain and think vulnerable. But then, she didn't look at Hunter and think that either.

"Not *me*. Doesn't really mean anything to me."

"It doesn't mean *anything* to you?"

That pulled her up short for a second, and sent her mind

careening down a rabbit trail. An image of Hunter taking a woman into his arms in a bar, taking her home. Taking her clothes off…

It meant nothing?

The idea made her feel scalded and she wasn't even imagining herself or anything. Not like she *would* imagine herself with Hunter. She wasn't even thinking of herself with a different man. She would never imagine herself with…

No.

Except the shirt she pictured floating to the floor suddenly looked familiar and the girl in her vision had a long, dark braid.

She blinked.

"Not at this point," Hunter said, his tone dry.

She should drop it. But she didn't. "Did it ever?"

"Let me cast my mind back. Yeah. I guess. Your first time, you worry about doing it right. And then after that, you worry about it less. But in terms of getting hurt?" He cleared his throat. "No. No, I know what real hurt looks like in relationships. Because I watched my parents. And I never had any desire to be a part of anything like that."

Yet again, he was talking about his parents, and while she knew about them, she hadn't heard him talk about them so…so personally. It felt like a heavy and strange gift, and it made her want to be careful. With what she said. With who she said it to. It made her want to hold the knowledge close and treat it like it was special, and it was such an odd feeling.

"So…I guess knowing up front that I didn't want any relationship to become anything… That's protection, right? That all by itself." She fiddled with her seat belt. "I don't want anything. Like, relationship stuff. But I don't want to get made fun of or look like an idiot. Or like somebody more than they like me."

"Well, that's exactly the kind of thing I mean. So you put on a little bit of armor. And if that happens to be an outfit that makes you feel good, then that's one way of having armor. If it's making him think that maybe you aren't interested, that's armor."

"What's your armor, Hunter?" She genuinely wanted to know, because... She just did.

Because he'd given her some truth, and now she wanted more.

"Whiskey?" He said it, light and funny, and for some reason it sounded like a lie.

"No. It's something else, isn't it?" The words scraped at her throat.

"It's not caring," he answered. "That's it."

She looked down.

"I want to learn to do that. But I think that's it, that's exactly what I'm getting at. If it doesn't feel like a rare opportunity, if it doesn't feel like something that's hard to come by, then I think I'll care less. But I've got to rip the Band-Aid off."

"That is one way of looking at it."

"It's weird," she said. "Watching Wolf and Violet. And Sawyer and Evelyn. Because I didn't really believe in that stuff."

"What stuff?"

"Happy marriages. I don't know. I guess I'm still waiting for them to leave. For them to leave my brothers. For them to leave the babies. I... Maybe for them to leave me too."

That was her deepest, most unspoken fear and she'd never been able to admit it to anyone. Even saying it to Alaina would have felt like a betrayal. Of Wolf and Sawyer, and her sisters-in-law. But she could say it to Hunter. She didn't know why, only that she could.

"They're not going to do that," Hunter said.

"How do you know? All we know is people who leave," she pointed out.

"Yeah. Historically." Silence passed for a long moment. "I don't think they will, though."

"Why? How do you figure out who will and who won't?"

"Because not everybody in the world sucks." He looked toward her, and she shifted, until she realized he was just changing lanes, checking his blind spot and not her at all. And she didn't know why that made her feel silly. "And I think they genuinely love your brothers."

"Yeah. I guess."

"My mom should have left," Hunter said. "Before she did."

"Well, she shouldn't have left you." Because mothers shouldn't leave their children. Especially knowing they wouldn't be taken care of. At least her father hadn't been cruel.

"No. I guess not."

"I don't think that I could ever handle that. The relationship thing. It makes me feel claustrophobic." Except that was a lie. It wasn't the enclosed space she feared. It was the space left behind when people decided to leave.

"We have that in common," Hunter said.

She thought about her brothers, about their lives. Their happiness. The thing was she did believe that Evelyn and Violet would stay. But she couldn't imagine ever trusting somebody enough to believe that they wouldn't leave. To really believe it.

"What soundtrack goes best with self-pity?" Hunter asked.

"Well, I am glad that you asked that," Elsie said, "because it so happens that I have a curated playlist for when I'm marinating in the sadness of my past."

"Well, if you can plug your phone in, my truck will play it."

"Excellent," Elsie said.

She fired up her favorite playlist, which she thought was a work of genius, and settled back in the plush seats.

The familiar scenery of pines and ferns gave way to less familiar scenery of I-5, which would take them the whole way north.

The farther behind them Four Corners got, the more her excitement grew. Maybe she should get out more. Maybe she should have tried to go somewhere else for a while.

"We should get there by dinner. We can throw our stuff in the motel and go somewhere to grab food."

"Oh yeah, I'd like that."

"What do you like?"

She tried to think of something she couldn't get in Pyrite Falls, but the list was too long. "I don't know! Everything?"

"Thanks, Els, that narrows it down."

She didn't put a lot of thought into anything but food until they were about a half hour away from their destination, and then she thought back to what he'd said about the motel.

"We're staying at a motel?"

"Some roadside place? Kind of shitty. I changed it to a suite when you decided to come."

"What does a bad roadside motel suite look like?" She was genuinely curious.

"I don't know, but they claim to have a kitchen, a dinette set and ample sleeping arrangements."

A strange, unsettled feeling crept up her back and made

her shoulders tense. It was something about not being at Four Corners. Something about being far away from home and Wolf and Sawyer and everything normal.

Like a weird sensation of being in free fall.

She could do whatever she wanted and no one would know.

Well, no one but Hunter. And what was she even thinking of anyway?

The feeling had been fleeting, but bright and hot and when she'd tried to grab it and make sense of it, it just didn't.

What *anything* was she thinking?

Why had her stomach swooped down low while her breath had overfilled her lungs?

"Ranking my food preferences," she said. "Indian, Thai, really good steak, Italian."

"All of that would work for me."

It was easier to anticipate a good meal than it was to try and parse the feelings she'd just had a minute before.

She looked at Hunter's profile, and something strange echoed in her chest. Hunter was that kind of handsome you couldn't really deny. And she had known him all her life. When she looked at him, she saw Hunter. The way the sunlight filtered through the truck now, highlighted the dark whiskers on his square jaw.

"Hunter," she said, because honestly, she couldn't really believe that she hadn't asked this question before. She had been curious about the way that he saw her. But now she wanted to know how women saw him. What he did. Because wasn't that part of the answer to this whole man/woman thing. "Why are you... I mean... Why do women like you?"

He turned toward her, just quickly, the corner of his lip turning up incredulously, one eyebrow lifting. "Elsie," he said, her name spoken like he was talking to a sad child.

And as she continued to stare at him, she realized why it was such a dumb question. Because he was beautiful. That was why. All of that male beauty had been in front of her for all of her life. But it had never been aimed at her. It had never been…for her. It had just been there.

Like the glorious mountain range that she could see in the distance every day when she got up and looked out the window of her cabin. Like the river and the meadow, like a sunset. That was all. Right out there, something that she could enjoy all the time, but something that she sometimes just took for granted.

Something she didn't pause and stare at all that often.

"What, like… Okay, fine. You're hot." And it made her squirm in her seat to say that. Hot. What a weird thing to call Hunter.

"Thank you."

"It's not a compliment. It's an observation. But I just mean, there're…cowboys everywhere. But I guess you just have a…particular…"

"So did your brother," he said.

"Sawyer?"

"Yeah. Although, to be fair, Sawyer never spread it around quite like me or Wolf."

"How was Wolf…?" Wolf was just so grim. Or he was, before Violet. "What's that deal?"

"He's intense," Hunter said. "So I've heard women say."

She shimmied her shoulders, doing the best outward expression of deep revulsion that she could. "I don't want to talk about my brothers. They're all settled."

"Which is not what you want."

"No. But I don't like feeling… I've been protected from a lot, Hunter, but some of it I never asked to be protected from, and the rest… You can't protect someone from their mom leaving, you know that. But then at the same time I feel like I get all the credit of someone who can work the ranch but when it comes to my personal life I still get treated like a child. And that isn't fair. I've been through the same shit you all have. Why shouldn't I get to flirt and drink and sleep around and…" She snorted. "What the hell am I supposed to do with all my demons?"

"Some things aren't healthy," he said. "Especially in the name of demon control."

"And you don't do them?"

He laughed. "Oh hell no. I do them times ten."

"Well, maybe I want to do them too." It sounded so stupid. But he'd shared with her about his parents. She wanted to share this. "I want…" She leaned against the passenger-side window. The glass was cold and her breath spread a fan of condensation over it. "Nobody has ever chosen me. Sawyer and Wolf are stuck with me. My mom ran away. My dad didn't give a shit. I just think it would feel really amazing to have a man look at me across a bar and choose me—and yeah, for a night is fine."

"So you really do want to…date."

"I said I did. I'm not a man, I'm not just thinking with my…well."

He didn't laugh. "All right, when we go to dinner tonight we'll practice that."

"What?"

"A date."

For some reason that made her palms feel sweaty.

They got off the freeway, and into town, and they drove around some of the side streets for a while until they spotted a restaurant that looked like it might be Indian fusion. He looked it up on his phone and confirmed, and while

Elsie wasn't entirely sure what Indian fusion was, she was willing to have some.

They got out of the truck after they parked, and Hunter opened the door for her. And there was something about it that made her unbearably self-conscious. The restaurant itself was pretty, with ornate silver lanterns studded with jewels hanging from the ceiling, and gilded mirrors that hung behind the bar. There was no one up front, and Elsie sat on the barstool and looked around. It was filled with patrons, and she wondered if it was the kind of place where you were supposed to have a reservation. Or at least have a certain standard of dress. She was just in those same jeans and a T-shirt.

"I'll get somebody."

He walked away and left her sitting at the bar. And she felt…antsy. Then she heard his voice behind her.

"Evening, miss. If nobody's brought you a drink yet, I'd be much obliged if you'd allow me."

She turned slowly, and her amber eyes met his, and for some reason it felt like a punch in the stomach. Because this was Hunter, but it wasn't Hunter. Standing here in this restaurant, where he should look out of place in a black T-shirt and jeans and a black cowboy hat, talking to her like she was a stranger.

And every female eye in the place was on him. He was… he was even more unquestionably good-looking here. The more refined setting making his rough masculine beauty stand out in sharp relief.

His brown eyes had flecks of green and gold in them, and it seemed more apparent for some reason right now.

Or just maybe she'd never really looked before.

Never seen before.

But there was something about him now that demanded

she did. That demanded she looked closer. That threatened to make her feel like she was falling.

"Sure," she said, trying to keep her breath steady. "I—I'd love a drink."

"What'll you have?"

Beer. Normally she would ask for beer. Should she ask for something different? He felt different. Maybe she should be different. "I've never been here before," she said. "Do you know what I would like?"

Just for a fraction of a second, she saw surprise flicker in his eyes. Her stomach went tight with a sensation of deep satisfaction that came from somewhere wholly female.

That she'd surprised him.

"Yeah," he said. "I know what you like."

That made her mouth go dry. And she felt a strange sort of echo between her legs. She fought the urge to press her knees together.

He leaned over and got the bartender's attention.

"The lady would like a daiquiri. I'll have an old-fashioned."

A second later a hostess came and assured them their drinks would be brought to their table. The table was upstairs, right next to a window that overlooked the city, light shining below. It was so strange. So...so different from anything she was used to. And she had never thought that city lights could be beautiful. Right now they felt nice.

"A daiquiri?" She wrinkled her nose.

"I chose that because you would never order it for yourself," he said. "They're expensive, and I bet you think they're girly. But I think you want one anyway." He smiled, slow and easy, and she couldn't tell if they were still playing a part or not.

"All right, maybe *pretend* Hunter knew what *pretend*

Elsie wanted, but now I am going to be stuck with a sixteen-dollar drink that I probably won't like."

His gaze was relentless, and so was his grin, and in no way acknowledged the pretend part of this that she wished so badly he would. "You're going to love it, Elsie."

She huffed, because her chest felt tight and it was better than sitting there with that. Better to seem indignant.

She took the menu from the center of the table, drawing it toward her. She was very thankful that it was structured around small plates so that she could try absolutely everything.

"You're enjoying this," he said, grinning.

"Yes. I never go anywhere, and there are things I've always wanted to try, but haven't ever."

"I didn't know you were a foodie."

"I don't know that I'm a foodie, I'm just hungry. And I would like the food I eat to taste good when I eat it."

"Fair enough."

"Have you done a lot of traveling?" In her memory, she didn't really remember him being gone all that much, but she of course wasn't all that aware of the things he'd done in his early twenties.

"Not a ton. But definitely spent my fair amount of time up in Portland, causing hell in my spotted youth."

"Maybe that's the problem. Maybe Alaina and I just need to go raise hell out of town."

"Honest to God, I don't like the sound of that."

"Why not? Why do *you* get to do it?"

"Because I'm a man." He held up his finger. "And before you go accusing me of sexism, it is actually just because of men that it makes me worry about you."

All of her umbrage deflated. "Well, that's fair."

"You and Alaina could cause a hell of a lot of trouble."

"True."

The drinks arrived, and the waitress took their order, and Hunter looked at her while she regarded the glass sitting in front of her.

"Okay," she said. "I'll try it."

She leaned forward and took a sip of the drink, and dammit, but she loved it.

"It's disgusting," she said.

"Liar," he said.

"No," she said. "I hate it."

"You are a dirty liar, Elsie Garrett."

He smiled at her, and her stomach turned over. And she had the sudden realization that the truth was all his beauty had never been for her. It had always been for other women. And so she had never really stopped to think about it in that way.

But what would it be like? To be a woman on a date with Hunter McCloud. Wondering if he would touch your hand, or put his arm around you. Kiss you. Invite you into his room...

You are staying in his room.

Something like terror streaked through her, but it was centered a lot more firmly between her thighs than most terror typically was.

And the image she'd seen earlier was back, glaring and bright and impossible to ignore.

"Fine," she said, eager to get on less teasing territory. She and Hunter teased each other all the time, though. It shouldn't feel so strange now. "I like it. I guess you do know what I like."

But that did not feel less loaded.

"Points for me."

"Yeah, there was a time there where I thought... Maybe

I'd leave ranching behind," he said. "Maybe I'd leave Mc-Cloud's Landing altogether. So I went a few places. Tried some different things. But in the end, family's family. Even if the patriarch of mine sucked."

"Right. Well, I don't remember mine all that much. And Sawyer and Wolf don't suck. So I always figured I would stay and...be a Garrett. I feel kinda bad that I'm doing work at McCloud's Landing. But I really love the work. And I'm appreciative of it."

"You're in a tough spot, aren't you?"

He sounded like he pitied her and that was really a terrible thing. She didn't want to be an object of pity.

"I'm not," she said. "I'm really not. I'm in a great spot. My brothers are awesome, and I can do the equine therapy while still being so close to them. And still doing work on Garrett's Watch."

"I just mean there are some things that make it so we never feel all that free. You're tied up in a lot of obligation."

"Yeah. I guess so. But you must..." They never talked about this. At least they hadn't until recently. The subjects had been edging into unknown territory lately, but she worried this was a bridge too far. He joked about Gus, but she knew that the topic of his brother, and the injuries he'd sustained at the hands of their father, and what had happened to their father before he disappeared, was kind of a touchy subject. "You must feel some of that for Gus."

He nodded. "Yeah. It's unavoidable. Gus took care of us. Gus took care of what needed taking care of. And he paid for it."

"You feel like you have to stay and help him?"

"We're all obligated to something. But I'm not stuck. No. Because the fact of the matter is, when I was younger especially, I don't think feeling obligated to Gus would've been enough to keep me here. Not if I didn't really want to stay. Your brothers are my friends. And I care a whole hell of a lot about them. They're part of it too. I always found it easier to spend time at your place. Especially after Mom left. And…things got worse then and hell. Look what happened to Gus. I guess in some ways, now I feel like I owe Gus some labor."

"Well, it's a good thing our families had each other, really."

"Yeah," he said. "Good thing."

One thing that hurt was knowing that the McClouds had not been safe at their place. Their land hadn't been a haven. Not like it had been for the Garretts.

Their dad might've been disinterested in his kids, and not a particularly great partner. But he had never hurt anybody. Not physically. And he hadn't been mean. Even though Elsie couldn't remember them that well, they'd had wonderful grandparents. Loving and sweet. There had just been more for them than there had ever been for the McClouds. And it made her feel pity for Hunter. And she couldn't recall having ever felt that before. It was a strange mix of sensations, all while sitting there realizing how handsome his face was.

She was relieved when a basket of flatbread was put down in front of them, followed by myriad chutneys and meat in spicy sauces, rice and cucumber salad.

Hunter himself had gotten a pot of something extremely spicy and was eating it without breaking a sweat.

"You want to try it?"

"I'm skeptical," she said.

"Come on now, Elsie Garrett, I've never known you to turn away from a challenge."

She picked up a spoon so that she could take some, but

before she could, he dug his own spoon in, took some food out and held it out to her.

She only stared for a moment at the spoon he held outstretched in front of him. He expected her to…eat off it. Like she was a child.

"Just hand me the spoon."

"This is what I'd do for a date," he said, his grin making her feel itchy.

She eyed him skeptically, then leaned in, her eyes on his as she opened and took the spoon into her mouth.

And suddenly it was like an electric current was arching between them, conducted through the spoon, and when her lips touched it, it was like a pop went off inside her.

She leaned back, suddenly, chewing quickly.

"Okay, that's intense," she said. But she couldn't really taste the food. Instead, her heart was beating wildly, and the thing that burned the most was his gaze.

"It's good, though."

"Yeah," she said.

She was only halfway through the daiquiri, but she was pretty sure it had gone to her head, and she decided to leave the rest sitting there.

They moved on to talking about the plan for tomorrow, when they would head to the ranch, and what they would be doing. And she was grateful to leave the flirting lessons behind.

But what she hadn't really considered, was that once they were done with dinner, it was time to head over to the motel.

Oh well. Whatever. At least they would have their own sleeping quarters in the suite. Presumably.

It was a long yellow strip of a building, with red doors that had gold letters tacked to the outside.

They parked out front. Elsie grabbed her duffel, Hunter his, and they went into the little lobby area. It had a rack of brochures proclaiming the sites around the area, and a small, floral couch with paper cups on a table beside it, and two silver canisters she assumed held coffee in the mornings.

The man at the counter smiled at them in a way that made her feel uncomfortable.

And she realized exactly what he was assuming.

She shrugged her shoulders up around her ears, on the pretense that she was just choking up her hold on the duffel bag.

Hunter signed some papers and got a set of actual keys.

"Room 203," Hunter said, leading the way out of the lobby.

They walked along the cement sidewalk all the way down to the end.

"I am told there's a view of the river," Hunter said dryly.

Especially funny considering they each had cabins that were mere steps away from a river. And they were at them every day.

He stuck the key in the doorknob and turned it. When he opened the door, Elsie burst out laughing. "Oh my gosh," she said.

The kitchen area had glaring yellow tile with some busy pattern on it, the cabinets painted red, with big chips in the paint. There was a step up to the left, and a bed featured prominently there. Then there was a lattice divider with the couch right next to it.

"There's only one bed," Elsie said, suddenly feeling a strange prickle of...panic.

"Hang on," he said. He moved one of the cushions on the couch. "Yeah. Hide-a-bed."

Elsie frowned. "Not exactly as advertised."

"No. I wasn't aware that a lattice half wall constituted a separate sleeping quarters. Or that a hide-a-bed was considered a bed unless it was noted as such." He chucked the cushions off and folded the bed out. It was the old-school kind, with the bar that ran in the center.

"No worries. I'll take this," he said.

"Oh," she said. "Are you sure? It's just… I wouldn't want you to hurt your back."

"Elsie," he said. "I'm thirty-four. I'm fine."

"Well, I know you're thirty-four. That's why I was worried about…" She trailed off.

"Honestly."

He went over to a closet and found some extra bedding, and set about making the bed while she took her duffel bag up the step to the lumpy-looking queen bed with the big sunburst headboard. She plopped the duffel on the end of the bed and started to rifle through it, looking for her pajamas. She hadn't really anticipated…well, them sleeping in the same room. She was not the most okay with it.

She stomped off to the bathroom, which was equally tacky, with a blue sink and toilet, and a counter with little daisies. She changed quickly into her sweatpants and purple thermal top, stashing her bra deeply in the other clothes that she had, so Hunter wouldn't see it.

Because the idea of Hunter seeing her bra was suddenly horrific.

She felt an echo of that feeling she'd had when she sat on his chest on the field and she hurriedly shoved that away.

When she got out of the bathroom, Hunter was already lying down in bed with the lights off.

She noted that he wasn't wearing a shirt. And then she looked away. *Forever.*

She climbed between the sheets and ignored the fact that it was comically early.

They were going to have an early start tomorrow. And tonight had just been... Well, it had been exactly what they'd agreed on. It wasn't Hunter's fault that it made her feel weird. It wasn't Hunter's fault that she didn't have any experience with men, and it made even this obvious farce feel like something it shouldn't.

She heard his breathing go even. And Elsie ended up falling asleep, but with great difficulty, listening to the sound of Hunter McCloud breathing only a few feet away from her.

CHAPTER SIX

HUNTER FELT LIKE literal hell the next morning, and he got up before the sun, went for a jog, then went and grabbed coffee from a neighboring chain before heading back to the motel room.

Of all the dumb fucking things.

He had felt edgy going back to the room, edgy after that... It was supposed to be... It was stupid. He wasn't even that cheesy when he picked up a woman.

I know what you like...

Hell.

But there was something about the way that Elsie responded to it that was screwing with him. And he didn't particularly like it.

He'd thought it was the best course of action to go to sleep as quickly as possible, to do something to break the weird tension that should not exist between him and a woman he had known since she was a baby. Him and his best friend's younger sister. She was practically *his* sister.

But she's not.

Whatever.

They had work to do today. And it was going to get them back on even ground.

"Rise and shine, sleeping beauty," he said.

She was still beneath the covers, her dark hair tangled and wrapped around her face.

The covers were up so high he couldn't even see her. But she had one bare foot sticking out the bottom of the blankets. And he chose not to look at that.

She stirred, turning over and sitting up, stretching.

And his eyes went to the last place they ever should.

To her cute little figure. To her damned adorable, pretty, breasts, which were way too visible beneath that purple waffle print shirt with… Hell.

It had *owls* on it.

And he could see her tits. And they were…they were good. They were very good. And that was the thing he didn't need to know. That Elsie Garrett had the prettiest set of *small boobs* he'd ever seen. And he was pretty sure he was only noticing them because she had mentioned them. And normally he didn't even like them small. Well, that was a lie, he'd take them however he could get them, but, it wasn't his preference.

But he was suddenly obsessed with hers.

"I brought coffee," he said.

"Oh good," she muttered sleepily, getting out of bed.

Those pants she was wearing were soft, and they cupped her ass in a particular way, which he noticed when she bent over to straighten the blanket.

"I'm sure even this dive has housekeeping. You don't have to make your bed." He sounded like a dick, and he just… There wasn't anything he could do about it. Because he felt like a dick.

Because he was looking at Elsie's body.

And thinking things.

She straightened and rolled amber eyes—which seemed especially bright this morning—at him. "You're grumpy. Drink some coffee." She padded over to where he was, and he was extremely conscious of her bare feet.

He didn't typically do mornings with women.

In fact, he never did. He didn't spend the night with women.

But this wasn't "women." This was Elsie. And it was remarkably different than "women."

"Is there sugar in there?"

"No," he said.

She scowled, and opened the cabinet in the kitchenette, finding a hot chocolate packet and getting it out, taking the lid off the coffee and dumping the powder in.

"That's disgusting," he said.

"Sugar and caffeine," she said. "Best start to the morning in my opinion."

"Flawed opinion," he said.

"You were so charming for, like, five minutes last night," she said.

"Yeah. Well, that was… You know what that was."

He wasn't sure *he* knew what it was.

"Right," she said.

"Drink your coffee," he said.

Because now he just felt like an ass. It wasn't her fault that he was being a horny jerk.

He wasn't going to *do* anything. It was Elsie. So what if he noticed she was good to look at. A lot of women were. And he didn't have any intentions on sleeping with them.

Elsie was… Elsie. And the thing was, he wasn't all that comfortable thinking of her as a woman. Because he felt protective of her. That was the thing.

That was the thing.

They finished their coffees, then got into the truck, and neither of them said much on the way to the ranch.

Until they arrived.

"Oh wow," Elsie said, sitting up straight and looking

around the facility. It was pristine. Dark green buildings with bright white trim, perfectly manicured lawns. They parked outside the main barn, and were met by the primary caretaker of the place. And he took them to the paddock where the five horses they were interested in were housed.

They got a quick rundown of where everything was and were essentially left on their own.

And one thing he couldn't get over was Elsie's absolute delight over being around horses. Always.

But he related to her on that level. Horses, in his experience, were better than people. And he knew that she agreed.

That was one of those things. If they were under your skin, they were under your skin. If you understood them, then that was it. They understood you.

There was an old Appaloosa that Elsie fed a sugar cube to, and then let out of the stall.

"You want to go for a ride?"

And he found that he did, even though he did it every day.

"Sure." He led one of the other horses out of the stall, and they tacked up, looking at a map that was posted at the end of the barn, deciding where they wanted to go.

The horses were as docile as expected, and there was no real attention to be paid to anything.

"Well, it would be easy to start with horses like these. Entirely broken completely ready for what we're after," he said.

"Yeah," she agreed. "It's amazing how big this place is. Just totally different than… I mean, obviously Four Corners is huge. But so much of that is for cattle.

"Yeah," he said.

"Do you remember that you're the first person that ever put me on a horse?"

He stiffened. "No. I don't."

"I do," she said softly. "I was, I dunno, four maybe? My grandma was still alive, and it freaked her out."

"Oh yeah," he said. "I do remember that. She was hollering at me because I put you on a horse that was way too big for you, and I was fourteen, and an idiot, and had no business being put in charge of a kid. That was the real issue," he said.

"We didn't always fight," she said. "That was the best day of my life. And I thought that you were my hero."

"Your grandma definitely disagreed," he said. Now he remembered. He remembered that he got a tongue-lashing to the end of days.

"She said, 'Hunter McCloud, if you injure one hair on my granddaughter...'"

"Yeah, and she didn't have to finish the rest, because I knew. I knew that I was going to meet Jesus a whole lot sooner than I anticipated."

"That definitely sounds like her."

June had been the best and softest adult influence in his life growing up.

She might've been hard sometimes—especially when it came to Elsie—but she had cared for Hunter like he was one of her own grandkids.

"I knew that I loved horses that day," she said. "More than anything. I dunno, I guess it felt like fate. It always has. Sometimes I was just so lonely, and I would go out to the stables and...smell them? And there's always been something about the way they smell that made me feel better. That made me feel different."

"When did you feel lonely, Elsie?" He couldn't help himself. He wanted to ask the question. Because she had her brothers, and she had Alaina.

"Sometimes I just missed my mom," she said. "And I don't even remember her. So that's about the silliest thing that I can even think of, but I did. I missed her. And there was nothing really that I could ever do about it, and nothing I could say.

"Poor Wolf and Sawyer, they remembered their mothers. They really missed them, not just a feeling they thought they ought to have. That's all I could ever miss. This idea of something that I never even had an experience of."

"Look," he said. "You miss your mom whether you knew her or not. Because we all know we're supposed to have one." He never wasted time missing his, though. She had to leave. She had to. And it never would've worked to…

"Your mom left before I was born. I only ever knew any of you after. And your dad…after."

He looked at Elsie, and his chest was a tangle of things he couldn't sort out. He wondered what she'd seen. What she knew about his home life, not because she'd been told, but because she'd *seen* it.

The idea that she'd been touched by any of it…

Shit, it knocked the wind out of him.

He wanted to protect her. And that was the damned silliest thing. It was all in the past and he couldn't protect her from it any more than he could go back and protect his brothers.

"Yeah. I'm sorry you were ever exposed to my dad."

"I wasn't much. Sawyer didn't want me around him. But sometimes it was either that or be with mine by myself."

"Did you ever…"

"I never saw anything," she said.

The relief he felt was…

"I didn't want you to… Hell, I'd feel terrible if you ever saw him being violent."

"You were the one who got hit," she said.

"Yeah, but that's just how it was. You weren't part of it and I'd have never wanted you to see." To see him get hit. To see him in a weak moment.

"I didn't," she whispered. "So many of my memories are good. Because of Sawyer and Wolf and…and you."

He and Elsie had lived their childhoods pretty much together. But he hadn't remembered when he'd put her on the horse until she'd mentioned it.

He'd been hiding away from his father, hanging out at Garrett's Watch, like he often did in those situations. But he remembered Elsie had wanted to ride a horse so badly. And he had thought then…honestly what he thought now. That she'd find a way if he didn't help. And she would likely get herself in trouble.

"Some things don't change, do they?" he asked, though he'd meant to ask himself.

"Like?"

"Just… Nothing."

Except that some things did change. Like him being forced to look at Elsie and see a woman. So there was that.

"Thanks for dinner last night," she said.

"Yeah." He found it easier to think about last night than this morning.

"I just… I've never had anyone take me to dinner."

He really didn't want to get into the list of all the things Elsie Garrett hadn't done. Or maybe he should. Maybe he needed a real stern reminder of all Elsie hadn't done.

Like kiss anyone most likely. And for sure no sex.

That was supposed to get his mind right out of the gutter. Right off that dangerous path he was on and had been on since…

He couldn't even say quite when.

Instead, it intrigued the hell out of him. Made his mind want to linger on it. On the implications.

He shook his head. "Come on, Els, let's head back."

When they got back to the barn, Ira Hodge, the owner of the place, was waiting for them and greeted them warmly. He told them all about the years he'd spent doing equine therapy and then invited them to use his table at the country club tonight. Which Hunter basically pretended to understand since he'd never seen a country club this side of a teen movie.

Hell, he'd committed to taking Elsie shopping, and now she'd have a place to wear a dress.

He ignored the warning alarm that sounded in his brain.

"A country club?" she asked when they were back in the truck and headed to the center of the city so they could shop.

"Yeah, well. Another dinner date."

"*Practice* dinner date," she pointed out.

"Yep."

He imagined this was the kind of place that would at least require a jacket, so he'd be picking something up too. He took them to the kind of department store he'd normally never set foot in.

"You can find the women's section, right?"

She nodded, but her eyes were wide and he had a feeling he ought to go with her. "I'll meet you at the fitting room," he said.

He made a straight line for the men's suits and found a black jacket, pants and shirt, then headed in the direction Elsie had gone. But she wasn't at the fitting room. She was frozen in front of a rack of dresses.

"Well," she said when he approached her. "I looked at a price tag."

He chuckled. "Yeah…"

"What the hell are they made out of, finely woven unicorn hair?"

"I think the label is supposed to impress you."

"I'm not impressed."

He moved past her and grabbed three dresses off the rack and handed them to her. "Here."

"How do you know they're my size?" she asked.

He looked at her, then at the dresses. "They'll fit."

"What, you just know that? Like you just know a woman's body and…" Her cheeks went scarlet and then she hugged the dresses right to her chest angrily and stalked to the fitting room.

He tried the jacket on and figured he'd leave the rest up to chance. He was making sure he could move freely in it—he had broad shoulders and it made coats tough—when Elsie slinked out of the fitting room.

And it was like time slowed down.

She leaned against the door frame, and he looked her over. At the way the black dress hugged her figure like cling wrap, and ended midthigh, showing her long, toned legs and…for some damned reason it was the socks for him.

Her white socks, which came up to the middle of her ankles and which she'd left on for *some damned reason*.

"Hell," he said.

He hadn't meant to say it out loud and that was the second time today Elsie Garrett had created words in his mouth he had never meant to be there.

"Is it that bad?" She winced.

"What? Hell no. It's… How can you look at yourself and think it's bad?"

She blinked. "I don't look like me. I look like I'm trying too hard."

"It's your body, Els. How could it look like anyone but you?"

It was just that he'd never really looked before. He'd never really known.

And he shouldn't look now, because that wasn't the point. Not of any of this. He was getting her dresses and creating confidence in her for Travis.

So Travis could put his hands on her and kiss her and well, shit, Hunter really didn't like what he was doing. Sawyer *should* punch him in the face.

"I don't know…"

"Get all three," he said.

"I can't."

"I'm your boss and I'll get them."

"Well, that's inappropriate."

"I'm also HR."

"You are not."

"Elsie," he said, his tone warning, "don't argue with me. Not now, anyway."

And by some miracle, she obeyed. Then she turned to go back into the dressing room and his eyes lingered for a little too long on her ass.

She paused, then turned back. "You look good too."

"Guess we're country club ready."

She reappeared looking more manageably *Elsie*, and he took the dresses from her and paid, in spite of her protestations. "It's all work stuff," he said.

She'd grumbled anyway. And he'd made her choose a pair of shoes.

But Elsie grumbling was comfortable.

They went back to the motel and Elsie vanished into the bathroom and he took the opportunity to quickly change into the suit. And black had been the right choice because it went with his cowboy hat.

Elsie reappeared and it was like a gut punch. She had the black dress on with a pair of low black heels and as much as he'd liked the socks, the heels were something else.

"I don't have makeup or anything." She fiddled absently with her hair.

"You don't need it," he said.

She stopped fiddling.

"Well, thanks."

"I'm serious. You look beautiful."

And he shouldn't have told her that. He didn't need to be the one to tell her that, but he knew she was hungry for it and, well, it was true. So why not say it?

You know damned well why.

"Thank you," she said. She cleared her throat. "You clean up pretty good yourself."

"I consider that high praise from you, Elsie Garrett."

"Pity about your personality," she added, her smile getting impish.

He walked over to her and held his arm out, and Elsie looked up at him with something in her eyes he didn't want to understand. Slowly, hesitantly, she slipped her arm into his.

And the two of them walked out of the motel room and toward the truck.

It was a fairly quick drive to the country club, which was everything he'd imagined one might be. Needless pillars that seemed to be there for the sake of gratuitous marble, and shiny floors and gray plush chairs with buttons that seemed to strain against the over-ample stuffing.

And Elsie looked awed. It made him like it.

She put her arm in his this time without him having to pause.

He gave the woman at the front Ira's name and they were ushered to a glossy wood table and given menus. Elsie's eyes lit up when she saw steak.

It reminded him of a wedding reception. Down to the live band with people dancing to Frank Sinatra tributes.

And for a minute it was just such a strange, out-of-body experience that it was easy to forget who she was. Easy to forget who he was.

"So the point of this is to have a membership to fanciness?" Elsie asked, while chewing on a bite of steak.

"That's my take," he said.

They'd ordered the same thing.

"I can see the appeal."

"Can you?"

She laughed. "Nah. I'd get bored. I like a jukebox and some beer. But the steak…well, the steak is pretty good, and I am a connoisseur."

She would be, considering beef was what the Garretts did.

She ordered lemon cake for dessert, he ordered the flourless chocolate torte, and she had a second glass of wine. Then she looked up at him with overbright eyes and it was familiar and upsettingly new all at once.

"You have to ask me to dance," she said.

The band was playing Louis Armstrong, and frankly things did seem wonderful right now.

"Dance with me."

"That wasn't a question."

"You told me to ask you, Elsie, so I already know you will."

She sniffed and lifted her wineglass, tilting it all the way back to get the very last drop and if he'd wondered about whether or not she was tipsy before he knew she was now. "A lady wants to be asked."

"All right, my lady, would you like to dance?"

"I would." Her cheeks went pink and everything in him lit up in a warning. Because this wasn't just him noticing her braless. It wasn't just him noticing her legs or figure or ankle socks.

She was pink. And noticing some things of her own.

He stood still and reached for her hand, and she took his. Her hands weren't soft. She wasn't soft. But she was. Strong and soft along with it.

And he took her hands and led her out to the dance floor. And he had danced with Elsie Garrett any number of times, but never far from home. And never when she was in a dress like that. And never when he had a restless, edgy thing snarling inside of him and reminding him that he was a man and she was very much a woman.

Reminding.

Was it a reminder? Or was it a discovery. Something new altogether.

It didn't matter either way. Because it was never going to be anything other than this moment. It couldn't be. For her sake, and for his.

For his sake? No. It was all out of concern for Elsie. Elsie didn't have any experience. For him…

He was practiced at sex with no strings. It was who he was. What he did.

That was what worried him more than anything about Elsie. That she thought she was heading right toward the same thing that he and her brothers did regularly, and she was going to come out unscathed. But Elsie had been protected somewhat by Wolf and Sawyer, and it was such a commonplace thing that she didn't really fully realize how protected she was. She was softer than they were. She was better than they were, when it came right down to it. Just a hell of a lot better.

And he didn't want her to go running to spoil that because she had some vague idea that there was something she was missing.

And what can you do about it? Like you can protect her from herself.

He was trying. And trying to protect her from himself while he was at it. This was just the dance.

That was all. And whether Elsie was beautiful or not didn't much matter. Whether he liked the feel of her in his arms didn't matter either. She was Elsie Garrett. But for some reason, despite how much he reminded himself of that, he couldn't quite make it mean something. Or rather, he couldn't get it to mean what he wanted it to mean. He wanted it to be an instant deterrent. Something that made him jump across the room like a scalded angry cat.

But it didn't. It stood, it fascinated him. She was Elsie Garrett. And she was absolutely, wickedly enchanting in a way he had never imagined his friend's little sister could be. In a way that no woman like her ever had been to him.

He wasn't sure he had ever known a woman like her. He had never known *anyone* like her, he decided. That was a fact. At the end of the day, Elsie was a singular creature, and always had been. Typically, she was singularly driving him crazy, but... But.

He quieted his thoughts because Hunter had never had very much use for deep thinking, and this was why. And then realized that was a mistake because the minute he let his thoughts fade into the background, it was even worse.

Because then, he was just focusing on the way she felt.

And it was the strangest thing, holding her in his arms like this, knowing how agile she was. How fit. Knowing what her body could do. In the sense that he knew she was an excellent horsewoman who was fearless and never said no to a challenge. Who was strong enough to best many of the men on the ranch in calf roping, and to beat them in a race.

And then he made the mistake of looking at her, which was worse than simply touching her, because it was a stark reminder that he knew this woman. Inside and out, but not in this way.

Not by touching her.

Not by holding her.

He didn't know her like this. He never should have gotten close enough to introduce himself to this. And it hit him then that he had been playing with fire from the moment Elsie had asked him to help do this. And every excuse he had given himself was... Wasn't it just that? An excuse? Because it ended here. With him holding her in his arms like he had the right. And suddenly, the world felt tilted because he didn't know what to make of that. Because he would've said that he never aspired to hold Elsie Garrett in his arms a moment in his life, but he wasn't an idiot, at least, not usually without intent. And he had told himself that his reasoning for all of this was noble. Hell. He knew better than that. He knew better than that. So what the hell?

Maybe he could simply get back on top of this. Maybe he could shut his thoughts down. Maybe he could even rethink all this. So that he got his mind back where it needed to be. So that he got himself sorted right back out, and never thought of this or touching her like this ever again. Maybe.

"Hunter," she said.

Her name was a whisper on her lips, and there was something strange about that too. That she was saying his name like a question rather than a curse, that she angled her body slightly and brought herself up against him. And he could feel her. Her pert, beautiful breasts and other feminine curves he convinced himself that Elsie Garrett just didn't have. And that he would never be able to unsee or unknow.

"Where did you learn to dance?" he asked.

"You," she said, but it was softer than she ever normally spoke.

"Me?"

"You always let me dance on your feet. At the bonfire."

He didn't need to think about all the things he'd taught her. From horseback riding to dancing. He really didn't. Not now.

"I'm not on your feet now," she said, looking up at him from beneath her lashes.

It was dangerous.

She was dangerous.

Then the song ended, and it was like a sign. One he heeded, unlike all the other obvious warnings that had gone off inside of him up until now.

He released his hold on her and didn't touch her at all as they went back to their table, as he took the bill and settled it. Didn't touch her at all as they walked out of the country club and waited for his truck to be brought up by the valet.

And he felt like he had his feet back under him when he was in his pickup, which was a piece of home.

Elsie was a piece of home, but that didn't seem to be doing anything to keep his head planted in reality.

"Thank you," she said when they were midway between the motel and the club.

He grunted in response.

Then she didn't say anything more. They pulled up in

the space nearest to their room, and he got out of the truck. Then went to open her door for her, but she was already out and headed to the room, and she was holding her shoes in her hands, letting them dangle from her finger.

And for one moment he let himself acknowledge that if she were anyone but Elsie Garrett, he knew exactly what he'd be doing once they were back in that room.

He'd take her shoes from her hands, and toss them on the floor, wrap his arm around her waist and…

He jammed the key in the lock and opened the door.

She looked up at him, but said nothing and went into the room. He followed behind and said nothing.

She went up to her bed and gathered up a bundle, then went into the bathroom and closed the door with a decisive click.

He stripped down and grabbed a pair of sweats he wouldn't normally bother with, and as soon as he pulled them on Elsie reappeared, in that same little owl shirt, with her dress wadded up in a ball.

And her bra hanging off her wrist.

She dumped the clothes, including the dress, into a duffel bag, then climbed into bed.

And he just stood there like a damned idiot, heat in his veins that had no business being there.

"Good night," she said.

"Good night."

And he couldn't escape the feeling that even though he hadn't touched her, he'd done something he could never take back.

This whole weekend felt like something he could never take back.

That's stupid bullshit. You've seen any number of hor-

rible things and you didn't let it change you. A weekend with Elsie in a tight dress won't do it.

She was just Elsie, after all.

CHAPTER SEVEN

ELSIE HAD FELT peeled and rolled in salt since she and Hunter had gotten back from Vancouver and she couldn't talk to anyone about it. She didn't even want to think about it in her own damned head, let alone talk about it.

Mostly because she couldn't even put it into words or coherent thoughts. Or anything other than feelings she didn't want. Couldn't identify.

And it wasn't even all the dinner dates, or sleeping in the motel room together. It was…it was what he'd told her about his childhood. What she'd told him about hers.

The stuff about his mom and how he was glad she left, for her own sake, like his didn't matter.

The reminders that he'd taught her to ride, taught her to dance.

And she'd been thinking ever since. About every horse ride, about every time he'd ever spun her in front of the campfire or in the bar.

But at the country club…

They'd been like different people.

She'd felt different in that dress, in those heels. And he'd held her different, she knew he had. It had been different.

Not awkward, and maybe it should have been. But it wasn't.

It wasn't.

She was raw with it, and she should just be amped to

see Travis, because wasn't she right in the pocket now? She was warmed up with the flirting so it should be all good. She'd been back from Vancouver for twenty-four hours and hadn't seen Hunter since. Or Travis. Or Alaina for that matter, and she felt jittery and thwarted.

But tonight was a town hall and that meant they'd all see each other. All the four main families, the employees and all their families.

Alaina texted about an hour beforehand and asked Elsie to come and help get chairs set up, and Elsie complied, driving her truck over to the Sullivans' and parking in front of the barn. Alaina came bounding out of the barn, her red hair flying in the wind. "So. Tell me everything."

For a moment, everything in Elsie's brain stalled out. And she wondered how Alaina knew.

And then she realized, and it was like getting struck by a freight train carrying horror as a cargo. She hadn't thought of Alaina once the whole time she was gone. And she hadn't thought about Alaina's feelings for Hunter.

Hell, she'd barely thought about Travis…

Alaina didn't know Elsie felt weird about Hunter. Alaina wanted to hear about the time spent with Hunter because she was hungry for any and all information she could possibly get about him.

Because she *liked* him.

Elsie refused to think that Alaina loved him, because whatever she thought, Elsie knew that she didn't.

She didn't know Hunter well enough to…to love him. She might know him, but she didn't *know* him.

Not like Elsie did.

"Oh, uh, I think we're leaning toward buying the horses," she said.

"That's not what I mean, Elsie."

Elsie knew it, and Alaina didn't know Elsie did because Alaina thought Elsie was dense about men and Elsie could see that completely evident on her friend's face.

"Right. Well. I mean, I don't know. We went to a couple of restaurants, I bought some dresses. I'm going to wear one out to the bar this weekend."

That was the plan. It had been the whole time.

She wouldn't wear the black one, though.

Just looking at it made her think of dancing with Hunter and made her imagine being held by him. And so she just wouldn't wear it.

"That's great," Alaina said.

He didn't mention you.

And she hated herself for thinking that. It was so damned catty. What the hell? Elsie had never been catty a day in her life.

And it was about Hunter. *Hunter.*

Who had always gotten under her skin, sure, but mostly it was in an irritating familial kind of way. Which was why you stamped out of the bathroom with your bra on display 100 percent on purpose...

She fought hard against that memory.

And also against the image of him in that moment.

Shirtless. In nothing but a pair of low-slung sweats, and she had wanted to stop and take in every detail of him. Of his body, which she had seen before.

But it had felt different there. Different and dangerous.

"The thing is... I just... Hunter isn't in the market for a relationship," she said.

"He has sex," Alaina pointed out.

The flayed, irritated wound that was Elsie throbbed in response to that.

"Sure," Elsie said. "But you don't want..."

"Why are you being a hypocrite, Elsie? You want to have sex with Travis."

"Can you stop saying *have sex* like that? Someone could walk in and there's just no pretending you aren't talking about exactly what you're talking about when you're carrying on like that."

"Fine. You want to *play Scrabble* with Travis."

Elsie rolled her eyes. "That isn't…"

"Why can't I play Scrabble with Hunter?"

"Because he's Hunter! He's not some random ranch hand who's going to leave before next summer. He is Hunter. He's…"

And the words died on her lips when Hunter walked into the barn. Gus, Tag, his wife, Nelly, Brody and Lachlan were there too, but they seemed fuzzy around the edges. And then her brothers were there and they seemed just as fuzzy, but Hunter never did.

He stuck with his brothers and didn't come and say anything to her, which irked her, irrationally. As much as Alaina, who sat next to Elsie as the meeting started and kept fiddling with her hair while making moon eyes over at Hunter.

When the floor opened up, Hunter took the opportunity to go up and talk about the trip to Vancouver, the horses, the cost of them and why he thought it was worth the investment.

Then it was Gus's turn to speak about the progression of the equine facility. Gus was the kind of guy who commanded attention by virtue of his presence. Even Alaina was looking at him, but Elsie found her gaze wandering to Hunter.

It wasn't until midway through the meeting that she reminded herself to look for Travis.

With a jolt.

She hadn't thought about him once since Hunter had come in.

She examined his profile. His blond hair. His jaw wasn't as square as Hunter's. His shoulders sloped slightly, his whole build quite a lot narrower than Hunter's. And he was several inches shorter, which had seemed completely fine less than a week ago. He was taller than her, so what did it matter if he wasn't…a lot taller.

She remembered how small she felt when Hunter took her in his arms and…

Gus was sitting down now and Fia was talking about the advances they were making in the farm stand and Elsie had somehow missed the transition.

When the meeting finished, the bonfire outside was lit and food was put out on tables, meat put on the grill, and the makeshift band that was filled with an ever rotating group of ranch hands started playing rowdy country songs.

And somehow Elsie felt distant from it. Like she was hovering above it rather than being right down in it.

She sat down with her family to eat, and when Hunter came over with his plate something in her chest lifted.

But then he sat down next to Sawyer and didn't even acknowledge her.

She felt…alight with fury.

Why was he doing this? Acting like they hadn't had a weekend together? Acting like nothing had changed? Like he didn't know her any better. Like they hadn't talked and danced and he'd bought her a daiquiri because he'd known she'd like it even when she hadn't and what the *hell*?

She stalked away from her family and went to the bonfire, where beer was being poured into red plastic cups. She took one gladly and knocked it back, glaring across the dancing flames at Hunter, who was sitting there, talking to her brothers like she was invisible.

So she went to the nearest group she could find—a combination of McClouds and Kings—and smiled. "Anything interesting happening?"

Landry King looked genuinely surprised that she was speaking to him, his dark brows rising slowly. He was a handsome man—the thing was, they all were—and Fia Sullivan always acted like she'd rather die than be in the same room as him. Or on the same side of a bonfire. As a result, the Sullivans tended to avoid him at all costs.

"Just a discussion about whether or not we should play beer pong," Lachlan answered. "We're split, for and against."

"We're not discussing beer pong," Arizona said, her amber eyes flickering with disdain. But then, Arizona was always filled with disdain and no one really knew why. Well, maybe the Kings did, but they were sort of an insular breed, so who could even say?

Then suddenly, she had a horrible thought that Arizona's feelings felt like a pickled version of the rage inside of Elsie right this moment.

But that was different. She wasn't... Nothing had happened between her and Hunter. Well, something had. And him acting like everything was normal was weird, and it hurt. But she wasn't... It wasn't...

"Hey, Hunt," Lachlan said. "You want in on a poker game?"

"See?" Arizona said. "He's a liar. Beer pong was never on the table."

"Well, I knew that," she said. Mostly out of loyalty. Because Fia hated Landry, whatever the reason, and since Alaina was Elsie's friend, she tended to keep to their opinions on the Kings.

"You can play too," Landry said as if she was supposed to be flattered by that.

But then Hunter walked slowly over to where they stood, and that just made her even more infuriated. Because he came over when Lachlan called, but apparently had no time for her.

"Yeah, I'll play."

And she was immediately overwhelmed by her desire to lash out at him. For sitting over there ignoring her so damned easily and for coming over here and ignoring her just as simply. It was like she was invisible. And she hated it.

In the moment, she thought she might hate him.

"Is that your poker face, Hunter? Or do you always look that dumb?" she asked.

"Wow," Lachlan said. "Elsie came to play. Looks like she might be out for blood."

"I prefer my bloodlettings to be a little bit more exciting. I could beat Hunter with one hand tied behind my back. Strategy isn't really his strong point."

"What did you do?" Landry asked, grinning.

"I didn't do a damned thing," Hunter said. "Elsie's just got a burr under her saddle as per usual."

"You're the burr, Hunter McCloud."

"Guess that makes you the moody mare, Elsie Garrett."

"Did we step into the middle of a fight?" Lachlan asked.

"No," Hunter said, his gaze so cool it made goose bumps break out on her arms. "There's no fight. Let's play. You got a card table?"

"Over here," Landry said.

There was a foldout table with red canvas chairs, and one in Realtree camo, set around it.

Elsie sat down, and so did Hunter. Far away from her.

And that was like a splinter right under the fingernail.

"We should play for chores," Landry said.

"I have enough chores," Lachlan said. "I don't want to play for any more."

"Yeah," Elsie said, running right over Lachlan. "Let's play for chores."

It would be sweet to make Hunter McCloud do her more menial tasks around Garrett's Watch. She'd enjoy the hell out of it, in fact.

"Only because you think you'll win. You've got a lot of misplaced confidence," Hunter said.

"Do I?" she asked. "Or does everybody underestimate me."

"I think everyone doesn't think about you half as much as you seem to think."

That shut her up, but her mouth continued to open and closed in rage, and she could feel it, and knew how stupid it looked, but she couldn't stop it.

"Five card stud," Lachlan said. "Aces and jacks are wild."

"Deal us in," Landry said.

Arizona grinned and leaned back in the chair, her expression as hard and unreadable as ever, even with a smile on her face.

The card game was fast and furious with promised chores being thrown into the pot. Everyone went around once. Except Elsie and Hunter.

It went on and on. And Elsie couldn't bring herself to fold. Even though her hand wasn't that great. She kept on putting more in. Knowing that if she lost she had an endless list of chores to do at his place.

She could not lose.

"This is getting pretty rich," Hunter said.

"I'm about to get rich," Elsie said. "Rich in free labor."

"That's a lot of confidence," he said.

"I'm very confident."

"You're a child, is what you are."

"Better than being a horse's ass," she shot back.

And it was like no one else was sitting there. It was just her and him and all of her fury. The rage that she had felt over how he had ignored her.

"You know who has too much confidence, is you. How the hell you think you know everything, when you're just a country boy who's never really been off the ranch, I don't know. You drive the same road to work every day. Working the same land your daddy did. Hell. You practically are your dad."

She wished she could stuff the words right back in her mouth the second she said them. Because they were just out there, and ugly, and about the worst thing she could have ever said.

"I call," he said, his tone flat.

She could feel the ripple around her. She knew she'd gone too far. It was the last thing she ever should've said. Hunter's dad had been the meanest man in creation, and saying that he was his dad was unforgivable, not to mention untrue. There was no call for it. She had… Well, she had definitely overstepped. But she couldn't let everyone see that. Couldn't let on that she knew. Or that she was sorry.

"Straight."

He rolled his eyes, practically in his head. "Royal flush." He had beat her so soundly it was humiliating. He shook his head. "Elsie, you're going to come at me with nothing more than a straight and a bad attitude? That's not good enough."

"Another round?" Arizona asked, and when even she was uncomfortable with the intensity of something, it was bad.

"I'm out," Elsie said, flinging her cards down and getting up from the table, reality setting in. She had just said that to Hunter in front of Arizona, Lachlan and Landry. And not only that, she now owed him well over a week's worth of chores.

She felt awful. Angry and mean and absolutely crispy.

It was just so damned awful. And so was she. She'd been so horrible and spiteful to him. And after the way they'd shared things on the trip.

But he was acting like the trip hadn't happened, so should she even feel guilty about that?

If they'd never danced and if they'd never…

Then maybe all the sharing didn't count either.

She walked past the bonfire and into the woods, standing beneath the trees, breathing in and out quickly. Trying to rationalize what the hell had just happened. Because that was…inexcusable. It just was. She heard a twig crack behind her, and she whirled around, and she knew it was Hunter, even though all she could see was his silhouette in the firelight.

"What the hell was that?"

And so she did what any reasonable girl would do in her situation. Where she knew she was clearly wrong, and had been in front of absolutely everybody.

She doubled down.

"You are being… You're being a dick," she said.

"What did I do?"

He didn't know? He *really didn't know*?

"Hunter you are ignoring me. You're acting like—like nothing happened."

Now that the words were out there, bare in the open, they just sat there. Vulnerable and horrible and she wanted to take them back, but she couldn't.

She was so used to just saying whatever she thought, especially with him, but now it was just a tangle.

"Elsie," he said, his voice firm and even. "Nothing *did* happen."

It was like a punch to the gut, and it made her eyes sting with unshed, shameful tears.

"Hunter..."

But it was true. So she had nothing to say. Nothing had happened. Nothing had happened, and she was acting like a scorned lover.

And she suddenly felt horrified. Horrible. She hadn't fully realized that what she was doing was acting the part of someone who'd had...a romantic interaction with another person. And they had not. They had not had a romantic interaction. They hadn't...anything. But she felt different. She felt different about him. And he should feel different. It should feel like something. How could he dance with her like that, go shopping for clothes with her and see her, and say those nice things to her. And hold her in his arms and...

She was mortified. And nothing inside of her would let him see that. Nothing would allow her to show it. She would rather die. She would rather kill them both. Wrap her arms around them and fling them into the bonfire. Because she was not going to ever let anyone know about any of this.

"You're acting like you barely know me," she choked out. "And you do know me. You taught me how to ride a horse, and you—"

"You listen to me," he said, moving closer to her. "Nothing happened. And I cannot treat you any different than I treated you before we went on that trip." His voice was rough now. Hard and almost desperate and it made that sharp thing in her chest sink even more deeply into her.

"Why?" The question came out choked. Broken.

And she just felt small and sad then, and was close to admitting that she was as hurt as she was willing to get.

"So you *do* know something changed," she pushed.

"No," he said.

But he was hostile with it.

"You do," she said. "That's why you're acting like this."

"What do you want to hear from me? Huh? You want to hear that you looked hot in a dress and I noticed? You want me to show people that I felt that? What good would it do, Elsie? What good in heaven or hell could it possibly do?"

"I—I don't know, but I'd—"

"You wanted me to help you pick up Travis. And that's what you should do. You should pick up fucking *Travis*. Because that makes sense. *This* doesn't make sense. You flipping a fit and trying to stab me between the ribs with your insults doesn't make a lick of sense."

She couldn't speak. All she could do was stare at him with stupid, ridiculous moisture starting to cloud her vision.

"You need to get yourself together, little girl," he said, his tone furious now, "because I can't do it for you. I *won't*."

"Hunter…"

"Pull it together. *Pull yourself together.*"

And he turned around and left her there. And she burned. Bright and hot with so many things she didn't have names for. Things she didn't even want names for.

And she pledged, then and there, that she was going to seduce Travis. And she was going to do it soon. And she was going to do it in front of Hunter. So he could see all that good work that he'd done. So he could see just what had changed.

Because she had.

He had thought she was beautiful in the dress.

But he wasn't *choosing* her.

What the hell kind of thought is that? Hunter McCloud? It's impossible, and if you were thinking clearly at all before you flipped this little tantrum you would know that.

She did. She was being... She just knew that she felt things, but she wasn't ready to assign meaning to them.

She wasn't. It made her want to weep.

To acknowledge that it mattered that he thought she looked pretty in that dress. To acknowledge that it made her feel good. That when he was standing there, and she could see that he was affected by what had passed between them, she had wanted to move closer.

It made her feel hopeless. Impossibly so.

Because Hunter McCloud drove her crazy. And there was no way that she could be attracted to him.

No way at all. There were too many reasons. Too many things.

Travis. This was all supposed to be about Travis.

Travis, who she had barely looked at once the entire time she was here.

Get back on the plan.

She would. She would get back on this. She would do what needed doing.

To restore sanity. Because she couldn't go having things like this happening ever again. For her pride and for the sake of Four Corners.

Because he was right. What did that mean? That she wanted him to acknowledge what happened? All the little undercurrents, because that was all they were. Just undercurrents. And there was nothing that anyone could do about them. Nothing anyone should do about them.

So what was the point? He had done exactly the right thing, and she had been wrong.

So she was going to forget this. She wasn't going to sit in

it, she wasn't going to unspool it. She wasn't going to look any deeper into it. She was going to forget that it happened.

Because there was no alternative.

He had accused her of acting like a child. And maybe she was. Because only a child would want their feelings acknowledged when those feelings were impossible.

So she would prove to him that she wasn't a child. That she was a woman.

She would prove it.

After she finished her chores.

CHAPTER EIGHT

HE TOOK A great deal of joy in outlining the chores that he was going to have Elsie do the next day at the ranch. It was a big, long list of bullshit that he knew she didn't want to do. Because nobody wanted to do it. Because every horrible task that had been put off was going to be dropped on her shoulders. Because she had lost big-time and spectacularly, and she had been fairly unforgivable in her treatment of him.

He didn't really care about the way she treated him, not generally. It was the way she'd intentionally compared him to his father. After he'd…

He'd talked about his parents on that trip.

They'd shared with each other.

Nothing happened.

Yeah, all right. He'd said that to her. He had pretty well pretended he felt nothing after that weekend when—yes—something had damn well passed between them.

But she knew his father had been a nightmare. When she knew that he had been one of the worst human beings on the face of the planet, and someone that he couldn't stand. And so, when she came into work the next morning, slinking like a shame-filled polecat, he held the list out toward her. "You're going to be clocking in some extra work today. And you're not getting paid for all of it."

"I can't believe you're holding me to a stupid bet."

"I have to hold you to the bet, Elsie. If you back out of it, then you won't have any honor."

She scowled. "What the hell do I care about honor?"

"You *should* care. You should care quite a bit."

He was determined not to revisit the scene of their tension. Elsie had seemed confused by it. It was partly why she was upset about him not acknowledging her, he was sure. But the bigger problem was he understood it. And he didn't want to. He didn't want to acknowledge that it was attraction that was arcing between the two of them. He didn't want to acknowledge that. At all.

But it was impossible to ignore. Impossible to pretend that it hadn't happened, that it wasn't happening.

Thank God she didn't understand. Thank God she was just angry in an indefinable sense.

Which relieved him when it came to the two of them and the tension that shouldn't exist. But it was the kind of thing that bothered him a little bit in terms of her going after Travis. Because that guy… He was not inexperienced. Hunter could tell by the way that he interacted with women in the bar.

He knew how to play the game, and he did it unrepentantly. Elsie might think that what she wanted was to play that same game, but she didn't know. She really didn't. And he knew that she was going to have to have a heartbreak. Most people did. But then, maybe like him, the heartbreak had come early. Maybe it had come from her family. Her mother. The neglect of her father. God knew that his own heartbreaks had been something other than romantic. Sex for him had always been easy because he didn't attach to people quickly. Part of him was pretty certain everyone he was ever going to care for had to be a preexisting condition. Come into his life before too much shit had happened.

He had his brothers, he had the Garretts.

And that was where things became absolutely impossible when it came to the stirring of attraction he felt for Elsie.

Because the Garretts were part of his clan. And those people... He didn't let go of them.

He just didn't.

So he would never get involved with Elsie, not like that. For a host of reasons. Not the least of which was that she was too young for him. Too sweet. Too innocent. Too Elsie. She drove him up the wall.

Why would he ever get involved with that little hellcat?

Involved. That wasn't even a word that applied to his sexual encounters. So. There was that.

"I don't know," she said, looking at him meanly. "I think that you could let this one go."

"No. I wouldn't let Landry King back out of a bet. I can't let you back out of it. And you well know that."

She huffed away from him. And that was the closest thing he'd ever seen to Elsie Garrett having a full-fledged girlish tantrum. And she was like that all day. The girl literally never chilled out. And there was something comforting in that. Because even if she wasn't usually quite this flouncy around him, she was often mean and snappish, so that was business as usual.

"Why is Elsie Garrett huffing around the property?" That question came from Lachlan, who was standing back on his heels, sweat rolling down his forehead from intensive hay bale moving.

"I really don't know," he drawled, careful to keep his face neutral.

"Nothing to do with the bet?"

"Oh yes. Everything to do with the bet. I just don't know why she's being such a sore loser."

Lach laughed. "Have you never met her before?"

"Look, her bad feelings aren't my problem. She shouldn't have gotten in my face."

"No," Lachlan agreed. "She crossed the line. But she's practically a kid, Hunter."

That hit him wrong. Especially coming from Lachlan, who didn't know Elsie half as well as he did and had no call to go making proclamations about what she was or wasn't. "She's not a kid," he said, thinking of her as she had been back in Vancouver. Very much against his will.

Lachlan's brow arched. "I just mean, she's a lot younger than we are. A lot younger than *you*. You could cut her a break. She was gunning for you the other day, and there has to be a reason for that. I mean, the two of you went out of town…" Suddenly, he didn't like the way that Lachlan's gaze was resting on him.

"What?" Hunter asked, daring him to say it.

If he said it, Hunter could hit him. And he could feel justified in doing it because *nothing had happened.*

And it would be a bullshit thing to do because whether or not he'd touched Elsie in that way, something had changed, and he was thinking of her like that. But on a technicality, he'd be justified. And he'd take the technicality if Lachlan would give it to him.

"You didn't…" Lachlan pulled a face. "I mean, nothing happened."

"What the hell do you mean by that?" He knew exactly what he meant.

"I've had any number of females be a little bit mad at me, Hunter, and usually it has something to do with…"

"First of all, *jackass*, women don't get mad at me after I have sex with them. They enjoy it."

His brother chuckled. "If they're not a little mad they can't have enjoyed it that much."

"Second of all," Hunter continued as if Lachlan hadn't spoken. "I would never do that."

"I didn't think so," Lachlan said, holding his hands up. "But she was pretty mad at you. That was personal."

"You know how she is with me."

"Yeah. She's the only Garrett who doesn't act like the sun shines out of your ass."

"Now this is going to be about me and the Garretts?" He was happy to change the subject. Even though he knew changing it to this was a little bit contentious.

"That is a fight for you and Gus to have," Lachlan said.

"I don't want to have a fight with Gus."

"Why not?"

"He'll punch me in the face. Anyway you all dance around this, so I guess this is how it is? You really are pissed I spent a ton of time over there."

Lachlan let out a harsh breath. "Hell, man, I don't know. Sometimes it felt like we could have used you here."

He'd sensed that. He'd wondered. Apparently he'd been right. They did resent him. They did resent that. He gritted his teeth. Guilt rising up inside of him. Memories. "I didn't want to be here. Not when we were kids. It's fine. I'm over it. It's not like we didn't spend plenty of time together."

"No. I know," Lachlan said. "But yeah, maybe it kind of sucks that you had an escape that wasn't just the mountains. But you had an escape, Hunt. You always had the Garretts. Why wouldn't you just…run away to be with them?"

Run away to be with them.

Like he wasn't a McCloud the same as they were. Like they hadn't suffered their dad's rages, all of them, even

Brody, because you couldn't be around it and not be ruined by it, even if the fists hadn't landed on your face.

That straw that broke everything.

"That's bullshit," Hunter ground out, except he knew it wasn't.

Lachlan shrugged. "Look. Bottom line, there was nothing to be done. Our childhood sucked. What are you going to do? There was nothing you could have done any different. Nothing any of us could have done any different."

"Yeah. Except actually buried our old man out back. That might have fixed some things."

Lachlan grinned. A grim sort of smile. "True. There is that. Still, whatever Gus did seems to have worked."

"Sure."

Lachlan was the baby. What the hell did he know?

He had to wonder, though, if there was some resentment. Gus had shouldered so many things as the oldest. And he was the one who'd borne the brunt of their father's temper. He was the one who had to wear it on his face, and along with that, the unfairness of the suspicion of what had happened to their father.

Hunter believed Gus. Gus said that he had told their father to never come back, after unleashing his own fury and giving him the beating of his life. It hadn't been a bloodless farewell, but it hadn't been murder either. And he had a feeling that most everybody believed Gus well enough. But it was the suspicion that their father wouldn't be so easily cowed that he imagined made the rumor endure. Especially among the older folks in the community.

"Basically," Lachlan said, "I think we all live in an endless circle of frustration that there was nothing we could do to protect each other. And our parents were the cause of our problems."

"Not Mom," Hunter said reflexively.

He didn't want to get into this, not with Lachlan. Or any of his brothers. Now or ever.

"She could have taken us with her," Lach said, his tone grave.

"And then what?" Hunter asked. "Who would have the ranch?"

"It's just land," Lachlan said.

"Yeah. Tell that to Gus. And Tag. And Brody. It's not just land. It's who we are. It's our blood. And Gus's blood specifically is soaked into this ground. You know that."

"No wonder you don't like spending extra time here. You still see blood everywhere."

He didn't in the way Lachlan meant, though. He found solace in the work because it made him feel like he was fixing something. Found solace in the land.

He didn't see blood. He saw his own failures.

And he worked to drown that out.

"It *is* everywhere," Hunter said. "There's nothing that can be done about that. But it's what we have. And what we do with it matters. So I'm on board with Gus's plans. It's something at least."

"Right. Well. This has been grim. You better go handle your hostage."

"She's not my hostage."

"Whatever. Whatever your deal is with her, work it out. Because whether I get it or not, the Garretts are your family. The same as we are. You don't want a little feud with the baby sister messing things up."

"She owes me a day of free labor, and she's going to give it. She's mucking stalls, oiling up some leather, turning the compost—"

"She is going to tear your throat out with her teeth."

"She shouldn't play dirty. And she shouldn't bet so far above her pay grade. That's the thing. She isn't a kid. She's a grown woman, and she chose to tangle with me. So she's going to get what she has coming."

"Yeah," Lachlan said, his eye taking on that same look that it had earlier. The one he didn't like.

"Stay out of it."

His baby brother lecturing him was something he could happily do without.

"Oh, I'm not in it," he said, backing up with his hands held high. "In fact, to be very clear, I have no investment in this at all. I'm just commenting."

"Yeah." But he was feeling scratchy with his brother now, and he went out looking for Elsie, who he found sitting on the floor of the barn, with oiled up saddles all around her, bridles and other leather items, a cloth and rage. Her hair had fallen into her face, her cheek was smudged with something black and she was moving the cloth seriously in a circle around an old saddle.

"You hungry?"

She looked up, the fury in her eyes not remotely hidden. "Do I get bread and water?"

"No. But I might throw a sandwich your way. And maybe a beer."

"I packed my own lunch, Hunter. I don't need your belated shows of concern. You're the one that sent me out here doing menial tasks. But they're hardly going to kill me. Just irritate me."

"Sure," he said, annoyed by how much he sounded like Lachlan.

"I don't need you to hover."

"You need to get your next assignment," he said.

"I'm tired," she said, looking up at him, her brow beaded with sweat.

"Should have thought of that before you bet me all this work. And before you said I was like my father."

"You're acting like a mean bastard now." Her expression was defiant.

"Yeah, but I'm not going to lay a hand on you. Different enough from my dad for you?" In context of the tension that had been mounting between the two of them, it was a different sort of promise. But if Elsie noticed, she didn't seem to indicate it. She swiped her face with her forearm, and he didn't know if she was trying to wipe oil off her skin or dash away some sweat.

"Great." She spread her hands wide, the rag dangling from her fingers. "What is my next assignment?"

"I need you to go up in the hayloft and get the moldy hay out. There was a leak in the roof, and apparently a bunch of it in the back got wet. I patched the leak the other day, but…"

"Great. I would love nothing more than to clean up mold." She got up from where she was sitting and crossed the space, beginning to scale the ladder. And for some reason, he found that he couldn't look away.

She climbed with rage-driven determination, the muscles in her shoulders and arms clearly defined. Her waist was long and lean, and her ass looked damned cute in her Wranglers. He didn't care what anybody said, he would always like what those jeans did for a woman's body. He was a cowboy. He liked everything that went with it, and that included cowgirls.

It was just that Elsie wasn't his typical cowgirl type.

But Elsie wasn't *typically* anything. Not the least of

which someone he should *typically* look at. She disappeared up into the hayloft, and he felt a surge of relief.

"You sure you don't want food?"

"No," she said, invisible now. It was just her angry voice floating down from on high.

"See you later, then."

"I hope not."

And as he shut the barn door behind himself, he gritted his teeth, determined to forget what had just transpired. Not his conversation with Lachlan, not his fight with Elsie, but that moment when he had allowed himself that visual tour of her body.

She was Elsie Garrett, and he had to remember that. No matter what had happened in Vancouver, no matter how she infuriated him, it didn't matter.

Lachlan was right. The Garretts were his family. As close as his own, if not closer in some ways. After his mother had gone it had seemed easier. Hell, it had been necessary because for a while there... For a while there, looking his brothers in the face had seemed an impossibility. Making himself scarce at McCloud's Landing had been the easiest thing to do. Obviously, he took his responsibilities on his family ranch seriously. And he was a horseman, at the end of the day. He had never found beef to be a particular calling, so he had never felt compelled to go work at the Garrett Ranch.

But then, it was sort of funny that Elsie was in his.

He pushed that out of his mind too. He pushed everything away.

He was going to go eat some lunch, and the way that Elsie Garrett spent the rest of the day was not his problem.

CHAPTER NINE

ELSIE WAS SWEATY and filled with rage by the time the day finished. She had kept thinking that she might mellow out as the hours wore on, but she hadn't.

She had thought that maybe her guilt would take over. Because she had been mean to Hunter. That was undeniable. She should not have said all that to him about his father. It had been over a line, and she knew it.

But she couldn't shake her own completely understandable anger over the way that he had ignored her.

And the fact that she didn't want to overthink it, didn't want to consider what it might mean that she felt the way that she did...

It was much easier to stay angry.

And so, angry she stayed, all the way to the bitter end of her chores list. But she had done everything perfectly. He would not be able to complain about a damned thing. The leather was oiled beautifully, the stalls were brilliantly mucked and she had cleared out the loft, leaving not a single speck of nasty, moldy hay behind. She was muggy, and she stank to high heaven, had pieces of straw wedged into her hair, and wood slivers beneath her fingernails, and all she could think of was that she deserved to jump into the swimming hole.

She kicked her shoes off and started walking down toward the creek. She walked gingerly, shoes in hand, enjoying the feel of the cool earth shaded by the tall trees beneath her feet. If she could focus on the earth, on the world around her, then her anger became much more distant. The sound of the breeze in the trees, the blue of the sky above. The sun felt less like an enemy then, and more like her companion, warming her skin rather than trying to heat her up from the inside out and cook her alive.

Perspective, she supposed, was everything.

As was being finished with her annoying to-do list, instead of just starting out.

She looked around and didn't see anyone, then unsnapped her jeans. She had a pair of athletic shorts on underneath, she just didn't really want anyone to watch her stripping off.

She shoved them down her legs, leaving only the little purple shorts behind. She had on a white tank top that she knew would likely be see-through after her jaunt in the water, but she figured she wouldn't have an audience. She stood on the edge of the jagged rock formation that lined the creek, ready to make the ten-foot jump down into the watering hole below. She knew that this time of year the water went well over her head so there was no risk jumping.

She was just about to go in when she heard a voice behind her. A very unwelcome voice.

"Did you finish everything up?"

And she didn't think. Not even a little bit. She turned and saw a fully clothed Hunter McCloud standing only a foot away from her, and then he took a step toward her. And she launched herself at him, wrapped her arms around his neck and pulled them both off the edge of the rocks.

They plunged down into the water below, which was a hell of a lot colder than Elsie had been anticipating. But clearly she had amnesia.

And the added weight of Hunter, who she was still connected to, dragged her down farther and faster than she had anticipated.

He was so densely muscled he was not as buoyant as she was.

She released her hold on him, and sputtered up to the surface, just as he popped up behind her.

"What the hell, woman?"

She started swimming away from him, frog kicking her way toward the opposite bank. "Elsie," he said. "I swear, I am going to skin you alive, you evil little rabbit."

He was swimming, but slower than she was, likely owed to the fact that he was still in his boots. His hat had surfaced and was floating somewhere next to him, and he grabbed hold of it, putting it on his head, even though it was wet.

But he kept up his pursuit.

"My boots are full of water."

"And you're full of shit," she sputtered back. "Seems fair."

"That doesn't make any sense."

"It does to me," she called back.

"Where do you think you're going?"

"What do you think you're going to do when you catch me?"

She scrambled up out of the water, but he was very close behind her, and grabbed on to her ankle as he hauled himself up behind her. Then he took hold of her waist and brought her down onto the grass, heaving himself up over the top of her. He wasn't touching her, his palms planted on either side of her, his knees to the left and right of her thighs. Water was dripping off the brim of his hat, onto her nose, and his angry eyes were blazing into hers. "What was that?"

"Revenge."

"You little weasel…"

"You can keep calling me any number of animals," she said. "I'm not going to be insulted."

"Polecat. Varmint. *Badger*."

She bared her teeth. "If I were a badger you wouldn't be so close."

But suddenly, she became overly aware of how close he was.

And how the position wasn't…innocent. Well, it was, because he was angry, and her legs were tightly closed, and he wasn't making any kind of contact with her, but she felt… she felt the heat of his body radiating off him. Or maybe it was just his anger. But either way it was something.

He lowered his head closer, in defiance of what she had just said.

"Marmot. Digger squirrel."

She arched up toward him and bit him. Right on the side of the neck. And he growled. Went stiff beneath her teeth, and she pulled back quickly, breathing hard. Feeling every inch like one of the scared little rodents that he had accused her of being. Her heart was thundering wildly, and she felt like something that had been cornered in its burrow.

His eyes were blazing into hers, but the heat had changed. It was different now. And suddenly, he moved, grabbing hold of one hand, then another, and pinning them up over her head. She was suddenly unbearably aware of her breasts. Of the fact that her shirt was see-through, and this position forced her to arch up toward him.

And she would've said that he was just mad. But Hunter would never hurt her. And none of his physical handling of her was about hurting her. So he was just…touching her. And this was…

There was no circumstance in which he would chase

Sawyer down and pin him to the ground, even if he had grabbed hold of him and dumped him in a creek. That was the problem. There was no equivalent thing he would do to a man, which meant that he was thinking of her as a woman.

And if they were a different man and woman, maybe the interaction would've been playful, but they were them, so it was tinged with anger.

If she had to wonder where the anger actually came from.

If the anger was actually more about the fact that this...

This was wrong. In every way. Impossible, improbable.

And not...

She scrambled away from him, pulling her wrists out from his hold. She stood up, brushing the sand and grass from her bare legs.

"Consider us even," she said.

"We are not even," he said. "You can't just say whatever the hell you want to me."

"Did I hurt your feelings?" He should've called her a hedgehog, because right about now she had her spikes turned out, trying to repel him, trying to hide any vulnerability that she might inadvertently display.

"No, Elsie, because life has taken enough potshots at me that you're not going to hurt me. But there are certain things that are off-limits. And anything to do with my old man is one of them, and you know that. That's the problem. You know that. And you're running around like a hissing, spitting—"

"Polecat?" she suggested.

"Yes. Like you can say anything to me, do anything to me. Like I'm not a man. I am. And I am not your personal punching bag, or your testing ground. Don't play with me.

Or eventually, something's going to happen that you're not going to like."

There was a threat in those words that was different to a threat that promised violence. A sensual undercurrent that she would've said she couldn't have recognized before this moment.

But now she felt like she couldn't unsee it. Couldn't eradicate it from the fabric of who she was. And he was right. She was pushing him, testing him. But it wasn't because she didn't know he was a man. She wasn't playing. She was upset and she…she had been having difficulty figuring out why.

But it was because while nothing had happened in Vancouver, lines had been crossed that they couldn't go back over. She had always known that he was a man, but now she had seen what other women saw in him.

And what she wanted more than anything was to be looked at and desired, and for one moment, for more than one moment, Hunter McCloud had looked at her like a woman he could want. And it had done something to her. To everything that she was made of. The very material she'd been stitched from. She didn't want it. She wanted to want Travis. And she was cut up, tangled up, in this thing with Hunter.

"I know you're a man," she said. "But I'm a woman."

"I know," he said, the words scratchy.

She looked at him, at the stretch of ground between them. And she realized it couldn't go on like this. She felt almost panicked with that realization. That she needed to do something to fix this. To change it.

But she didn't have any amazing insights or solutions. She only had a mass of feelings that she didn't know how to deal with. At all. And she didn't want to run away from him. Not again. Because he was Hunter and she was Elsie. And they had the relationship they'd had for all these years. Antagonistic though it sometimes was. But he wasn't a predator, and she wasn't his prey. And she wasn't afraid of him, or anyone else. So she stood her ground. And she looked at him.

And there was really no further indignity to be had. She had vomited her feelings all over him that night at the bonfire, and she was standing there reduced, having absolutely shown that she wasn't fine or over any of it. Or handling it in any way at all. There was no pride left for her.

"Forget it," she said. "I'm sorry. I made a mistake. Telling you that I wanted…something after Vancouver. I didn't know what I was saying. I didn't… I didn't understand."

"You do now?"

He rocked back on his heels, and he touched his neck. Right where she had bitten him. And it sent an arrow of desire down straight between her legs.

And she couldn't deny it. Couldn't pretend. Not anymore. Because these feelings were more real, more raw than anything Travis had ever made her feel. Than anything any casual fantasy she'd ever had about anyone or anything had ever made her feel.

She had never really known what it was to be attracted to somebody. She'd had vague longings about how she wanted someone to make her feel. How their attention might appeal to her. Or change something inside of her. Yes. She had experienced that. But this was different. This was outside of herself. This was…big. And she couldn't control it. She didn't like it. But she also had to acknowledge that it was teaching her something. A lesson she wasn't entirely certain she wanted to learn.

"Yes," she said. "But it doesn't change anything, does it?"

"Even if it did, would you want it to?"

She shook her head. "No. No. I'm me and you're *you*. And that's…that's it."

And she felt sad. Just indefinably, horribly sad.

"I'm not running away," she said.

She hadn't meant to say it out loud.

He frowned. "I didn't say that you were."

"I didn't… I just… I'm not. I'm not. You're Hunter Mc-Cloud."

"And you're Elsie Garrett."

"Right. So that's…that's that."

She stood there, and she just stared at him. And it hurt. Because he was the most handsome man she had ever seen, and now she knew what that meant. Now she knew why it was more than just looking at a mountainside. Now she understood that it wasn't simply a matter of aesthetics, but something that went bone deep. Something beyond what the eye could see. Chemistry. She had never understood that before.

She did now. She just wished it wasn't with him.

"I'll see you around, Hunter," she said. Because there was nothing else to say. There was nothing else that either of them could say. There was certainly nothing else they could do.

She wasn't running. She was just walking away.

She turned around, and she headed back toward home. Back toward safety.

And she didn't look back. No matter how much she wanted to.

CHAPTER TEN

HUNTER WAS INVITED to dinner at Garrett's Watch. Sawyer's house specifically, and he hoped very much that Elsie wouldn't be present. Of course, he also hoped that she would be. Because he wasn't sure that he enjoyed dinner at Sawyer's half so much if he couldn't spar with her. And wasn't that ridiculous.

When he walked in, it was only Sawyer and Evelyn, and June. And he wished that he wasn't disappointed by that.

June immediately ran to him and he scooped her up, giving her his hat like he always did, but his mind wasn't here.

He kept seeing Elsie as she had been standing there on the riverbank. Soaked through, the outline of her bra showing beneath the flimsy fabric of her tank top, her hair wet and dripping, her expression vulnerable. He had wanted to... Well, he had wanted to reach out and take her into his arms. And it had been more than enough of a reason to turn and walk the other direction.

But it was her that had walked away in the end. And he would question why he hadn't been the one to do it for the rest of his days.

Right when Evelyn was putting pot roast and potatoes on the table Wolf and Violet came through the door. And that made it weird that Elsie wasn't here. That made him take her absence a little bit personally. And he probably should. But again, that made her the smart one. If she knew he was coming for dinner, right now she should probably stay away. He hadn't stayed away. Just like he hadn't walked away.

He was batting zero right now.

He wished she were here, though, not just because he wanted to see her, but because the amount of domesticity surrounding him made him intensely uncomfortable. That was an understatement.

He had never been part of a family like this.

And he knew the same was true for Wolf and Sawyer. Wolf's and Sawyer's mothers had left, just like Elsie's, and their father had been a piece of work, though he wasn't the nightmare that Hunter's own was. Still, they had never… It had never been like this. And he wondered how either man knew how to do it. And why they had wanted to in the first place.

But he supposed the answer had a lot to do with Violet and Evelyn. Because both Wolf and Sawyer had had their pick of women in town. And none of them had ever managed to snare them. Or even get them remotely interested in long-term relationships. Though, in the case of both Sawyer and Wolf, their children had been a big part of that. In Sawyer's case, it had been becoming a single father, and knowing that he wanted there to be a mother in her life so that she didn't grow up like Elsie, surrounded by men who had no sensitivity at all. And both had decided to commit to Violet after she'd gotten pregnant. But he could see that both Sawyer and Wolf loved their wives, even if they had come to be in their relationships through unconventional means.

Actually, he supposed they were about as conventional as the marriages that had existed in the West once upon a time. Marriages of convenience—that had turned out happily.

He wondered sometimes if his own parents had loved

each other. Ever. But then, that would assume his father had been capable of love. And he didn't think he had been.

"When is the baby expected?" he asked, shifting June to his knee as he sat at the table, trying to dig deep and find the charm that he was theoretically known for. He had been short on it lately, and all he needed was for Wolf and Sawyer to notice.

"June twenty-fifth," Wolf said, grinning. "A little girl cousin for June. In June."

"That's great," Hunter said. And he did not say that he couldn't reconcile this man, who was so happy about his impending fatherhood, with the man he had known all of his life.

Maybe it was even more of a reason to entrench himself in McCloud's Landing.

The idea of putting distance between him, Sawyer and Wolf didn't hold any appeal. But looking at this was...

It was painful.

And he hadn't imagined something like this could be painful. He hadn't known he'd care about it. He'd figured they could be married. They could be fathers. He could do his thing because he didn't want any of that.

But the reason he didn't want it felt heavy right now.

Because he could see—easily—why they were happy.

And it made it all that much more real that he wasn't going to be that kind of happy because while his father had scarred Gus on the outside, he'd gotten plenty of his own on the inside.

He heard the front door open from his position at the table.

Elsie.

He knew it without having to see her.

And he heard her, because she was stomping. But by

the time she entered the kitchen, the scowl he could hear embedded in the stomp was managed.

"Hi," she said, nearly sounding chipper as she sat down at the table.

"Hi," Sawyer said at the same time Wolf said, "Hey." And both of them were looking at her like she was crazy.

If Violet and Evelyn thought anything strange about Elsie's appearance, they kept it wisely to themselves.

"Did you all hear I lost a poker game against Hunter the other night?" Elsie grinned, then tilted back in her chair and put her boots on the table.

Evelyn grimaced. "Honey. Sweetie. Oh, the table."

Elsie looked at her sister-in-law then swung her feet down. "Sorry. Anyway, yeah, I lost about a week's worth of chores to him but I did them all yesterday."

Sawyer looked over at him. "You don't look savaged beyond all reason."

"I'm a woman of honor," Elsie said. "I'd never go back on a bet."

She'd wanted to, though. In fact, tonight was a total change in demeanor from where she'd been when he'd seen her yesterday.

This was the Elsie she'd been all the *ever* before Vancouver. And it was the Elsie that should have been more familiar to him. But for some reason the Elsie who was fraught and tension filled seemed…more real.

The Elsie he'd held in his arms and all but pinned to the ground yesterday.

The Elsie who'd been so soft beneath his hands…

He cleared his throat for no good reason but to jar himself back into the present. Evelyn took June from his arms and set her in her high chair, and he was grateful because holding a child right now felt wrong.

"I have her doing everything I haven't wanted to do for the last year. And all the things Gus, Brody and Lachlan didn't want to do along with it," he said.

"You're not usually such a graceful loser," Sawyer pointed out.

Elsie turned crimson around the edges. "Well. I might not have been all that graceful in the moment."

"Are you repentant?" Hunter asked.

She looked up at him from beneath her lashes. "No."

This was more like their usual banter. And yet it wasn't. It felt nothing like it.

Because when she looked at him like that...

It was like something wholly new.

"That's typical," he said, the words scraping his throat raw.

"You're a hard case, Elsie," Wolf said.

"You raised me." She served up a heaping helping of roast beef and potatoes, and he spent the rest of the night practically outside his body.

It was a weird-ass sensation.

He didn't like it.

And when it was time for him to go home, he was surprised to find Elsie saying her goodbyes at the same time. When they stepped outside, it was dark, the sky clear, stars twinkling overhead like diamond dust deep in the heart of a mine.

"It was good to see you," Elsie said.

And it occurred to him then that she was really trying to be the bigger person. That she was really trying to go out of her way to choose to make this better. To make it all okay.

And he had to respect that. But something in him didn't like it.

"Good to see you too."

"Do you have plans tomorrow night?"

The question knocked him back a pace. "What kind of plans?"

"Oh nothing. It's just… It'll be nightime. I have nothing to do. No dinner plans. I figured I would head to the bar."

He nodded slowly. "Sounds like a plan."

"Hopefully…hopefully everything will go well."

"I'm done teaching you," he said. The words sounded rustier than he intended. The fact that he said them out loud was actually unintended.

"In what sense?"

"In the sense that you don't have anything left to learn from me." And he was grateful for the cover of darkness. Because if he could see her face… If he could see her face, he would close the distance between them. "You go in that bar and you'll be able to get any man you want. But you make sure you want him."

That was his last warning. And the rest of this… It didn't have anything to do with him. He wouldn't let it.

He'd spoken his piece. And what else he did from here on out was his business. He just didn't want her doing anything just for the sake of it. Because she was bullheaded. Because she had set her mind to something before she had fully realized the implications of it.

She nodded slowly. "Sure."

"Good."

"See you tomorrow?"

"At the bar?"

"Yeah," she said.

"Probably not. I think I'll stick to home."

"All right. Maybe I'll see you when I report back to Mc-Cloud's, then."

"Yeah," he said. "See you then."

And then he walked back to his truck, and just like Elsie yesterday, he didn't look back.

"This is a good dress, right?" Elsie asked, looking across Alaina's bedroom, eyeing herself critically in the full-length mirror.

"Yes," Alaina said definitively. "And Hunter said he's not going tonight?"

"No."

"Do you want me to come?" Alaina asked. "For moral support?"

She considered that. "No," she said. "I think if you were also hoping to pick somebody up it would be different."

She shook her head. "No. I might go loiter around some of the common areas and see if I get a Hunter sighting, though."

She ignored the stabbing feeling in her breastbone. "That sounds like a good idea," she said.

Because there was no point in the stabbing feeling. No point at all.

And she had gone to her brother's house last night for the sole purpose of affirming her position with Hunter. For making sure that she could be normal around him. And that he could be normal around her. And they had managed it, hadn't they? And she had told him that she was going to go after Travis, and he hadn't done anything to stop her.

Did you want him to stop you?

The very idea made her go red all the way to the roots of her hair. No. She didn't want him to stop her. She wanted him to let this all go back to normal. She wanted him to let this die down. Obviously.

"I can see that. Having your friend watch you be sexy is uncomfortable," Alaina said with deep pragmatism.

"There are whole flocks of girls who don't seem to have a problem with it," Elsie said. "They descend on the bar in groups, and they all...shake their hips. In front of each other."

"In front of God and everybody," Alaina said, stretching out on her stomach on the bed. "My mother would have had choice words for women like that..."

"Because your mother really had choice words for your father, but reserves them for other women instead."

Alaina snorted. "Fair." She reached into a bag and pulled out a handful of candy. "She's not perfect. She's just my mom. Of course, neither is my dad."

"Hey, they're both still in contact with you."

"Yeah," she said. "I shouldn't complain."

"You have every right to complain. Just because my mom abandoned me when I was an infant and my dad is dead, doesn't mean you're not allowed to complain about your own parents."

"Did you really tell Hunter he was just like his dad?"

The back of her neck prickled. "Who told you that?"

"Fia heard it from...I guess from Arizona? I'm surprised that she was speaking to a King, quite honestly."

"Why does she hate Landry so much?" She was curious now more than ever for some reason, also happy to sort of guide the subject to Fia, and off what she'd said to Hunter.

Maybe it was natural for her to be extra curious with her trying to gain new perspective on men, women and the fallout that occurred between them.

"The standard reasons I would assume," Alaina said. "Some kind of high school infatuation? They slept together and it ended badly?"

"All this time? Just because they..."

Alaina lifted a shoulder. "Look, I don't know that for sure. She's never admitted to it."

"But it *has* to be that."

"You would think. Why else would they act like that?"

"He doesn't act like anything. He acts like he barely knows her."

Alaina shook her head gravely. "Men. That's even worse, don't you think?"

It was.

Elsie shifted uncomfortably. "Do you really think that a relationship is permanently ruined when something like that happens?"

"I think it's only a problem if you have one person that's in love, and one person who just wants a good time," Alaina said, as if she was deeply knowledgeable on such subjects. But then, in fairness, Elsie had asked.

"That makes sense."

Her mind went back to Hunter. They could *not* become Landry King and Fia Sullivan. They just couldn't. It would ruin everything. The very idea filled her with grief, and she would have said that she didn't like Hunter enough that the idea of not speaking to him would fill her with grief. But one thing was certain, they could be hissing and spitting around each other like...

Her eyes drifted back to Alaina.

She really should be more concerned about her feelings. Except... It was just that... She really didn't think that Hunter would be going for the complication of her either. Especially not when he made it very clear that Elsie herself was too complicated.

Alaina would be less complicated for him.

It wasn't like he was best friends with Fia.

She looked back at the mirror. "Yes," she said resolutely. "This is good. And I feel...ready."

She didn't. She was lying. But she couldn't do this if she didn't make herself ready, if she didn't take this step... Well, she was going to drive herself insane. She wanted to go back to the way things were. She wanted to be obsessed with Travis again. Because it was easy.

And that was something she never would've thought to associate with her infatuation with him.

It had felt easy. Now when she had been breathlessly worried that he might never pay attention to her.

But she could hardly remember the person that she'd been that night in the bar when Hunter had offered to teach her to flirt.

It was like a whole other body ago, not just a couple of weeks.

"You look amazing," Alaina said. "I expect you to text me and let me know exactly how everything goes."

"You know I will."

She would. Because tonight, she was going to succeed in her plan.

Tonight, she was going to fix what she had inadvertently broken.

It had to work.

It had to.

CHAPTER ELEVEN

HUNTER HAD BEEN called a fool any number of times in his life, but he was gunning for top title by showing up to Smokey's Tavern tonight, and he knew it. When he had already told Elsie that he wouldn't come. When he had already said that he was going to stay home.

He'd told her, and he'd told himself.

Because there was no point coming out to the bar tonight to watch her try to hook up with Travis, when the very idea of it made his gut clench tight. But that was the problem.

He had spent the last twenty-four hours thinking about that. About what that would look like. About how it would all go down. And he couldn't deal with it. He couldn't handle it.

So all the while, telling himself that he wouldn't, he had gotten ready to go out tonight. He had told himself he wouldn't actually go to the bar all the way up until he walked through the front door. But now here he was.

And there she was.

She damned near made him feel like his heart was going to bust straight through his chest. And it was like the room—the world—had been tilted onto its side. She was Elsie Garrett, but suddenly that wasn't the problem with his attraction to her.

Suddenly, it was the reason.

Her. All of her.

All she was, all he knew.

Elsie sidled up to the bar, leaning over a drink. She was wearing a red summer dress that flared out just above her knees, with little white flowers on it. It looked innocent, with its sweet little sleeves and scoop neck, with a tantalizing drawstring right there at the center of her breasts.

His mind made it anything but innocent.

It took a moment for him to register that she already had a drink. She *already* had a drink.

Which meant she'd accomplished part one of her mission.

And that was when he saw Travis walking across the room and sitting down beside her. And he looked…well, he looked intent.

Hunter looked away, grinding his teeth practically to dust.

This was what he'd taken her out for. This was the whole point. And he'd known it. Then as well as now.

They'd reaffirmed that. After the poker game. After she'd flung him into the water and he'd called her a varmint and he'd fought the urge to press his body against hers as he'd pinned her down on the riverbank.

After dinner at Sawyer's when they'd parted like the almost-friends they were.

He'd made up his mind. So had she.

But he didn't like it. Not in the least. Not one bit.

Thankfully, though, Sawyer and Wolf were nowhere to be seen, since they were now family men, and his brother Brody was there, sitting at a table.

He crossed the space and sat down in the chair opposite him.

"I'm hoping to find a date," Brody said. "So you can sit there until one appears, but I don't want it looking like my evening's not free."

"Same," Hunter said. "I know when to make myself scarce."

"Yeah. I know you do. You aren't Lachlan. You won't overstay. And you aren't Gus, so you won't scare away potential dates."

Hunter huffed a laugh. "How long has it been since Gus got laid?"

"Too fucking long," Brody said, grinning. "That's why he's such an insufferable ass."

"I don't think that's why Gus is an insufferable ass," he said, keeping his eye on Elsie.

One of the waitresses, who was wearing a formfitting dress and a little green apron tonight, came over to the table. Dulce, that was her name. And she was damned pretty. He imagined that if he really wanted to, he could go home with her. Or she with him. He wasn't really picky.

"Hi there," she said. "What'll you have?"

"Whatever you got that's local," Hunter said.

"Same," Brody added.

"Sure." She winked and turned away, walking back to the bar with a little sway to her hips.

"She's cute," Brody said.

"Yeah," Hunter agreed. "But I don't want it to be weird when I come buy beer."

"Fair," Brody said. "Still. If no other women show up... I'll take weird."

"That's a low bar," Hunter said.

"My bar is eternally low, little brother."

"Well, that I do know."

"So, what happened with Elsie?" he asked.

That was right when Dulce reappeared with two beers and set them down on the table, which gave Hunter enough time to think about how to respond. Or hope that Brody forgot what he'd asked.

"Some onion rings too," Brody said. "That'd be great."

"Onion rings?" He stared at his brother after the waitress left. "I thought you were trying to get laid."

Brody lifted a brow. "Onion rings are not going to stop me from getting laid, Hunter."

"I think you've got an ego problem."

Brody shrugged. "I haven't got a problem with it."

"Maybe onion rings would be good..."

"Don't deflect. What was going on with you and Elsie?" Dammit. "Lach said she was madder than a wet hen during the poker game the other night, and that she was TO'd at you the other day when she came to do work. He told me what she said to you. I'm shocked you didn't turn her over your knee and take a switch to her backside."

He would love to go back in time and pay his brother not to put the image of him spanking Elsie Garrett in his head. His brain was already a pretty messed up place right about now, and he didn't need Brody adding to it by introducing an idea that was inescapably erotic into the mix.

Hunter scowled. "Don't you and Lach have anything better to do than chatter like a pair of old biddies?"

"Not really," Brody said, grinning.

He sighed.

"She was just being Elsie," he said. "You know how she is. She's like a bobcat with a hangnail when I'm around. There's nothing I can do about it. And nothing I did to deserve it either. Ain't my fault."

"You didn't let her get away with that shit about Dad..."

"No. I took her to task."

"Good. You should defend yourself. You don't need to let bullshit like that stand." Brody paused. "You know it's bullshit, right?"

"I don't think I'm like Dad," Hunter said.

Brody looked benignly innocent. "I didn't say you did."

"You actually looked concerned. Which is unlike you."

"Not really," Brody said. "I worry about you enough. I'm a pretty callous bastard all things considered, but you're younger than me—"

"But a year, for heaven's sake."

"I worry about you."

"I don't have any hidden concerns I'm like Dad, Brody." And as he looked at Brody, all pretty and unscarred and Dad's favorite, he had to wonder if it was Brody who really carried that concern. But Hunter just didn't even know how to... how to say it to him. Especially right now when his whole world was a mess. "Worry about Gus." Defaulting to worrying about Gus was what they all tended to do when he wasn't around. "If someone said something like that to him..."

"Gus isn't fragile," Brody said.

"No. Gus is basically a mountainside. But he could be eroding underneath and you never know. That's what worries me about Gus. He's hardheaded. And he's impossible to get to. He'd never tell us if he was falling apart."

"A smile covers up things just as well as the frown, Hunt," Brody said.

That hit him square in the chest. His brother smiled at him, and Hunter smiled right back. And it all felt a little bit pointed and far too close to the truth of who they both were. But rather than going deeper...

They just smiled.

"Whatever," Hunter said. "It's handled. Just the same kind of petty squabbling when I'm out with Elsie."

"Right. Well. Glad you cleared it up."

"Cleared."

"So, are we obligated to intervene with her and that douchebag?"

"Which douchebag?"

He knew which one.

Brody shrugged. "I don't know his name. All these little upstart ranch hands look the same to me, and they're all gone just as quickly. But do you honestly think that Sawyer wants her messing around with him?"

"Is he a particularly egregious douchebag?" Hunter asked, as if he hadn't been more involved with all of this than he cared to admit.

"Yeah, I think so," Brody said. "I don't like him. I don't like anything I've seen of him. He's charming. But it feels fake to me."

"Says the man who is all fake charm?" Hunter pressed.

"It's different," Brody said. "I can identify a guy who's an operator when I see one. The kind that only cares that he has a good time. He doesn't give a shit about the woman he's with. And I worry. That he's not going to care if she's drunk and her ability to say yes is impacted by that. That it's going to be all about him. I don't want Elsie in a situation like that, do you?"

The picture his brother painted made him see red, instantly.

"Hell no," Hunter said.

"Well, just keep an eye out."

Except, Hunter knew that Elsie wanted *him*.

She was still flirting with Travis, but Hunter was the man she wanted. Down there at the riverbank they'd both admitted it, in between all the things they'd said to each other.

She was choosing Travis because they'd stood there and felt the futility of it stretch between them.

Not because she wanted the ranch hand.

That didn't make Hunter feel better.

Then Elsie finished her drink, and she was laughing,

and Travis grabbed her hand and led her to the dance floor.
Pulled her up close to his body and held her the way that
Hunter had just days ago.

Rage burned in his gut.

Mine.

Mine.

The word pounded in his head, in his blood.

He kept on watching as Travis's hands skimmed dan-
gerously close to Elsie's ass.

"You okay?"

That man was touching what belonged to him.

He looked across at his brother. "Fine," he said.

Except he was not *fucking fine*. He couldn't stand it.
Couldn't stand to see that little wet-behind-the-ears bandi-
coot pawing at Elsie.

Elsie, who was a particular kind of beautiful that was
honestly too good for this guy. This guy who liked to go out
and hook up, and who didn't care if the girl was drunk. Because he was going to go with Brody's impression of him.

This guy who didn't care about a woman's pleasure.
Only his own.

This guy that Hunter currently wanted to punch in his
damned face.

And then he stood up, and he didn't know what the hell
he thought he was doing.

Except he stopped thinking at all as Travis's hand moved
down to Elsie's ass.

But she was looking up at him with a smile on her face.

Maybe she did want Travis.

And Hunter walked straight out the door.

Straight out the damned door, because what Elsie wanted
mattered.

And then he turned around and punched the side of the

bar. Punched it. He heard a crack, and he hoped to hell that he had broken a knuckle. But it sure as hell felt like he had. His skin was bleeding, profusely, dripping down his arm.

"Fuck," he shouted.

He had just punched a wall because of Elsie Garrett.

He had punched a damned wall.

Because of the twenty-four-year-old virgin he'd known forever. Who didn't know how to flirt or kiss or anything.

Because she was dancing with a man who wasn't him. And what the hell had he planned to do about it? What the hell had he planned to do about any of this? There was nothing to do. Nothing at all.

Elsie wanted Travis.

But he could still see her standing on the banks of the river. Wet with white cotton stuck to her gorgeous figure, her eyes filled with the kind of vulnerability he knew she hated.

She'd made it clear she felt something...

Yeah, well. He wasn't listening to himself. He was an unreliable narrator. And he couldn't be trusted.

That was just how it was.

And he decided then and there he was going to leave the tab for his brother.

Because if he went in there...

He couldn't do that. He had to leave. He had to leave right now.

But then he was headed back into the bar. He was going back into the damned bar. Even though he had just decided that he was leaving.

And he was walking right over to the dance floor with blood dripping down his forearm. "I'll cut in," he said.

Travis looked at him, and so did Elsie, who then looked down at his hand. *"What the hell did you do?"* she asked.

"It's nothing," he said.

"It's *not* nothing."

"I'm fine, and I'm cutting in."

And he grabbed hold of her hand and pulled her up against his body, and started to move in time to the music, with Shania singing about her lover's boots being under the wrong bed.

And wasn't *that* quite the soundtrack for the evening.

"What are you doing?" she asked as he pulled her up against his chest.

And Travis receded back to the bar. Pansy.

A real man would stay and fist fight him. He'd have a fistfight with Travis.

Happily.

"Checking your progress," Hunter said.

"You're *interrupting* my progress," she said. "And what did you do to your hand?"

"I punched a wall," he said casually.

Because why lie? Why lie to Elsie when...

This was absurd. The entire thing was absurd.

Her eyes met his and he felt it, down in his gut. "Why did you punch a wall, Hunter?" she whispered.

"Because I can't stand that *fucking guy*," Hunter ground out. "And I can't stand him having his hands on you."

Elsie's eyes darted back to Travis, her cheeks turning pink. "But..."

"Oh, there's nothing to say to that," he said. "Nothing at all. Because you're right. Hell, we agreed already it didn't matter. You're Elsie. I'm Hunter. It's absurd. I have no right to have any feelings about it whatsoever. And you were angry the other night. Weren't you? Pissed as hell at me. Madder than anything. And you have every right to be. And here I am, and I can't deal with it."

"Why?"

"Good question."

"No." She shook her head. "Don't deflect. You're the only one that can answer the question, Hunter. So answer the question. Why? Why does it bother you to see me dance with him?"

She was daring him to admit it.

"Because he put his hands on you."

She looked at his knuckles, at the blood there. "Does that mean…you want to put your hands on me instead?"

It was a ballsy question asked with her typical Elsie Garrett bravado. But there was an underlying vulnerability to it that killed him.

"I don't know what I want," he said, his words rough as gravel.

"I guess that makes two of us."

"But I do know that I think it's pretty damned absurd that you've got me punching walls."

"The entire thing is absurd," she said. "And you said it yourself. There's nothing anyone can do about it. There's no damned point. To any of it."

"You were here to pick up Travis." It came out as an accusation. It came out sounding…hurt, and he hated that.

"I wasn't going to go home with him," she whispered, leveling her gaze at him.

"Good."

He let go of her and looked down at his bleeding hand. And it was like he was really seeing himself for the first time. Bloody knuckles, completely at the end of his sanity.

He must look unhinged. He *felt* unhinged.

And for what? Why intentionally tempt fate, the devil and all manner of sin and terrible ideas?

Why was he doing this to her?

To them?

He had no idea. He just knew that he hadn't been able to stop himself.

Then he turned and walked out of the bar. Let the door swing closed behind him. He braced his hands on his knees and bent over for a second, trying to catch his breath.

He wasn't terribly surprised when he heard the door open, and heard angry footsteps following along behind him.

He straightened and turned around, faced with Elsie in all her fury.

"What am I supposed to do with that?" she asked.

"Like you said," he returned, "there's nothing to do with it. There is nothing for either of us to do with any of this."

"What is it?"

And she was so honest, so pure, and he could barely stand it.

It was all already ruined, that was the problem. They were out in the parking lot at Smokey's, where every damned person inside knew them. They were shredded. Him literally. Bleeding onto the asphalt because of this.

It was broken already.

There was no stopping it.

And the last sane thought in his head—as he closed the distance between Elsie and him—was that he never should've come back in this bar.

And that it wasn't too late to leave.

But he didn't listen to himself.

Instead, he wrapped his arm around her waist and pulled her up against his body, and before he could think about what he was doing, before he could think about anything, he lowered his head and kissed Elsie Garrett right there in the parking lot.

CHAPTER TWELVE

SHE WAS DYING. Or something. She was floating underwater, and flying through space, and also somehow more in her body than she had ever been. Breathless, weightless, wondrous.

It was nothing like she had imagined. It was so much more physical. His whiskers were rough, his hold was tight, and she felt every bit of the hard work that he did in his strength. In his lips. His mouth was hot, and it made her hot all the way down. Made her stomach feel tight, and also like it was in a freefall. Then he angled his head, forcing her lips apart and sliding his tongue into her mouth, and she gasped, flinging her arms on top of his shoulders to steady herself, to keep herself from melting. From falling to the ground. She was so close. So very close. She had never felt so protected and so…so perilously close to perishing all at once.

And she was now. Every bit of her.

She felt like she had been lit on fire and left there to burn. Out in the open. Where everyone could see. Worst of all, where *she* couldn't hide. Where she couldn't pretend anymore that this wasn't what was between them.

She was attracted to him.

No, that seemed weak.

She *wanted* him.

And it was why she hadn't been able to look at Travis at the town hall.

Because she'd only had eyes for Hunter, and that was…
impossible. Ridiculous. She couldn't… She couldn't want
Hunter like this. Not when they were both so broken and
damaged they didn't know how to be in relationships. Not
when they could destroy something brilliant and wonderful
by doing this. Because Sawyer and Wolf would…

That was what made her pull away from him. She was
gasping for air, her heart thundering so fast and hard she
could barely breathe.

But the thought of her brothers, well, that had basically
ruined everything.

"We… I…"

"Elsie—"

"Hunter," she said, mostly because she was trying to
remind herself that it was Hunter. Hunter that she had just
kissed. Hunter that had just *kissed her*.

And she wanted to cry because this wasn't what she
wanted. This wasn't her fantasy.

Her fantasy of being wanted. He was supposed to help
her learn how to flirt. She wasn't supposed to want something from him. It wasn't right or fair. It wasn't fair.

And she felt like everything that had been exposed after
their time together was being reinjured. Being examined
and inflamed and…

None of those words were sexy. But the problem was,
this was just as painful as it was sexy.

And she realized, standing there in front of Hunter,
that she'd actually never wanted a man before. She hadn't
wanted *that* with Travis. She'd had this vague idea of what
it would be like to be kissed. What it would be like to be
touched, and she had told herself that she wanted it.

But she hadn't. Because she hadn't really known. And
now Hunter had touched her. He had touched her and he

had shown her just what an idiot she was. Because this was being flayed down to the bone, and it was just a kiss.

Hunter.

Hunter McCloud had kissed her. Hunter, who she would've said only weeks ago was basically the most annoying person on the planet. And now she felt like her reality had been turned upside down and she didn't know anything. About him, about herself. About the whole world.

And so, Elsie Garrett did what any self-respecting woman in her situation would do. She ran. She ran to her truck like her boots were on fire and her ass was catching.

She slammed the door and fought tears as she turned the ignition on.

And she saw that Hunter was coming after her, so she peeled out of the driveway as quickly as she could and drove away.

She was an idiot. She was a damned idiot. And she cursed herself the entire way back to Four Corners, which was the direction Hunter was also going. Or maybe... Maybe he wouldn't go that way. Maybe he would stay at the bar. Maybe he would pick up a woman who knew what to do when a man kissed her. A woman who didn't freak out and run off.

She drove back to her cabin and shut the door behind her, leaning against it, her heart pounding hard against her breastbone.

And then she took stock of what she felt.

Her legs felt like jelly, that place *between* her legs felt swollen and slick. Hollow. And it was humiliating. Because everything she had felt when they'd danced in Vancouver was magnified by about a thousand degrees now.

She was trying to catch her breath, and couldn't.

And then two whole minutes later, when she still had

her back up against the door, there was a solid knock that landed just between her shoulder blades.

"I clearly ran away from you," she said.

"I had to check to make sure you were okay," he said.

She flung the door open and looked at him. "Do I seem okay to you?"

"No. You seem freaked out. And I wanted to make sure that…"

"That what? That I wasn't as freaked out as I appeared?"

"Yeah. That."

"You kissed me," she spat, as if it could take the impression of his mouth off hers. As if it could do something to minimize the heat.

"Yeah. I did."

"That's insane."

"I agree."

She realized something in that moment.

That if she moved toward him, he wouldn't be able to resist. That if she put her hand on his chest, if she pressed her breasts against him, that he would respond because he wanted her. And she knew that. She knew it, like it was a new kind of knowledge that hadn't been there before, and suddenly was.

She didn't feel so weak or scared right now. Not at this moment.

Instead, she felt a little bit powerful. And she didn't quite know what to do with it.

She didn't know what to do with this. With this wealth of knowledge that felt suddenly opened up to her even in the midst of her ignorance.

That was what it had felt like. A stunning moment of ignorance. How could she not have *known* that she was attracted to Hunter?

Because now she couldn't not see it.

Now she couldn't look at him and see anything other than a man. A man that was beautiful.

A man that women wanted.

A man that made women weak.

And he wanted her. Even more miraculously.

She wondered what he saw, standing there, because what she saw was… It was like a revelation. Right there in her little house that she had lived in for all of these years. On this property she had been born on.

Very near the barn she had been born *in*.

And yet it was like seeing with new eyes. So many familiar things, but Hunter was no longer one of them.

She studied his face. The intensity in his dark eyes, that mouth that had been on hers. His square jaw, the strong column of his throat, and when had she ever noticed a man's throat before? But there was something indescribably sexy about it. That even that was different. Sure, they both had a neck, but his had an Adam's apple.

Something she'd never pondered in her life.

His chest was broad and thick and deep, well muscled. And she had felt it when she'd been pressed up against him, and she thought again of when he'd gone to bed shirtless in the motel.

And how she'd had to look away because it had done things to her she wasn't ready to confront. Same as she hadn't wanted to confront what she'd felt when he'd turned all that flirtation right onto her. Or when she'd sat on his chest on the football field.

Then he'd pressed his lips against hers and there was no more pretending she didn't know.

And she felt rotten with it.

"I'm okay," she said softly.

"Are you?"

"Yeah," she said. "I'm okay. I... Hunter, I... They can't know. Not ever. I don't know what would happen if..."

"Oh, I know," Hunter said. "They would peel my skin off my bones and hang me from the nearest tree as an example."

"And they wouldn't do that with just any guy."

"I know," he said, his tone grave.

He wasn't just any guy. He was Hunter. He was the man who had taught her to ride a horse. He was the man who had taught her to dance.

And he was a man who had shown her what it meant to be a woman and feel powerful with it. And she could never, ever have him. Alaina...

Alaina.

There were so many reasons that this couldn't happen, but *Alaina.*

And it wasn't because she thought Hunter was going to want Alaina, it was just that... Of all the things... Of all the things, and she hadn't thought about her best friend even once during all of this, during her entire emotional breakdown.

She had just been annoyed with her.

It was the crappiest thing. It really was. And she just felt like the biggest jerk in the entire world.

The saddest. And the most frustrated. And...

She had *needed* Hunter in her life. In about a thousand different ways. For so many years, and if this happened, and she ruined the friendship between Sawyer and Wolf and Hunter—if Hunter was effectively removed from their lives—she would never be able to forgive herself for that. Ever. Not ever.

"You have to go," she said. "Nothing else can happen."

"Absolutely," he said, his agreement firm.

"Nothing."

And she realized that as they were talking, they had moved closer to each other. And she was close enough that she could smell his skin. His hard work, and sunshine. The grass and the hay.

"Nothing," she repeated.

"I agreed with you."

"Hunter," she said.

And then she was in his arms. And he was kissing her again. And she didn't want talk. She didn't want to do anything but be in this moment. She said that it was impossible, and he had agreed, but here they were. It wasn't stopping them. It couldn't.

It should, because there were about a million reasons they couldn't kiss. That he shouldn't be walking into her cabin right now, that he shouldn't be shutting the door behind him.

She should stop. And she should tell him to go away.

But she didn't want him to go away.

He had told her not to do this with someone she didn't want. He was the only person that she wanted. What she had thought was wanting, it wasn't anything. It was just thinking somebody was cute. It wasn't the same.

What she felt for Hunter was something deep. Something beyond her reach.

Something she could hardly understand, much less resist. If she didn't want to. She was done with it.

The fact of the matter was that even though she walked around pretending that she was brave, half the time Elsie Garrett felt like the motherless child she was. She felt unloved, abandoned and unwanted, no matter how much Wolf and Sawyer had rallied around her and been the most wonderful brothers she could've ever asked for.

She felt a deep hole inside of her soul. And there was something about the way that Hunter looked at her that satisfied it.

Even if only for a moment.

Then there was this. The way he kissed her. The way he touched her.

His mouth was firm and hard against hers, decisive. They were in private now. She had thought that he was out of control in the parking lot, had thought that he was being unrestrained, but it was nothing compared to this. He cupped the back of her head with his strong hand, and used it to guide her, to direct her movements. He parted her mouth beneath his and tasted her. Deep.

It made her want to cry because had she thought that she was going to go into this with Travis?

Had she really thought she'd be able to do this with him when it was Hunter she wanted?

She hadn't known. She hadn't known *anything*.

And the depth and breadth of her ignorance was becoming more and more apparent the deeper Hunter took the case. The deeper they walked into her cabin.

She put her hands beneath the hem of his shirt and felt hot skin, his hard stomach. She pushed it up farther, up to his chest, and she remembered how beautiful it was. With just the right amount of dark hair and sculpted muscle.

And suddenly, she was desperate to see him. Desperate to see him in a moment when she was able to look. When she didn't have to be embarrassed about the fact that she was attracted to him.

She pulled away and looked up at him, and just for a moment, she was overcome by the strangeness of it all. She felt like she was standing in the center of a deep ocean. And somewhere behind her she knew there were shadows.

She wouldn't let herself fear them, not now.

Not long ago, she had looked at him and her primary emotion had been annoyance. A little bit of affection, given everything he had taught her, but mostly, he'd gotten under her skin.

But that was a distant memory.

Now she looked at him and she saw something entirely different, and she felt something…

Something that she had never imagined.

She was out here in the middle of the ocean, and she should be afraid that she was going to drown. But she wasn't. Her desire for him was all around her. Fathomless. Above her, below her. Pressing in on all sides, but she didn't want to turn away from it. She wanted to embrace it.

So she did. She pushed his shirt up over his head and cast it onto the floor, and embraced it and him. And he didn't protest. Instead, a hard growl reverberated in the back of his throat, and she swallowed it down.

She had never been this close to another person before. And it somehow seemed both wildly *wrong* and totally *right* that the person be Hunter.

They parted again, and she put her hand flat on his chest. "Well, you did teach me how to ride."

He closed his eyes. Like he was in pain.

"It seems relevant for now," she whispered.

"It doesn't have to be…*everything*," he said, breathing hard. "Not now."

She shook her head. "It does. It does." She said it twice, affirming it, not just to him, but herself.

He picked her up and carried her to the couch. Her heart

was thundering so fast she thought she might pass out. But she didn't want him to stop.

He kept on kissing her.

Kissing her until her mouth was swollen, and her face felt prickly. His body was hard and muscular over the top of hers. And she wrapped her arms around his neck, pushed her fingers through his hair and sighed at the delicious sensations that he created inside her.

He moved his hands down her back, around to the front, palming her breast, his thumb flicking over her tightened nipple. She arched against him, silently begging him for more. She had never felt anything like this. She had never imagined that she could feel like this. This was the promise that had been laid out in front of her on the banks of the river. And it was more, better than she had ever imagined it could be.

He pushed his hands up underneath her top, his thumb skimming the edge of her bra cup, where it met sensitive flesh.

She wiggled.

And she looked up at him. It should be strange that it was Hunter, but it wasn't. He might have thought it was a little bit cheesy when she brought up the fact that he had taught her to ride. Taught her to dance. Suddenly it all made sense to her. It all became clear. This was right. It was the way things were supposed to be.

It was the way *they* were supposed to be.

There had never been another man for this moment. And she had been a fool to think that there was.

It wasn't about love or anything like that. It was just about the way her life was built. The way it had been structured. It was just about the fact that he was him, and she was her.

And that mattered. It always had. He was… She would never be able to explain exactly what Hunter McCloud meant to her. Because it was too complicated. Because he got under her skin in a way that nobody else did. In a way that nobody else ever had. But he was also that mountain.

Who was always there, unwavering, and would be there, no matter what. No matter what she called him during a poker game, no matter if she threw him into a river.

Because here they were, with that not too far in the distance, and now he was holding her like she was something precious. Even though she had been a spiteful varmint, and he had been happy to call her out for it.

She clung to his shoulders, arching against him as he kissed his way down her neck, down to her collarbone, and pushed her T-shirt up over her head, leaving her in only her bra. He kissed his way down the valley of her breasts, over the top of the fabric, down her stomach. And then he made his way back up to her lips.

As she was watching him. She knew that she should probably have her eyes closed, but she was held captive.

Because this was another look at the Hunter McCloud that she had never known. The Hunter McCloud that she'd heard rumors of, that she knew women loved, but that she had never herself experienced. Dark and handsome and intense.

She had always imagined that he would be funny.

When she had let herself imagine it.

When she had let herself really wonder why it was women couldn't resist him. She had figured that he was that charmer. With a quick and ready smile, because she had seen that in him. But it wasn't that. He was intense, and he was focused. And it was all on her. It was so intent she thought she might break apart with it. Thought she might burst into tears because of it.

It was everything, always. And she had not been prepared for that.

He reached up and unhooked her bra, flinging it down onto the floor. And she knew a moment of complete and total embarrassment. Because what would he see when he looked at her body? At what she thought was an entirely average rack. If not slightly below average.

"Remember when you asked me what a cute figure was?"

She nodded, feeling self-conscious.

"You asked me if it was small boobs."

"I did," she said, her throat scratchy.

"It's not. You are perfect. And beautiful. I spent a hell of a long time ignoring that on purpose. Because why would I be looking at you?" But his eyes were filled with wonder now, and he was drawing his thumb down her cheek. "How could I ever look at you? You're Elsie Garrett. You're Sawyer and Wolf's little sister. But you're not. You're *Elsie*. You are strong and fierce, mean, funny and brilliant. And you have a damned fine body."

"I… Thank you."

Then he kissed her again, and swallowed anything else she might have said, which was a relief because she didn't think any worthy words could come out of her mouth at this point. Not when she was feeling quite so overwhelmed. She would probably just embarrass herself. She didn't really want that.

He unsnapped her jeans, moving his hands down beneath the waistband, beneath her panties, and she cried out, bucking against his hand as he stroked her there, where she was embarrassingly wet and aching for more of his attention. But she didn't have time to beg for more, because he kissed her again. His mouth hard and intense on hers. That kiss going deep as he carried her to heights she had never known existed.

He created a white heat between her legs that was almost uncomfortable, stroking and teasing her until she was panting, until her hips were moving in time with his stroke, until she was gasping, begging for release. Then he pushed one finger deep inside of her, and stars exploded behind her eyes.

It didn't end, and she didn't want it to. And it terrified her all at the same time. She'd never felt anything like this before. And it had come from him. Hunter was the only one who could do this. He was the master of her desire just now and if he stopped touching her, it would end. And if he didn't, it might go on longer than she could bear it.

She opened her eyes, and looked into his and the wave peaked, a sharp sound exploding from her.

His mouth crashed down onto hers and he swallowed her cry of pleasure. Kissed her until it subsided. He kissed her and kissed her, and her desire wouldn't bank. Wouldn't stop. She started shaking, and turned her head to the side because she needed a reprieve.

He gathered her up against his bare chest and held her, her breasts pressed tightly against his chest, while she tried to find her normal breath. And she could hear his heart, pounding like hers was.

Hear his breathing, shattered like her own.

"Hunter…"

"Just rest for a second," he ground out.

He maneuvered her so that her rear was pressed right up against the evidence of his desire, and she really wanted to see it. She really wanted to see *him*.

But he was shushing her like she was a wild horse, and her heart was beating so out of control she thought he might not be far off from the truth.

"Hunter…" she said again, her voice shaking.

"That's enough for tonight," he said. "But I'll stay for a bit."

"Why?" She suddenly felt bereft. "Why is that enough for the night?"

Even as she said that, she sounded hollow and afraid and she knew he was right. But she didn't want him to be right.

"Because I think we're both wrecked," he said.

"So?" Why did she always have to *push*?

"Because I know that you're a virgin," he said. "And I know that you've never done any of that before. Believe me, Travis would have taken you up on the offer to do everything tonight. But he's the kind of guy who doesn't let grass grow underneath his feet. I've let a whole field grow underneath mine, and I don't mind. I'll be here. You'll be here. There's plenty of time. It'll be worth it. To make sure that you're ready."

"I'm ready," she said, even while she trembled.

"Maybe I'm not," he said.

She was raw and shaky inside, and it felt so important just then to know if he was too. "How come you're not?"

"Because this is different," he said, his voice rough. "Because you're you. That matters to me. I have to figure out—"

"You're not going to talk to my brothers."

"No," he said, looking horrified. "I am not. This is between you and me, Elsie. Nobody else needs to know about it. Not because I'm ashamed of it. Or you. Just because…"

"No," she said. "I get it. Because no one here can keep a secret worth a damn and we don't need that kind of trouble."

"No, we don't."

She felt like she'd been in a car speeding down a highway only to have the brakes put on too fast. An adrenaline high making her shake, and at the same time, she felt desperately tired.

And he was promising her that this wasn't it.

"I've got to go to Vancouver. Again," he said slowly, tracing a line up and down her arm with the tips of his fingers. Soothing and arousing all at once. "I have to go and pick up those horses. I think you should come with me."

Her breath left her lungs in a rush. "So that we can…"

"It would be better, don't you think? To be away."

She imagined him coming to bed with her in that motel that they shared. Not across the room, but in her arms. Over her. Strong and masculine.

It made her shiver.

"I take that as a yes?"

She curled herself into his chest and nodded.

"Good."

They lay like that for a moment, and finally, her shaking stopped. Finally, she felt like she could think, even just a little bit.

"You should get a Band-Aid for your hand." She peeled herself away from him and stood, and her jeans started to slip down her hips, so she redid the button.

She left her shirt off as she went into the bathroom to grab some Band-Aids. A little bit of hydrogen peroxide. Which she knew hurt like a son of a bitch, but he had cut himself and he needed to be disinfected.

She went out to the couch, where he was laying still, no shirt, his jeans resting low on his hips. And she could see that bulge right there, letting her know that he did still want her.

She cleared her throat and looked at him, trying to play more bold than she felt.

"I can help you with that," she said, looking meaningfully at his fly.

Of course that was an awful lot of confidence borne from nothing. She had no idea if she could help *him with that* or not. She'd never seen a naked man *like that*. She'd never touched one. Certainly never brought one to pleasure.

"No," he said, his voice hard.

She was both relieved and offended by the refusal.

"Why not?"

"Because I said no."

Disquiet wound its way around her soul. "Is it too weird for you?"

He shook his head, a strange expression crossing his face. "It's actually not weird for me at all. I don't really know what to make of that."

She knelt down beside him, taking his hand into hers and looking down at his knuckles. They were blue and swollen. "You broke your hand," she said.

"It's all right," he said, trying to wave her off.

"You broke your hand," she reiterated.

"Probably not my *whole* hand, or I wouldn't be able to move it."

"You punched the side of the bar?"

"Yes," he said.

She unscrewed the lid on the hydrogen peroxide and pressed the cloth against the top of the bottle, tipping it upside down and saturating it. Then she applied the medicine to his knuckles.

"Hell," he said, his breath hissing through his teeth.

It reminded her of another moment. When he'd come

to Garrett's Watch when he'd been eighteen or so, with a black eye.

She'd only been eight, but Sawyer and Wolf had been out, and she'd fished a steak out of the freezer for him to put on his eye because she'd seen the boys do it when they were hurt. He'd said he'd fallen off a horse. And suddenly…

"Hunter. Do you remember that day you came over and you were…you were hurt. I tried to patch you up, but I was a kid and—"

"Yeah," he said, his voice rough.

"What happened?"

"It was my dad," he said. "I didn't want to worry you. It was…" He cleared his throat. "Dad was going after Lachlan like he always did—he was mean to all of us, but man he had it in for that kid—and I couldn't take it. I went right for him and it was…it was insane. That was…that was when Gus…handled it."

"You mean when Gus…"

"I never saw my dad again, Elsie, but Gus swears he just threatened him. It was one of those things where… My dad had a way of making us all feel like scared little boys even though we were all bigger. A lifetime of abuse will do that to you. And Gus, well, there were reasons we didn't push back. But something went off inside me that day and I couldn't stop myself."

They'd always been there for each other. The truth of that settled over her now. He'd been there for her, taught her things she needed to know. When he'd been hurt she'd been there for him. It had been a pivotal moment in his life and she hadn't even realized it.

"Why did you punch the side of the bar?" she asked softly.

He didn't say anything for a moment. Then when he did speak, his voice was rough.

"Because it messed me up. Thinking about you being with him."

She looked up at him. "And it made you mad." A little bloom of pleasure popped in her midsection.

"Yes," he said.

"And you wanted to punch him," she said.

"So badly."

She felt giddy. "But you punched the side of the bar instead?"

"Yes. I was going to leave. I was going to leave you to it because you wanted him. But then I couldn't."

"I didn't want him," she said, drawing the cloth gingerly over his wounds. "I just thought I should. Because I thought…" She looked up at him, and she felt like her chest would crack open. "I just thought there was no point wanting you."

"There's not," he said, his words instantly dashing that spark of hope in her. "So don't go looking for meaning. Or a point. Because you're not going to find it. But…"

"We can have a good time?"

"Yes," he said. "But that's not exactly right either. You could probably have had a good time with Travis. By all accounts he knows what he's doing. But there's more to sex than just thinking someone is attractive. There's chemistry. And that's something that you and I have. Real and certain. And it's not common. I'm not doing this for you. I'm not teaching you or doing you a favor. I want you. And I couldn't stand the idea of him having his hands on you. That's why we're here. I want to be very clear about that."

She nodded, feeling overwhelmed by his intensity.

"You know," she said, "I thought that you were probably more charming and funny."

"I usually am."

She put bandages on his knuckles, and he got up and collected his shirt. But she was sorry that he was leaving. Really very sorry.

"How come you aren't charming and funny with me?"

"Because I'm not supposed to be here," he said. "Because I was never supposed to touch you, much less... like this. And I know that. I know exactly what I'm doing wrong. I know exactly the way I'm sinning, and I don't want to stop." He shook his head. "But I can't bring myself to be charming about it."

"Does that make me different?" She smiled a little bit in spite of herself.

"You're not like anyone, and I think you know that, Elsie. Because you know me. How many times have I ever brought a woman around?"

She thought about that. Because he didn't. Hunter didn't bring his conquests to the ranch. He didn't seem to keep them around for more than a night at all. In fact, she only knew that he was a womanizer because she had heard about it. She'd seen him talk to women at the bar, and then disappear, but she had never seen the women again.

He didn't hook up with women he knew. Bottom line.

Though, she supposed he hadn't really hooked up with her. They hadn't finished. But maybe that made her different too. And she didn't know why she should like that so much. Only that she did.

"Your hand is all fixed," she said.

"So it is," he said, flexing his fingers. "Two days. We go up to Vancouver."

"Two days," she confirmed.

"Are you going to be able to be chill around me?"

She rolled her eyes. "Hunter, it would take more than you to dismember my chill."

"Apparently, you do a very good job at getting rid of mine."

And that, well, that made her feel *wonderful*.

"Sorry about your hand," she said, except she could hear that she sounded cheerful.

She shouldn't be celebrating his broken knuckles. But they were for her. So she did. Even if just a little.

"I don't think you are."

"I'm not," she said. "You were right. This is very basic. I... I am no better than anyone else. I am glad of your ridiculous display. I am glad that I made you break your hand."

"Great. I'm not especially. But here we are."

"Here we are," she said.

Silence stretched between them, and so did tension. She was about a second away from asking him to stay. Asking him to get into bed with her.

"I'll let you get some rest," he said, moving away from her.

She nodded. "Just remember that you're the one that said that. Not me."

"And that is important for you to say, why?"

"To make it clear that I'm not the one who can't handle it."

He stared at her. "All right," he said. "Maybe I can't handle it. Maybe I can't handle the fact that a few weeks ago I saw you only as my friend's little sister, and a pain in my ass, and now I want to lie back down on that couch and do unspeakable things to you. Maybe I can't handle that. If that shocks you or bothers you, that's too bad."

Her face went red. "I am not shocked or bothered.

Thank you. Though, a couple weeks ago you were only my brother's friend who was not unannoying to me. So there."

"Is that what we're doing now? Trying to score points?"

"It's what we always do."

He leaned in, his mouth a whisper from hers. "But not this."

And he kissed her. Soft this time, and it made her flutter. Made her feel like she was floating. Elsie Garrett had never felt like she was floating a day in her life.

But she had a feeling she was going to have a hard time making it feel like her feet were connecting to the ground over the next few days. And she was going to have to act like everything was normal.

Hunter collected the rest of his things and moved toward the door.

"I'll see you at work tomorrow," he said.

"Yeah. I'll see you at work."

CHAPTER THIRTEEN

"Where the hell have you been?"

When Hunter pulled in the driveway he was shocked to see his brother Gus standing there, bathed in the headlights.

"Since when do you check up on my whereabouts?"

"Since you and I were supposed to meet to discuss the timeline for bringing those horses in from Vancouver."

Well. He had completely forgotten about that.

"I went out. Sorry."

"Right. Where were you, exactly?"

"Does it matter?" he asked.

Gus crossed his arms, his expression grim as hell. "The fact that you won't answer tells me that it does."

Hunter sighed, feeling exhausted and wrung the hell out. And he had taken himself to the edge with Elsie without getting any satisfaction and he was absolutely not in the mood for Gus to suddenly get involved. "Gus, don't act interested in my life. It doesn't suit you."

"Who said I wasn't interested in your life, Hunter? Sounds like somebody has some daddy issues."

"That would be all of us," Hunter said.

"True enough," Gus replied.

"Anyway. Sorry. If you want to talk about timelines—"

"It might escape your notice that you have a couple of pretty young things around Four Corners deeply interested in you."

Hunter stilled. "What exactly do you mean by that?"

"I think you know. Alaina and Elsie." He looked at Gus and he tried to figure out where this was coming from. And he also decided to see if he could play it off.

"What makes you think that?"

"I was at Game Day, Hunter, and I was watching the way they act around you."

"Elsie likes that ranch hand. Travis," he grunted.

"She doesn't," Gus said, shaking his head. "Look, Hunter, I'm not charming like you. I'm not easy. I watch people. And I see what's going on, and I'd have let it go, but I have a concern it's all escalating."

And right then, he kind of hated his brother. Because the thing about Gus was he didn't jump in and talk and joke with everyone else. He hung back. He watched. Gus had an entirely different experience of the world and everyone in it than the rest of the McCloud brothers.

Hunter wasn't vain about his appearance. He had no reason to be. But he also knew that he was the kind of good-looking women found easy.

That wasn't true for Gus. Hunter's looks drew people in, Gus's tended to repel them first, and while Gus never issued a complaint on that score, never seemed bothered by it, the fact of the matter was it shaped the way he dealt with people.

And when it came to judgment, he wasn't wrong. He never was. He just wished that Gus had been looking the other way the last few weeks.

"It's Elsie," he said, trying to keep his tone dry, trying to play off the fact that he had just kissed Elsie. Touched her to orgasm. Trying to play off the fact that he was planning on taking her virginity sometime in the next few days.

Dovetailing nicely with the conversation about picking up the horses, actually.

"What does that mean?" Gus asked, repeating his own dumb words back at him.

"She doesn't have feelings for me." That he *did* believe was true. They were suffering from an excessive amount of chemistry, but that wasn't the same as having feelings.

"I don't believe that. But it's complicated, because Alaina's got eyes for you too. Or haven't you noticed?"

He hadn't noticed Alaina at all because yeah, Gus was right, he didn't care.

He *was* a little surprised Gus had noticed.

"I wondered if you hadn't," Gus continued, "because it seems to be Elsie that preoccupied you."

That the way he felt about Elsie was apparent was like a stick straight through the gut.

"Elsie is like a sister to me," he said, the words feeling shockingly disingenuous at the moment.

"Sure," Gus said. "Though I've never seen Sawyer look at her quite the way you do."

And if Gus could see it, could everyone? He and Elsie had been locked in...it was like their own world. They'd gone away and things had shifted and frankly, they'd both been obsessed with what was happening between them and ignored a lot of what it might look like to other people.

"Do you have a point to this?" Hunter asked.

"Yes. Watch what you're doing. And who you're doing it to. Those girls are lifelong friends, and I know you, Hunter. Women like you too quickly and too easily, and you don't feel the same things back."

"You don't have the right to tell me what I feel. Not for anything or anyone, least of all Elsie Garrett."

The denial was intense and firm, and quite a bit more

than he had intended on issuing. And if he had hoped to leave his brother in the dark about the things that he really felt, well, he had failed.

But the problem was, not even he knew what he felt. He just damned well knew it wasn't nothing.

"I don't want them to get hurt."

"I don't need you to tell me how to live my life. I would rather die than hurt Elsie. And I don't have any designs on Alaina at all. I cannot control what that girl feels for me."

"You could tell her that you don't feel anything."

"Well, see, Gus, this is where we see that whatever judgment you have for me and the way that I conduct myself with women, you certainly never had a long-standing attachment to one either, or you would know that walking up to a woman who's never declared any sort of intention toward you, and informing her that nothing is going to happen is actually insulting."

Gus shrugged. "I don't see how telling the truth is insulting."

"Yeah, because you don't bother with charm."

"When you lead with this face, there's no point. You know how to bullshit, Hunter, that's what you're good at. You make people feel at ease. I can't do that. So I don't try. But I also don't accidentally get into entanglements. I have to go looking for them."

"Yeah, why don't you go look for one instead of getting into my business."

"Do I need to intervene with this thing with Elsie?"

"What do you mean by that?"

"Do I need to have a talk with Wolf and Sawyer, because if it comes down to it, I will."

He gritted his teeth. "Elsie's twenty-four years old. And she's a woman. Whatever she wants to do, she can do it. If you want to talk to Sawyer and Wolf, go right ahead. I don't have a whole lot of friends, but I'll stand by her choices."

Gus looked at him hard. "So, something is happening."

And Hunter couldn't bring himself to play games.

"Do you want me to deny it? I'm not ashamed of it." He couldn't lie, that was the thing. The weird-ass thing. He couldn't make Elsie into a dirty secret when she felt way too special for that.

He didn't want to expose her because she didn't want that. But that was all.

"And what do you expect to happen?" Gus crossed his arms and stared him down, like some kind of overprotective parent taking him to task.

Something they'd never had at all, so where that came from he didn't know.

"I don't know. Because I don't know what she wants. I can't give you the answers that you're looking for, Gus. And I don't know why the hell you want them."

"Because I have protected your ass for your entire life, Hunter, whether you realize it or not. And I want to protect it now. You're in deep with somebody that is bound up in our lives. Not just this present project, but everything else. You're right. You don't have a lot of friends. I don't have any. So forgive me for caring about yours. And about Elsie. Because I've seen more hurt on this godforsaken land than I can stomach."

Hunter stood and looked at his brother, his face etched in rough stone, his expression hard. "Gus, you don't need to keep protecting me. I'm not a kid."

And he felt… It felt wrong.

Because Gus didn't know. He didn't know the whole truth about their mom leaving. And while Hunter might not flat out blame himself, he would always feel ashamed about what had happened. He would always wonder if his words had a more profound effect than an eleven-year-old's words should have, because his mother was just so damned vulnerable.

And he would always wonder if what he'd meant to protect her had ended up wounding her beyond repair.

He would always wonder if somehow…

He was the reason she'd left without them.

She should have gone, of course. But why not take them?

He would always wonder that. And he would always wonder how much of what he'd done had brought the hammer down on Gus and Lachlan especially.

"We'll always be those kids," Gus said. "You can't erase what's inside there," he said, pointing to Hunter's chest. "Any more that I can erase what's here." He pointed at his own face. "In the end, it's all the same. It's just that people can see me coming."

"So, your point is that you think I'm too broken to be with Elsie?"

"I'm glad that Tag is happy. I am." Which wasn't a no. "I encouraged him to get with her, in fact. In the end."

Great. Somehow Tag was all good and Hunter was just a mess.

"So why not me, Gus?"

"Because Tag was in love with her. You're playing with a lot of emotions not knowing where it might end."

"No one ever knows when it will end or how." He wasn't ready to talk about things ending when they hadn't even begun. He wasn't ready for them to be things.

"I actually do know who I am, Gus. And I do get that I… I'm well aware. If I could… If I could not want her, I wouldn't." It was a dumb thing to say, really. But it was honest.

And suddenly, something in Gus's expression changed. *Understanding.* Hunter wanted to ask, but it just wasn't how they did things. This whole moment was out of character for Gus. Coming and getting in his business wasn't typical of him. And he wondered why he had been spurred to do it now.

He really, really wondered.

"Well, *that* I get," Gus said.

"You just have to trust me that I would never hurt her."

"I don't think you would on purpose."

"Yeah. Sometimes people get hurt."

That was fatalistic. But it was true.

Gus nodded again. "I can't really argue with that."

"I'm taking her to Vancouver with me. I'll have the horses back here in the next few days."

"All right."

"Gus… I do appreciate that you're looking out for me. And for her. You can let your guard down now, though. Now it's just regular life stuff. Nobody's in danger anymore."

Gus didn't say anything to that. Instead, he nodded slowly and turned to walk away. And Hunter watched his brother until he faded into the blackness.

It left him with a strange feeling of disquiet in his soul. But determination all the same.

Because he had to stand there and justify what he was doing with Elsie. He had to stand firm in that. He had fewer answers than he wanted. But he also knew one thing. If turning back was possible, he would turn back. But he had punched a wall. He had chased her down because he couldn't leave well enough alone.

And it tangled together with all the guilt that lived deep

down inside of him, and even with all of that, he knew that he couldn't stop. He knew that he wouldn't stop.

That in and of itself was confirmation. Even if it was rather inglorious confirmation.

In his experience, life didn't give you much better. So, he was going to take it.

It was a damned surprise that he was able to go to work the next day and put in some time with Wolf and Sawyer without spontaneously combusting with the force of the sins he had committed the night before. Because damn, it was the only thing he could think about. And he knew that he was in the wrong.

But was he?

He'd defended himself to Gus last night, and honestly ever since then he'd been working through all the shit in his own soul and still couldn't...

Even as the sun rose up over the mountain and he tried— he really did—to feel a sense of guilt as he imagined his hand skimming over Elsie's curves, as he imagined slipping his fingers down between her legs and feeling her all soft and wet for him, he couldn't. He didn't really want to either. Elsie was a grown woman. And he had no doubt about that after last night. And he...

He couldn't explain. But his chest was tight from wanting her, and his body was on fire with it.

He had never felt anything like what had passed between them. And he wanted to follow it. He just did.

"You seem subdued this morning," Sawyer commented.

"Meaning?" Hunter asked.

"You're usually hassling us."

"I've got no hassling to do," he said, because apparently there were limits to the shamelessness, and that extended to harassing the brothers of the woman that he had partway corrupted last night.

Leaving her had been the hardest thing he'd ever done.

"What the hell did you do to your hand?" Wolf asked from his position on the horse beside Hunter.

Damn. He had forgotten about his knuckles for a minute while he thought about Elsie and how good it had felt to kiss her. How good it had felt to touch her.

But now he remembered, and the searing pain in his fist was a reminder.

"Nothing all that interesting. Got mad about something stupid. Hit a wall."

"You hit a wall?" Sawyer asked.

"Yeah," he said. "I was trying to fix something. At my house. Got pissed off and punched the wall. And it was apparently a lot stronger than I am."

"You're not one for temper tantrums," Wolf said.

"Well, I don't know. Maybe I'm more like my old man than people think."

He tried to say that with some levity, but given what else he had said only recently, it came out flat.

"I heard Elsie said that to you," Sawyer said. "At the poker game. In front of people. That that was what the whole conflict with the bet was about, even though neither of you mentioned it the other night at dinner."

"Who said that?" Hunter asked.

"Landry."

"Right. So Landry decided to speak to you, but about my business. That seems on-brand for a King."

They didn't involve themselves in the broader social context of the ranch, unless it was to be a pain in the ass.

"He just mentioned it in passing yesterday. Asked if I'd heard about it, or if you'd put Elsie six feet under for it."

"No. She was mad at me. You know how she is. I don't take anything she says all that seriously."

But he remembered her face last night, and he remembered her saying she just wanted to be chosen, and he knew that he was a liar. Because he took her pretty seriously.

"Well, she shouldn't have said it either way."

"You don't need to make excuses for her behavior, or talk about what she ought to do," he said to Sawyer. "You're not her father."

"I am aware of that," Sawyer said. "Given that I actually do have a child. But it doesn't matter. I care about the way she treats you."

Well, if Sawyer had any idea what had gone on last night, he would care about Hunter's feelings a hell of a lot less. Of that he was certain.

"She's a good kid. She's a good worker," Hunter said. "That's it."

"Great."

"I'm taking her up to Vancouver tomorrow. Finishing off this horse sale. Going to tow up the trailer."

"Sounds good."

"Yeah. Should be fun."

"Fun," Wolf said. "Not something I would normally characterize a road trip with my sister as."

"Hey, don't give her such a hard time," Hunter said. "She has it tough, you know? Being raised around all us jackasses. Maybe she would be sweet if things had been different."

He didn't want her sweet. Or maybe, more accurately, she was a particular brand of sweet that he quite liked. She was... Well, hell. She was Elsie, and he liked her the way she was. His very own kind of sweet and sour, and she tasted like nothing else. Suddenly, he felt himself getting hard, right there, in front of her brothers sitting on the back of a horse. He willed himself back into submission. But he was thinking of her flavor now.

What the hell?

He just… He tried. He did try to remember how he had seen her only recently. Hell, how he had seen her for most of her life. Why was it impossible to remember who they'd been for all those years? Why was he so consumed with who they'd become in just a few days.

Maybe it's been longer. And maybe you don't want to go back.

Maybe. Maybe that was the problem. Maybe she was too perfect. Maybe she was too perfect for him. Maybe she was too close to something he hadn't even known he craved.

This salty, sweet-and-sour Elsie Garrett.

"You know what I mean," Hunter said. "She never had a chance."

"Yeah, I guess that's true," Wolf said. "It is kind of too bad that she had to be raised by the three of us."

"*I* did not raise her," Hunter said.

He balked at the very idea.

"You've been a pretty big part of it."

He just felt uncomfortable. About all of this. Talking about her.

"Because now he felt he knew things about her that they didn't. And it wasn't his place to talk about it. It was her personal stories.

He had some stories that they didn't have. He couldn't betray her.

He had kissed her, and he knew what it looked like when she wanted somebody. And he knew how desperately she wanted to be wanted in return.

Should he feel guilty about that? Should he feel like he was taking advantage?

But he did want her.

He just *did*.

And he remembered the bleak look in Gus's eyes when he'd said that, and he knew whatever the truth about his brother was, he related to that feeling.

"Yeah. Well. Looks like we got everything under control for the morning. I've got to head back to McCloud's Landing. So, I'll see you around."

"Yeah," Sawyer said. "See you around."

He gave a double tap on his horse's flanks and urged him forward quickly. And he took off in a flat-out run toward McCloud's. It would take a good while to get back there, but it felt good. The morning air stinging his face, the sky a rosy glow around him. But it wasn't long before he heard a second set of hoofs pounding in the dirt. And he didn't even have to look to know, he *felt* who it was before he saw her.

Elsie, with her braid whipping behind her, and her body pitched forward in the saddle as she encouraged the horse forward.

"Let's see what you're made of," he murmured, kicking it up a notch, and Elsie kept up all the way, until she passed him. And he watched as she moved, weaving through the trees, kicking up dirt behind her in big clumps. She was amazing. This was almost as beautiful as the way she had arched against him last night. The way she had cried out her pleasure. Almost. This was something incredible.

And so was she.

And he didn't feel guilty. Because right now he felt like he had something to learn from her.

Right now, he felt like he wanted to change something

fundamental inside of himself so he could better be there for her. Better be whatever she needed.

And that was a strange damned thing to feel after the bare minimum encounter they'd had. Especially when he'd never felt it for a woman before.

He didn't quite know what to call it. Didn't quite know what it was.

They arrived at McCloud's Landing. Breathless.

Elsie dismounted, sweat dripping down her forehead, a big grin on her face.

"Good morning," she said.

"Hot damn," he said.

"I didn't know that you would be out riding this morning."

"Same goes," he said. "I expected you to drive."

"Well," she said, "I was in the mood to clear my head. Woke up a little bit…" She blushed. And it was the sweetest thing he had ever seen.

He smiled. And the smile she gave him back lit him up brighter than the rising sun.

"Same," he said. "I also saw your brothers."

Her smiled turned to a grimace. "Well, that's horrifying."

"It didn't horrify me." It hadn't. If anything, it made him more resolved, same as the discussion with Gus. "But just so you know, I told them I punched the wall because I was trying to fix something at my place and it frustrated me. So if it comes up, that's what I said happened to my hand."

"You're lying to them," she said.

"I don't really have a choice. They asked what happened. You don't want me to tell the truth. That I punched the wall in a jealous rage over their little sister."

"I'm not *their little sister*. I mean, I am, but that isn't the definition of who I am."

He chuckled. "I am aware. But that isn't necessarily what they think, and I think you know that."

"You seem to have a lot of opinions about what you *think* I know."

"I'm a man of many opinions."

"Hunter, I just… I don't…"

"You don't have to say anything. You can just talk to me like you always have."

She looked wild-eyed and helpless in that moment and he wanted to draw her into his arms and hold her, but he knew it wasn't the time.

"What's going on, Elsie? You were enjoying my discomfort the other night and now you seem to be the one on edge?"

"Why aren't you?" she asked.

"I am. In some ways." Physical ones. "But all these irritating conversations with your brothers and mine…well, they confirmed that this is what I want right now. I'm willing to accept this. Because I know that I stand behind it."

"I can't really explain what I feel? And that freaks me out a little bit, Hunter, because I never have a problem telling you what I think. But now I'm afraid I'll say the wrong thing. I haven't been able to talk to you since we got back from Vancouver. I've either said nothing, or said too much. I've been a nightmare and I've been a mess. But the problem is, I haven't known what I wanted, and… I know myself. I'm Elsie Garrett, and I love horses. I love Four Corners. I decided that I wanted to have sex, and I set my sights on somebody, and I directed myself there. And it isn't going according to plan. I don't even think I want that person anymore."

Everything in him went hard. "You better the hell know you don't want him."

He would tear down the damned mountains with his hands if she did.

"Fine," she said. "I don't want him. I know that I don't. I absolutely one hundred percent know that I don't. I do not want that man. And sorting out that I want you... Hunter, I don't know how to reconcile the change between us. I don't know what it means."

Seeing Elsie so uncertain, he wanted to reassure her. He wanted to be the one who could do that because he was the one who'd unsettled her, and he just wanted to fix it.

"I was thinking about that this morning," he said. "Just a few weeks ago I had never noticed the way that your nose curves like a ski slope. And that you have about five freckles scattered on your face. That your lips are the color of cherry blossoms, and your eyes are like amber more than brown. I hadn't noticed any of that. It was right in front of me the whole time. And I didn't see it. I guess it could feel wrong to know it all now. I guess I could be upset about it, but I'm not. I'm just...thankful for the beauty. How can you be upset that you see more than you did before?"

His heart was pounding. He felt like... In some ways, he felt like the virgin. It was weird. But he had meant every word. He felt like there were aspects of the world around him that were new, all because of her. All because her eyes were more amber than brown. All because of those freckles. Like each and every one was a revelation, that had brought with it world-changing knowledge.

Lord have mercy.

She looked away. "Oh. I—I don't know. I..."

"You're beautiful," he said.

She shifted and looked up at him, her eyes glassy now.
"How?"

"Do you need me to tell you about your freckles again?"

"No. It's just, I feel very ordinary, Hunter."

"You are far from ordinary, Elsie."

She looked at him sort of shyly, and he could see that
this wasn't just Elsie speaking her mind. This was Elsie
digging deep and speaking her heart, and it was different.

They were different.

"I've been here my whole life, around people who have
known me my whole life. And I—I don't feel special. I don't
feel special at all. My mother walked away from me when
I was a baby, and I don't think my dad ever held me. How
can I be special enough for you to think I'm pretty? It's
not that I think I'm ugly or anything like that, but I know
you've been with, like, a hundred women."

"Well, damn. You make me sound like I'm disgusting."

"I don't mean it that way," she said.

Because she was Elsie, he believed her.

"Right."

"Just… Look, it wouldn't have made me feel special that
Travis wanted to sleep with me. It *didn't*. Last night when
I was having a drink with him, and realizing that it could
happen… It didn't mean anything to me. It really didn't. It
just… I didn't want him. And I knew that he wanted me, but
it wasn't about me. It was just about the fact that he's a man
and he's perfectly happy to have what's available to him. I
never expected him to tell me that I was beautiful. I never
expected him to make me feel good about myself. But you
doing it… When I know that you could have any woman,
especially one who actually knows what she's doing, and
not one who had never been kissed… I don't know. It means
something to me, and I… It makes my chest hurt, Hunter."

His own ached in response. "Elsie—"

"My own mother didn't want me. My dad was there and he never even held me. But knowing that you want me, that you are choosing this, even though Sawyer and Wolf—"

"You might be giving me too much credit. I'm not sure that I *chose* this. It's something bigger than me. This isn't me wanting to teach you something, this is me surrendering. I don't know how to see you any different now." He had never the hell talked about his feelings for this long before with anybody.

This was all different than knowing each other's history. They were talking about how that history shaped them. Made them feel. Talking about what they meant to each other.

He had never put this much thought into anything. It just mattered. And he couldn't make it not matter. That was the thing. That was the thing.

And he suddenly wanted to give Elsie the whole world. But it wasn't his to give, and he felt like it was inadequate at best.

And he could feel it all building between them, and he didn't know if he wanted to take a step back from the edge of the cliff, or grab hold of her and leap off.

Like she'd done with him down at the river.

He felt stronger and somehow weaker than he ever had.

"This changes things," she whispered.

"I think things changed a while ago." It was too late for them to protect themselves from it, and in that moment, he was sure they both realized it.

That whatever was going to happen...

It was too late to stop it.

But they could ignore it all for now.

He could feel her put a wall up. And he was ashamed to admit, even to himself, that he was glad for it.

"Enough talking," she said. "We have work to do."

"Sure do," he said.

And it was a relief. The interruption. Because she was right. While they were here they had work to do. And when they were in Vancouver… Well, that was a different story altogether.

For some reason, being away made it seem manageable.

Because here, at Four Corners, it all seemed too tied to dangerous truths about the past.

It all seemed too big.

Vancouver would make it easier.

Lord knew it couldn't get any harder.

CHAPTER FOURTEEN

"You're going out of town again?"

"Yes," Elsie said, feeling annoyed for some reason by Alaina and her questioning. It was a natural thing to ask. She would be asking Alaina the same question if Alaina was going somewhere. And she would probably want details. But Elsie was not going to give details.

"So, what happened with Travis?"

She stiffened. "Nothing," she said.

"Nothing?"

"No," she said. "It's fine. I'm good with that. I—I mean… There's always next time."

"That's true," Alaina said. "I mean, maybe you have the right perspective. There's no point being upset because it didn't pan out once. He's a guy. He's likely to come around eventually."

"Maybe when the pond dries up," Elsie said dryly.

Alaina gaped at her. "I didn't mean that."

She knew that Alaina hadn't meant that, and she didn't know why she was being mean.

You do. You don't like that she likes Hunter. Because now you like Hunter.

Well, maybe, but she hadn't *planned* it. It had all sort of run together. From the flirting lessons to this thing that wasn't anything other than… It was physical.

She just hadn't understood how powerful physical could be.

Not until the kiss.

Not until he'd touched her and taken her to places she'd never imagined before.

Even now it made her shiver.

Even now it made her want more.

It was complicated, of course. Because he was Hunter. Because apart from whatever this was, they'd always had… feelings for each other of a kind. They were like family in some ways. Obviously a pretty poor analogy right at the moment, but they were entwined in each other's lives. So that added an edge.

She wasn't made of stone, and anyway, Hunter was her… her friend, sort of. So, it was only natural that she would feel something for him given what had happened. What was going to happen.

And she didn't owe Alaina an explanation for anything, because Alaina and him… She wasn't in a relationship with him. And she wasn't going to be.

Something inside of Elsie hardened. Went small and mean and fierce. And she couldn't quite say what or why. Jealousy. Petty jealousy.

"Anyway," Elsie said, "Hunter and I are going back to Vancouver."

She had a chance. To be honest. To say that there was something going on between her and Hunter. To let Alaina know now, so that she wouldn't be hurt. So that Elsie wouldn't be lying to her. By omission if nothing else.

Except, what was really happening with her and Hunter? It didn't need to be Alaina's business. It wouldn't go on for very long. It couldn't. There was no way. So there was no point being… Well, there was no point being weird about it.

She could let things go on as they were.

"You have been spending a lot of time with him," Alaina said, her eyes suddenly getting sharp.

"I always spend a lot of time with him," Elsie said. "He's basically a fixture at my brother's house."

"True," she said. "Did I tell you that my dad called me?"

Elsie frowned. "No."

"Yeah, it was to wish me happy birthday."

"Your birthday was over a month ago," Elsie said, frowning.

"I know," Alaina said. "I don't think he forgot or anything, I just think this was the first time he got around to it."

Guilt gnawed at her. She had her own parental issues, but she figured it was easier to have a mother that was absent from your life completely, than to have parents who dipped in and out of your life the way Alaina's did.

At least Elsie knew better than to ever expect anything from her mother. As far as she knew, her mother could be living off-grid at a commune in Sedona. It was as likely as anything else. Maybe a penthouse in New York City. She didn't know. She had never called Elsie, on her birthday or otherwise. And there was something complete about that. Again, it came back to control. She didn't have to worry about when her mother would drop in and disrupt her life. Not in the way that Alaina's did. When Alaina's father had left the family it had destroyed everything the Sullivans had once been. Eventually, their mom had wanted out of the ranch, out of that life.

Alaina said she couldn't blame her. Elsie figured you could always blame someone for leaving.

"And was it a good conversation?"

"Well," Alaina said, "I might've told him to go to hell. So, probably not."

"It's no less than he deserves."

"Yeah," Alaina said. "He's still my dad. But whatever, I'm not bothered by it. It just is what it is."

That was Alaina. Fiery in response, then acted like everything was just fine, as if the explosion had never happened.

"Yeah. How does Fia handle that?"

She knew that if her dad tried anything like that Sawyer would be livid.

"I didn't tell her. It just upsets her to think about Dad. I know that it… I was really young when he left. It makes me sad, but I don't know. I think you can't miss what you don't really remember. I just wish that he wouldn't call at all."

"Yeah," Elsie said. "I understand that."

"I'm sorry," Alaina said. "I know your dad is gone and your mom has never made contact with you. Does it bother you when I complain about my parents?"

"Not at all," Elsie said, and she felt especially like that right now because she was being uncharitable toward her best friend in the entire world because of feelings that she had about a boy.

She had never thought she would be the kind of person who let a boy come between her and her friend.

The problem is, Hunter's not a boy. And you're not a girl.

Right. Well, that was a problem. One that she didn't really have a solution to.

Because it made everything more complicated.

It isn't complicated. It's sexual.

She told herself that with utter confidence, but she only knew a sliver of what that meant.

It's enough. He put his hand between your legs, you had an orgasm. So...you do know.

She did know. And yes, she felt defensive of Hunter, but it would fade. Because he wouldn't be hers forever, that was the thing. And she was going to have to live at Four Corners knowing that he was carrying on with other women sometimes, and she was going to have to be okay with it. And it was entirely possible that someday one of those women would be Alaina.

Everything inside of her rebelled against that.

Against all of it.

"Look," Elsie said, "we have our different struggles. But at least with my parents it's certain. My dad is dead, and it doesn't get much more certain than that. My mom… She doesn't care. She never did. Come to that, my dad never did either. But there's no fixing it with him. I can't even be tempted to. Because he's gone. Black and white. This weird half-in-and-half-out thing that your parents do? I wouldn't like that."

"You seem so certain about everything," Alaina said.

"So do you," Elsie said. Granted, it was in a different way than Elsie was. Sawyer and Wolf had raised her to stand firm in who she was, and they'd formed a protective circle around her from the time she was a kid.

They were, and always had been, her protectors against the things that were out there raging in the world, and it had given her space to be her.

Alaina never accepted defeat. Elsie had watched her friend find ways to forge new paths and land on her feet time and time again.

Whether it was trying to emerge with dignity when being dragged soggy from a pond, or smiling through her dad's inability to remember her birthday while listing all the good people in her life and all the reasons she didn't need him, Alaina was a force.

What Elsie feared was what might happen if she broke something in that force, if she was part of the string of people to disappoint Alaina.

In the end, she didn't tell her anything. And she didn't feel as guilty as she probably should have. That she felt, well, Hunter was hers. Whatever was going on between her and Hunter was also hers. She loved Alaina. She did. And she had to remember that, and not allow herself to be small and mean.

She was basically living for Vancouver. And she couldn't recall a time when she hadn't simply been anticipating the next sunrise. This was…different.

And it was…good.

Maybe this was it. Maybe this was part of growing up. Maybe something like this just couldn't be shared with a friend—or anyone—at a certain point.

Alaina had always been so important to her, and that wasn't going to change. Not ever. But what was happening between her and Hunter was just… It was different. It was different, and it was theirs. And it was too precious to be shared.

It was one thing to joke about sex without having any experience of it. But she had tasted it now. In the way that he had made her body feel, the things that he'd done to her, it wasn't something she could joke about. It wasn't something she could share. She couldn't really explain, it was just true.

"Well, if you learn anything interesting in Vancouver, let me know," Alaina said.

Everything inside of her turned to stone.

"Yeah," she said. "I will."

But she wouldn't. Because there were certain things that just had to stay hers. That was how it was.

But everything would be fine. Because after this… After this, she would know.

She would've learned.

She didn't know exactly what she expected, only that… it was just something she had. With Hunter.

Something they needed trying.

He had said it wasn't about teaching her, it was about wanting her.

That was something that she needed more than she had realized. Something she needed more than she would've ever expected. She hadn't thought that she was desperate for validation or some kind of boost to her self-esteem, but she had to admit she didn't mind it.

Not at all.

It was such a strange thing because she'd felt in pursuit of Travis. But Hunter was standing there, not running. Hunter was moving toward her, all intense and certain and adding that to the equation was something she wouldn't have been able to imagine.

It made her feel more and less confident all at once.

In the end, it would all be okay. Because there were so many things in her life that just weren't okay, and she had to live with them. So this would be fine. It would be, because it was Hunter.

Hunter was one of those people who was there for her. He had been. He continued to be. And he always would be. No matter what. And that meant that she had nothing at all to worry about. Just a change in her life. But it would sort itself.

She had faith in that.

HUNTER HAD EVERY intention of taking Elsie back to that motel because it was very near to the ranch that they were headed to. But when he went to make the reservation, he found that it felt wrong. He couldn't do it. She deserved something better. She deserved something special. And that was how he decided to book the nicest room at a hotel downtown and, you know, it felt a little bit weird to be engaging in this in a premeditated fashion when he had just been talking to her brothers the day before, and would undoubtedly see them later today. But she deserved something premeditated. She deserved something with effort. Because one thing he couldn't quite get over was the way everybody talked about her. And he was part of it. He had been. Like she was a termagant and a problem, and one that everybody loved quite a bit, but like she was...a mascot or a kid or something. And not a woman, never a woman. He just didn't see her the way they all did. Not anymore. She was a woman to him. And a woman deserved to have time put into her, especially a woman's first time.

A bolt of desire went through him. Maybe he should feel bad about it. About all of it. But he couldn't bring himself to.

No. He shouldn't feel guilty about it.

Because Elsie deserved to be wanted.

Not wanted because she was a woman, and she was beautiful. Because the man wanted sex and she was there.

No, Elsie deserved to be wanted for everything that she was.

He wanted her.

Travis didn't want her. He wanted *a* woman.

Hunter wanted *this* woman.

He wouldn't appreciate the gift that her first time was. Because it was.

He wondered if she ever stayed in a place as fancy as that one. He hadn't. He never had a reason to. This wasn't the kind of thing he usually did. This...wooing, he supposed.

But he wanted to do it for her. Somebody ought to. Deserved it.

And as for him, he didn't really know what he deserved. He had never spent any amount of time pondering that. Because it had never really mattered. Nothing in life had ever really come down to what he deserved.

He'd taken beatings that were just the result of his dad having a bad day.

And in the end, it hadn't mattered if he deserved it or not.

His father had lost his ranch. But he hadn't gotten even half of what he deserved. He *deserved* to have Gus kill him. He *deserved* to rot in prison. Bottom line.

His mother hadn't deserved to be hit for most of her life. She had fallen in love, that had been the extent of her crimes. She hadn't deserved to be trapped with a man who treated the people in his life worse than pack mules. Beasts of burden for him to unload his anger on.

No. None of them had deserved any of that. So maybe he didn't *deserve* Elsie. He didn't *deserve* her innocence, he didn't *deserve* her desire.

But he *wanted* it.

And he'd spent so much of his life taking hits he didn't want. Didn't deserve.

Wanting seemed enough right now.

"So," came a voice from behind him, "are we going to talk about the other night?"

He turned and saw Brody. And he wasn't necessarily in the mood to deal with Brody, who was obviously referencing his grand exit from Smokey's.

He didn't really like this new trend of his brothers being up in his business.

"I don't think that we have anything to talk about."

"You saw Elsie Garrett with that other guy and you lost it. Practically ran out of the damned bar. You came back in with a bloody hand, then you stole her from her dance partner, *then* the two of you left and I didn't see you again."

"Yes, Brody," he said. "All of those things were done in full view of everyone in that bar."

"Yeah. But I talked to Wolf Garrett, and he mentioned

how you lost your temper and punched a wall *at your house*, and busted up your knuckles. Which you and I both know isn't true. So while that was done in full view of everybody, you don't want them to know about it. Which tells me that you are messing with Elsie Garrett."

His brother zeroed in on the truth in a way that made him squirm.

But he was not *messing* with her.

It was something else. Something deeper. Something that he'd never felt or experienced before ever in his life. But he didn't have words for it, and he certainly didn't know how to explain it to Brody.

But then, he didn't owe Brody an explanation.

His brothers were acting like Elsie was a kid, and she wasn't. They were acting like they knew her when they didn't, not like he did.

Elsie was his friend. In her own right. She didn't belong to Sawyer and Wolf, and she wasn't beneath him.

She didn't need mindless protecting.

Hell, he wondered why no one was worried about Hunter. From where he was standing he thought Elsie might have the power to destroy him with the right words.

He gritted his teeth. "I am not *messing* with Elsie Garrett. Can you think of anything stupider than that?"

"In terms of whether or not you want to wear your colon outside of your body as decoration, courtesy of Sawyer and Wolf, no. I can't think of anything stupider. In terms of just the reality of the fact that she's an attractive woman—"

His fury was immediate. "Don't talk about her that way," he snarled.

"What, don't notice that Elsie Garrett hasn't been twelve for a damned long time? She's cute. That's just a fact."

"Yes, she is cute," he said, feeling so possessive now

he couldn't see straight or hide it. "That's not for you to notice."

"I'm not the one getting in fights over her."

"I didn't get in a fight. I took her off that guy on the dance floor and he *let her go*. He *let* me do it. Which as far as I'm concerned shows he's an idiot who never deserved to dance with her in the first place. I don't let go of something that I want."

"Hunt, you might as well come clean. There was something going on between the two of you at the poker game, and there's obviously something going on between you now. You can't tell Sawyer, you can't tell Wolf, you need somebody to run interference because you aren't hiding it very well. So if I were you, I would chill out, and tell me what's going on.

"I'm not going to tell Gus," Brody continued. "That guy has a sense of humor failure deeper than that well we have out in the back pasture, and I don't want anything to do with it. Because he will likely tell on you, and join Wolf and Sawyer in dancing on your grave."

"Gus already knows," he said, his voice hard.

"Well, damn," Brody said. "Now I feel left out."

"If you think you already know, Brody, why should I tell you?" he asked, walking into his cabin and grabbing the duffel bag he had in their already packed and ready to go for Vancouver.

"Well, because I'm looking for any explanation that's not what I think."

"You think I'm sleeping with her?"

"Hell, no," Brody said. "I think you *wish* you were sleeping with her. If you had slept with her, you wouldn't have been *sitting there* while she was talking to Travis."

Damn his brother for knowing him this well. And damn

him for being unable to keep a secret. "Well. Fair. I haven't slept with her."

"You want to?"

"Like you said," he returned, a muscle twitching in his face. "She's cute."

"A lot of women are cute, Hunter. You and I both know cute isn't worth all this. This is something else."

It was something else. Something new. Something…

"Fuck." And the truth of it all was buried in that. "I want to sleep with her."

"You're taking her to Vancouver."

"I am *going* to sleep with her, jackass."

"Right. So…did you want a proper Catholic funeral or…"

"It's not like that," he bit out.

"What do you mean it's not like that? You just told me it's exactly like that."

"She wants to…she wants to get some experience. I'm happy to oblige. It was going to be me or him. And you tell me, who do you think it should be. Me or him?"

"I don't want to weigh in on this debate. Because I don't really want to know where you put your junk."

"You're digging into my business. Like hell you don't want to know, you practically demanded an accounting of where I want it to go."

"Fine. But I don't want… Look. Obviously, that guy is someone I don't trust. And I would be worried about having her anywhere in proximity to him. But I don't know how you could think this isn't going to blow up in your face. Or your junk."

"It might," Hunter said.

And he accepted it as he said it.

"Doesn't that matter?" Brody asked.

Yeah, it mattered. It mattered a hell of a lot.

Which was why his willingness to go forward with it meant something.

"She's worth it," he said, surprised at the conviction with which those words came out. He walked past his brother, down the dirt trail, toward his truck. He slung the duffel bag in the back and turned around. "I don't know how else to say it. She's worth it. And I am willing to risk whatever might happen to make this special for her."

He'd had to defend himself to Brody, to Gus, and most of all to himself, and he came back to the same place every time.

"To make it *special*," Brody said.

"Yeah," he said. "Because that's how it is. I care about her."

"Damn," he said. "I don't know what to say."

"Yeah, neither do I. I didn't plan this. You have to know I wouldn't. It was never my goal to end up in this situation. It just is. So…"

"Right. You in love with her or something?"

The words shocked him. Like a bucket of ice-cold water over the top of his head. And he couldn't help but laugh.

"Well," Brody said, "glad you think it's funny, but I just kind of figured if a man was willing to risk life and limb—and other appendages—to be with a woman because he thinks she deserves something special, he must be halfway in love if he wasn't already there."

"What does love even mean?" Hunter asked.

Brody just stood there for a moment. "Fair enough. Can't say I know the answer to that. I know what it's not."

"No shit," Hunter said.

"What do you feel for her?"

And he couldn't seem to separate that from memories

of screaming and violence and just utter sadness. Broken vows and kids who were caught in the middle.

He had never been able to.

Because everything related to him and family was like a shattered mirror, and when he looked into it, he couldn't get a clear picture of who he was or where he fit.

And he sure as hell couldn't look at all that broken mess and figure out the feelings.

Had his dad loved anyone?

Had he loved their mother once?

Had he thought he'd loved them?

Had she?

Had Hunter loved either of them? Both of them?

Did he still?

That was the problem. It was all just fragments, and he couldn't work out a damned thing.

It made all this splintered too.

"I don't know," Hunter said. "I've gone out of my way to never have feelings for a woman. You know how it is. You know what we saw. You know."

"Yeah," he said. "I remember it. A lot better than I'd like to. Hell, I remember it better than things that mean a lot to me. Things I wish I remembered better. Learning how to ride a bike. Touching a woman's breast for the first time."

"Sure," Hunter said, snorting.

"The thing is," Brody said, "maybe love isn't real."

"Well, that's a cheerful perspective," Hunter said.

"I'm serious. I just think it comes down to…what you choose to do or don't. I mean, you could choose her. Who the hell cares what you call it? You're never going to choose to be Dad."

"I'm not afraid of that."

"That's not why you avoid relationships?"

"Is that why *you* avoid them?"

Brody's face went to stone, a rarity. His brother's infuriating grin was a staple on his face. A face that had never once felt their father's fist. That hard look coming from him was something next to devastation. "No. I avoid it because I can't see a scenario in which anyone ends up happy."

And like that, Brody had said it better than Hunter ever could have.

"No. I can't imagine it either. And I wouldn't wish that kind of thing on any woman. If I can't imagine what it looks like to be happy with somebody for six months, let alone six years, sixty years? What's the point. All I can see is this ranch. All I can see is this life. I can see a couple of really nice days with Elsie Garrett. And I want them." That sounded anemic. Insufficient. He felt right now like he'd die if he didn't have them. "Because I have a chance to give her something good, and I want to do that. And maybe I… maybe I want something good too."

Brody nodded slowly. "You should, Hunt. There's nothing wrong with being happy for a while. Whatever that looks like."

"I don't know if I have anything more in me than a couple good days, though."

"I hear you," Brody said.

"Don't tell anybody or I'll kill you," Hunter said, climbing up in his truck.

He didn't want anyone stopping him. He'd take the consequences if they came down later.

But later.

"I believe you," Brody said.

"I know you do."

"Good." He started his engine, then drove the truck straight to Elsie's.

She appeared, quickly scampering out to the car with extreme verve. She got into the truck and looked over at him, her eyes wide.

"Nothing has to happen, Elsie," he said, his heart suddenly thundering hard.

How did she do it? How did she make him feel like the virgin?

"Oh, I'm not nervous," she said.

"You're not?"

"No," she said. "I—I'm excited."

"Good."

They started out on the road, and his breathing was labored. And damn, he wanted her. This was...this was insane.

"So, is there anything I need to know?" Elsie asked when they were about twenty minutes away from Four Corners.

"Well, we're getting three of the horses..."

"About *sex*," Elsie said. "You taught me everything I needed to know about flirting. Is there anything I need to know about sex."

His stomach went tight.

"I mean, I don't know. I think you—you probably know well enough the kinds of things that happen," he said.

"Do I? I'm glad that you're confident."

"You said you did," he pointed out. "You said you were clear on the logistics."

"I did, I did. But now I feel like there might be more."

"Well, what do *you* think you need to know?"

"What you like?"

"You," he answered. "I like you."

And he hadn't meant to answer back quite so sharply, or definitively.

He sneaked a glance at her, and she was cherry red. "Me?"

"Yes, you. You little termite."

"Why?"

"Didn't I tell you? You're beautiful. But you know, you're also infuriating. You're a massive pain in the ass. I have known you since you were a *small* pain in the ass, you make me crazy. You make me take my life in my own hands by carting you off property to hook up with you when I know full well that Sawyer and Wolf would have an honorary Game Day using my dead body as the football if they ever found out. So I guess the thing is…I want you even though I shouldn't. I want you because I can't *not* want you. And I think you're the sexiest woman on God's earth. At least the sexiest one I can remember ever seeing, because I can't remember anyone or anything else. And I want whatever it is that's going to happen between us. I want you to realize that. This isn't choreography you need to learn. You do what you want. Whatever you want to me."

His blood started to run hot, his body getting hard.

"Whatever I want?" she asked.

"Whatever you fucking want."

He felt delicate fingertips on his thigh, and everything in him went hard. Then her fingers migrated upward, toward his arousal. He gritted his teeth, desire coursing through him like a river.

"I can't wait to see you," she whispered.

His breath hissed through his teeth, and he shifted his weight. And then her hand was there, over his hardness, and he was doing his best to keep his eyes on the road.

"I'm going to crash the truck," he said.

"Well, don't do that," she said. "It's a very nice truck."

"I know it's a nice truck," he said. "Varmint."

He steered the truck off the road onto the shoulder. They were in a secluded part of the highway lined with trees, and there were no other cars around. And he hauled her up out of her seat, undoing the seat belt as he did it, and brought her over onto his lap, placing either of her legs on the sides of his thighs. And then he brought her head down and kissed her.

Hard.

Poured every ounce of his desire and frustration into her.

And every bit of him didn't want to wait until they got up north. Didn't want to wait for that hotel room. He wanted her here, and he wanted her now. He wanted her in this truck, on the side of the road, he wanted her and he didn't know if he could wait.

She curled her fingers in his hair, grabbing hold of him and making a little kitten sound as she kissed him, deep and hard, and this time she didn't run away. She rocked her hips against him, she gave him as good as she got. She parted her lips and thrust her tongue into his mouth like the bold, quick study that she was.

Because she was Elsie Garrett, and she was fearless, and he should've known that. No nerves for his girl.

But they couldn't. Not here. Because he had gotten that hotel. Because he wanted to make it special. Because he wanted to make it perfect. Because he wanted to rip open his chest and give her something he didn't have a name for.

And when they parted, his heart was pounding, and he was sweating. And he was so hard it hurt. He couldn't breathe for wanting her. And all he could do was stare at her, with the sunlight streaming into the truck, and the thick green pines as a backdrop. Elsie. Out in nature. And he knew. He needed to have her outside. Out in the field, where she would be surrounded by nature. In her element.

His body growled with desire.

"Elsie," he said. He lifted his hand and cupped her cheek. "You are something else."

She blushed and scrambled off his lap, breathing hard as she rested her head against the seat. "Let's go," she said.

"It's for the best."

He started the truck and eased back out onto the road, and they were quiet for a ways.

"Where are we going?" she asked when they made it to Vancouver and did not go the way they had last time.

"I thought… I thought maybe the motel wasn't quite the order of the day."

"Oh," she said.

He turned onto the off-ramp that took them downtown, and they were surrounded by glass and chrome buildings, the kinds of places neither of them had much experience with.

"What did you do?" she asked.

"Like I said. I thought it should be special."

"Oh," she said.

"Do you hate it?" he asked. "Because if you hate it, I'll take you to the motel. I'll take you anywhere. Elsie, whatever you want, I'll make sure you get it."

And he didn't know why those words felt so drastically short of what they should be. Because he didn't know what the words should be.

He had never done this before. And he suddenly felt compelled to let her know that.

"I've never done this. I've never been to a place like this. I never planned on taking a woman to a place like this."

This…

This wasn't like anything else. She wasn't like anyone else.

"I just wanted you to know that. This isn't some kind of game that I run."

"I know," she said.

That trust, that easy belief in him, just about broke him open.

And then he pulled the truck up to the front of the hotel and let the valet take it from there.

ELSIE FELT LIKE an imposter wandering through this fancy place. She was wearing blue jeans, and a black tank top. She didn't look anywhere near up to the standard of the high-gloss marble in the lobby. The ceiling was tall, and there were multiple seating areas all around the place. A shiny-looking bar off to the right.

"You check in online now," he said. "Your phone can open the door."

"That's...that's very strange," she said.

"Yeah."

She looked at Hunter, who was also wearing jeans and a black shirt, but for some reason, she didn't think he looked out of place. He looked beautiful. And handsome. But suddenly, she was nervous. Because he had brought her to this place. He had brought her to this place with her jeans and her duffel bag, and she just wondered if he did want her to be something that she wasn't. He had said that he didn't.

But she...

Her chest was exploding with all of these weird underexplored feelings and she didn't like any of them. She had never really worried about whether or not a man found her attractive. Even when she wanted to pursue Travis she was more worried about letting him know that she was interested, not him thinking that she was good enough. Not him thinking that she was pretty enough. And she knew that Hunter said that he did. He had affirmed it. Over and over again. He had been as encouraging as any man could be.

And when he had pulled over earlier and hauled her on his lap like he couldn't wait, she had been thrilled.

He pushed the door on the elevator, and let her go in first. And she was thankful when no one got on with them.

"I got a text that said we were on the twenty-fifth floor."

"That is very high," she said. Which was about the lamest thing that could possibly come out of her mouth.

"You ever been in a high-rise?"

She shook her head. "No."

"Me either."

"Why are we in one now?"

"I told you."

He had.

Tears stung her eyes. "I'm sorry," she said. "You told me. But I have a hard time believing it."

She leaned against the back wall of the elevator, and her throat went tight, and she wondered why in the hell she was on the verge of tears in front of Hunter. When everything was going the way that she wanted it to. When she was actually quite happy with the state of things.

"Elsie," he said, crossing the space and putting his hand on her face. "What's wrong?"

"This is what I wanted. I wanted somebody to want me."

"It's not enough for me to want you. You have to want me too."

"I do," she said.

"Then what's the matter?"

"I don't believe it. And you keep telling me, but I still don't believe it. Because…"

"Because life is a bag of shit."

She laughed, resting her head against the back of the elevator wall. "Yeah," she said. "It is."

"That's all this is," he said, taking her hand. "Me wanting to give you something that isn't terrible. I'm sorry if I'm messing it up."

"You won't," she said. "It's just you wanting to give me something so much, and I... I have such a hard time believing it, because Sawyer and Wolf have always been so good to me. But..."

"It's different."

"Yes," she said. "It's different. And I think that this is amazing, and I think that you're amazing."

"Well, reserve your opinion until you see the room."

"The actual room? Or are you talking about..." She looked down at the front of his jeans meaningfully, and immediately embarrassed herself. And she wondered where the more confident version of Elsie had gone, who would've just said the word *penis* in front of him and not given it a second thought. Okay, maybe a second thought, but she was giving it about fifty thoughts right now, and she just hardly recognized herself in the moment.

"Elsie," he said. "You are something else."

He checked the numbers on the wall, then they walked down the hall, and he flashed his phone in front of a gold doorknob that made an unlocking sound when he waved the device in front of it.

He opened the door, and her heart expanded. It was a huge room. With a couch, a desk and a view of the city below.

And a bed. A giant bed.

"There's a big tub too..."

And then suddenly, she just couldn't wait anymore. She really couldn't. She turned on her heel and wrapped her arms around his neck, pressing her mouth to his.

And he slammed the door shut behind them, holding her hard against him, moving his hands up and down her back.

"Do we have any reason to wait?"

"Not a single one," he said.

And he stripped her tank top off and threw it down onto the plush rug of the glorious, beautifully appointed hotel, and she took his T-shirt off and did the same.

And she remembered the barriers that had stood between them when they were in that ratty motel only a couple of weeks ago.

Weeks? It felt like an entire lifetime.

And she could scarcely remember when Hunter hadn't been this to her. This man that she desired so much, who made her feel feelings that were too big for her chest, who made her want things that she didn't have words for. Hunter.

"I'm sorry that I'm so annoying," she said, kissing him.

"You're not annoying," he said, reaching around and unhooking her bra, throwing it onto the floor. "Sweet Lord," he breathed.

"Well, neither are you," she said.

They kicked off their shoes, and worked off each other's clothes, and before she knew it, they were both naked. Completely naked, in front of each other for the first time.

She had never seen a naked man. Not a fully aroused one.

And he was, well, he was a whole lot more than she bargained for. Not that she'd had any idea what to bargain for. She had no real idea of anything. And that was the thing that had been driven home so firmly over the course of this whole situation. She just didn't know anything. She had thought she was brave, and she had thought that she could go boldly out there and make for herself a little physical relationship that would give her something that would touch her skin and nothing more.

But she had been naive. She had been silly.

But she wasn't going to think about it now. Not when her heart was pounding so hard, not when desire was a thunderous pulse between her thighs. Not when Hunter's hands were on her body, not when his whole body was exposed to her, proud and thick and hard for her.

"You're beautiful," she said, reaching her hand out and wrapping it around his arousal. She squeezed him, moving her hand up and down his length, and his breath hissed through his teeth, his head falling back. And Hunter, desperate for her, was the most erotic thing she had ever seen.

Because he had made her desperate. She knew what that was like. She understood why women lost their minds over him. She really did.

But this was something else. This was more. He wanted her.

And that was the aspect of this that… Over and over again, it was catching her off guard. Over and over again it was filling her with joy. And over and over again it was bringing about this sense of deep grief that she could scarcely make sense of.

It made no sense at all. This should all be good. All happy. All perfect. All lovely.

And yet it felt like something else altogether. It felt like dying.

"Elsie," he whispered against her mouth, and she ignited.

She was the one that was important to him right now. He was putting his relationship with her brothers in jeopardy for this. And that was a whole new revelation. He wanted her more than he wanted to keep the peace with Wolf and Sawyer. And sure, none of them were announcing what was going on here, but it was a risk. And he was taking it. For her.

And she could think of nothing more wonderful. Nothing more incredible than that.

He was holding her, and it was terrifying as much as it was exhilarating. And it reminded her. It reminded her of how he told her the truth, even though it was hard.

That mothers didn't come back. That people left and stayed gone.

Yes, it was hard.

Yes, it was horrible.

But it was true, and he had been the one to tell her. But not without giving her comfort. Not without holding her. Like he was doing now.

He was showing her the world. How it was. The way things were between a man and woman, and it was terrifying, because it wasn't the fun romp that she'd imagined. She felt like her chest was going to split right open. She felt like a woman being torn in two.

It was wonderful. But it was terrifying all the same. There was nobody else that this could have ever happened with. She was so certain of it now. How would she have been so stupid to think that it could have ever been Travis? It couldn't have been.

It was Hunter. It was always Hunter.

He slid his hands down her back, her butt, and around her thighs and lifted her off the ground, wrapping her legs around his waist and walking them both over to that big bed.

She shuddered as he laid her down on the soft mattress, his hard length sliding through that slick cleft at the apex of her thighs.

It was wonderful.

Pleasure and pain all rolled into one, like everything of value ever was and ever had been.

But this wasn't like anything else. She was on the edge of something terrifying, the edge of something that might destroy her. And he was holding her. So strong. So gentle. All at once.

She never had somebody there to walk her through slowly.

She had brothers who had thrown her into the deep end of the swimming hole. Who had challenged her to run faster, push farther.

Hunter wasn't doing that. Hunter was giving her all of the tenderness required, along with exhilarating joy. Pleasure. His hands were rough on her skin. She knew her hands were rough too. Because they both worked. That same kind of work. That was where the similarities ended. Because his whole body was hard, sculpted muscle.

She felt small and fragile by comparison, and it didn't scare her.

Being with him like this didn't scare her at all. It made everything feel wonderfully right and it made her feel more like a woman than she ever had. Made her understand why it was a glorious thing.

It never felt like an advantage to her. It had only ever made her different.

Younger and female and more work for Sawyer and Wolf, even if they had never treated her that way.

But she loved being a woman in this moment. Held like this by Hunter McCloud.

And her throat was thick with emotion.

She remembered that moment back in the bar when she had thought about him leaving with another woman and she'd felt like prickles had broken out on her skin. It had felt uncomfortable.

And she wondered if it had been this way then. And

she just hadn't been able to admit it. If she'd thought that it was Travis, because she had thought that some blue-eyed greenhorn with an angelic face was easy.

And nothing about this was easy.

But it was exquisite. And she wanted it.

Wanted him.

"I was going to open a bottle of champagne," he said, his lips hovering over hers, his body pressed against hers, chest to chest, side and thigh.

"I don't care about champagne," she said. "I just want you."

It felt like such an enormous weight on her chest. Driving them both forward. She knew that he felt it too. Felt this keenly as she did. That he wanted her exactly how she wanted him.

And even if she didn't know the way that need coursed through a male body, she knew the way that it moved through her soul, and for some reason right then, looking at his eyes she knew that their souls were one. That they matched.

That they were the same.

She knew it as surely as she knew the sun would rise tomorrow. Back at Four Corners, and over this city that was new and strange and nothing like she'd ever been in before.

This was like nothing she'd ever had. She really understood now. Why he felt the need to do this. Because they weren't together for familiarity. Or because there was no one else.

They had made this choice together. She wanted him because she did. And it didn't matter if there was a whole lineup of hot cowboys, or any other kind of man. Hockey players, basketball players. Tall, athletic, whatever. She didn't want him because he was a cowboy. She didn't want him just because he was in proximity. She wanted him because he was Hunter.

"You know that it's going to hurt, right?"

"Everything you learn hurts at first," she said, thinking back to getting thrown off a horse for the first time, or learning to cope with being saddle sore. Pain didn't bother her. Not at all.

He shook his head. "What a world, that you had to learn to be okay with that."

"Just makes you stronger," she said.

"You're as strong as they get." He kissed her neck, her collarbone. "But I'm going to make you weak."

The promise was wicked, the words making her shiver. And he went down and fastened his mouth to her breast, licking and sucking her until she was trembling.

He was right. She did feel weak, but she felt strong all at the same time. Felt like she might tremble all apart, but be put back together as something new.

Something better.

All the pieces fixed back into place with magic.

And the magic was him.

Them.

He kissed his way down her body in an erotic choreography, down the skin of her tender thigh, and back to her center.

And she gasped. Hunter wasn't tentative there. He took her. Tongue going deep, his mouth certain as he zeroed right in on that source of her pleasure, as he tortured her in the most divine fashion she could've ever imagined. Then he continued to laugh at her as he added his hand, pushing a finger inside of her and stroking her deep. She squirmed, a whimper rising in her throat.

And there was nothing outside this. Nothing outside of

him. If Four Corners existed, it was less than a memory. That place where she had spent so much of her life was somewhere far off in the distance, and all the people who had always been there... They were so dim in the face of this moment. The brightness that she found here.

He added a second finger, and she felt herself stretching slightly, her hips bucking up off the bed. And it did hurt a little. But it was glorious. And she found herself lost in it. In him.

Begging, moving her hips in time with his thrusts, when her release broke over her. Shocking her. She grabbed the back of his head, arching her hips and holding them steady as a sharp gasp escaped her lips.

He rolled away from her and looked up, his expression so wicked that it made the bottom fall out of her world.

She moved down the bed to him, stroking his face, moving her hands through his hair. She knew him this way now.

Hunter.

No one else ever touched her like this, let alone tasted her like that. She knew what it was like when he desired a woman. She knew.

Right now she felt like she might know everything.

She lowered her head and kissed his mouth, tasted her own desire there. "Take me," she said, words coming from somewhere inside of her she hadn't even known existed. "Please."

And she meant that, as desperately as she had ever meant anything in her life.

Take me.

"Gladly."

He left her on the bed, got up and went for the duffel bag, where he retrieved a box of condoms. She was thankful that he had the presence of mind to do that, because she didn't. And hadn't she been so blasé about all that? Using condoms, and throwing the word around, like it was common sense. Because she hadn't realized that common sense often didn't feature when you wanted someone.

Because she had never really wanted anyone.

He came back to her, pressing her body down into the mattress as he settled between her thighs, moving his hands down her back to cup her ass, as he started to push his way into her body.

It did hurt. He was so big. Thick and beautiful, and too much.

Except he couldn't be too much. Because he was hers.

That truth beat fiercely inside of her, to the rhythm of her pulse, a certainty that she knew, more than she knew just about anything else, and she didn't care if it made no sense. He didn't need to. Not to anyone else.

This was their world. There was nothing beyond it.

She wanted to stay with him here for the rest of her life. Holding him in her arms, being held in his.

And then he thrust the rest of the way home, and she gasped as he buried himself to the hilt, filling her so impossibly full.

"You okay?" he asked against her mouth.

"Yes," she whispered.

And she could hardly speak, because her throat was so tight, because she was full to bursting with unshed tears, and she didn't know how she was going to be able to make it without dissolving.

But then he began to move, and the delicious friction awoke the desire inside of her.

Any pain faded, and need replaced everything else.

She wrapped her legs around his waist, meeting him as he thrust into her.

It felt right, and natural. Easy as much as it was hard.

And it was hard.

This wasn't the place for gentle, it wasn't an easy intro-duction, it was a baptism of fire, and it was no less than what she needed. Utterly and completely.

"Hunter," she whispered, and she felt his body shudder.

He flexed his hips against hers, and this time, she was aware of her orgasm building, deep and intense, the build frightening her, because she could tell that it was going to eclipse the one she'd had previously, and she had no idea how she was going to survive it. But then, he thrust home one last time, and she shattered.

Gasping, she clung to his shoulders and trembled as she rode it out, crying out his name over and over again.

He lowered his head and bit her lip, growling as his own release shook him.

She was all wrapped up in it, the exhilaration, pain and need.

The ecstasy.

And when it was done, he rolled over onto his back, bringing her with him, cradling her to his chest.

She had been right about one thing. She felt a little bit broken. But as for being put back together? She didn't know if that was possible.

CHAPTER FIFTEEN

"Room service is on the way." He looked up at Elsie as she emerged from the bathroom, swamped by a large bathrobe, her dark hair piled on her head. Her skin looked damp and pink from her shower, and he wished more than anything he could have been in it with her. But he had sensed that she needed space.

Because she'd said to give her a minute, outright.

He wasn't all that intuitive and if she hadn't said so... well, hell. He'd have joined her.

"That's nice," she said, shy now, hanging back slightly.

"You don't even want to know what I got you?" he asked.

"I'm sure that it's good," she said. She looked around the room. "This place is...amazing."

"Not as amazing as you."

She wrinkled her nose. "I don't know how I feel about that."

"Being complimented?" He got up from the bed, and her face went red, her eyes flickering over his body. He hadn't bothered to cover up. He wasn't embarrassed to be naked in front of her. He was comfortable with his body overall, but there was something about being with her that just seemed... It seemed right. He had thought that this change would be weird, but for him it wasn't. Obviously it wasn't quite the same for her. Of course, she had been a virgin up until an hour ago. So maybe that was part of it.

"By *you*," she said.

"I hate to break it to you," he said, moving closer to her. "This is how it is." He wrapped his arm around her waist and brought her in for a kiss. "Don't get skittish on me now," he said.

She snorted and pulled away from him. "I'm not skittish."

"You seem skittish," he said.

"I'm skittish of nothing," she responded, but walked over to the window and peered out the curtains. "It's dark now."

"Time flies."

"I guess." She turned around and looked at him. "Did you give an excuse for why we had to spend the night? This is just a pick-up trip, not a whole evaluation."

He shook his head. "No."

The fact of the matter was, he wasn't sure he felt like constructing an elaborate story. Or lying. He wasn't ashamed of what had happened between Elsie and him.

Of course, he wasn't going to say that. Because he had a feeling that would send her running for the hills, wearing only the bathrobe.

"You better put something on if room service is coming."

He grinned and got off the bed, putting on his boxers. "Better?"

"I don't know. It seems like getting that much of the view is a slightly bigger tip than is warranted."

"Are you flirting with me, now?"

"Well, you taught me how." She smiled slightly, and he thought she might be relaxing a little bit. "This feels like a different life." She looked back out the window before letting the curtain drop.

"It's all the same one," he said, keeping his eyes trained on her.

The heavy knock on the door signified the arrival of room service, and he pulled his jeans on before answering the door and bringing the tray into the room.

Elsie's eyes lit up when she saw the array of food. Steak, vegetables and salad. Twice-baked potatoes. And a couple of big pieces of different kinds of cake.

He'd also gotten a bottle of champagne.

"Champagne?"

"Some things deserve celebrating."

She grabbed hold of the bottle with both hands and sat on the edge of the bed, and he just wanted to keep this moment in his mind forever. Elsie sitting on that plush bed with her dark hair in a tumble, clutching a champagne bottle. Like a thoroughly debauched princess.

She deserved that. The pleasure, the comfort.

"This is kind of going above and beyond when it comes to job perks," she said dryly, tugging at the foil around the top of the bottle, clearly uncertain about how to open it.

He took the bottle from her, and aimed it the opposite direction, popping the cork with ease.

Then he poured a measure into a glass and handed it to her before pouring some for himself.

"This isn't about the job," he said. "This is just us." He raised the glass.

She offered him a funny little thin-lipped smile, but took a sip of the champagne, her eyes brightening.

"You like it?"

"Yes," she said.

He took the food and set it on the bed, presenting it to her.

"Are we eating in bed?"

"We have to go to the Running Y tomorrow, and then

we have to go back to the real world. I think we should do as much in bed as possible while we're here, don't you?"

She laughed softly, her dark lashes fanning over her cheekbones as she lowered her gaze. "I guess so."

He felt so hyperaware of every detail of her. And he wanted to exist in that for as long as possible.

He took his own tray and carried it onto the bed with him, settling across from her.

She grinned. "This is ridiculous."

"Indulgent."

"I'm unfamiliar."

"I know. And you should be more familiar with it. Because you deserve it."

"I always thought that was such a funny thing. The idea that any of us deserve anything. I didn't deserve to have my mom leave, any more than you did. So I don't really know why I would deserve anything good either. It's just life. It's either crap. Or you have steak and a naked man in a hotel room."

"And I assume that's a good thing?"

"It's been pretty good so far," she said, cutting a bite off the steak and popping it into her mouth. "Yes. Very good."

"I don't know. I figure it has to balance out. If we didn't deserve to have our mothers leave, then maybe we deserve to have some nice things."

"I just think it's random."

"And you just have to enjoy it when the random doesn't suck?"

"Basically," she said.

"I'm not sure if I like that or if it's grim."

She shrugged. "I don't know that it's particularly grim or not. It just is."

"Yeah."

"I told my mom to go," he said. And he hadn't meant for the words to come out of his mouth, they just had. But maybe it was because she had given him something she'd never given anyone else, and he wanted to do the same.

Or maybe he'd just been lonely for all these years and something about Elsie made him less lonely.

"You… What?"

"I told her to leave," he said, his chest feeling oddly tight.

"Why?"

"My dad was a monster, Elsie. He hit her. He beat her up badly. And at the time, she wouldn't report it. The sheriff knew, but he wasn't doing anything about it. He said that he couldn't. Just… Gus was getting angrier and angrier, and Dad was escalating things with him. The abuse was just starting to trickle down. And I thought… I thought maybe…maybe if she left, Dad wouldn't be so angry." He chewed on those words because he felt guilty for them. For having those thoughts when he was a child. For believing that on some level any of them had been the cause of the abuse that happened around them.

But he hadn't known then. Hadn't understood that it was the abuser who was responsible for his actions. He had grown up in a bubble of it, so to him, it had seemed like it must be something to do with the boys. Something to do with his mother. That they made his father angry in much the same way his brothers made him angry when they pulled a prank on him or something.

It had seemed reasonable then.

But it was all tangled up, because he hadn't been angry with his mother or anything like that. He'd worried for her. For all of them.

And he knew… He knew she stayed for him, because he was the youngest. She'd said so.

And so he felt like it was his responsibility to let her go. That he was the only one that could do it.

And he could remember just how it was. Being eleven years old and filled with conviction. So certain that he had to shove down whatever he wanted. Whatever his own fears were, and tell his mother to go and be happy on her own.

"I saw her in the barn, and she was crying. She had a bruise on her face. Because he'd done it again. And that was just a fresh one from that morning. She had…so many others from other times.

"And I told her that I didn't need her to protect me. I said I could take care of myself because I wasn't a little kid anymore. I was close enough to being a man. And that she didn't have to be trapped just because of me. I said I'd be all right."

Elsie was staring at him, her eyes bright. And then she reached out and touched his forearm. "Hunter," she said. "How could she leave you? You were so brave. What a selfless—"

"It wasn't selfless. Like I said. I thought maybe…maybe it would just be better. But it wasn't. Gus just became the target, and I didn't have my mom.

"She was the adult. That's the thing. I come back to that, over and over again when I think of my mom," Elsie said. "If ever I'm tempted to think that maybe there was something wrong with me… Maybe there was. Maybe I was an ugly baby. I was born in a barn, after all. She dropped me right there in the hay. The thing is, I don't think she ever wanted me. And I think she was trying to hold me and for as long as possible, not go to a hospital, not admit it. I think I was born in a barn because my mother desperately didn't want me to be born. But none of that is my fault. I didn't choose that. She was the adult, and she was the one with the power to make the decisions about what was going to happen. With me, with her life and with mine. She didn't need to leave me at Four Corners. I'm glad that she did. I could have spent my whole life with a mother who didn't want me, and not had Wolf and Sawyer there. Not had Four Corners. Not had you. And that would've been terrible. But in the end, she didn't know that. She didn't know that it would be okay. She didn't know that I would be okay. She just made the decision. She made it for me, she made it for them. And that's exactly what your mother did. She didn't know what your father would do when she left, and think about Gus. Everything did get worse for Gus, and she just left him."

He shook his head. "I told her to go. And if my brothers find out..."

"Nothing. You were an eleven-year-old boy doing your best. You were trying to be the man because your father wasn't one. All of you. It isn't your fault."

Something tugged at his lips that he would've called a smile if his chest hadn't felt like it was full of glass.

"Thanks," he said.

"You're not the only one who knows stuff."

He chuckled. "I guess not."

But he knew that. Because Elsie was wise, since she had to be. Because like him she had been dropped into a life with a whole bunch of adults who hadn't cared all that much. And had had to make her own way.

But he'd been there for her. And he would always be there. He knew that then as certainly as he ever had.

He cared about Wolf and Sawyer and he always would. But this had changed things. Now Elsie was something to him that they could never be. And not just because he wasn't attracted to them. Because he and Elsie had shared this moment. Because he'd told her this secret.

"It hasn't been such a bad life," she said softly. "I love Four Corners. I love my life there. You asked me why I wasn't fixing to leave... And it's because I can't imagine anything else. And maybe it's because sometimes I think about it. What it would've been like if she had taken me with her. And it makes me feel scared. Terrified. My dad was no prize, and he died when I was young. But I can't imagine my world without Sawyer and Wolf. Without the Sullivans. Without you. Without the experience that I've had with horses and with working the land. With living in that place that holds the memory of my family name... Even if my family hasn't always been great, we have a legacy in Garrett's Watch. And it matters."

"I understand that. That feeling. If we hadn't enough stake of McCloud's Landing, my father would have been the one to let it die. He would've been the one in control of that. And he doesn't deserve that legacy. It's ours. He can't have it. And for that reason I'm glad we didn't go. Because the land is ours."

"Just make sure of that."

"I know he did something terrible to Gus, but Gus won't talk about it. He burned him."

Elsie's face nearly crumpled with horror. "He what?"

"I think he... I don't know exactly what happened I just... I know he did it to Gus. And I wonder if Dad would have killed him. If he could have."

"Hunter I—I don't know what to say. I was afraid it was your dad, but I never... I don't know I never really thought about it. I remember Gus before. Just barely."

"Yeah," Hunter said. "He's never been the same."

The scars weren't only on his face.

"He never told you exactly what happened?"

"We don't talk about things like that. We talk about food and sex and horses. About the ranch."

Elsie's nose wrinkled. "Gus talks about sex?"

"In fairness, that's mostly Lachlan and Brody. Formerly Tag, but now that he's married, he plays his cards a little closer to the vest."

"I'm glad that you told me." She put her hand on his chest. "All of it. Since you can't talk about those things with your brothers."

"Yes. I'm glad that I told you to."

When she finished her dinner, he moved to feeding her cake, and then he started to hold bites hostage for kisses, and soon after that, the cake wasn't the only thing on the dessert menu.

And he couldn't help but feel this was an isolated moment that was now slipping through his fingers. And he hated it. With everything that he was.

So he chose to push that thought out of his mind. And focus on Elsie. Because that was about the only thing that made sense in the whole world.

And it wasn't until this moment he'd realized that nothing had ever made sense to him before.

And for the first time in his life, when he fell asleep, it was with a woman in his arms.

And when he woke up in the morning, she was still there.

CHAPTER SIXTEEN

ELSIE WAS TENDER, and more than a little bit emotional when she woke up the next morning. She hid in the bathroom for longer than necessary, taking another shower, even though she'd just had one last night. She let the water roll over her skin, and if there were tears sliding down her face, she didn't know. And that was exactly how she wanted it.

She didn't need to know just how deeply all of this had affected her. She didn't need to know.

Flashes of last night went through her mind as her hand skimmed over her bare curves. The way that Hunter had kissed her. The way that he had touched her. It aroused her even now. She felt irrevocably changed by that. By his touch. By everything. She felt…new, but not in a strong way, but the way a butterfly was when it came out of its cocoon, wet wings and shaky legs.

This wasn't what she'd expected. All these feelings. Closeness and pleasure that made her feel weaker and stronger all at once. A giddy sort of happiness that terrified her and made her feel shy and exposed. She had signed on to see a penis. She had signed on for an orgasm.

She'd had much more than one orgasm, and she realized now that innocence had nothing to do with whether or not you had seen a penis.

It had something to do with the way your emotion shifted.

It had something to do with the way having a person inside you made your soul feel changed. Touched.

The way they had the power to rearrange things in your own body whether you told them they could or not.

She emerged fully dressed, and was thankful that Hunter was dressed too.

"Time to head over," he said. "Checkout time is soon anyway."

Which meant it was near eleven, which blew her mind. She hadn't realized how late they'd woken up. As if he was reading her mind, he spoke. "It was a long night."

"Yeah," she said.

She studied his face, so familiar and so new all at the same time. And she looked for that little boy. The one who had stood there and told his mother he would be all right if she was gone. That he didn't need her. That self-sacrifice that he'd offered up then and there, and she had taken it.

It killed Elsie. To know how brave he'd been. How misguided. And how his mother had taken the promises of an eleven-year-old and used them as license to leave her boys with a monster.

It made her feel cut up. Devastated. She didn't feel her own maternal abandonment that deeply; it shocked her to feel it so heavily for him.

"You okay?"

"I'm okay," she said. "I'm just…thinking."

"Thinking loud enough that I can almost hear it, but I still don't know about what."

"Just last night."

It felt strange walking out of the hotel room with him. Wearing her same jeans and tank top. Carrying that duffel bag. Because all these things were the same. Just like the truck they got in to leave. And yet she was different. They were different.

It was a half-hour drive out to the ranch from the center of the city, and she watched as the gray concrete landscape gave way to something much more familiar.

And she waited. Waited for her insides to feel more like usual as the trees began to outnumber the buildings. As the fields grew and expanded, carrying more cows than people.

But she didn't feel like herself. She felt like that woman she'd been last night. So aware of him. Of his body, of the ways in which she wanted him to touch her.

Kiss her. Taste her.

Would she always think about this? She was never going to be able to go back to just being near him.

She was going to have to… She was going to have to figure this out. And she wasn't looking forward to it. Wasn't looking forward to having that conversation.

Not at all.

When they pulled up to the ranch, Elsie suddenly felt shy. Because she had met the ranch owner, and she wondered if she would look alarmingly different now that she was no longer a virgin.

Oh, she hadn't even thought about that. When she got home was Sawyer going to look at her and know? Was Alaina?

She felt a stab of guilt, because she hadn't thought about Alaina at all. Even when she had been talking about how much the Sullivans meant to her, she had not thought about her friend, or the ways this would hurt her.

You decided not to think about it. You decided to do it anyway.

She had.

And for what? Because…because no one could ever

know. Because it would have to end here. In this moment outside of time. They were going to have to draw a line around it. There was nothing else for it.

She had never come here with him intending for it to be one night. She had thought... She had thought that whatever was going on between them could continue on after this, but she could see now that it couldn't.

Because it was all weird and strange in this place that they'd been before without being lovers, and when they got back to the ranch it was only going to be that much more pronounced.

That fancy hotel with room service and champagne, that hadn't been the Hunter and Elsie that worked at Four Corners.

That had been the Hunter and Elsie that went to the country club and had a fancy dinner. The Hunter and Elsie that had danced. That had flirted.

Out-of-town Hunter and Elsie. Those two slept together, and they were going to have to be the only two that ever did. Because real world Elsie and Hunter could not have that relationship.

They would never be able to carry on. They would never be able to get on with their jobs. With their lives. With the relationships that they had at Four Corners that they had a deep responsibility to.

"Calm down," Hunter said.

And she was thankful that picking up the horses didn't take very long. They were loaded into a trailer right there, and Hunter hitched up. And the owner of the ranch wasn't even involved in the transaction. It was a ranch hand that she'd never seen before, and it made her feel calmer.

And when they were back on the road, she knew that she couldn't wait to speak.

"We really could've done this in one day."

"Yes," he said.

"Wolf and Sawyer are probably going to realize that."

"Not unless you give them an itemized list of all the things we did. And if you do, I hope that you make sure to talk about my staying power."

She wasn't sure if she was horrified or relieved at the joke. Because it was like him to tease her. But weird to have him tease her about this. "I will not," she said, sniffing loudly.

"Skittish."

"I'm not skittish! I want all your body parts to stay where they are."

"Because you like all my body parts."

"You are an unstoppable egomaniac."

He nodded. "Yeah. Pretty much."

"But seriously."

"No one's going to question it," he said. "You don't need to worry."

"Right. Because they would never suspect it."

"Not in a million years," he said.

"They trust you."

He nodded slowly. "I should feel worse about that than I do. But the thing is, you trust me. And that's what you wanted."

"Yes," she said. And even though she didn't like what she had to say next, a small well of pleasure bloomed in her chest. Because she had been the important one. Not Sawyer. Not Wolf. What she wanted had mattered more. And maybe what he wanted too. But it had been her. So the pleasure of that was all the same.

It was complicated, sure. But there was joy in it.

And that joy was all theirs to share.

Which was sort of a wild, reckless epiphany. They had shared their bodies. He'd shared difficult things about his life.

And they shared this.

"We can't do this at Four Corners," she said, blurting it out even as her mind spun out, racing ahead and imagining them doing just that.

"We can't?"

"No." And that dampened her joy.

But right now they were talking. And they had something special. And what if they broke it if they pushed their luck?

She didn't want to break them.

"I don't see why we can't."

"I can't," she said. "Just going to Running Y… I was freaking out. I think everybody can see that we had sex."

"The thing is, Elsie, maybe they can."

"Don't say that to me. You should be trying to make me feel better."

"Why? You want me to lie to you?"

"No," she said. "I don't want you to lie to me, but I don't want you to say that. I don't want you to agree that maybe the fact we had sex is stamped on my forehead somewhere."

"I don't know that it's stamped on us, I just think when two people have chemistry and when they've shared intimacies, it can be pretty obvious."

"So, does that mean that when a random woman walks into Smokey's I'll be able to tell whether or not you had sex with her?"

"No," he said. "Because I haven't shared intimacy with anybody else."

That made her feel like she'd been punched in the chest.

She felt afraid of what the sex had made her feel. All that it opened her up to and he was just...

Fearless.

"I don't... I don't even know what that means."

"I know you, Elsie Garrett. I've never known a woman that I had sex with. Much less spent the night with her. Much less spent the whole night holding her. After telling her about my childhood trauma."

That made her eyes feel scratchy, and she resented him for that. "Well—well, what the hell. What the hell even? What am I supposed to do with that."

"Maybe say that we should keep on having sex?"

"But we *can't*," she said. "And you said that what I wanted mattered."

"What you want does matter. The thing is, though, I just think that the problem isn't whether or not you want it. It's that you're afraid."

She hated that he knew her then. She should have slept with Travis. Travis, who didn't really know her. Travis, who didn't really care. Because this deep insight Hunter suddenly seemed to have into all that she was, was really very inconvenient.

"I'm not afraid," she said, even while she feared a little bit that she might be. "Not for me, anyway. Honestly, you're hot, and you're a charmer, but that won't hold weight with Wolf and Sawyer. They'll be so pissed and it'll wreck stuff and I like... I like our lives, okay?"

"If you don't want to keep doing this, Elsie, we don't have to."

"I just, I care about Four Corners. I care about what happens there. And there are too many people in my life who should have cared who just didn't. And you do care about me. And Alaina—"

"I don't care about Alaina."

"She likes you."

"I know," he said. "Gus told me. But I didn't encourage her and I'm not into her that way. So for me, she's not part of this."

That both pleased her and hurt her, somehow. Because she loved Alaina deeply, but also she didn't want Hunter thinking much about her. "I have to, though, because she is my only friend."

"I'm your friend."

"Yes. I care about that. So let's just be friends."

The words fell from her mouth. Flat. She had never called Hunter McCloud her friend in all her life, and this was about the dumbest time ever to do it. She despised that. She despised the words even as she spoke them.

"Suit yourself, Elsie."

"Are you... Are you okay with that?"

"I'm not okay with it," he said. "I'm going to have to be."

She stamped her foot. And it echoed on the floorboards of his truck. "Can't you just make me feel better? Can you say that it's okay?"

"No," he said. "Because I'm not in the business of making you feel better, little girl. I'm in the business of telling you the truth. So, no, it's not okay. That meant something to me. That night in the hotel room. I compromised my friendship with your brothers, and I would do it again in a minute, but I didn't do it for just one night."

"What did you do it for, then?"

He didn't have a response. The road noise echoed in the car, too long. Too loud.

"I thought so," she said.

"Elsie..."

"No, that's the thing. We can keep doing it. We could.

But to what end? Just until we make Sawyer and Wolf mad at you, and Alaina mad at me. Until it gets to where things are going to be awkward between us forever. Until there's more nights that we spend together than…" But of course they could never spend more nights together than they had apart. Because that would be a lifetime. Because she had known him for a lifetime.

And they would never have a lifetime.

She just didn't believe enough in that. She hoped that Wolf and Sawyer would have it with their wives but she…

She thought it was probably a pretty rare thing.

"If that's the way you see it, even if I'm not ready. Even if I don't want to. Well, maybe you're right. Maybe there's no point."

"Yeah, well. It must pain you to admit that I could be right. But I am. About this."

"Okay," he said. "If you say so."

She leaned in and turned the radio on, and didn't even bother to hook up her phone. She didn't care about her playlist. Not right now. She just wanted to drown out the awkwardness. Just wanted to drown out the feelings that were echoing in her chest.

And she thought so many times about starting an innocuous conversation as they continued to drive, because she had to find her normal voice with him, so that when they got back home things would feel right. They would feel normal. But she couldn't find it. She couldn't find it in her.

And she just felt miserable.

"Buck up," he said when they pulled onto the long dirt road that provided access to the different parcels of land that made up Four Corners.

She *did* need to buck up. They were here now and it

would only be a few minutes before they were around other people.

They went straight to McCloud's because they had to drop off the horses. And when they got there Gus and Alaina were there. Her friend being there was such a shock, she started breathing in short, sharp bursts and her vision went blurry.

"Don't worry," Hunter said, squeezing her hand quickly, and before she could say anything about it, he got out of the truck.

She sat there for a moment, trying to get her bearings, and she realized that Alaina was staring intently into the truck cab.

Great.

She tumbled herself out of the cab and went back toward the horse trailer.

"Show me what I bought," Gus said.

"Hi," Alaina said brightly when Elsie got closer. "Gus said I could come see the horses."

Elsie felt prickly with discomfort. "That was nice of him."

Alaina rolled her eyes. "I mean, he's not really nice," she said.

Gus's facial expression didn't change, but Elsie had a feeling he heard that.

In general, his presence was disconcerting. There was a dark intensity to him that the other McCloud brothers just didn't have. Of course, she had never seen him be anything but gentle and kind. If anything, he was like a big benevolent protector. He just looked dangerous.

And didn't seem like he had any softness to him at all. Hunter was rock-solid. All lean muscle, and she had spent a whole night exploring his body, so she should know. The thought made her face feel hot.

But Gus was even thicker. All muscle. Not an ounce of softness on him.

It made him all the more menacing along with that face full of scars.

"Sure he is," Elsie said.

Her friend scampered to the back of the horse trailer, and of course Elsie realized she wasn't actually here to see the horses, but to see Hunter. And guilt shot through her. Because it was all well and good for her to make decisions about what she was going to do, and how she was going to be okay with all of it, and quite another thing to actually do it.

And to face Alaina in the aftermath.

Alaina started to pepper Hunter with questions about the horses, which he answered with ease, and Elsie was thankful for that. Not one bit of body language gave away the fact that he knew Alaina had a crush on him. He treated her like he always did. With a fair amount of polite cordiality and nothing more.

But of course, by the time that was done and Alaina offered to drive her back, Alaina was chattering excitedly about how friendly he'd been.

And it was grating on Elsie's nerves.

"You're quiet," Alaina pointed out.

"I'm tired. It was a long day on the road."

"Yeah, were you guys doing things at the ranch?"

Guilt twisted at her chest. "Yeah. We spent some time getting a little hands-on—" she grimaced "—instruction."

"Maybe I do want to help work at the ranch," Alaina said. "It might be interesting. Gus was explaining the plan for the place. I'm surprised that he cares so much about it."

"Why? He's always been—"

"Overbearing? Overprotective?"

"I don't know. He's…he's him."

"Definitely," Alaina said. "I just didn't think all the 'him' he was extended to caring about giving therapy to people with emotional baggage." Suddenly Alaina's face softened. "Well, of course he…"

"He pulled you out of the pond." Knowing what she did about Gus now, Elsie felt the urge to remind Alaina of his good character.

"No, I know. He's just so hard, he…he's difficult."

"Yeah, I know."

"It's amazing, how different they all are."

Because they had different experiences. Because Gus carried scars outside, and Hunter carried them inside. And Elsie knew about it now.

And it was another thing she had to keep from her friend.

She waved to Alaina when she got dropped off at her house.

Her friend pulled away, and Elsie stood there, staring at the house, staring at her truck. Everything felt different now. She felt different. And she did her best to push the feeling away. Because she was back home. It should all be a reminder of why things needed to stay the same. But she didn't want them to.

She swallowed hard and headed toward the house.

Everything would be fine. Everything would go back to normal. She would make sure of that.

She and Hunter had known each other for too long to let one night change anything.

He was still Hunter. He would go right back to being Sawyer and Wolf's friend who annoyed her.

There was no other option.

CHAPTER SEVENTEEN

HUNTER DIDN'T RECOGNIZE himself the next day, waiting for work to start. Because he had never felt excited to see a woman before. And he was anticipating seeing her. Elsie Garrett, who he had seen nearly every day for more years than he could count in his head.

He felt a sense of anticipation. And frustration, because he knew he couldn't just walk up and kiss her.

Still. He waited outside the barn to see her familiar, athletic figure walking toward him. And when she finally was there, everything stopped.

She looked the same. Wearing a cowgirl hat, with her dark hair done up in a braid that was draped over her shoulder. She was wearing a white tank top and a pair of jeans, holding her gloves in her hand as she moved closer to him.

"Morning," he said, willing himself to keep his boots planted to the dirt. To not walk toward her. To not pull her into his arms.

"Morning," she said.

"You're five minutes late," he said, the statement coming out a little bit more terse than he meant it to.

"Sorry," she said, frowning.

"Well, we have extra animals now. More work to do. Plus, gotta get everything up and running."

"Yeah, yeah," she said. "Alaina wants to see about doing some work here."

"She'll have to talk to Gus," Hunter said.

"I'll tell her that," Elsie said, walking past him and into the barn, and he stood back, looking at the way her ass moved when she walked. And he felt…unrepentant.

Because she was ready to be done. He wasn't.

That had never happened to him before. And it was… Hell, the virgin was the one who had broken things off. He thought he might have to give a speech. On expectations. On things not being permanent. But she'd given him the speech.

And he still wanted to tease her.

Didn't matter that things had changed between them, that urge was still there.

"Your ass looks real cute today."

She whipped around and shot him an evil glare. "I am your friend, remember?"

"Fine, your ass looks real cute today, *buddy.*"

"Your ass is pretty cute too. It'd be a shame if I kicked it."

"Don't threaten me with a good time, Els, I'm liable to take you up on it."

She started rustling around for tack, grabbing a bridle and making her way over to one of the new horses' stalls.

So, he did the same.

They each got out a mount, and started putting them through the paces.

"If you mean playing darts…"

"I didn't."

"You're shameless."

"I thought you'd like it. You were filled with complaints about how intense I was when we actually…"

She looked around, her eyes wide.

"No one knows," he said.

Discounting the fact that Lach and Gus were way more in his business than he'd like.

"Can you tease me and make it not about sex?"

"No," he said, grinning and moving closer to her.

And he could see a blush in her cheeks and a smile tugging at the corners of her mouth in spite of herself and his heart started beating faster.

Like he was a kid with a crush.

And it was… He couldn't remember having so much fun.

"You're the worst."

"I am one hundred percent the worst."

He took another step closer and for a moment he thought she was going to lean in, but then she rocked back a step and cleared her throat.

"Has Gus gotten any further on permits?"

"Yeah," Hunter said. "He mentioned last night that everything is approved. So next, he's bringing on an expert and we're going to get things started soon."

"Great," she said.

He rode away from her and pushed the horse harder than was strictly necessary, but it was good to see what the animal could do. It was fit and hearty and sure-footed, and made for a pleasant trail ride, all things considered.

That he was hard for his best friend's sister, that she didn't feel like his best friend's sister anymore. And that she didn't want him back. Yeah, all things considered.

When he returned to the barn, Elsie wasn't there. And he was almost relieved. Because he didn't need all that. Didn't need to be dealing with her and everything just now. He felt like he was too close to snapping his leash, quite frankly.

He got his horse put away, and right when he got out of the barn, Elsie rode in, dirt on her face, and all over her.

"What happened to you?"

"Nothing," she snapped.

She got off the horse and started to remove the animal's tack.

"Like hell nothing happened to you," he said, looking at the back end of her jeans and seeing a whole dust cloud.

"It's fine. And it isn't the horse's fault."

She bent down and started cleaning the animal's hooves.

"What happened?"

"I fell off, okay? Par for the course. I ride horses all the time. It's not a big deal."

"Well, I need to know what happened, because if we are going to be sending vulnerable people out on a horse, we need to know what causes the problem. Yes, people are going to fall off horses here. It happens. But we have to try to mitigate risk as much as we can."

"I don't… I don't think it's going to need mitigating. It's…"

"Just tell me what happened."

"I got distracted. I went on part of the trail I shouldn't have… Look, I'm just… I'm upset. Because I'm good with horses, and I shouldn't have been distracted. And frankly, I'm lucky I didn't cause the horse to turn an ankle. As it is it was just a stumble, and I fell. And thank God she's okay, but I could've caused her injury and—"

"Elsie," he said, reaching over and grabbing hold of her. "Talk to me."

"I don't want to talk to you," she said, jerking out of his hold. "You caused the problem."

She finished with the horse and got her put away in her stall.

"I'm the problem?"

"Yes, Hunter. You are the problem. If I hadn't been distracted thinking about you, then it wouldn't have happened.

And the fact that this has impacted my professional life is unacceptable."

"You were thinking about me?"

"I *fell off a horse*, keep focused."

"Yeah. You fell off the horse because you were thinking about *me*."

"Don't... Don't look pleased about it," she said.

He realized he was smiling. "I'm not pleased," he said. Because he wasn't. She was right, the horse could have been hurt. But worse in his estimation was the fact that she could have been hurt.

"This is what I do. It's who I am. If...if sex is going to make me bad at my job, then I should just go back to being a virgin. This is why nuns marry God, Hunter. Because they're not distracted by thinking about naked men. They can focus."

"I'm not following you at all," he said.

"I don't care if you're following me. I don't care about you. You just... You're just Hunter," she said. "You're just annoying. And you are—"

"Shut up," he said, grabbing her arm and hauling her to him, kissing her mouth with a ferocity that roared through him like a beast.

And just like teasing her earlier had felt right, this felt right.

It couldn't just be one thing—it had to be everything because they were...they were everything.

She wrapped her arms around his neck and kissed him back for a reckless, heated moment, and neither of them could breathe.

Then she pulled away. "No," she said.

"It's not finished, Elsie," he said, his heart thundering

hard. "If it were finished, then you wouldn't be thinking about me naked."

"It is finished," she said. "It's finished because it has to be."

"But it's not finished, because it isn't."

"What about when it is?" she asked, her voice breaking. "What about when it is? If it was this hard after a night, it's only going to be harder later. And I don't want to deal with that. I don't want to deal with it. It's just... There's already been too much. There's already been too much, and I don't want to put this at risk. I can't explain it to you. Because I would've just said that you were Hunter and you annoyed me and you drove me crazy, but I can't stand the fact that it's making it impossible for me to work with you. I can't stand the fact that it's making it difficult for me to focus on my work, which I love more than anything. I can't handle that it's made me less at my job..."

"You had a bad moment, it wasn't you being less."

"It feels that way. So answer me that question. What happens when it's finished? Because the very idea of that terrifies me. And I don't think that I can face it."

And he knew he was going to have to be the one to expose himself a little bit here, because she was scared and it made him want to be scared right with her.

"I can't tell you everything that's going to happen," he said, grabbing her chin and pinching it between his thumb and forefinger. "I can't see the future. But I can promise you this. I won't leave. I will never leave you, Elsie Garrett. I will always take care of you. I will always be there for you. And it doesn't matter what we are. That is the truth. It was true when you were a kid. It's true now that you're a woman. Nothing could ever change that. Nothing."

He was breathing hard when the words finished. As they

settled there between them. But it was true. The absolute truth, and he meant it with his whole heart. He couldn't promise anything else. Hell, he couldn't understand much right now. But he knew that to be true. That whatever they were, he was committed to her. In a way that he had never felt committed to another human being in his life.

"You won't?"

It was that question that undid him. The vulnerability of it.

"No," he said. "You can trust me."

And he knew that he hadn't done a damned thing to earn that trust, not really. Not when anyone took into account his track record with women. Or the models he had in his life for parents. For loyalty.

Except…he never tried before. That was the thing.

She made him want to try. Except, with her he couldn't afford to fail, so it was going to have to be more than a try. And he was up for that.

And then, she was kissing him. She flung herself into his arms, like she had dropped all of her concerns and it made her weightless.

"Come with me," he said against her mouth.

"Okay," she said.

He took her hand and led her out of the barn, walked her down a side trail that led to a place he'd never taken anyone to before. Not anyone other than his brothers.

"Where are we going?"

"The Lost Boys' hideout," he said.

"The Lost Boys?"

"That's us, Elsie," he said.

"You're the Lost Boys," she said.

"Yeah. Because the grown-ups were pirates," he said. "And this was where we used to hide out."

In reality, it was just a shady spot in the meadow, surrounded by trees, which made it feel carved out. The place that they went when their dad was being an ogre. Because they knew he wouldn't follow. It was near the river, and there was still a hammock that Gus had strung there between two trees.

He wondered if they ever came down here anymore.

He hadn't walked down this way in years. It was cool and secluded, and he felt a little bit like he was showing her the inside of him. But he wasn't sure he minded.

Because he wanted her to see. That she mattered. And that he meant everything he'd said.

"You can see the old fire ring," he said. "But this is the best part."

Holding on to her hand, he led her through the shady patch and up a hill, following the narrow trail until the trees broke. Until they were standing on top of a round, grassy hill covered entirely in wildflowers. Purple, yellow and dark red, waving in the wind along with the slim blades of grass. The sun filtering through like magic.

"This is the Enchanted Hill," he said. "There's magic here. And nothing bad can touch you." He smiled down at her. "Gus told me that."

Elsie's eyes were suddenly shiny, and he realized how sad this was. It was just something he had accepted. Part of his life. But looking at it through Elsie's eyes, he saw it. The vision of the little boys they'd been, hiding out, with their oldest brother constructing fantasy worlds to keep them from feeling hopeless.

And he thought he probably didn't give Gus enough praise for all that he'd done. That he didn't even really understand the weight that his brother had carried all of his life.

More than the scars. He had tried. All those years he had

tried. With no role model, no nothing. He had just done it because he knew it was right.

And that realization flipped some of the sadness in him.

Yeah, he had it tough. But he'd had it good too.

His brothers, the Garretts…

And Elsie all on her own.

There was a lot of tough at Four Corners. But there was a whole lot of good along with it.

"We are extraordinary," she said. She nodded decisively. "All of us. You know how Alaina's parents just… They're always playing these games, calling in, making her feel bad for not keeping in touch with them when they're the ones who left. And the Kings… Who even knows. But I doubt their father was any better than yours. Not that they would ever tell anybody."

"Never," Hunter agreed.

"But we have this. We have this magic." She looked at him, pressed her hand flat to his chest and let her fingers slide up to his shoulder, around to the back of his neck. "We have this magic," she whispered.

He kissed her lips, and he understood: this was the place he'd imagined laying her down. This was the place he'd fantasized about having her.

This meadow, where he had memories of childhood. Memories of himself. Memories of things that were much more real than he'd ever shared with another person. And he wanted to see her lie down in it, surrounded by these flowers.

When he'd been a boy he thought they were the most beautiful thing he'd ever seen. But it was Elsie Garrett now.

"It's a hell of a punch of magic," he said, kissing her deep and long and gripping the bottom of her tank top and pulling it up over her head. He admired her body, the way the sun fell across her skin, the way it gleamed golden in the light.

She looked shy for a moment. "Nobody's gonna see," he said. "Don't worry. Trust me. I told you I would protect you."

"Yeah," she breathed.

He took her bra off, and the vision of her bare breasts in the sunlight about killed him dead.

He opened the snap on her jeans and pushed them down, taking her boots and underwear with them. And then she was gloriously naked in the sunshine, and all he wanted to do was join her.

There was something so erotic about it all, but something free. Childlike all at the same time. To be naked outside like you didn't believe anything could ever hurt or embarrass you.

Like you were bulletproof.

He pulled her up against him, luxuriating in the feel of her soft body against his.

And she clung to him, and it was the clinging that undid him.

He brought her down to the soft grass, and kissed her. Fiercely. As if everything in him was dependent on a taste of her lips. And she was different than she'd been the first time. Different than the girl he'd had that night in a fancy hotel. Because this was Elsie in her element. Elsie brought back to nature.

She was his cowgirl.

And he wanted to give her a chance to ride.

He reversed their positions, her legs draped on either side of him. He reached behind her, and pulled the rubber band off her braid, sliding his fingers through it slowly and letting her dark hair fly free.

"Beautiful," he whispered, staring at the way her hair fluttered in the breeze, at the pink tips of her breasts.

She cupped his face, dragging her fingertips down his jawline. "You too," she whispered.

"Ride me," he said, gripping her hips, his fingers digging into her skin.

And only right then did he remember his promise. That he would protect her.

"Shit," he said. "Protection."

She scrambled off him and went to his jeans, searching hopefully for a wallet, which she found quickly, and pulled out a condom.

She tore it open, then gave it back to him. He sheathed himself quickly, bringing her back over him. "I told you, you can trust me," he said.

And that broke her. She smiled, but stopped at the same time, moving herself over his body, and bringing herself down over him slowly. He thought he was going to die. As he entered her body, inch by excruciating inch. She was so tight. So perfect. For him.

And when she began to move, it was a revelation. The sun behind her, beams of light crowning behind her like a halo as she rocked him. Destroyed everything he'd ever believed about himself and about the world and rebuilt it into something he didn't recognize.

Something he had never really thought could exist.

Pleasure was like a wild beast inside of him, roaring for its satisfaction. But it was nothing compared to the riot of emotion in his chest. It was what made this undeniable. It was what made it all-consuming.

He held her hips, bucking up inside of her, even as she rode, and when they reached their peak, it was together. Crying out their pleasure with no thought to anything but desire. And if it carried out on the wind, he sure as hell didn't care.

She collapsed on his chest, and he wrapped his arms around her. Stroking her hair, kissing her face.

"Don't you tell me it's done," he said.

"I wasn't going to," she said softly.

"Thank you," he said. "For trusting me enough."

She nodded, and he realized his chest was wet, and she was crying.

"You okay?"

"No," she said.

"I don't know if I am either." He let his fingertips trail up and down her shoulder. "But I'd rather be not okay with you."

"Than what?"

"I don't know. Not okay by myself? Perfectly fine by myself?"

She wrapped her arms around his neck and buried her face there. "Yeah. Me too."

"But?"

"No but. Except I should probably get back. I'm supposed to have dinner at Sawyer's tonight."

"Right. Well, you wouldn't want to miss that."

"I'm just going to have to get home and clean up and…" She looked up at him. "We are going to have to be careful."

"How about we just don't plan it. When you start making proclamations things go bad."

"You just made a whole lot of proclamations," she said.

"I did. But when I make them they end with you climbing on top of me. So I'm in favor of them."

"That is…that is deeply male of you."

He grinned. "But you like it."

She socked his shoulder, and he let his head fall back in

the grass. Because she had punched him. And he was still inside her. And things felt right.

"I have to go," she said, moving away from him.

But she didn't run. She got dressed slowly, and he held her hand all the way back to the barn. Until they might see somebody. Then she pulled away.

But he didn't.

He hadn't given much thought to his lack of care over whether or not anyone found out. And it was clear that she cared, so he was going to have to at least give that some consideration. But he wondered why he didn't.

What it meant.

He supposed it couldn't really mean much of anything.

"I'll see you," she said.

"Don't give me that," he said. He gave a quick look around, then kissed her. "Now I'll see you."

As he watched her walk back to her truck, he felt a sense of certainty lodge itself in his chest.

But he knew that she wasn't ready to hear about it. Not at all.

CHAPTER EIGHTEEN

THE NEXT FEW days went by in a sensual whirlwind. She and Hunter worked, and they had sex. Nothing like the long, leisurely sex they'd had in the hotel when they'd spent the night together—it was always quick and dirty, somewhere outside, somewhere in the barn. On lunch or toward the tail end of the workday.

And Elsie felt like her head was spinning. Pretending like everything was fine and normal when she saw her brothers, when she saw Alaina, and being completely caught up in everything that was happening between the two of them all the rest of the time.

And then it was already a town hall, and she'd forgotten that she was supposed to help get everything ready for the evening.

She had to tell Hunter that she couldn't come to the barn, and all she could think of was how disappointed she was that she wasn't going to be able to have sex with him again.

She was entirely preoccupied with that thought when she walked into her sister-in-law's kitchen.

Violet, nine months pregnant, was sitting at the kitchen table with a piecrust rolled out in front of her, and Evelyn was standing at the stove stirring the pot.

"There you are," Evelyn said brightly.

"Yeah. Sorry. I'm completely thrown off. It was…going

to Vancouver last weekend. Ever since, I haven't had any clue what day it is."

"Understandable," Evelyn said, smiling.

She felt a little bit guilty about lying to Evelyn, but in a sense it was true. Because she really hadn't known what day it was, or which direction was up or down, or even her own name for the last week. It was just that it had less to do with Vancouver and more to do with the constant orgasms.

"Where's Bug?" she asked, speaking of her niece.

"She's with Sawyer. She doesn't last as long out on jobs with him as she did when she could just ride in a front pack, but she gets a kick out of spending as much time with him outdoors as possible. I imagine it's a lot what you were like."

For some reason, that made her feel guilty. Maybe because she was sneaking around and lying to everybody. Maybe she was just going to live under a cloud of guilt until all of this finished.

The idea of it being finished made her feel something worse than guilt.

"You can start filling muffin tins," she said, handing her a giant pastry bag filled with batter. "We need to make a hundred muffins."

"Why don't you just make a giant-ass cake," she grumbled, moving to the muffin tins that were all lined up on the counter.

"Because this is fussy and fiddly," she said, grinning. "And I like fussy and fiddly."

"Can confirm," Violet said.

"Oh, you love it," Evelyn said, grinning. "I can't tell you how wonderful it's been to have a professional baker on hand as a new sister."

Elsie looked at the two women, and she suddenly felt

like she was standing on another side of a glass pane from the two of them. She could confide in them. But she hadn't done anything to get particularly close to them since they'd married her brothers.

Yes, she was completely friendly with them. And she had been from the beginning. But it wasn't the same thing. She hadn't learned to do the girl-talk thing. She had been raised by men, and had entrenched herself in that.

And she couldn't confide in them now, no matter how much she wanted to. To ask them if it was normal to be obsessed with the man you were sleeping with. To ask them what she was going to do when everything came to an end, because it would. And she was terrified by the prospect. But even more terrified at the idea of anything else.

"Are you okay, Elsie?" Evelyn asked. "You seemed different the last couple of weeks."

"Yes," she said. "I'm fine."

Evelyn frowned. "You know, when I first met you, I really admired how open you were. But I thought you reminded me a lot of somebody who hadn't really been hurt yet. And as much as I know about your parents from the time I spent hearing Sawyer talk about his life, I know that isn't true. You definitely had your hardships."

Elsie felt uncomfortable with that characterization because in many ways it was actually true.

"Well, I have," Elsie said. "But in the way that I don't really know any different. Sawyer and Wolf took care of me. And I never had parents who were any better than the ones I had. Absent and uninterested. My life didn't really change that much when my dad died. And I felt like I should be sadder than I was, but... I've been protected. So you're right. I haven't been hurt."

And as soon as she said that her throat went tight. Because she felt like the problem was that hurt was inevitable. And she could suddenly see the path to it in a way she never had before.

"So…" Evelyn said.

"Nothing's happening," she said. And she started to aggressively fill the muffin tins.

"Well, the way that you said that makes me not believe you," Evelyn said.

"Well, doesn't matter if you believe me or not," Elsie said.

She looked away from Evelyn, but then her eyes landed on Violet, who blinked slowly. "Yeah. I don't believe you either."

"Well, it doesn't matter if you believe me or not."

"Hi," came a cheerful-sounding voice.

Alaina. Of course. Alaina was coming to help them get the food together because the Garretts were responsible for the desserts, and Elsie had asked if she would. And she had completely forgotten.

"Come on in," Evelyn shouted.

And Alaina appeared a moment later with a giant bowl of dough in her hands. "Pastry dough at the ready."

"Perfect," Evelyn said. "I'm almost finished cooking down the raspberries for the Danish. And then pie filling is on the way."

"Hi," Elsie said, trying to smile, but she had a feeling it looked more like a grimace.

"What's the matter with you?"

"As it happens, we were just discussing that. I was saying that she has seemed very distracted."

"I'm not distracted," Elsie said.

"You do seem weird," Alaina said. And then suddenly

her expression changed. "Did you... Has something happened with Travis?"

And suddenly, Elsie was weak with horror and relief. "I... You know not Travis, but there are some things happening and..."

Alaina looked slightly wounded, like Elsie had hurt her by not telling her about all this. But if she only knew...well, she'd be a lot more hurt if she knew.

"Really?" Evelyn asked, arching a brow. "Like...some *things*?"

"Uh, yes," Elsie said, suddenly very aware that everyone was looking at her. "It's just...you know, not a huge deal or anything, it's just... I have a lot on my mind."

"Well, which guy?" Violet asked. "I want to rate him."

"Rate him?" Elsie asked.

"Yes," Violet said, very seriously. "A ruggedness scale."

Evelyn laughed. "Yeah, rugged. I like them big and rugged."

"Same," Violet said, smiling slightly.

"No, we are not rating," Elsie said. "It's no... I can't. No. I'm embarrassed."

"I'm enjoying this," Violet said. "And I feel like I'm owed," she continued. "You know, my best friend is my aunt and I have to hear about how deeply satisfied she is with my uncle. She's ten years younger than him. My dad was really... Anyway, it's a long story but the point is, I'm enjoying getting to horrify someone else."

"Well, stop," Elsie said. "I don't want to be horrified. But that's it, that's all there is to say."

"No, it's not," Alaina said. "Is the guy we can't rate good in bed?"

Her face went hot. Because she wasn't thinking about Travis. She was just thinking about Hunter.

"I don't have anything to compare them to," she said.

"You don't need to," Violet said. "When you know, you know."

She was molten now. "Then I know. It's good. Good enough that I'm distracted. But I don't really need to have this conversation with everybody," she said.

"It's not a big deal," Evelyn said, waving a hand. "You're a grown woman."

"Yeah, Sawyer may not see it that way," Violet said.

"Oh, don't tell Sawyer," Elsie said.

"I don't keep things from Sawyer."

"Just don't bring it up," Elsie said. "I doubt he's going to randomly ask if I'm still a virgin."

"No," Evelyn said, laughing over the pot of berries. "He definitely isn't going to do that. In fact, I think he would rather die."

"Don't kill him. I like him."

Evelyn laughed. "So do I. You have my utter and total promise that I will not kill him."

"Well, I appreciate that," Elsie said flatly.

"Why didn't you tell *me*?" Alaina asked.

"Because you have no chill," Elsie said, which was at least a truth in the middle of this lie. "Look at you, blowing everything in front of everybody."

Alaina had no idea how big of a deal it was. She wanted to yell at her for being a silly virgin, and then she realized…they weren't even talking about the same thing. Because she was lying to her friend. She didn't know what a big deal this situation was because Elsie hadn't told her what was happening.

But how could she? How could she tell anybody what was happening? She didn't know what was happening herself.

And that thought made everything feel muted after that.

Everybody brushed the moment off and carried on, and a couple of hours later they were loading baked goods into a big truck to drive over to the meeting site. But on their way out the door, Evelyn stopped her, leveling her gaze at her in a fashion that was far too knowing.

And she wished that Violet and Alaina would come back, which was frankly the first time this whole day she had wished for an audience.

"It's not a random ranch hand, is it?"

Tears filled her eyes, and she hated that. How quickly and immediately emotion seemed to be right at the surface for her now. It had never happened to her before. Not like this.

"I…"

"You don't have to tell me what's happening. In fact, it's probably for the best if I only suspect. All things considered. I told you that I don't keep secrets from Sawyer, but I would never intentionally hurt you or throw a bomb into the middle of your life. You need to be careful."

And a few weeks ago, Elsie wouldn't have had any idea what that meant. Why would you need to be careful, for any reason other than not getting pregnant? But she understood now. She also understood that whatever careful was, she was a long way past it.

"I am," she said, nodding, amazed that she had managed to force the words around the giant lump in her throat.

Evelyn smiled, her expression entirely sympathetic. Far too sympathetic for Elsie's well-being. It made her feel small and fragile. And she didn't want any of that.

"It's impossible, isn't it? When you have feelings for someone."

She didn't want to hear this. She didn't want to have this conversation. She didn't want it at all. She didn't want

Evelyn to look at her and see her soft, vulnerable middle. She didn't want this to be something anyone knew about. She didn't want…

She didn't want her own feelings to be so out of control.

"I don't have feelings for him," she said, holding on to her elbows, and squeezing her arms tightly around her body.

But her mind was forced back to the meadow. To his admissions about his childhood. And her whole body hurt.

"You don't choose them," Evelyn said.

"*You* did," she answered. "You came here to marry Sawyer. It was a good thing when you started to have feelings for him."

"Yeah, I guess so. But he didn't intend to have any for me. He just did. We couldn't help it. We have chemistry, and I thought that would be it. I thought it would be the biggest part of our relationship, and the rest would be loving Bug. It would be loving this place. The whole family. And that he would just be part of it. But that isn't how it stayed. I started to love Sawyer very much very quickly. Whether I wanted to or not. Whether I thought it put me at risk or not, it didn't matter. I couldn't stop my heart from doing what it was going to do."

"Well, you don't have to worry about me," Elsie said.

"I hope not. I love you."

The words stuck in Elsie's throat, and all she could do was try to smile back. She hadn't had a whole lot of women in her life. Her grandmother had been the biggest influence, and she'd died when Elsie was so little she could hardly remember her.

Evelyn's gaze went soft and overly sympathetic. And Elsie wanted to tell her to stop that. But she knew that it wouldn't be very sisterly. Especially not in the context of how sweet Evelyn was being.

"Let's go," Evelyn said.

And they got into the truck then and headed to the meeting. When they got out, Elsie instinctively looked for Hunter. Her gaze found him immediately.

The families all settled in for the meeting, and the Garretts sat next to the McClouds. Which gave Elsie an excuse to sit next to Hunter. Easily. But she didn't touch him, no matter how much she wanted to. And she was keenly aware of Evelyn's furtive gaze following the two of them for part of the time. She wondered how she had become obvious enough for Evelyn to figure out that it wasn't Travis.

But the whole right side of her body burned where Hunter wasn't even making contact, and really, she could see how it was obvious.

Except, it wouldn't have been obvious to her. Not before. She never would've looked for this kind of subtle change between two people. Because she wouldn't have understood.

Now she felt an unbearable sense of ownership over him, and it was nearly impossible to not put her hands on him when it felt natural to do it.

She wanted to move. She regretted sitting beside him. But there was nothing she could do about it.

Gus spoke, giving an update on the ranch along with a timeline for the opening. And Lachlan McCloud's friend Charity, who was veterinarian for most of the horses in the community, explained her role in the proceedings.

Charity had gone to school on the ranch, the only child of an elderly single father—the town of Pyrite Falls' previous veterinarian. She looked between Charity and Lachlan and wondered. But she couldn't see anything between them other than friendship. At least, the intimacy that she felt with Hunter didn't exist there.

The intimacy that she could see between Evelyn and

Sawyer, Violet and Wolf. Well, she was acting like sex was giving her X-ray vision, which she supposed wasn't terribly reasonable.

But still, she looked at Landry King, and then across the room at Fia, as if it might give her some insight into the two of them. Because she and Alaina had wondered often what the situation was there.

She couldn't see anything.

But that didn't mean they hadn't...

It just meant they didn't have any intimacy. Anyway, they were across the room from each other.

She was being silly. But anything to distract herself. Anything to keep her brain off what was going on.

And was Travis even here? She hadn't bothered to check.

And she still didn't. Because she just didn't care.

The meeting concluded, and they all went outside for the customary bonfire and meal.

And she found herself twitchy and distracted the entire time. Which was a shame because the food was great.

She was looking forward to music, to the tempo of everything picking up, so that she would feel less like she was under the glare of the spotlight. Looking forward to darkness, and everybody getting a few more beers into them.

Everybody was always happy for an excuse to do that, so it didn't take very long, thankfully. The music started, the tempo fast and fun, the band, which was always a different collection of contributors, with fiddles and guitars and laptop steel, kicked off with some classic Dolly Parton, and got everybody on their feet.

Pretty soon, the most dominant light was the glow from the big fire, the sparks rising up into the air. Elsie stayed at the table, sipping slowly at her beer.

And then she felt him before she saw him.

"You should dance with me," he said.

She looked around, and there was no one right around them, much less paying attention to them. "We can't dance."

"Why not? It's not that unusual. I drag you out on the dance floor all the time."

How did she explain it? That it was obvious. That things had changed between them, and if they touched then it was only going to become all the more clear. How did she explain things that didn't make sense even to her?

"I just—"

"Dance with me," he said, his voice going low, the sexiness of it making her shiver.

His eyes were so intent on hers, and she couldn't deny him anything. Even though it was really stupid. Even though it was a dumb idea.

He reached his hand out, and she took it. Because there was no other choice. Because this was Hunter, and she couldn't deny him anything, much less want to deny him anything.

So she took his hand, and the minute their skin touched sparks fired through her whole body. And everything slowed down. The world shrank, and it felt like it was only the two of them, which was so dangerous because they were surrounded by everybody.

"It's a fast song," he said, his hand on her waist, which she felt like he wouldn't have done before, but she couldn't really remember. Maybe he would have. Maybe he would have, and it was just that she was so unbearably aware of the placement of that hand now. Because she knew what it felt like to be touched by him with no clothing on at all.

Because she knew what it was like to touch him the same way.

And it didn't matter that the dance was fast, it felt like

it might be slow. And she felt like she was floating. And one song faded into another, and she knew that it wasn't normal for them to just keep dancing with each other. Like there weren't other people there.

Usually, she ended up dancing with the Sullivan sisters. She didn't just dance with one of the men. It was common for them all to trade partners around. And only the couples ever stuck religiously to the person they went out on the dance floor with.

But she couldn't bring herself to let go of him. Couldn't bring herself to release him to anyone else.

The music changed, and it got slow, and she looked around as Hunter pulled her close. "No one is watching us," he said.

She scanned quickly for her brothers, and didn't even see them. They might've gone. They had babies, after all. And Violet was extremely pregnant, so it was likely she had been done with everything a long time ago and Wolf had escorted her home.

She was satisfied then that no one was paying particular attention to them. And she looked up at Hunter, chancing a small smile at him.

"So twitchy," he said, smiling.

"So *dangerous*," she returned.

"I like a little danger."

His voice. She would never be able to hear it and just… hear it again. Because she could feel it now.

"Well, I think you might be flirting with a lot of danger."

"I know I am," he said. "But what does it matter?"

But she had a feeling they were talking about two different things, and not because he didn't understand her.

"Would it be so bad?" he asked. "If people knew?"

She looked away from him because…how could people

know? How could they ever know? It would make this private thing between them mean something. It would make it…real.

It wouldn't be hers to hold and examine only when she could manage it. It would take on a life of its own and it was already so much…

"Elsie," he whispered.

It was too much. She couldn't take it anymore. She slid her hand down his shoulder, grabbed his hand and led him away from the bonfire. Into the darkness of the trees.

"Hunter…" she said breathlessly.

But she didn't have to ask for what she wanted, because he knew. And then he was kissing her. And she nearly wept with relief.

It was torture. Sitting with him like things hadn't changed. Dancing with him, having his hands on her and not…

Danger.

The word went off in her brain like a flash bomb, but she didn't care. Because she was kissing him. She pushed her fingers through his hair, and marveled at how familiar the texture was now. The way the whiskers on his jaw felt beneath her fingertips, and how it wasn't strange.

She moved her hands down his well-muscled back next, and she felt like it was a roadmap of Hunter that she knew by heart.

She knew him now, and yet it still felt fresh. Still felt new each time he touched her. Just as urgent, just as exciting.

And it made her forget. Everything.

Everything but this. Everything but him.

"What the hell is going on?"

She jumped back from Hunter, and horror hit her square in the chest. Because there was Alaina. Standing just inside the trees with the bonfire all lit up behind her.

"Alaina..." Elsie said, trying to find the words.

"How could you!" Alaina asked. ".You knew, you...you knew!"

"We didn't plan this," Elsie said. "I didn't plan it, I—I'm sorry."

"Sorry? You're sorry?"

Alaina turned on her heel and stomped away. "I have to follow her," Elsie said.

"You want me to help you handle it?"

"No. You don't owe her anything," Elsie said, the conviction of that burning in her chest. "She likes you, and that's...that's her problem. It's not my fault. But how I've handled all of this is," she said. "And that isn't your fault. And she is my friend. So I need to deal with it. I'm sorry. I have to...have to go with her."

She ran after Alaina's retreating figure. Her friend went all the way behind the big barn. Elsie could hear her sounds of distress, and her heart twisted. "Alaina, "I'm sorry," Elsie said. "I should've told you. But I didn't know how. Because I didn't know how to tell anybody."

"How long has that been going on? You just let me talk about him. You let me make an idiot of myself talking about the man that you're... You're sleeping with him, aren't you? You lost your virginity and *you didn't tell me.* And it was to him. And you didn't tell me. You made me sound so stupid, Elsie. Have you been making fun of me behind my back?"

"No," she said. "I would never make fun of you, Alaina. It isn't funny. If I thought it was funny I would've... I wouldn't have tried so hard to protect you."

"Did you tell him?"

The accusation cut Elsie. Straight to her heart.

"He knew already..."

"You *told him*?"

"Gus told him! I didn't."

Alaina looked mortified. "Gus knows?"

"I swear we haven't talked about it enough to actually get into who knows what. I—I love you, but this wasn't about you."

And she could see it. The moment Alaina Sullivan decided she'd land on her feet. It was who she was, and Elsie had always admired her for it, but right now she had to wonder...

How much of it was Alaina masking her pain?

Not wanting to feel it.

"Hey, it's... Look, Elsie, it's a little embarrassing but I just had a crush on him. We wanted to...get some experience and this is what worked out for you. I'll be fine."

"Alaina..." She wanted to fix it. Alaina's face was oddly serene and casual all at once and it was the defense of it all that hurt Elsie.

She'd started it. She hadn't shared. And now Alaina was putting up walls of her own.

"No, I'm good. I just... Hey, I guess it's my turn, right?"

"It wasn't about that with him." Elsie swallowed hard. "I didn't tell you because I didn't want to hurt you. And also because I was embarrassed. Because this wasn't about getting experience. It's complicated and—"

"You know, you're right, Hunter is too complicated," Alaina said. And then Alaina put her hand on Elsie, almost sympathetically. "Better you than me working all that out. But I hope it doesn't come back to bite you."

Elsie almost laughed. Alaina had switched the whole thing and was now acting concerned. Acting like she hadn't had a temper explosion a moment ago.

"I mean, I don't actually know if it will or not," Elsie said.

"Then you must really like him. Honestly, Elsie, don't

lose any sleep over it, okay? I just wanted to do it with him. You'll have to tell me what it's like."

"Alaina, just…don't do anything…"

"That you wouldn't do?"

And she sat with that for a minute because really, what could she even say to Alaina? She and Hunter were caught up in something that had nothing to do with making smart choices.

They were chasing a flame and they were…reckless and heedless and it was the greatest thing she'd ever experienced in her life.

Like that day they'd ridden their horses so fast and far, until they were out of breath. It was a kind of freedom she'd never experienced before and she didn't know where it all went. So how could she lecture Alaina on anything? How could she tell her what to do?

"I'm going to go put out feelers."

"Or you know, you don't have to do anything right now."

"You're good with the Travis thing, right?" Alaina asked.

"I'm… Well, yeah, I mean, I don't… I'm not… Hunter is the only guy I'm interested in," she said, and that cost her a little.

Because it was an admission of all those deeper things that scared her.

"Good to know." Alaina winked. She winked. And then she went practically skipping back to the fire.

Elsie just stood there, unable to really parse what had just happened. It was classically Alaina, in many ways, but it was…it was surreal to see it in action like this.

Hunter reappeared then, moving toward her. "Are you okay?"

"Yes," she said. "I—I guess. She's going to be fine. I—I

feel like I'm not sure if I'm a bad friend or... She wasn't mad. I mean, she was, but mostly about being tricked."

And she felt like if nothing else a barrier had been removed. She was standing there, looking at Hunter and there was just... There was no reason not to stretch up on her toes and kiss him. So she did. She kissed him, and everything in her went warm. She kissed him and she felt free for a moment. And she pushed out of her mind all the things Alaina had said about being careful. About her getting hurt. There wasn't any reason to dwell on that.

"Take me to your place," she said.

"Gladly."

They skirted around the edges of the bonfire with his hand in hers.

She felt warm and excited. She felt...happy.

This was Hunter. Her Hunter. And all of a sudden things were right with her friendships. Because Alaina was okay. And all right, she might be a little bit mad, but she was Alaina. She would find a way to make it all work. And she had admitted to exactly what Elsie had believed. That she had been attracted to Hunter, but she didn't have deep feelings for him.

And then there was Hunter. He was her friend. And there was all this stuff happening between them, but the bottom line was they liked each other. Sure, there was an edge to their teasing. There always would be. It was just how they were.

But now there was something more with it. Something deeper. And that was only a good thing. Right?

They got into the truck, and she took her shoes off, put her feet up on the dash and let her head fall back as he rolled the windows down and let the night air flood the cabin. They didn't talk. He put the radio on, put on some music, and she started to sing. He put his hand on her thigh. And he sang along with her. It was such a casually intimate gesture. And it made her heart squeeze.

Scooting to the center of the bench seat, she tilted her head and let it come to rest on his shoulder. And by the time they got to his place, she was warm all the way down.

They went inside, and he kissed her hard. "It's been too long," he said.

"It hasn't been that long."

"Ever since I tasted you, I just wanted more. It's been a lifetime. It's been a hell of a thing. I'm not... I'm not quite right when you're not in my arms."

His words were gruff, intense, and they made something sharp and painful expand in her chest. And there was something greedy underneath it. Something desperate. Something pleased, but in an uncomfortable sort of way.

Need.

She needed to hear him say things like this.

She had spent so much of her life feeling like she might be abandoned at any moment, so to hear someone say that... It was a revelation.

It was something she had always wanted, but was afraid to ask for. Something she felt if she had to ask for it, wouldn't mean as much.

"I want you," he said.

"I'm giving myself to you," she responded, smiling at him because she couldn't help it.

Because he was intense when they were like this, but he was still Hunter, and that was the magic of it.

It was not like she was with a different person. But like she had found a whole other dimension to him.

Like she knew him better than anyone, because he might've slept with a whole lot of women, but how many of them knew him the way that she did? None. They were

Hunter and Elsie. And nobody was them. And now they had seen each other naked too.

She had been in this little cabin so many times. They'd gone fishing together often over the years. And he was taking off her clothes here. Laying her down on the bed. Teasing her, tasting her. And it was one thing to do this sort of thing outside or in a hotel, but another entirely to bring it here. To this place that was familiar. To this place where they'd been Hunter and Elsie—who scrapped all the time and irritated each other for sport. And Hunter and Elsie, lovers. Which was an intense sort of word that made her feel right. Hot.

He brought his hand up to cup her breast, teased her nipple as he looked down at her. "You okay?"

"Yeah," she said.

"You're all right with everything with Alaina."

"I feel bad. I feel like I should've done something different. I was afraid. And that wasn't fair."

"And now?"

She smiled, or she tried to. Through her arousal, through the pain in her chest. Through the maelstrom of conflicting emotions that were fighting for dominance inside of her. "I'm not afraid."

And she was used to giving him bracing honesty, and she had maybe lied a little bit. But it was different now. Before, she had just said what was on her mind, and it had been about her. It hadn't much mattered what it meant to him. What it meant to the moment. And now...that was different. She cared what he thought. And she didn't know how to explain what was happening inside of her, and she was afraid of what he might say. She didn't know why. Only that everything felt... The stakes felt so high now, when for all the years before they just hadn't been.

But while they were Hunter and Elsie, who had known

each other forever, they were also something more. Something new.

And it was that part that felt uncertain.

That part she wanted to protect.

So he kissed her, and she let herself forget. She let herself forget that she had any concerns at all. She let herself forget complication and embrace pleasure. And the rising tide of joy that came along with it. With his focused attention, his hands on her skin. The declarations that he made with his lips against hers.

How much he wanted her.

How beautiful she was.

How special she was. And she ate it all up greedily, and didn't offer the same words in equal measure. She didn't quite know why she did that. Except opening her mouth at all made her feel exposed, and she was trying to hoard all of the good things to shore herself up.

And not let any of it back out.

But he didn't seem to mind. He kissed her all over. Brought his mouth down between her legs and brought her to screaming pleasure.

He made love to her until they were both exhausted.

Until they fell asleep in Hunter's cabin, firmly entrenched in their life at Four Corners, firmly bonded to each other.

And when Elsie slept, she slept so deeply she didn't even dream.

Because his strong arms around her were dream enough.

WHEN HE WOKE the next morning, Hunter was overcome by a deep, hard conviction.

This was what he wanted. This. Waking up with her. Waking up with Elsie Garrett. In his arms and his bed, in his life.

Alaina had been a huge source of concern for Elsie, and Alaina knew now. So, there was really only one mountain left to climb. Or rather, two.

He got up and opened up the fridge, got out some eggs and bacon and started to cook up breakfast. A few minutes later, Elsie came padding down the hall, her hair a wild tangle, her eyes sleepy. She was wrapped in his bedspread, comically large over her petite figure.

"Good morning, sunshine," he said.

"I smell bacon," she said.

"Have to replace the calories you burned."

"I think we burned a lot," she said.

She came and sat on the chair at the little dining table next to the kitchen, drawing her knees up to her chest, her bare feet pressed to the edge of the seat. The blanket covered up anything good, but honestly, everything about her was good. He liked her feet. Her knees. All of her, pretty much. Yeah. He liked it all.

"You got plans for the day?"

"I feel like I need to… I don't know. Maybe go see Alaina. I feel like I need to make amends for the fact that I've been a bad friend."

"You're not a bad friend. But hey, do what you need to do."

"I will."

"You know… Really appreciative of all of this. Of…"

"Are you…are you thanking me for sex?" she asked, her eyes going wide.

"That's not what I was trying to say."

"You are appreciative." She waved her hand, still mostly concealed by the bedspread. "Of this."

"Well, yes. I am. Though, I like to see you not wrapped in a puffy blanket."

"You are appreciative of my body."

"Yes," he said. "I am. But I actually meant... The work that you do on the ranch, you helping me go up north and get those horses. Everything we are. Everything we've been. That I can talk to you about anything, and I told you more shit about my childhood than I've ever told anybody else, and you don't look at me like I'm a project, or like I'm broken. That we can laugh. That we can make love, yes. I'm just thankful for you, actually. And I was trying to be romantic or something."

She snuggled deeper into the blanket. "Sorry. I didn't realize."

"Yeah, well. I'm not ever romantic. Not really."

"But you feel like you want to be romantic now?"

"Yeah. Doesn't feel like enough."

His chest felt like it was full to bursting.

He just...he just wanted everything. Because he loved her. Bottom line. He loved her. And he wanted to spend his life with her. He had never felt this way about another person, and he had never seen it coming with her. But somehow, it all made sense. Right then, it all made sense. His whole life.

They had both lost their mothers. They'd both lived through more than anyone should have to. They dealt with the fear of abandonment. They dealt with a hell of a lot of pain when it came to family. They loved this land. They were both hardheaded as hell. What was everything for if not for this?

She was a firecracker. She gave as good as she got. She made him laugh, even when they talked about stuff that sucked. She was his other half in a way that transcended age, or the fact that they had known each other since she was a kid. It actually all just fit.

"You know you're really damned cute," he said. And then he served her up a plate of bacon and eggs.

"You too," she mumbled, pulling the plate toward her, and starting to eat. He just watched.

She looked up. "Oh my gosh, you look like you're waiting to pounce on me."

"That's because I am."

She smiled somewhat shyly at first, and then pushed her plate toward the center of the table. "Well, then, what are you waiting for."

He grinned and crossed the space, picking her up out of the chair, bedspread and all, and carting her back to the bedroom. "It's been too long," he said, grinning when she was underneath him, the blanket stripped from her, her naked body pressed against his. "It's been, like, three hours."

"It's too long. It'll never be enough."

CHAPTER NINETEEN

IT HAD BEEN really difficult to leave Hunter's. She hadn't anticipated that. Just how it would all feel if they brought it into real life. How easy it was to imagine herself waking up there every day. It…it scared her a little bit.

What did you think it was going to be?

She hadn't thought. That was the thing. She hadn't thought even a little bit at all. She had convinced herself that she had. But she hadn't. Because she hadn't really been able to imagine intimacy on this scale. And what she really wanted to do was talk to her friend. But things were weird with Alaina. Whatever she said.

Still, she found herself heading over to Sullivan's point anyway, and when Fia opened the door, she smiled brightly. "Alaina's not here," she said.

"Really?"

"Yeah. She's down at the lake."

"Oh."

"You should head down there. She took a bunch of food and drinks."

Elsie frowned. She had no idea who Alaina could be with. Since it was usually them who was down at the lake.

"All right. I will."

"See you later, Elsie," Fia said.

Elsie waved, then got into her truck and drove down to the lake. Alaina's truck was there, and so was another one.

Travis.

Alaina hadn't been kidding.

And Elsie didn't feel jealous about it. It was difficult for her to even recall how she'd found Travis all that attractive. That wasn't the issue. No, the issue was she didn't know what her friend was doing.

And she really hoped that she was going to be careful.

You were going to do the same thing. You're a hypocrite.

"Hey," she said, waving.

"Hey," Alaina responded, her eyes sparkling. She was sitting in a lounger at the beach, and it wasn't actually just Travis out there horsing around on the dock at the center of the lake, but a couple of the other ranch hands as well.

"How's it going?"

"Great," Alaina said, smiling. "I'm expecting to make a conquest."

"You seem excited about it."

"I am."

"Just, you know…be careful."

"Yeah. Well, since you're not a virgin, maybe you can give me some pointers."

She tried to rack her brain to think if she could offer anything to her friend. But everything between her and Hunter felt specific and singular, and it didn't feel like it would be valuable as a generic sex pointer.

"Don't let the wet spot freak you out?"

Alaina frowned. "What?"

"It… Nevermind. I—I… Nothing."

"So, now that you're not lying to me—"

"Yeah, that's what I came looking for you for. I'm just really sorry. I was a bad friend. I was a really bad friend. I should've trusted you. And I didn't. But it was honestly because of me. It's because I completely freaked out. I couldn't handle it." *Can you handle it now?*

"That's okay. It's you and Hunter. Honestly, I never saw it coming. I didn't even think you liked him."

"I didn't. I mean, I did. I told you that I did. I—I've always cared about him a lot."

"Are you in love with him?" Elsie asked.

"I'm… No. It's not… I don't want… Nothing has changed. I don't want that kind of relationship. And, anyway, *you* might be okay with it, but there's Wolf and Sawyer to worry about."

"They probably wouldn't care as long as he married you."

"I'm not marrying him," Elsie said, feeling jumpy.

"Why not? You love horses, you love the ranch…"

"But why? You show me a good marriage on this ranch. My brothers aside. And Tag. They don't count."

"Why don't they count? Because it's inconvenient for you?" Alaina was seeming far too wise right now, and Elsie didn't like it. Considering she'd spent all that time being a fool and protecting her from nothing, and now she was being nice and forgiving and actually trying to make her feel better.

"Hey. Maybe this is why I didn't tell you."

Alaina sighed. "Elsie, the thing about life is that you have to take it as it comes. And then you have to make it your bitch. I expected one thing to happen, because you know how I am. Once I decide on something, I want to get it. So I knew eventually I was going to figure out how to get Hunter. That's not what's happening. So what'd I do? I took life as it came. He's cute," she said, pointing to Travis. "And I bet he knows what he's doing. I'm going to get my education one way or another. I'm not going to lose sleep over what could have been, or who could have been. There's plenty of fish in the pond, and all of that."

"You make it sound easy."

"It can be easy. There's no reason to marinate in stuff you couldn't control. You can't help it that your mom left. I can't help that both my parents left. But I don't have to sit around feeling upset about it. I didn't choose it. So why should I take the consequences? I don't have to feel bad about myself. I don't have to sit around feeling bad. Like, this is the problem with Fia. She's mad forever about whatever happened with her and Landry. Why would you do that? Why would you ever sit in pain like that? What good does it do to be mad at other people about things you can't control? Maybe they should have been better, but they're not. So the way I see it, you got a good guy who likes all the same things you do, and you can have a whole life with him."

And it was so tempting, so very tempting. But also terrifying. Just the very thought of it. Letting herself want that. Letting herself believe it was possible. Because she couldn't believe it. She just couldn't. It was impossible to believe that it could ever be real. That it could ever last.

Because what Alaina said was all well and good, but it just wasn't something that Elsie could fathom. Forgetting what other people had done, choosing not to let it hurt you.

"Have a beer," Alaina said. "Hang out."

"Oh, I…"

"Don't be a pick-me girl, Elsie. Just because you have a boyfriend doesn't mean you need to be with him all the time."

"He's not my boyfriend," Elsie said.

"Did you sleep at his house all night?"

"Well, yes."

"Did you have morning sex?"

Elsie squirmed. "You are a virgin."

"Not for long."

"Yes. I had morning sex."

"He is your boyfriend," Alaina said sagely.

"He is *still a secret*."

"Well, how much longer can it last? Either you're going to have to break it off with him, or you're going to have to be honest. Because nobody likes to be lied to, Elsie."

Elsie sat with that, her chest burning. "Fine, I'll have a beer. I will hang out at the lake."

She needed a reprieve. And actually, there was something about a lake day that felt normal. She was being honest with Alaina, who seemed completely happy to have redirected her intent.

Maybe things could just rest a while. Maybe she didn't need to make any decisions. Maybe she and Hunter could be what they were. There was no harm keeping it a secret. For a while longer. It would probably reach a natural conclusion at some point. The thought made her feel desperately sad.

But everything ended. Everything. So it was best to just be prepared. It was best to just accept it. No reason to do anything else. No reason at all.

CHAPTER TWENTY

WHEN ELSIE LEFT, Hunter sat there next to the remains of breakfast for a long time. It had been in the back of his mind what he had to do. But it had only become more and more obvious this morning.

Elsie was so guarded, and he could understand why. And there were so many things that she had never talked to her brothers about, and he could understand why that was too. There were just so many secrets. All bound up in hurt. In fear.

The things that he hadn't told his brothers because he was afraid of their rejection. The questions that Elsie had never asked because they hurt her too badly.

And he couldn't bear their relationship being another one of these secrets. And it was time.

He walked over to the main part of McCloud's Landing, and was about to get into the runaround truck when Gus appeared.

"What are you doing?"

"Going to talk to a man about a horse?"

"That's weird. Because you brought the horses back already."

"That sounded almost like a joke, Gus."

"No. Couldn't be."

"I need to go talk to Sawyer and Wolf." Well, he had to talk to Elsie first. But it would be Sawyer and Wolf after that.

Gus nodded, and he sensed his older brother's approval.

And he realized something too. He didn't ask enough questions. He was too content to let things lie. They all were. Too content to let their pain and trauma sit there. Like a big elephant in the room.

"Gus, what happened to you the night you got your burns?" They'd never talked about this. But Hunter was done with not talking.

Gus looked away. "Dad was drunk one night. I got into it with him. In the barn. I was thirteen or so. So you might remember it, but you wouldn't remember it very clearly. And I don't think anyone ever spoke of it. I told him he was the reason that Mom left. And that I hated him. I took his liquor bottles and I started throwing them on the ground. He pushed me back into a stall and locked me in. And then I realized a bit later that he had set the barn on fire. He meant for me to die, Hunter."

"Gus—"

"No. It doesn't matter. That's why I always protected all of you. Because I knew what he was really capable of. I really knew."

"I'm sorry," he said, and he knew that it was inadequate. Knew that it would never be enough. Not for all his brother had been through. And they had never talked about this. They had gone to Neverland, and eventually Hunter had gone to the Garretts'. Because he hadn't been able to cope with mistakes he felt like he'd made.

But the mistakes were never theirs. They were just children. And all of the secrets that they carried, all of the burdens, had never helped them. They had only protected the adults.

"I'm so sorry, Gus. I'm so sorry that protecting us—"

"Hey, it wasn't like I was just benevolently protecting

you. I was an asshole who wanted a fight, and the bigger asshole just about took me out."

"Shit, I didn't know he really tried to kill you."

"Obviously, he thought better of it, or I'd be dead. I was a kid, Hunt. He would have killed me. But you know, he knew I'd never tell. And I knew I got to walk around reminding him. Just how bad he is."

"Do you think he... Do you think he was ever sorry?"

Gus looked off to the horizon. "No. That's why I made sure he lost everything."

"I love you, Gus, I really do."

"All right." Gus cleared his throat.

"You're the best."

"Hunter," he said, looking grave. "I'm sorry. I'm sorry that I got in your business before. About Elsie. I'm sorry if it seemed like I didn't respect you. Or like I was saying you might not be good enough. That wasn't it."

"You're protective. I get that."

"It's more than that," Gus said. "I... I can't really explain it. But you deserve to be happy. And you should be. So go on. I hope they don't kill you."

"Will you back me up if they try?"

"Hell, no. You banged their sister. If they kill you, I have no choice but to support them."

"Thank you," Hunter said, getting in the truck and heading out toward Garrett's Watch.

He was gratified to see that Wolf and Sawyer were both in the driveway, obviously getting ready to go out and work together. How nice for him that he got to kill two birds with one stone, and entirely possible that the two birds would turn around and kill him.

But first he had to find Elsie.

Where are you?

The lake.

He drove on over to the lake and was surprised to find her there with Alaina and Travis and a couple of other ranch hands.

Immediately, his hackles were up. He just really didn't like Travis.

And he didn't have it in him to be chill anymore. He walked over to Elsie and wrapped his arm around her and kissed her on the cheek. She pulled back and scrubbed at it, looking around.

"We're not subtle, kid," he said.

The guys were staring, and Alaina was open-mouthed. "I need to talk to you," he said to Elsie.

"I thought you just wanted to swim."

"I didn't know you were at the lake when I texted," he pointed out.

She sighed. "Yeah, okay."

He took her hand and led her away from the others. "I want to go talk to Wolf and Sawyer."

"What?" She looked like he'd just said he wanted to start walking on all fours and start life over as a cow.

"I want to tell Sawyer and Wolf about us."

"Why?"

"Elsie, this is stupid. We either go till we get caught, which is going to get our asses handed to us, or we stop. And I don't want to stop."

"I don't want to stop," she said, looking upset.

"Or we tell them. I'm not ashamed of it."

"But…but to what end?"

"To the end that you're not my dirty secret. And I'm not yours."

"Hunter…"

"You know how it was with Alaina. If you could go back and change something…"

She closed her eyes, and he could see her pulse beating hard at the base of her throat. "Yeah. No, you're right. I would tell her. Not telling her was a mistake."

"So I need to talk to them."

"Why do you need to do it? That seems like macho bullshit."

"Yeah," he said, touching her cheek. "It is. You cool with that?"

"I'm not really cool with any of this."

"But you know I'm right."

"Don't push your luck, McCloud."

He kissed her cheek again. "I'll come see you later, okay? You going to be home?"

She shrugged. "Should be."

"Okay. See you then."

He got back in his truck, filled with resolve. And when he got to Garrett's Watch, Sawyer and Wolf were sitting outside the barn. Hunter just hoped there were no weapons nearby.

"We need to have a talk," Hunter said as he got out of his truck.

And two very serious sets of eyes turned on to him.

"Do we?" Sawyer asked.

"Yeah. It's about Elsie."

"It's about Elsie?" Sawyer repeated.

"Yeah," he said. "It is. I… Well, she and I…"

"Hold on," Wolf said, stepping forward. "That sentence better not be about to end the way it sounds like it's going to."

"I care about her," Hunter said.

"Hold up," Sawyer said. "What exactly are you saying?"

And he realized he wasn't saying a whole lot. Or at the very least, he wasn't saying enough.

"Are you sleeping with her?" Wolf asked, suddenly getting menacing. "Because I swear to God…"

"That's not the point. Whether I slept with her or not isn't the point."

"So you did," Sawyer said. "What the hell. I oughtta knock your head off. My sister. My baby sister. My *baby sister* that you used to carry around on the ranch—"

"I'm in love with her." He realized what he had to say, the minute the words came to him. Because it was true. Because it had been true. It had been true this entire damned time. "I love her. And I'm willing to do whatever goes with that. I never thought I would. I never thought… Hell. I've never been in love. And I didn't keep it a secret because I was sneaking around, I did it because she didn't want anyone to know. I did it for her, not to…to take advantage or lie to you."

"You are in love," Sawyer said, his tone flat. "With our sister."

"Yeah," he said, trying to wrap his mind around the enormity of it.

"You," Wolf said. "Are in love, with our sister, who pretty much hates your guts."

"In fairness, she likes me a lot better lately than she used to."

"What the hell happened?" Sawyer asked.

"I don't know," he said. "Because if I could explain it to you, I probably would've stopped it before it got this far. Because do you think I want to be in love with her? No, I don't. I didn't want to be in love with anybody. Because I… Hell. *Hell.* You know. You know my life. You know what I was raised around. I didn't want anything to do with any of it, not any more than the two of you wanted anything to do with being in love."

Wolf and Sawyer looked at each other, and if it wasn't all so damned fucked up, it might've been funny.

"Were you going to hit me or…"

"Yeah," Wolf said. "I was pretty well prepared to hit you a few times."

"Great. Go ahead."

"But you love her," Sawyer said.

"Yeah," Hunter said. "You can still hit me if you want. She's still your little sister. Innocent, and all that."

"Probably not anymore," Wolf said, not making direct eye contact.

"Well," Hunter said. "No."

"And you didn't ask her to hide it," Sawyer said. "She asked you to, and you were just…"

"Respecting her," Hunter said. "I told her that I didn't care who knew. I was happy to let everybody on the ranch know. Hell, I was happy to let them know before I realized I was in love with her."

"*Why* are you in love with Elsie?" Wolf asked.

"Why would I not be?" It wasn't that he didn't have a specific answer. It was just there were too many. It was like looking up at a sky full of stars and trying to pick just a handful. But he did it anyway. "Because she knows exactly what it's like to be left behind, and she made herself stronger for it. Because she isn't afraid to call me out when I need it. Because she's the best horse wrangler in the whole place. Because I can talk to her in a way that I've never talked to anybody before. And she listens. Because she's beautiful. Because there's a thousand more reasons to love her than to not love her. And because… I can't imagine life without her." He nodded. "I've lived life without a lot of people. I don't have a father that's worth anything. And my mother left. I'm fine with that. I could be fine if you guys never spoke to me again. Sorry. I'm not okay without Elsie."

It was all clear. Sharply, beautifully clear.

"Well, hell," Sawyer said, shaking his head. "I—I don't know what to say. You love her."

"I do," he said. "Big surprise to me. Didn't expect it. Gotta say."

"Yeah. Well. You never do," Sawyer said. "You never do."

"He got married and he didn't expect it," Wolf said. "So I wouldn't really listen to him."

"Says the guy who got a woman pregnant."

Wolf shrugged. "Worked out."

"Yeah. Well, I hope that you guys will still be my friends. Since I'm hoping you'll be my brothers-in-law."

Both Wolf and Sawyer looked deeply uncomfortable with the thought. "Well. I guess that's… Yeah. I mean…"

"Not only that," Hunter continued. "It'll be nice to get advice. Because I've a feeling I'm going to need it sometimes. I don't know how to be right for her. I don't really know how to be right for anybody. But I want to be. For her. And you know, she's…difficult." He smiled.

Because she was *his* difficult. And he liked it.

"Yeah, well, don't say we didn't warn you. But if something goes wrong, we're going to kill you," Wolf said.

"Even if it's her fault," Sawyer said.

Hunter nodded slowly. "That seems fair."

"I thought so."

"I have a feeling, though, that she's not in the best place," he said. "It's complicated."

"Look," Sawyer said. "There's a limit to what I want to

know. But I can't imagine how the hell…you and Elsie. I just would never have ever…"

"Whether you believe it or not, it started with good intentions. What I didn't want to see was her getting involved with that Travis asshole without a little oversight. Because that's what she was going to do."

They both recoiled.

"No," Wolf said. "That guy seems like an asshole."

"That's my opinion," Hunter said. "But I'm not going to say that my motivation stayed pure. Obviously."

"Rather have you for a brother-in-law, that's for sure," Wolf grumbled.

"You sure? I'm a McCloud," he said. "Bad blood and all that."

"That was just your dad. He's a bad seed," Sawyer said. "There's a lot of McCloud blood here on this soil, as much as the Garretts and the Sullivans and the Kings. And if it wasn't good blood, nothing would grow. So overall, no matter what's happened, no matter what we've done… I think it kind of evens out."

And he liked that more than he would've thought. Needed it more than he would've imagined.

"Yeah," he said. "Maybe that's true."

"Yes, true," Sawyer said. "Because I'm never wrong."

Wolf shook his head. "Your ego is a problem."

Sawyer shrugged. "Evelyn doesn't mind it. Hey, Hunter. You and Elsie should come to dinner tonight."

"I… Yeah. Sure. We will."

Hunter got into his truck, and as he drove down to her house, the realizations that tumbled over him seemed so clear now.

Of course he loved her. Of course he had.

And when he looked back over the course of his life, he wondered if there had ever been a moment where he hadn't.

But his feelings had just been waiting. Waiting to grow and change along with the two of them.

They'd always been just right for where they were.

Now it was time for more.

And he could only hope that she thought the same way he did.

Because as far as he was concerned, as he drove his truck down the familiar path that would take him to her house, his road had always been leading here.

From the very beginning.

CHAPTER TWENTY-ONE

SHE WAS TERRIFIED that the next time she saw Hunter he would be in a body bag. But no, he wasn't. He was back with a dinner invitation. And Elsie was…

Completely not okay.

Because what was the point? Because it was going to end. Of course it was going to end. Everything ended.

People left. It was what happened.

It was…

She could have lost Alaina with her behavior, and it had been such a stark reminder that relationships were not unconditional. They were very, very conditional. And it was only because Alaina was so changeable that theirs was salvaged. It certainly wasn't because Elsie deserved to have her friend speak to her.

Her sister-in-law set up dinner outside on the deck that overlooked the river below. And it seemed fancy. And that made her even more nervous.

"Hey," Hunter said. "It's just you and me. No worries."

She nodded. "I'm not worried."

They got out of the truck and went toward the deck, and Hunter put his hand low on her back. She flinched slightly. But he didn't move it.

"You be you," he said. "I'm going to be me."

And there wasn't really anything she could say to that. But when they got up to the deck, she did pull away from him slightly. Sawyer and Wolf were looking at them both with flat eyes, and Violet and Evelyn were barely suppressing a grin.

"Thanks for the invite," Hunter said.

"Don't be weird," Elsie said. "You wouldn't normally thank them for the invite. This is weird," she said. "And I don't like the weirdness."

"It's different," Sawyer said, clearly trying to behave.

Her sister-in-law brought out dinner, and Elsie knew that she was being slightly feral. But there was something about it all that was just...

And it wasn't until June toddled out onto the deck and jumped onto Hunter's lap, and he plopped the hat on her head, that it crystallized for her. That her chest seized up with a particular kind of horror.

Because he was making declarations to her family. And declarations ended here.

With babies in family dinners, and marriage. And people left when those things happened. That was her only experience of it. She was the baby that had been born in a barn that had ruined her mother's life so much she'd had to run away from her.

And Hunter was just a kid whose mother had done the same. And what did they know about anything? What did they know about breaking cycles?

She had been certain that her friend would withhold her blessing, and that would be an excuse. She had been certain that her brothers would be furious and she could use them. But all of the barriers were gone, and she was just left with this. With this pain. This fear. This unimaginable sadness that she wasn't the person people stayed with.

And it just pounded in her like a drum. Unending and

horrible. And when dinner was through, she couldn't get away quickly enough.

"Stay and have a drink," Evelyn said.

"No," she said. "I'm tired. Early morning and…" She trailed off and moved quickly out of the house. And Hunter followed behind her.

"What's the matter?"

"It's just… It's weird," she said, loading up into his truck. He began to drive them back to her place. And he would want to stay but she needed to breathe. She had just never felt…anything like this before. She was so…so scared. There was no beast. No monster at the gate. Except she could feel it. In her heart. In her soul.

"I just… It's the whole domesticity thing," she said. "I don't know that I like it. It's not really what we signed on for."

He was silent for a long time. They parked in her driveway, and he turned off the engine. And he still didn't speak. It wasn't because he didn't have anything to say, she could sense that. He was saving it. And that made her nervous.

When they walked into the cabin, he turned to her. And she knew that there was nothing she could do to stop him from what came next.

"Hunter—"

"I want to get married."

CHAPTER TWENTY-TWO

HUNTER HAD KNOWN this was where it would go.

Maybe he always had.

From the moment he'd punched that bar wall.

From the moment he couldn't leave her.

Maybe he'd known even then.

He had spent his whole life trying to ignore the deep things. The heavy things. He had spent a long time telling himself he wasn't a deep thinker. But maybe that was just because the logical conclusion was right there, and always had been. The conclusion he hadn't been ready for.

But he was going to have to get over a whole lot of stuff. Going to have to heal because Elsie Garrett deserved a man who was whole. Because she had been through too much on her own, and she needed to be able to trust that he could go the distance. Because he needed to be able to promise her that he would. Unequivocally. Absolutely certain this was why he had wanted to give her everything. Lush hotel rooms and date nights at nice restaurants. Why he wanted to make love with her in the field. And in this house.

Because it was everything. *Her.* She was everything. She deserved to be spoiled, and she was one with nature. One with him.

He wanted to show her everything that he had to offer.

He wanted to be her world. Her whole damned world.

He knew he could be what she needed. He could be everything for her because this was right. He felt it down to his bones.

"Elsie Garrett," he said. "I love you."

She stepped back, her eyes wide.

"You don't mean that."

"I do. I love you more than anything. Hell. I don't care about anything else. That's the thing. Nothing matters as much as what I feel for you, nothing at all. I love you and that means that's all there is to it. It's all that matters."

"It's not all that matters," she said. "It can't be… Because…"

"Why?"

"Because. I have let…this…*love* turn me into something unrecognizable. And if that's possible…when does it stop, Hunter? I have… I have turned into a person that I don't know. Being okay with betraying my friend. I did it because I wanted you. And that can't come from love. And if it does, then love isn't a good thing. Not for me. I'm sure my mom thought she loved my dad too, but she left, didn't she? She left and she didn't come back. And how close… How close am I to becoming her? And how will I ever know? Because all you have to do is start deciding that the people around you don't mean as much as what you want, and before you know it you're leaving your baby behind, and you never come back and see her and you…"

"Stop that," he said. "That wasn't love. It wasn't love that made her leave."

"No, it was *me*," Elsie said. "So maybe it was all…in me all along, all this…stuff. This… Maybe I'm just not worth it. I claimed that friendship was the most important thing to me. Loyalty. Trust. But what did I actually prove? That I was willing to hide things and lie when it suited me. I was willing to call the pain of the people I care about collateral damage when I wanted something enough. I don't like this person that I've become. I don't like what I've turned into. Because when does it stop, Hunter? When does it stop?"

"Yeah, well, maybe all that doesn't matter," he said. "Because maybe it's all for us. Did you ever think about that? Maybe we're the only ones that matter." The words flowed from him with conviction. As if his chest had been cut open and everything was just pouring out. "Fuck everyone, everyone but us. I love you. And maybe that's all that matters. Maybe it's all that ever mattered. Maybe everything...every hard thing—my dad being an asshole, my mom leaving, your mom leaving, your dad being dead, me spending time with your family, my friendship with Sawyer and Wolf—maybe it all just led here. And maybe there will be collateral damage, but it's worth it."

"We are not the center of the world," Elsie said.

And logically, he understood that that was true.

But in his heart, he felt this with an intensity that defied everything. "I don't care about anything else. Because I thought... Elsie, I thought that I wasn't worth a damn. I thought that I broke my family in deep and profound ways, and I thought that was my only purpose. To break things. My mother was tied to my father because of me. Because I was the youngest. I had to figure out how to help let her go. But I knew that doing that made things harder for my brothers. And I thought that's all I could do. Make it harder. Make it worse. What if I was meant to love you? All along. From the beginning. What if the whole world exists so I can love you?"

"That is insane," Elsie said, her eyes filling with tears. "It is insane, and I don't even know what to say to that."

"Say that you love me. Because the sun shines so that I can love you, and fields are out there full of flowers all so that I can love you. And sometimes things are bad, just so loving you feels better. I'm convinced of that. You are my faith. And you are my hope. And most of all, Elsie Garrett, you are my love." He moved forward and cradled her face in his hands. "Wretched little varmint, you are everything and I love you with all that I am. With all that I have. There will never be anything more important. And I don't care what anyone thinks. I don't care what happens next. As long as you love me."

"I can't," she said. "Because love shouldn't make you a smaller, meaner person who doesn't care about the people around you."

"It won't make you small and mean. Not once you realize you don't have to protect it. That's what you're doing, sweetheart. You are just protecting yourself. You don't have to. Because I'm here to do that. I'm here to protect you. I promise."

"And what about when you aren't, Hunt?"

"I already told you that moment won't come."

"Look how much we've changed. Just in these past weeks."

"But what about all the change that was good? I talked to Gus about his scars. I told you all about mine. I'm ready to talk to my brothers about…all the hard things I've kept inside forever. I became the man I needed to be through you, for you." he said. "This was the path." He needed her to understand. He needed her to. It was so hard, something he had only just come to realize himself. "I need you to understand that this was the path all along. It wasn't a random shift. This is where we were headed the whole time. This is fate, Els. It is. You are my fate."

"I don't believe that, Hunter," she said. "I don't. I don't…"

"I believe in it enough for both of us," he said, grabbing

hold of her and pulling her toward him. "I believe in you. I believe in us. Whatever you want to call it beyond that, I don't care. You're all that matters. Every last bit."

"Well, I can't do this. I…"

He kissed her to show her, to show her how deep he believed. In them. In this. She kissed him back, a sob rising in her throat, one that he captured.

"I love you," he said.

"It's not enough," she said. "It's not enough."

"What do I need to do? I will do it. I will do whatever you need me to. I will give you whatever you need me to give you."

"I need you to leave," she said, tears falling down her face. "I need you to leave. Because I can't… I can't be this. I can't be this person that I don't recognize. This person that I lost control of. I have to… I have to fix myself. And this was just supposed to be…to teach me to flirt. I wanted to have sex. I didn't want forever."

He looked at her, and for the first time he felt like he might be out of hope.

And then a glimmer started again. And it damned near killed him. He remembered Elsie was twenty-four. She might not be ready. It had taken him this long to get to this point on the path, and he thought that sex had brought them there, but that didn't mean it was true. And if loving her meant letting her go for a while, until she was ready to see, then he was going to have to do that. Even if it killed him.

And it would. He would punch a number of walls about her being gone, away with other men. Thinking about all the life she was living. But he had to give it to her. He had to. That was what she needed, to find her way to him, then he would have to give it to her. And he would.

"Whatever you need," he said. "Whatever time you need, it's okay. You can have it."

"Not time…"

"I love you," he said. "I always have. And there's not a limit on that. Time or otherwise. I will always be there for you. I'll wait until you're ready for me."

He turned and walked out of the house, and he felt like he had left his heart behind. Bloody and battered on the floor of her cabin.

And dammit all, as mad as he'd been at that wall in a fistfight with his own emotions over wanting that girl, he was more incredulous now. She wasn't just making him jealous. She had broken him. Little Elsie Garrett had broken him, because what they could be was so clear to him, and she couldn't see it. There was no amount of fortification that could have prepared him. No amount of pain in his past. Nothing was this. Nothing had ever been this.

He got in his truck, and he didn't know where to go.

Go to the Garretts'.

Go to Gus.

He would go to his brothers.

It was time they had a talk anyway.

ELSIE WAS CRUMPLED. Lying on the floor like she had been stabbed in the stomach. She'd spent the whole night in agony.

The truth of the matter was, she'd stabbed herself. She was the one that had caused all this pain. Her own and his. She was the one who was responsible for all this.

She had ruined everything. Everything. She didn't even know where to begin picking up pieces. It was impossible to say.

She had broken their friendship. Broken Hunter. Broken herself.

She'd been so worried about hurting her best friend.

And in the end she had.

But it wasn't Alaina.

It was Hunter.

What would Wolf and Sawyer say when they found out?

They'd just had dinner with them last night and now she…

She pulled into her brother's place just after noon, hoping she might catch him for lunch.

She wasn't disappointed. It just so happened that Evelyn, Violet, Wolf and Sawyer were there.

"Hi," she said. "I came to…talk."

"What did he do?" Evelyn asked, leaning out of her chair, holding her fork.

"Nothing," Elsie said. "It was me." She wondered if she sounded as disembodied as she felt.

"Elsie?" Sawyer asked.

"I'm sorry. I am sorry that everyone got dragged into this. I'm sorry that Hunter is hurt. I can't do this, though. And I didn't want everyone involved. They got involved. And I can't…" She dissolved then. Dissolved into sobs.

And then Wolf and Sawyer were holding on to her, keeping her steady. "Don't," she said. "Don't comfort me. I'm the one that did this. I'm the one that…"

"Hey," Sawyer said. "We all make bad choices when we're running scared."

"True," Wolf agreed.

"I'm not scared," she said. "Just impossible. It's impossible because I messed everything up with Hunter and I'm afraid. I'm afraid that…"

"You're just afraid," Evelyn said. "And who wouldn't be?

With the life you all had. But fear doesn't do anything for you. When there's not a snake in the grass, Elsie, fear isn't helping you. And serving it doesn't offer you anything."

"But what if…"

"Yeah. I asked that question always," Sawyer said. "What if. That's what it's like to love somebody. You have your moments. Your whole days, where you ask yourself what if. Because you get to where you can't imagine your life without them. But you can't fix that fear, you can't fix that wound by removing them from your heart. Because they're already there. Believe me, I tried."

"Same," Wolf said.

"But I thought I was fearless because I hadn't been hurt."

"I was wrong," Evelyn said. "You are just very good at hiding it."

"I want to keep hiding it," Elsie said. "For me and everybody."

"Well, it's too late. We can all see it. But you're still breathing." Violet smiled. "You're not a failure just because you had a moment of faltering courage. Wolf had the same problem."

She looked over at her brother, who was the strongest person she'd ever known, and the most reluctant to show an emotion, and she expected him to dispute that. But he didn't.

"Yes," he said. "I did. Because you know what, this stuff is scary, Elsie. And it's easy to feel like you're in over your head. But you have to remember that when you're with somebody who really loves you, they'll be there to help you out when you fall in. They will bring your head back up above water. Because that's what love is."

"What if I fail?" Elsie said. "What if I fail. That's the

thing that I can't stand. I don't know my mother. Not at all. What if I'm like her. And how would I ever know?"

"I would hope," Sawyer said, "that you would be a lot more like us. We are not perfect, not by a long shot, but we are the ones that stayed. We are the ones that raised you. Look at us. Staying."

"It's just…"

"Are you really afraid of that? Are you afraid of the things you can't control?"

She didn't know what to say to that. Instead, she didn't say anything, and she sadly ate lunch, and then half of a pie.

"What if…what if I'm just not enough," she whispered finally. "My mom left me. When I was a baby."

It was Sawyer who knelt down beside her. "My mom left me too. And look. Look what I have now."

"How do you know you're good enough?"

"If Hunter is half the man I think he is, then what I want you to do is look at his face. Look at how he sees you. Look at how he loves you. If you can see yourself the way he does, then you'll know. When Evelyn looks at me," he said, his voice rough, "that's when I know."

Elsie remembered Hunter's face.

And suddenly it was like seeing clearly for the very first time.

And she knew.

CHAPTER TWENTY-THREE

HUNTER LOOKED AT his brothers. He had never told them any of this. And it was something that he wasn't looking forward to. But it explained a lot. And it was time. He didn't want to hang on to any of this bullshit anymore.

"I told Mom to leave."

"What the hell are you talking about?" Gus asked.

"I told her to leave."

Tag, Brody and Lachlan all regarded him from around the table. "You were eleven years old," Tag said.

"Yeah," he said. "I was."

"You can't possibly blame yourself for an adult deciding to leave because an eleven-year-old told her to," Brody said.

"I did. For a long time. But you know, I told Elsie Garrett about it, and hearing her repeat it back to me… It made me realize how stupid it was. But I distanced myself from all of you for a long time because of it. Because I felt responsible for it. Because I felt responsible for how things went with Dad after. And Gus…"

Gus's face turned to stone. Hard, and just as rough. "What happened between me and Dad is between me and Dad. Both what happened here," he said, gesturing to his face, "and what happened when he left."

"I felt like I didn't deserve to be one of you. I felt like I did something to betray you. To betray us and—"

"You knucklehead," Gus said. "You never betrayed us.

Our family was messed up. It is messed up. The only thing that ever mattered to me was that I could protect you."

"You did that," Brody said, "and then some. And it isn't fair that you had to."

"That's what older brothers are for," Gus said. "We protect people."

"What's all this about you talking to Elsie Garrett about us."

And that was when he knew he had to tell them. And he had a captive audience for that. A skeptical and captive audience.

And by the time he was done, they were all silent.

"Well, shit," Brody said. "I never thought you would fall in love."

"Two down," Tag said, looking a little triumphant.

"Hey, I am not resolved," he said. "Don't go celebrating yet."

"She'll come around," Tag said.

"What if she doesn't?"

"She will."

"True love and all that," Lachlan said.

Gus laughed. "True love. No such thing. You can choose to make something work, or not."

"And you would know that how, Angus?"

"I told you. I'm the oldest."

"Wish you'd get yourself a wife so that you could get this place cleaned." The smart-ass remark came from Lachlan.

"If the right one comes along. Maybe I will."

Nothing about love. Nothing quite so sappy for Angus McCloud.

And his brothers didn't hug or cry, but things felt better with them. He didn't feel quite so separate. And that had been the point of the whole thing.

By the time he got in his car to go, he'd had a beer too many, but it was a quick jaunt to his cabin. When he got there, a familiar truck was parked in the lot, and his heart went up to his throat. And he didn't even care. Not anymore. That his emotions were…well, that they existed. Because he loved this ridiculous woman. She was standing barefoot in the dirt in his driveway in what was practically an evening gown.

"Dammit, Elsie," he said when he got out.

"I'm so sorry," she said, and she burst into tears.

"Don't you apologize to me," he said, moving in and pulling her in for a hug. Just a hug. "Elsie, baby. You don't need to apologize to me."

"Yes, I do," she said. "Yes, I do. Because I ruined everything. I made a mess out of it. I made a mess out of us."

"No, you didn't. It just took you a little while longer to get to this place on the road."

"How did you know?" she asked. "How did you know this whole time?

"I didn't. Because it snuck up on me. Soft at first, and when it hit it was like a freight train. But I love you, Elsie."

She looked up at him, and the wonder in her expression took his breath away. "You really love me."

"Yes."

"You see me…you know I'm a baby who was born in a barn, whose mother left her, whose father didn't love her, and you love me like *that*."

"Only if you can love me. I'm the son of a violent, horrible man, Elsie. The son of a mother who didn't stay. But I know who I am when I stand here with you. You're my reason. My forever. My fate."

His chest felt like it was cracked open, and that was all right with him. All right because if he bled, it was for her.

And that was a purpose that he could embrace. This all-consuming love. This wonderful, bright, brilliant, sharp, life-changing love.

"You're mine," she said. "You were right. It was all worth it to be standing here."

"I'll love you forever. And I want you to marry me."

"I want to do that. I don't know how to do it. I don't know how to be married. I don't know how to be in love. I just know that I am."

"I know you are," he said. "Because this was us. From the beginning. It was always going to be yes."

They walked hand in hand from the driveway and on down to the river. Right by his favorite fishing spot. And while they walked, they talked.

"You act like you've always known."

"Maybe I did. And maybe you did too. Maybe there's some fate to it. The person that's with you from the beginning." He brushed his thumb over her cheekbone. "The one that's always there to protect you."

"Like you protected me?"

"And like you protected me." He kissed her lips. "Remember when you put those bandages on me? When you were just a little girl. Because my father had finished beating the hell out of me?"

"Yes." She blinked. "I do."

"Elsie," he said, "I really do think you have a cute ass."

And she laughed, then balled her fist up and hit him on the shoulder. "I thought we were being romantic!"

Then he grabbed her around the waist, and heaved them both into the river.

When they came up, they were sputtering.

Well, Elsie was howling.

"Don't you know, you vile little polecat," he said, pressing his forehead to hers. "This is romance for us."

And while she laughed, she kissed him. With cold, wet lips that he loved more than anything.

"Hunter," she whispered. "I love you."

He pushed her wet hair back from her face, and in that moment, he felt everything. "I love you too. And I will never leave."

Elsie smiled. And it was like the sun had come out from behind the clouds after thirty-two long years of rain. "I believe you."

EPILOGUE

ELSIE GARRETT HAD literally been born in a barn, but she cleaned up pretty nice if she said so herself.

She was a much prettier bride than she had ever anticipated being. Actually, being a bride was something she had never anticipated. And she was thrilled to be surrounded by her friends as she married the man of her dreams.

Even if she hadn't known he was the man of her dreams.

Particularly precious was the presence of her best friend, Alaina, who was ready to stand with her as her bridesmaid.

Alaina might have had a long road to her own happiness, but the wedding ring that sparkled on her finger now was almost as bright as the smile on her face.

"This is nothing like we imagined, is it?" Alaina asked.

"No," Elsie agreed, looking ahead at Hunter. "It's better."

And she lifted up the front of her dress and began to walk toward the lake, began to walk toward Hunter.

She looked at all the people who were gathered there by the lake. Their cousins. Eli, Connor and Kate, their spouses and their children. All there on Garrett land together.

Then Sawyer and Wolf each took an arm. "We're ready to give you away," they said.

"I hate to break it to you," she whispered, "but I gave myself to him a while ago."

"Thanks for that," Sawyer said.

"Consider it practice for both of you. For your daughters."

And she looked at her brothers and smiled.

Because here they were, the Garrets. All happily married. And it turned out, there was no curse, after all. Not when you traded out fear for love.

In the end, love was stronger.

If only you would let it be.

And she knew they all intended to. From now on to forever.

* * * * *

HER WAYWARD COWBOY

CHAPTER ONE

Thirteen Years Ago...

Arizona King loved a man she could never have.

For one, he was twenty-nine years old, and she was eighteen. For another, he was in love with another woman.

She hated that woman.

That woman back in Texas who had his heart.

That woman he was pining over even as he worked on her daddy's ranch in Pyrite Falls, Oregon, the middle of dadgum nowhere.

She'd never felt anything like this before, not even when Billy Maddigan told her he thought she was pretty in fourth grade. And Billy had been quite a catch around Four Corners Ranch.

Not that the pickings were overly abundant at the ranch.

At least not outside the four main families and ew, gross. No.

Women liked her brothers, and she never wanted to hear a blasted thing about that. The Garretts and McClouds were like family as well, and she couldn't imagine ever entertaining a naughty thought about any of them.

But Micah...

He made her heart hurt.

He had eyes that were blue like the sky and hair as dark as the earth. Or maybe as dark as her favorite cow.

That might not be super romantic, but cows were often a reference point for Arizona, as Four Corners, and specifically King's Crest, her family's portion of the broader operation, had a hell of a lot of cows.

But today she wasn't going to think about that woman, Lacey, who had broken up with him before his move out to Oregon, and who had left him—in his words—pretty messed up. Today, she was focusing on the fact that they were out riding the range together and it was a beautiful, glorious day out on the ranch. And he was even more beautiful than the day itself.

She felt free out here. And it was good to get away from the house for a while. Good to get away from their parents, all the associated drama in the King household.

This was what she loved.

A beautiful view, a great horse. And a beautiful man.

She knew that she was pretty. She also knew that he seemed unaffected by that.

Though, he did seem to like spending time with her.

"You're doing a great job," she said. She tossed her hair over her shoulder and gave him what she knew to be a pretty flirtatious smile.

"I'm hardly a greenhorn, Arizona. Though I appreciate your approval of my skills."

"Well, you knew the terrain out here. It's a little bit different."

She was given to understand that the terrain he was used to traversing out in Texas was much flatter compared to the mountainous rugged spaces in Oregon.

"I got the hang of it pretty quick."

Such a man. Couldn't take a compliment if it meant having to admit he hadn't known everything from day one.

He circled his horse around so that he was facing her,

and her heart jumped up in her throat. She was used to cowboys. She was around them all the time. But the thing was… She loved cowboys. Everything about them. The way they wore their hats, the way they wore their jeans, the way those jeans fit their asses and thighs.

She liked their cocky swagger, she liked every damn thing about a cowboy. Most of all this one. He had a square jaw with dark stubble across it, and piercing blue eyes that made her feel like she might be transforming into one of the flighty, feminine Sullivan sisters from the ranch next door. They meandered around talking about Jane Austen and shit like that. Arizona wasn't a romantic.

He made her feel like one.

Which was a real shame.

You couldn't be a romantic and be a King. There was no way. There wasn't a single ounce of romance in her blood, just like there wasn't a single ounce of it in her home.

He made her wish that maybe…

Well, he made her wish all kinds of things.

"I'll race you to the edge of the pasture," she said, spurring the horse on and giving herself a head start. He let out a whoop and went on after her. And she laughed, exhilarated, her hair flying in the wind. And when she reached the edge, she hollered in triumph, but then he was right there. Right there, on the back of his horse.

She grinned at him, and he reached out and wrapped his hand around her arm. His hands were rough. From all the work that he did, and it was so easy for her to imagine them trailing over her bare skin. They looked at each other for a long moment, and she thought her heart was going to gallop straight out of her mouth. Then he dropped his hold on her and jerked away quickly.

"Better get back to work," he said.

"I suppose so," she said, sounding breathless, and it wasn't from the physical exertion.

She'd seen it, though. Right in that moment. He had looked at her and there had been...heat. And she knew she was a little bit too young for him, and she knew that he still had all those feelings for Lacey. But he had feelings for her too. In spite of it all. When she went to bed that night, she dreamed of him.

She *loved* him.

So fiercely. All these months of their friendship building like had bloomed into something more. He made her feel things that she'd never felt before. He made her want things she'd never wanted before. And it wasn't about sex—well, not strictly. Though that was definitely a part of it.

He made her feel like maybe, just maybe, she could find a way through that outer shell that surrounded her heart and find a way to care for someone. Really care for them.

She saw him everywhere. All around the ranch, and in her dreams. Sometimes she worried she was the one putting herself in his path. But then she noticed he did it just as much.

Like one warm August night when she was out at the lake.

The moon was bright, and she was on the swing that hung over the water. She loved to come out on nights like this. It was her favorite.

"Arizona."

It was his voice. She knew him. They had spent hours talking. And she had told him so many things about herself. He made her feel emotions that she never had before. Emotions her father had always discouraged.

He made her want to open herself up. Be raw. Be honest. He made her want to be different than she was.

"What are you doing out here?"

"Came to find you."

He walked over to her and took her hand, and she couldn't breathe. She was still up on the swing, watching the moon glitter over the surface of the lake. And then he slowly lifted her down from the swing, like she weighed nothing. And she was so close to him that she could hardly breathe. She put her hand flat on his chest, stretched up on her toes. And then he brought his head down to meet her. He kissed her.

Her first kiss.

"Yes," she whispered, fisting his shirt in her hand.

"Careful," he said, stepping back.

"What?"

"I can't… We can't…"

"Why not?"

"I'm twelve years older than you," he said.

"I know that. I don't care." Then she stopped and looked at him seriously. "What about Lacey? *That* I care about."

"I don't love Lacey. That was… It was something to talk about, but it wasn't love."

"Well, then, nothing is stopping us."

"I don't want to hurt you. And I'm not… I've never had a serious relationship and I just feel like…"

"Well, neither have I. We're actually on the same ground."

"You are incredible." He kissed her again. "And… Maybe let's just see how things go. Slowly."

"Okay."

They sat at the edge of the lake for the rest of the night, talking. About how his mom drank too much, and his dad had run away when he was a kid. How he didn't even remember him.

"That's not the kind of dad I would be."

"You want kids?"

She hadn't thought about kids one way or the other, because she was too young to think about things like that. But she would have his. If they could just have this, forever, she would be the happiest ever.

She couldn't talk to anybody in her house. There was Penny, but she was a kid. And her brothers were impossible. And her dad... Well, he actively discouraged any kind of talking about feelings or anything.

This generation is self-obsessed and soft, he was fond of saying.

If you didn't talk about your problems, maybe you wouldn't have so many.

"I don't know," he said. "I've got a lot of anger. I don't know that I'd be the best dad."

"Well. You *know* that you have the anger, though. A lot of people don't know that about themselves. So I actually think you would be a pretty good dad."

And she felt like she could fly. They were talking. And kissing. And there was maybe a future.

When she woke up early the next morning, she was eager to meet him.

She put her boots on, and left her hair so that it was a little bit bigger, then ran downstairs. Just in time to see his old pickup truck zooming by the main house. And he had a trailer attached to it. That same trailer he had brought out from Texas. Like he was...

Like he was...

And she took off running. After the truck. Like a fool. Ran in the cloud of dust behind it, and even though there was a big-ass trailer covering up his back window, she knew that he had to see her. She knew that he did.

"Micah!"

She called after him, like a fool. Tears streaming down her face.

But he never stopped. He never looked back.

And that was when Arizona King learned that she wasn't half as tough as she'd once believed.

Because the man who had given her her first kiss had broken her heart clean in two. And she didn't think that she would ever be the same again.

CHAPTER TWO

Thirteen Years Later...

"THERE'S A PICKUP truck out on the road."

Arizona King pushed her hat back from her eyes and looked up from the table she was sitting at out in the front yard of the King family home. She and her brother Landry were playing a game of poker to pass the time.

"Are you expecting anyone?"

"No."

It was a blue truck. An old beater. It looked... It looked strangely familiar, and for a moment she was lost. Back in a moment thirteen years ago that made her skin crawl to remember.

"But any number of us could be expecting someone," she said.

"Why would Denver or Daughtry or Justice be expecting someone?"

"Could be Penny. Maybe she got herself a new truck."

He snorted. "Likely not."

But as the truck got closer, she could see that the license plate was different.

It was a Texas plate.

And then she really did think she might pass out.

There was no way she'd ever live that down, so she had

to do her best to stay upright and conscious or Landry would torment her over it for the rest of her life.

Just like if he ever knew that thirteen years ago she had chased Micah Stone's blue beater truck down the road running as fast in cowboy boots as she possibly could, screaming and crying like she was dying, he would mock her until the end of days, because that was the only way the King family knew how to interact with each other.

All these other families all around them, so nice, borderline functional in spite of the way that their parents were. The Kings were not like them. They were close, but in that way soldiers tended to be. They'd survived a whole lot of shit, and they'd banded together for better or for worse. They weren't necessarily sweet to each other. In fact, you would be hard-pressed to find people less sympathetic to each other's trauma than the ones who shared that same trauma.

"Texas," Landy said, questioning.

"I don't have any idea who that could be," she said, and her voice sounded a little bit too loud.

He looked at her, one dark brow raised.

"Really?"

"I don't know any Texans," she said, testing him, daring him, because why would he remember one ranch hand who had passed through the area thirteen years ago? They had any number of ranch hands.

The truck pulled up to the house, and she could see a tall, rangy figure behind the steering wheel, big cowboy hat on his head.

And she knew a moment of total deflation, because that was not Micah.

Did you really think it was?

The truck opened, and said rangy figure, who looked

like a teenager, stepped out. And she couldn't deny that he looked… Well, it might not be Micah, but he looked like him. Enough to be…

Well, enough to be his son.

"Howdy," he said. "I'm Daniel Stone. I was here to see if you might be hiring."

CHAPTER THREE

MICAH HADN'T CURSED so many times in a single sentence since… Well, last Saturday. At least. He didn't claim to be a saint. But Daniel was gone, he was fucking gone, and his ex-fucking-wife hadn't noticed. Just hadn't noticed for days. And that was why the hell he didn't like Daniel going to Dallas to visit that woman.

Because she didn't pay attention to him.

And every damned time he went there was some kind of trauma for Micah to undo.

Daniel should've stayed out on the ranch with Micah. Maybe they would've butted heads about it, but they always got over it. It was Lacey that always did something to fuck everything up. And this was just one example of that.

"How many days has it been, Lacey?" he asked, about to lose his patience completely.

"I was gone for a couple of days, darlin', so I don't know."

"Our *son* was in Dallas to visit *you* and *you* left for *a couple of days*," he said.

"He's practically a man, Micah, settle down."

"He's thirteen years old," Micah said. "And he might be six feet tall, but he's still a kid. He doesn't weigh a buck ten soaking wet."

"He probably doesn't want us interfering right now. I

mean, what kind of shenanigans were you up to at thirteen?"

"It doesn't bear thinking about. I don't want him up to those same shenanigans. And neither should you."

"I'm not like you. I don't worry about every little thing."

No. The problem was, Lacey didn't worry about a damn thing but herself. And that was their central problem. Always had been.

She'd been a sweet girl back when they were young. The problem was, she'd stayed that same girl. She'd just never grown up.

They'd dated in high school and split up for years, then met up again when they were twenty-nine and had given it a try for nostalgia.

But she'd been the Lacey she'd been in high school, and that hadn't worked. Because he didn't want drama and screaming fights, and she seemed fueled by it.

They'd ended it and he'd gone out to Oregon, looking for something new.

Then she'd called him out of the blue to let him know that she was eight months pregnant and it was his baby.

He wasn't an idiot.

He'd gotten a DNA test.

Daniel was his kid. And even if there had ever been any doubt when he was a baby, there couldn't have been any doubt thereafter.

He was the spitting image of Micah, down to getting all of his height and none of his muscle by age thirteen. Also, none of the brains either.

Micah was well familiar. And also with the dangers of looking a little too old and having no smarts to back it up. It scared the hell out of him. Because he knew exactly what kind of trouble his kid could be getting into, because he'd gotten in all that trouble. But the point of actually being a good dad was to try to spare him from that.

Micah hadn't had primary custody of Daniel since he was five. His and Lacey's marriage hadn't lasted long. Micah got Daniel in the summer, and the kid always thrived. Then he went back home to Lacey and things degraded. And this time...well, *this* time they'd clearly degraded in a uniquely awful way.

"He was looking at some old pictures on his phone," she said. "Talking on and on about some ranch you were at forever ago."

Four Corners.

He knew. He'd talked to Daniel about it a bunch of times. Four Corners was where he'd been when he'd found out Lacey was pregnant, and he'd had to leave and...

For some reason, a vision of Arizona King flashed through his head. Arizona King as she'd been then, of course.

She'd been so pretty.

He'd felt like a dick every time he'd looked at her and thought so. She'd been far too young, and she'd been enamored with him. It had felt good, even if it shouldn't have. She was beautiful and it was nice to have someone look at him like he was a hero. He just hadn't counted on feeling anything for her in return. But she was sharp and funny along with her beauty, and he'd found himself developing something of a crush on her. He'd kissed her. And it had lit his whole world on fire and...

And that had nothing to do with this.

Four Corners.

Daniel had been talking about Four Corners.

"Oh right, I forgot to tell you," Lacey said, her tone telling him she hadn't forgot, she just didn't care enough to be detail oriented. "The old beater truck is gone."

"The what?"

"That truck that I took when I left you. It's been parked in the driveway this whole time. The guys use it whenever they need to."

The guys he assumed were the men that she brought home on occasion.

"That thing still works?"

"Yes."

"You're telling me that our thirteen-year-old son stole my old truck, a truck that is twenty years old, and is possibly driving across the country."

"Sounds as possible as anything else."

"Fucking hell."

There was no other option.

For the first time in thirteen years, he was headed to Oregon.

And when he thought of Oregon the only thing he could picture...

Was her.

CHAPTER FOUR

ARIZONA LOOKED CLOSELY at the kid standing in front of her. He was tall and had a mature look about him, but he favored his father, which meant he wasn't anywhere near as old as he looked.

Unless Micah was a bigger liar than you realized.

Yeah. That was a possibility. Because when it came right down to it, she had fancied herself in love with the man, but what the hell had she actually known about him? Nothing. Not a damned bit of anything. She had believed all the stories that he'd told her, but she'd been eighteen. And an idiot. So what the hell did she think she knew now?

"How did you hear about the ranch?" Landry asked.

Because of course Landry didn't instantly recognize the son of a ranch hand who had been here for just a few months thirteen years ago. Because of course Micah Stone hadn't been a formative human being in the life of her older brother. Of course not.

"Oh, I just saw something about it. Online. Biggest ranch in the state of Oregon," the kid drawled, straightening up so that he looked taller.

"Bullshit," Arizona said. "You heard about it from your daddy, didn't you?"

She wasn't a nice person. The years had hardened her and twisted her. And if it hadn't been Micah leaving, it had been what happened after. The accident and then her father's unwavering lack of sympathy. His demand that she get up, pull herself up by her bootstraps, heal miraculously, or lose her spot at the ranch.

She was tempted sometimes to go spit on his grave. He wasn't buried in it yet, seeing as he was alive and all. But still. Spitting on his grave seemed like a decent enough idea.

"I'm eighteen." He tilted his chin up.

"Try again," Arizona said.

"Seventeen."

"Boy, you are a bad liar."

He shrugged. "I just look young for my age."

She had a feeling he wasn't any such thing. She had a feeling he looked older. And while there was a chance Micah had come out here with a kid waiting back home in Texas, there was also a chance…

"You're thirteen if you're a day. Your dad did not have a child when he was out here."

"How do you know? You don't look any older than I do."

And suddenly, she felt a little bit warm toward the man-child.

"Well, I am. Does your dad know where you are?"

The kid lifted his chin in defiance. "I don't answer to anybody. I drove myself all the way out here in that truck, I decided to make the trip. My mom doesn't give a shit where I am."

Well. That was interesting.

"She may not give a shit where you are, but I need to make sure that you don't have a warrant out for you or anything like that."

"No warrant," he said. "I just borrowed the truck, is all. But she doesn't drive it. It was my dad's."

And suddenly… Suddenly a cold chill swept over her.

"Wait just a minute. It was your dad's?"

What if he was dead? What if Micah Stone was dead. What if all the dark, fervent, angry wishing that she had done late at night had actually landed the man *in his grave*.

She didn't want that. She realized that right then.

She desperately didn't want it.

"Yeah, he lives in the country, and I live in the city with my mom. I usually spend summers with him…"

"So he's not dead," Arizona said.

"No. My dad's not dead."

"But you're about to be."

The masculine voice startled then both, and that was when she saw a tall, broad cowboy walk out from behind the truck.

She didn't see another vehicle, and she had no idea where he'd come from.

But she would know him anywhere.

Micah Stone.

Because there could never be another man that looked like that. There could never be another man who reached down into the frozen, prickly heart of her and made her feel. There never had been, there never could be.

The kid looked guilty and like a rabbit caught in a trap all at once.

"Damn, Dad," he said. "What the hell are you doing here?"

"I knew exactly where you'd gone, you little varmint. I talked to your mother…"

"I'm surprised she even noticed I was gone."

And she could see Micah steel himself against that comment. It was so strange. To see the years on his face, because in her mind he was forever the man he'd been back then.

The man who'd abandoned her. No matter how much

she'd wanted to, she could never make him into half the disfigured enemy she wanted.

No. He was as beautiful now as he'd been then. The nerve of him. The honest-to-God nerve. Why couldn't he be ugly?

Because what had happened to her after...

What had happened to her after had stopped her. Had compromised everything.

She would never have waited for him. She would've gone on and slept with every man that caught her fancy. Would've left this ranch. Would have...

If not for that accident. That accident that he'd caused. The one that her father had held over her head.

The one that had destroyed so much of her youthful beauty.

Micah had never even seen her naked. That was the thing that really pissed her off. Maybe that was silly. Maybe that wasn't fair. But it was how she felt. Her body had been wasted on her anguish for him.

Sacrificed on an altar she'd been too foolish to realize she was flinging herself onto.

Driving too fast while tears streamed down her face.

She'd been eighteen. And she'd wanted nothing more than to take it all back forever. But there was something she couldn't take back.

And when you were essentially a walking Tim Burton movie underneath your clothes...

She gritted her teeth and looked up at him. No. Not a scar. Just glorious weathering from the storms of life, and dammit all. Back when she'd been young he'd been attractive to her. And now... Well, he was the man she needed.

Why was that? Why was her sexuality so firmly Micah Stone? Maybe it was because that accident had frozen her in time. She'd often thought that. That it had taken all the pain that he'd left inside of her and turned it into an obsidian ball that just sat there, immovable. Time didn't erode it, or degrade it. Time didn't change it. And nothing could fix it. No matter how much she wanted it to.

Maybe this was lucky.

Very few people got the chance to stare their demons down, she realized.

Arizona had spent the last thirteen years being a bitch to basically everyone in her immediate proximity, using them as a surrogate for him.

Now she could just be a bitch to him.

"What the hell were you thinking?" Micah asked his son.

"I wanted to get away from Texas. I'm sick of it. I'm sick of Mom. I wanted to find what you said was out here."

"You can come work at my ranch," Micah said. "You've never shown the slightest bit of interest in it."

"This is different. This place is different. You said that… You said this was the prettiest place you'd ever seen. That it made your soul come alive."

And Arizona turned her own off. She didn't want to hear this. Didn't want to listen to it, and the last thing she wanted to do was to be standing in front of him.

Unprepared.

That was the dream, right? To face down the one that got away, while you were looking better than you ever had. But she couldn't do that. Because she didn't look better than she ever had.

She supposed her saving grace was her face. Her face had been protected by that airbag. But the rest of the twisted metal had done things to her body that…

"You think you want to work here?" Micah asked.

"Yeah."

Micah turned, but he didn't address her, he addressed Landry. "You got work for him?"

"How many child labor laws would I be violating?" Landry asked.

"A few," Micah returned.

"You're not seriously going to let your kid stay in Oregon, and live away from you?" She had thought him to be a pretty callous dick, but that would take the cake.

"Oh hell no," he said. "I'll stay here. Work alongside him. While I prove to him that this is harder than he thinks. And he's gone and made a romance out of something that's just sweat and tears."

Well, that sounded familiar.

"You expect us to train him just to let him go?" Landry asked.

"*I'll* train him," Micah said. "I've worked here before. I run my own place now."

"No skin off my nose," Landry said. "And we can use a little extra help right now anyway. I'm only paying for one of you, though."

"Works for me," Micah said. "Let's see if you can last thirty days, kid," Micah said to his son.

"I can last. What do I get if I win?"

"You can stay out here forever if you want."

"Yeah. I'll do that. Get away from you and Mom, have my own life."

"Sure. If you can hack it after thirty days, you're welcome to this life."

Just like that, Arizona was staring down a thirty-day prison sentence with no way to get out of it.

CHAPTER FIVE

LANDRY SHOWED THEM to their quarters. There was a row of houses nestled in trees at the edge of King's Crest. He remembered it well, because it was right in the same neck of the woods he stayed when he worked here the first time.

It wasn't the only thing he remembered well.

There was Arizona.

And time had only made a more beautiful woman out of her than she'd been at eighteen.

She'd been pretty enough to knock his socks off then, to make him feel guilty about thoughts he had toward her. Made him feel bad that he'd encouraged any kind of relationship with her, even though it was *mostly* just friendship. But damn… She still did things to him.

That was a hell of a thing.

His ex-wife didn't do anything for him anymore at all. Of course, her personality had soured that.

But he didn't have time to go thinking about Arizona right now. He had to deal with Daniel.

He rounded on the kid as soon as they were in the cabin.

"What the hell were you thinking?"

"I was thinking I was going to prove to you that I'm a man," he said.

"I didn't do anything to you, kid, where is this coming from?"

"You didn't do anything to me, maybe, but you left me

to rot out there in the city with Mom. I'm sick of it. Sick of all her boyfriends."

"I didn't leave you to rot, you little asshole, it's called a custody agreement. It's not my fault that the judge gave most of the time to your mom."

"Well, how the hell did you make it so that she's going to let you stay out here for thirty days with me?"

"I told her flat out if I was going after you, what happened when I found you was up to me. Given she's liable to get charged with neglect for how she handled it, she was agreeable."

"How did you sneak up on me this morning, anyway?"

"I flew and I had a car drop me off at the edge of the driveway. Apparently they even have rideshare services out here. But anyway, she agreed to let me deal with you as I saw fit if I came out here. I'll let her know we are staying for the month."

"She doesn't care about me," Daniel said. "Not at all. She just likes to use me to hurt you."

Micah stopped, his heart freezing in his chest. "I don't think that's true," he said. "Your mother might be a difficult woman, and she might show love in some different ways, but I do believe that she does love you. I do. I don't think that she…"

"She doesn't know what love is. That's why she keeps hooking up with these idiots all the time. She doesn't know that what she had with you was good."

Micah appreciated his kid being on his team, but the fact of the matter was, Daniel couldn't possibly remember how he and Lacey had been together.

"I thought you wanted to start a new life away from me too," he said.

"No, just away from… It isn't you, Dad. It's Texas. It's anywhere near Mom."

"I'm sorry," Micah said. "Of all the things I'm sorry about, that we couldn't give you a home with the two of us is the biggest one."

"Do you know that woman?" Daniel asked. Changing the subject. Because they both tended to be allergic to sincerity.

"Why?"

"I don't know, just wondering if she was here when you were here."

"Yeah. I know her."

"Man, she's hot. She's got huge…"

"I will kick your ass," Micah said. "You don't talk about women like that."

"I'm not being rude about it," he muttered. "Or saying anything that isn't true."

"We don't talk about a woman's big… You don't. Trust that every man in the vicinity that isn't a blood relation noticed without needing it pointed out, and just leave it at that."

"Oh," he said. And he seemed to be processing the fact that based on what Micah had just said, Micah had noticed.

Of course he had. He'd been inappropriately noticing Arizona King's rack for way longer than he should've been. And he'd noticed it today, in the company of his son, who was being a horny little asshole.

"I actually think maybe your life in Texas isn't as bad as you think it is. And you're about to find all that out working your knuckles to the bone on this ranch. You might be begging to go back to city life."

"I am never going to be begging to go back to playing New Uncle Roulette. Where the big question of the day is which dude with a hairy back is going to be standing in the kitchen looking for beer at 9:00 a.m."

Micah winced.

"All right, look, kid," he said. "We're going to work all this out. I swear. We're going to figure out how to come to terms with all this. How to make a better life. We got thirty days to build it, and I think we're going to be able to. Maybe we get back…"

"This place is pretty cool," he said, interrupting Micah.

"Yeah," he said, looking around, "it's not bad."

Rustic, and barely more than four walls with a toilet. But it wasn't anything he hadn't lived in before.

The thing was… The thing was, he thought he'd gotten away from this. And here he was, back in the middle of a complicated time in his life that he'd thought he'd never have to revisit. He'd made a successful life for himself, and his personal life had dissolved.

Maybe getting back to this place wasn't the worst thing.

It was the truth, he'd always said it was the most beautiful place on earth. He'd always said it was one of the best times of his life.

But he'd never intended to revisit it. Because if he'd learned anything, it was that you could never go home again. You just had to move forward.

And judging by the look on Arizona's face when she'd seen him today, he was right about that.

Anyway, he had no idea what the years had done to Arizona King.

He just knew that they'd done a hell of a number on him.

He'd missed her. All these years. He'd wondered what might have been, and even as he did he'd tried to tell himself that was pie-in-the-sky stuff. That men loved a what-if. A romance that had never really happened. A big fish story.

She was the one that got away.

But now suddenly he wondered if she was more.

If she was fate.

No. He wasn't twenty-nine anymore. He didn't have that kind of faith left in him.

"So this is a bunkhouse," he said, gesturing grandly around the space, as a plan began to form. "Workdays start early on a ranch, buddy. If you expect to make it thirty days? It's time to get tough."

CHAPTER SIX

When Arizona woke up the next morning his name was the first word that popped into her mind.

He was here.

He was back.

Micah Stone.

The thought made her chest constrict, made her heart thunder yet more rapidly. She felt silly. She felt eighteen. And she hated to think of that girl she'd been at eighteen. All smooth soft skin and brilliant dreams.

She didn't have any of that anymore.

She scrubbed an arm over her face and continued to lie there. But it was nearly sunrise, and she didn't have time for that nonsense.

She got up, and her brothers were already in the kitchen, standing around over pots of coffee—they had more than one coffee maker, there were too many people in the house for them to mess around with making not quite enough coffee every day.

Penny was there too. Penelope, their honorary sister, who had come to live with them back when she was in high school, after she'd lost her dad.

As if the King family was soft, gentle, or the right kind of people to be caring to somebody who had been through difficult times. They weren't.

But they had done their best. And it had something to do with what her dad had felt he owed Penny's dad.

Arizona had never been exactly clear on it. But then their dad had never made it his business to be clear.

He was not that sort of man. The sort of man who prized the affection of his children. He wanted their fear and their respect. He didn't necessarily wish to be known by them. Denver, Landry, Daughtry and Justice were seated around the table, Penny was tucked into the back corner, her blond hair tied in a bun, wisps of pale white falling into her face.

And when Arizona walked in, they all looked up and stared at her.

"What?" she asked.

"We have a new ranch hand?"

That question came from Denver.

"So what's notable about that?" Arizona asked.

She wasn't friendly. She knew that. She had a reputation for it, in fact. It was just that no one really knew or understood why. Sometimes she didn't really know or understand why. Was it all a defense mechanism because of her scars?

Outside of her family, people didn't realize she had them. Or at least, they didn't know the extent of them.

Yeah, they might vaguely remember the car accident that she'd been in all those years ago. There was any number of accidents and dramatic happenings that occurred to the people at the ranch. That was the thing. Ranching was tough work, and they tended to work hard and play harder. Over the years, a lot of things had happened. Hell, Gus McCloud had been *set on fire*.

His scars were on his face, and people couldn't help but be conscious of them.

But people didn't really think much about what had happened to her. It had been years ago. For all anyone knew she wasn't permanently injured. That she never wore shorts no matter how hot it was, never showed her arms, never swam in the lake…well, people wrote it off as being part of her prickly weirdness.

But *she* knew that she was scarred. She knew that there was damage that she would never heal from.

"Yeah. But… It's just weird. Right? He's Micah Stone's son, that guy that worked here years ago… And if I'm not mistaken…"

She narrowed her eyes and looked at her brother Denver. "I would be very careful about finishing that sentence, Denver. Because I'll have you know that nothing ever happened between me and Micah Stone. And nothing ever will. I'm not that kind of idiot. I didn't fuck around with ranch hands then and I don't do it now."

"You don't fuck around with anything," said Daughtry. "Much less human emotion and basic decency."

"Your opinion is noted, you marshmallow," she said.

"Would you like some coffee?" Penny asked, her voice soft and feathery, and Arizona felt ridiculously irritated by it.

"Put some metal in your voice, Penny," she said. "I know you're not still scared of me."

"Nobody wants their head bitten off by you," said Daughtry. "Maybe take it back a peg or two, all right?"

"I don't have to take it back *any pegs*," said Arizona. "I don't owe you anything. Least of all a smile."

"You're like a damned badger," Justice said. "Except badgers might be safer to cuddle."

"Fuck off," she said, pouring her own cup of coffee into a travel mug and stomping from the kitchen. Immediately after she did that she felt…regret.

She did that. Let her mouth run off with her and then felt…gross right after.

She didn't like to have conversations about herself, she didn't like to get caught up in discussions about the past. And she had woken up thinking about things she didn't like.

She didn't know why she was so awful sometimes.

She stomped out into the blue pre-dawn air and got into her truck. She started the engine and sat for a minute, her hands wrapped around the coffee mug. She let the liquid warm her through.

She didn't know why it was so hard. She didn't know.

And she was jittery because she was going to see Micah. No. She was not going to see Micah. She was going to let the foreman handle it—meaning Landry—and she was going to leave it alone. So she decided to busy herself in the back pasture where she knew no one else would be, but where there were holes to fix in the fence. It was the perfect place for quiet busywork.

And so when she ran into Daniel, she was shocked.

The sun was getting to be in the middle of the sky, and the kid was covered in dirt. Sweaty from a day of working hard.

"What are you doing all the way out here?"

"My dad told me to check the fence lines," he said, breathing hard, and she wondered if the kid had walked all the way over here.

"We've been working since four thirty."

"Well, now that is a violation of child labor laws. Have you had lunch?"

"No," he said. "I'm good. Dad said that it if I wanted to work the ranch, I had to be tough. I have to work on the same schedule as everyone else."

"Well," she said slowly. "Sure. But…"

And she didn't know why she felt any compassion for this kid. For the scrappy boy who was like a gangly man who hadn't grown into his testosterone yet. Except God knew their parents had never taken any softness or pity on them. While in many ways they had turned into functional humans, she didn't think that they were all that emotionally conversant.

Her behavior this morning was exhibit A in that.

Part of her—a part she hadn't known existed—just wanted better for this kid.

"Come on back to the house with me. I'm going to put together some food. And you can help me. That'll be part of your workday."

"That doesn't sound like ranch hand business."

She put her hands on her hips and stared the kid down. "Do I look like a cook to you? Or do I look like a ranch hand?"

"Well…"

His eyes flickered over her body, and his cheeks turned scarlet. Lord help her.

"I'm a ranch hand," she said. "And you, kid, need to take a break or you're not going to be able to get any functional work done. And I don't want to hear any whining about it."

"Yeah. All right."

"You can ride back with me."

"Oh," he said. "Thanks."

She got into the cab of the truck with the kid and drove him back to the farmhouse.

And the one thing she was grateful for was that even though she had run into Daniel, she hadn't seen his father anywhere.

CHAPTER SEVEN

MICAH COULDN'T FIND Daniel anywhere, and he was starting to get worried—which manifested itself as irritation. He had texted him three or four times and hadn't gotten a response. And finally, he lost his temper and called.

"What?"

"Where the hell are you?"

"Working. Like you said."

"Where?"

"At the ranch house."

He cursed and hung the phone up, then started to drive over to the ranch house.

He didn't know what was up. And he hoped that the kid wasn't making a nuisance out of himself. Yeah, he was being hard on him. He was running him maybe a little more ragged than was strictly necessary, but the thing was, Daniel didn't understand life.

He had it rough with his mom, it was true, but more or less, Micah had worked as hard as he could to give him a childhood, and the kid didn't understand that he was supposed to sit back and let things be easy. He didn't understand struggle. Not really. And he shouldn't be in any hurry to rush into one. Micah had no intention of hanging out here for the next thirty days. His plan was to get the kid so sick of work by the end of three days that they would be on the road back to Texas. His ranch could run on its own for a bit, but he certainly didn't intend to leave it for thirty days.

That said, he was not going to tell the kid that he was trying to get out of this. Nor was he going to openly welch on the promise in any way. One thing he knew about Daniel was that he didn't have the stability that he should be able to count on. And that was all Lacey's fault.

Well. You're the one that dated her and had a kid with her...

Sure. Maybe. But he had done the best he could to offer stability, and he still was.

Where the hell had she been? She hadn't even known or cared where Daniel was.

He rolled up to the farmhouse, and thought of Arizona as she'd been yesterday. He thought of her often. A part of a simpler life, a simpler time. And yet, right now, nothing felt...simple. Or easy. He pulled up to the house and walked up the front porch. He'd been here before, though it had been a long time ago. He'd shared beers with her brothers, talked about different things. In some ways, he felt like he was living in a flashback, except... Except, of course, his son was behind that door.

And when the door opened, it was Arizona who answered, wearing one of her tight T-shirts that drew his attention... Well.

Who's the horny asshole now?

"Why did you bring him in here?" he asked, his voice harder than he intended.

"He was hungry," she said, her expression defiant. "I thought he needed a lunch break."

"He had some granola in his bag."

"He's a growing boy. That's not enough."

"Are you a parent?"

"No. But I have common sense," she said.

"I'm trying to toughen him up."

"Oh my gosh. You're like a walking advertisement for toxic masculinity."

"Can I see my son, please?"

"Come on in," she said.

She was different. The girl that he remembered was wide-eyed and pretty, and this woman was no less pretty, but she was not wide-eyed. There was an edge to her that had never been there before, and he didn't know where it had come from.

He wanted to ask.

He found that he wanted to linger with her more than he should.

But then, that had always been the case.

Instead of lingering, he followed her into the kitchen, where his son was sitting, eating. He was surrounded by a huge spread. Pies, cakes and a big sandwich with what he was pretty certain was tri tip overflowing from the bread.

"Hey, Dad," said Daniel.

"This is not being a ranch hand," he said. "Being a ranch hand is staying in a terrible bunkhouse and eating beans from a can."

"Not when you're a thirteen-year-old growing boy," said Arizona.

"You cooked all this?"

She waved a hand. "Hell, no. My brothers are the grill masters, I would've thought you'd remember that, for all your drama about canned beans. My brothers grill, the Sullivan sisters do a lot of baking and share the bounty around. Something else I would've thought you'd remember."

"I don't remember the Sullivan sisters much," he said.

And he let that sit between them.

Let her ponder that.

She blinked, but that was the only indication that what he'd said had landed at all.

"Well. They make good food."

"Clearly." He looked at his son, who didn't even have the decency to look sheepish. But then, maybe the kid figured this was part of normal ranch life. The pretty woman taking you in and feeding you. It was not.

"Head back to the bunk, kiddo," he said to Daniel.

"But it's really far," said Daniel.

"You can drive the truck. And don't act like you can't drive now that you've driven cross-country."

His son shoved the last bit of his sandwich into his mouth, his expression suddenly keen. "Sure."

"Take five over there, and then I want you to go and find Landry King at one of the main barns—you remember where those are—and ask him what you should be doing."

"Yes, sir," Daniel said, bustling off.

"You and I need to have a little talk, Arizona King."

"Do we?" she said, her expression looking disingenuously sweet.

"The thing is, I don't want you being easy on my son. He thinks that he wants to grow up. He thinks he wants to be a man instead of the thirteen-year-old boy that he is. When he doesn't realize how lucky he is that he doesn't have a dad that's making him work to earn his keep."

"Yeah, look, I don't disagree with you. I felt sorry for the kid, that's why I brought him into the kitchen. He doesn't need a hard-ass lesson, Micah."

"That's the point. I want him to have a hard-ass lesson while I'm here. While we can still go back home and he can appreciate the fact that he doesn't live a harsh enough life to have to go work at a ranch 24/7. I don't even make him work at mine."

"Then why did he want to come here?"

"I assume he got into it with his mom."

She crossed her arms beneath her breasts. He wasn't going to think about them. He really wasn't.

"Right. Well. Have you asked him about it? Have you asked him why he wanted to be here? Have you asked him what he wants?"

"He wants to work here," Micah said, "and damned if I really know why. I guess I told him stories about the place and he seems to think... I don't know. Maybe he's having a hard time at school?"

He suddenly felt a little bit ashamed at what he didn't know about his son.

"He lives with Lacey most of the time. Not my choice. It's the court. He stays with me over the summer when school gets out. So I haven't seen him for a while. His mom is a particularly difficult case."

"You're not with her anymore."

"No," he said.

"How old is he exactly?"

"He's thirteen."

"I see."

"For what it's worth, I didn't know when I was here, and once I did know I left. Also, you were eighteen."

"I don't understand what that has to do with anything."

"I think you do," he said.

"Oh, what?" she snapped. "The whole you-disappearing-without-saying-a-word thing? That? You didn't owe me anything."

"But you're mad at me."

"Maybe I thought there was something between us. But I

recognize now that... That it was silly. Inappropriate, even. You're a lot older than me."

"I know," he said. "I am well aware of the age difference. Thank you. As I was then."

"But are you going to tell me there wasn't anything between us?"

He cleared his throat. "No. I can't tell you that. Because there was. But then, the night before I left, I got the call from Lacey. She was eight months pregnant. And she figured it was time to tell me that she was having my baby. So I went back. We tried to make it work again. It doesn't work between us. She isn't the kind of person who can have a stable relationship. She doesn't... She does not thrive in that space."

"Meaning what?"

"Meaning she likes drama. And a lot of men is a lot of drama. One man...less. And I don't share."

"Oh," she said.

"Yeah. Whatever. It's not about her. This is about Daniel."

"He's why you left," she said.

"Yeah," he said. "He's why I left."

And the moment stretched between them. And Arizona King, the reason that he remembered this place so well of all the places he'd lived, of all the places he'd worked, had just confirmed the thing he had always wondered. If she thought about him the way that he thought about her.

He'd felt like an ass at the time. Because he'd had no right. No right to look at her like he had no right to want her like he had. He definitely hadn't had the right to kiss her.

He hadn't been a man then. But he'd been too old. And it was the combination of those things that'd made it absolutely impossible.

He had grown since then. Made a lot of mistakes, and done his best to atone for them.

And then there was Arizona, the mistake that he'd *wanted* to make. Hell, he'd wanted to make it so bad he'd ached with it.

But he hadn't.

He'd only kissed her once, and never taken it further. But he'd dreamed of her.

He still did, if he were honest.

He took a step toward her, and she took a step away.

"Hey there, buddy," she said. "I don't need that kind of... anything. I'm not looking for it."

"Sorry."

"I just think that you should be easier on your kid."

"And I get that. In general. But this is all kind of in service to being easier on my kid."

"You want to make him leave? Is that it?"

"Yeah," he said. "I do."

"Well, I guess that is better than having a conversation."

"I don't get your investment."

"I don't know," she said, growing increasingly prickly. "I don't know what my investment is either. You're just some guy that I used to know, and not a particularly special one. But you did make that kid a promise. And trying to manipulate him? What's that going to do for him?"

"I'm not trying to manipulate him into anything bad."

"It doesn't matter if it's good or bad. How can you not understand that? The point is that you're manipulating him. And that is kind of a shitty thing to do. Believe me. Gentry King, my father, is a master at that sort of thing. He just wants you to do what he wants. He's not interested in knowing you, he's not interested in what you care about. He's the king, after all."

"I remember that you had issues with your dad."

She looked angry that he remembered that. "Yeah. He's great to work for. He's an asshole if he's your dad."

"I didn't have a dad at all. I try to be there as much as I can and I try to guide him. I'm not trying to be a hard-ass, but a man has to walk the line."

"Right. Well, I guess you aren't my dad."

"No," he said, his voice hard. "I'm not."

"Whatever. Just… You promised the kid this. And believe me when I tell you, if you want to have a good relationship with him, then maybe you should take that promise seriously."

"I do take it seriously. And you know, I recognize that I'm going to have to deal with the custody issue again, now that my ex-wife let him drive across the country without ever checking in on him."

"You *married* her?"

There was something on her face that looked hollow.

"I tried to do the right thing," he said. "But I'd be lying if I said that I didn't marry her in part because I wanted to make sure I got a fair shake when it came to custody. I wanted to be an ex-husband. Not just the ex-boyfriend. It felt like it might carry more weight."

"Right. Well, I don't know anything about that. And you know, what do I know about kids? All I know is that I was a pretty miserable one."

"Well, I hope you're a less miserable adult."

She laughed, and there was a bitter edge to it. "Depends on who you ask."

CHAPTER EIGHT

Arizona still felt breathless by the time Micah left the kitchen.

She was angry at him. And she had no call to be. He had never owed her anything, and now she had an explanation for why he had left all that time ago. She had no right to be mad. She had no right to have expected anything from him. He had gone back home to claim custody of his kid, and that was admirable. It was.

And yet… She still felt betrayed. That he had gone back to a life she hadn't known he'd had. That he'd married somebody else.

As if you didn't think he had.

It would've been different if she would've had a lover.

But not having a lover didn't have anything to do with Micah Stone. It was all the things that had come after.

It was all the things tied up in him… And he had gone back to have a baby with someone else. If she'd known that, would she have cried for him the way that she had? Would she have driven quite so fast?

Would she have broken her leg in those places, and split her torso up the side? Would she have left herself with all those scars?

She didn't know the answer to those questions.

Maybe she would've driven *faster*. Maybe it would've been worse.

Maybe she would just be dead.

And that would be a pretty piss-poor thing. To have died over some man who had never even slept with her.

She'd wanted him close, and now all she did was try to keep people away.

She was sick of herself.

Her family came in, loud and boisterous in the big cabin, and her brothers started to go through the fridge to get out the steaks that they'd taken out of the freezer earlier.

There was always beef to be had at the Kings'.

She'd said that she was a vegetarian for a while. She might as well have announced her plans to become a serial killer. It had not gone over well in her ranching family. As a result, she had stuck to her guns and avoided beef for two years.

Just to be in a fight about it.

It was Denver who'd said to her: *Why are you cutting your nose off to spite your face?* And it really was then that she'd realized she was *being* her dad, rather than being in a fight with him, and that felt like a silly thing.

So she had given up on the crusade. Because it had never been about her moral convictions, and had only ever been about making Gentry angry.

She'd thought perhaps the better part of valor was to eat prime rib.

It was better now in the house with her dad gone. Her mom had never been much a part of her life, and given how her dad was, she assumed that might even be a gift. He'd left the ranch to all the kids, and had gone his own way years before. And it was a good thing, it made everybody happier. More free.

Well, everybody but her. She didn't really do happy or free. And she supposed that was her fault. Her problem.

Because she was the cause of the accident. And she was the one who had never gotten over it. Who had never been able to forgive herself for what she'd done to her own body.

She didn't know what the hell to do with that.

And she decided that she really couldn't do family dinner tonight, so while her brothers were outside grilling, she pulled some leftovers out and heated them up, then beat a hasty retreat to her room.

They didn't live in each other's pockets, even though they did live in the same house, so she knew that nobody would notice that she was gone or care about why.

Anyway, they were all probably still mad about the way she'd been this morning.

She hated that part of herself. The one that made people want to avoid her. The one that made her family not all that sad when she didn't join them for dinner.

She was a bitch. She wished that she wasn't. She wished that she could be better.

She wished that she could find a way to heal.

Micah.

The word whispered along her body, and she hated it. She just hated it.

She scampered back through her bedroom door and down the hall, down the stairs. Her family was still sitting around the kitchen table, and it was dark outside. Nobody said anything when she ran out the front door.

She let out a long breath, and then took in another one. Smelling the sweet, hay-scented air, doing her best to revel in the ranch. Because she loved the ranch. Because she didn't want to leave it. Because for all that she was not exactly beloved by all the people here, because of her own behavior, this was her place.

Micah.

Yeah, he was the root of a lot of her problems. But she was the ultimate architect of her own disaster.

Then and now.

Sometimes she wanted to cry, but she didn't let herself do that, and maybe that was why it came out as f-bombs and anger. She didn't know why he was here—well, she did know, she knew that he was here because of his son, but what she didn't understand was…why. Why was the universe doing this to her?

It was such a hell of a thing. And she just wanted to be free. She wanted to be free of this pain.

But she was bound up in the loss of him and what had happened after.

Bound up in the insecurity that it had created, and she had started pushing people away. So that they wouldn't see her as ugly the way that she did.

Yeah. She just thought she was so ugly.

And what would he think now? *He thought you were pretty back then then, but if he saw you naked now…*

The idea made her shiver.

She wanted to be with him. That was the thing. Physically, time had not dulled the impact of him.

He had gorgeous eyes. A little bit of gray at the temples that assaulted his dark hair. His stubble was the same. There were lines now, fanning out around those eyes, bracketing his mouth. And she just thought… He looked better than ever. That was the truth of it. He was gorgeous.

She ran. It was two miles from their house down to Sullivan Lake. It was owned by the Sullivans, but they had an easement so that they could all use it. Each family had a segment of shore to call their own.

When she got down there, she breathed a sigh of relief.

The rope swing was there. Like it always was.

And she climbed up on it and swung back and forth, letting the night breeze blow through her hair.

Maybe there would be clarity here. Except she never had an easy time finding clarity in herself.

If it were that simple, she'd have done it before.

"How did I somehow know that you'd be here?"

She turned and saw Micah standing there, his hands stuffed in his pockets.

He was dimly lit by the light of the moon, but it was still impacting to see him there. Tall and strong and broad.

He was beautiful.

Just beautiful.

And she wasn't. She had seen the way he looked at her in the house, but he didn't know. He didn't know. He still thought that she was that young unspoiled girl that she'd been.

Actually, he probably assumed something a little different. That she'd gained years and experience in his time away.

Instead, she was frozen. Pickled. In her bitterness.

And she was sick of herself.

"And how exactly did you know I would be down here?"

"You liked the swing then too."

"You noticed."

"I shouldn't have. I felt bad about it. I wanted to figure out a way to be friends with you, but even being a friend... It seemed...like maybe it wasn't right. Because I was a lot older than you."

"You still are."

"It's different."

"Sure."

"But I felt connected to you just the same. And I remember coming down here and finding you and pushing you on the swing."

She remembered that too. She remembered his strong hands gripping the ropes of the swing as he held it back and let it fly.

But he didn't move any closer now. Didn't do it like he'd done it then.

"You were such a funny little thing," he said. "And we were different, but somehow, I thought maybe you understood me. Better than anyone else I've ever met."

She felt the same. It hurt her to hear him say that. She hated that he'd said that. Because it reminded her. A feeling like she could talk to him. A feeling like maybe they uniquely understood where the other was coming from.

He'd told her all about his life in Texas. She knew that he didn't have a father. She hadn't had to ask. Because she remembered all the things he'd told her.

Remembered and held them close to her heart. Remembered and knew she would never forget.

"I really do remember the stuff you told me about your dad. I know you didn't get along with him," he said.

"Nobody gets along with my dad," she said. "It's not a matter of getting along with him. It's his way or it's the highway. And there really is no other way about it. That's who he is. He doesn't brook any nonsense. And he considers a lot of things nonsense. That's the other thing. It doesn't matter what you think is reasonable or not. What matters is what he thinks is reasonable."

"Yeah. I seem to recall you having difficulty with them."

"We shouldn't have been friends," she said. She stopped swinging herself, letting the swing stop. "And we weren't, were we? Because when you left you never got in touch with me again."

"I couldn't," he said. "Because the thing is, we *were* friends. But I was also attracted to you, and I had to go home and deal with the mess that I'd made myself. And... I had to grow up. You were young, but I was hardly finished maturing myself. I'm not saying that I am *now*, but I've come a long way."

"Yeah. Well. I..."

"I want to know what's happened in your life since then. You can see what's happened in mine."

But she didn't want to say. She didn't want to tell him about what she'd been through. She didn't want to talk about all of her pain. She didn't want to admit that she was the least popular person at Four Corners. That even her own brothers would probably sell her out in exchange for other people. Because she was such a pain in the ass. Because she just wasn't... Because she had all this pain and anguish inside of her and she didn't know what to do with it. She never had.

Because she had never been understood, not once in her whole life, and then she'd gone and made it worse. That she had thought she met a person who saw her. Knew her. Got her, and then he left and...

"Why do you want to know anything about me? You're going to leave again. We both know that. What's the point in knowing me?" She jumped off the swing, and she felt that irrational anger rising up inside of her that tended to show up right when she needed to push someone away.

"Are we friends, Micah? Were we ever? Or were you just some guy sniffing around looking to get a piece of ass?"

"It was not like that. And you know it. I happen to think you're worth getting to know. I always have. The reason that Daniel knows about this place is that I talk about it. I didn't want to leave."

"But you never contacted any of us ever again. So how much could we have ever mattered?"

"Did it ever occur to you that you meant so much to me I couldn't contact you again?"

And then he turned away from her, and without a word, he walked away, leaving her with a jumble of confusion and feelings that she didn't know what to do with.

CHAPTER NINE

ARIZONA WAS DOING her level best to keep space between her and Micah. But she wasn't having similar luck keeping any kind of space from Daniel. The kid was everywhere. He was a nice kid, but kids weren't really her thing in general.

"Can I ask you something?" he said, coming up to her while she was grooming one of the horses.

"I have a feeling you're going to ask whatever I say."

"Yeah, maybe," the kid said. "It's only that… I want to learn more about horses. I mean, I'm at my dad's ranch part-time. But not all the time."

"Yeah," she said. "That must be tough."

"Yeah. I'd like to spend more time with him. But it's… The agreement he has with my mom. She's… She's difficult."

She felt uncomfortable. Like she shouldn't listen to slander about Daniel's mother, particularly given the tangle of a relationship she'd had with Micah back then.

"Sorry about that."

"What about you?" he asked. "How was your mom?"

"Well, she's dead," said Arizona. "So there's that."

"I'm sorry," the kid said, looking uncomfortable.

"Don't be sorry. I was pretty little when she died. I don't really remember her. My dad's the one who did most of the raising. He's hard. He thinks that life is going to break you, so you need to get really tough. Tough love, I guess, except he always forgets the love part."

"My dad's not like that," he said. "My dad is great. He tries. He's kind of hard, but he tries. He calls me every day on video call, when I'm with my mom." He smiled. "I'm probably closer to my dad than people that live with their dads all the time."

"But you still ran away out here."

"I just wanted to get away. I don't like school back in Texas. The classes are huge and I can't pay attention. I'd rather be outside working. I just… I don't like it. When the teachers get mad at me my mom gets mad at me and…"

"Right. So you were in a little bit of a tough spot."

"I shouldn't have made my dad worry."

"No," she said, "you shouldn't have. But I can teach you about horses if you want."

"Thanks," he said. "Can I help you with this one?"

And even though she felt like she was going to regret it, getting close to this kid, letting him help her out… "Yeah. All right. Come on."

CHAPTER TEN

HE HAD BEEN tempting fate, going and looking for Arizona a week ago, and he had managed to stay away from her since then.

He had also…taken some of what she'd said to heart. Oh, not the part where she'd gotten angry at him. There was nothing to be said about what he hadn't done all those years ago. He wasn't going to pretend that he was the greatest man of all time, but he had behaved appropriately with her, and he wasn't going to let her take his skin off about it. He might not have been able to help his attraction to her, but he hadn't taken it as far as he'd wanted to.

She had been young, it was true. She had been a woman. It was just that she had been a very young one, and he had scruples enough—even then when he'd been an idiot—that he wasn't going to take advantage.

But he definitely took on board some of what she had said about Daniel.

One thing he did remember from being here was that she had always had an adversarial relationship with Gentry King. He didn't want that for himself and his son. Hell, they already spent too much time apart, and that wasn't what he wanted, nor was it what he would've chosen but that was the life they had as decided by the court. There wasn't much he could do about it. He'd tried. But she was right. He had told Daniel that they would do this for thirty days. And he needed to try in earnest rather than just using it as a chance to teach his son a lesson.

And he told himself he didn't have anything to do with Arizona or the fact that she still captivated him. Even keeping a distance from her the last few days, he could observe quite a few changes about the way she was. She was angry now. He didn't really know why.

He felt compelled to find out, and did feel that it might be the better part of valor to leave that stone unturned. After all, he was leaving again. He had made arrangements for his ranch to be fully cared for without him being present, but he would be going back at the end of the thirty days.

To give Daniel his credit, he seemed to be having the time of his life. And the King brothers had made it their mission to give him a taste of just about every task the ranch offered.

And, at nights, Micah often went down to the swing to see if Arizona was there...

He wasn't perfect. There were things he thought might be best...and things he felt compelled toward. They were not always the same.

He was down there tonight. It was warm out, a beautiful summer evening. The moon was full, reflecting on the water.

And then he saw her, down at the lakeshore, her arms wrapped around herself. Even from far away he could tell how she was holding herself. Because even with all the years between then and now, he knew the shape of her.

The shape of her moods.

So much more often angry and combative now than she'd been before. Except with Daniel. She was great with him.

He made sure that his footsteps were loud as he approached. So even though she didn't turn, he had a fair idea that she knew he was there.

"Haven't seen you for a couple of days," she said.

"I've seen you. Even if it was just across the field."

She did turn then. "Maybe I did see you."

Yeah. He had figured as much. That they were in proximity to one another, they saw each other clearly enough.

"I've been thinking," she continued. "I want to finish what we didn't before."

"And what is that?"

"We never slept together. And I think we ought to. We both wanted to. But for reasons… It didn't happen. So here we are, circling each other again when we're both grown adults who know this time you're leaving. It doesn't change what we want. So why be coy about it?"

There was an element of boldness that was intrinsic enough to her character that he didn't question it. But there was something about this type of boldness particularly that had a false note ringing beneath it.

He couldn't quite make out what it was. Something soft and uncertain beneath all that bravado.

"It was hell, you know," he said. "Leaving here."

He didn't know how to tear down her walls, but he knew how to tear down his own. Having a child did that for you. And while he didn't always do things right with Daniel, Daniel had made him change. Deeply.

Because in order to parent a child in a difficult situation, a child who had one parent that couldn't grow up, no matter what, it seemed, you had to do a hell of a lot of your own work to make sure that kid wasn't a huge mess.

And all right, Daniel coming out here without telling anybody suggested that he might be more of a mess than Micah wanted to admit, but for the most part, he *tried*. So if he needed to be the one to tear himself down here too? He was willing to do it.

"I had to do it," he said. "Lacey called, she was eight months pregnant, and finally telling me about it. I asked her to get a paternity test. She did. By the time I got home, she had the ball rolling on that, and I provided DNA. Couldn't deny that the kid was mine. And I knew that I needed to make changes. I didn't think that she and I could make a marriage work. But I did wonder if we could make a family. So I thought we might as well go ahead and try and see what happened. I didn't think of it as marriage till death do us part. I thought of it as giving our family a fighting chance, because I knew that I would never be my dad. The man who donated genetic material and never showed up. I knew I couldn't be that. I also knew that I couldn't be the same person that I was when I left Texas."

He let that settle over him, in his bones. The truth of it. Before he continued. "My time here... It changed me. Mellowed me out a bit. I'm grateful for it. I think it is one of the reasons that I was able to be the father I am. That couple of years after Daniel was born... It was tough. Lacey was resentful, and was in and out the door. She had affairs. I didn't care so much for me. She and I didn't have a physical relationship at that point. I didn't care because of me. I cared because I knew she didn't love Daniel the way that I did, and it made me angry. How can you not love that kid with everything that you are? I couldn't understand it then. I can't understand it now. She left when he was three. I had full custody until he was five. That was when she decided she wanted to change the weight of the child support."

Arizona was listening, he could tell. Even though her gaze was fixed straight on the horizon line.

"That was tough. For a while I had him on weekends. As

he got older… I got him for holidays and all school breaks. It's not enough. I drive down to Dallas to visit several times when I don't have him, and sometimes he stays with me for a weekend. I thought a lot of times about selling the ranch, so that I could be closer. But… Then I'm worried that I won't have a legacy to leave him." He shook his head. "I'm not too proud to tell you that I spent a lot of time crying into my whiskey about it. Kids have a way of stripping away that thing. That thing that makes you think you're tough. Yeah. I think he took that away from me pretty effectively. I guess if something is going to make you weak, it might as well be your own kid."

"Why tell me all that?"

"Because you're holding something back. You're angry, Arizona, I can see it. And you're propositioning me like it doesn't matter. And hell, maybe you do just want to have a good time because the attraction that we felt before is still there. It is for me. But I wonder if there's more."

She tilted her chin up, her eyes squinting. "Let me tell you something. I didn't get softer in the years since you were here. I couldn't afford to. I got harder. Because sometimes life throws stuff at you, and it's not an opportunity to let your guard down. You've got to build a higher wall. A harder wall. I'm not tearing down a wall for you, Micah Stone. You're leaving again. I'm not destroying myself, and everything that I created to protect myself, for you."

"You just want to sleep with me?"

"Yes. That's what I want. It's a take-it-or-leave-it kind of thing."

He wanted more. He realized it in that moment, and he had to wonder if he was cursed. He had been bound for all these years to a woman he wanted less of, quite frankly. But they had a kid together, and he'd been forced to try and make something work. He'd done his best. He'd had to leave, had to go away, had to step up and be the best dad he could, to be worthy of Arizona.

Now he was here, ready to give her more. Everything.

And she didn't want it.

Refused to even give him a chance.

But she would give him this.

And maybe that was the bottom line. This was the opportunity. This was the moment. So he had to take it.

So he took a step toward her, and he let the future be its own problem. He took a step toward her, and he decided that what happened after tonight didn't matter. He took a step toward her, and he let his guard down. Then he wrapped his arms around her waist and lowered his head.

And finally, after all these years, he kissed Arizona King again.

CHAPTER ELEVEN

FOR THE FIRST TIME, Arizona wondered if she had miscalculated. She had decided that she was going to have this, because if she couldn't have everything, why not have what she wanted? Because since he was indirectly responsible for the thing that was holding her back from having lovers, he might as well be the first one.

Break the barrier, so to speak.

But now he was kissing her, and it was… It was so big and raw and real, and he was so close. It wasn't like she had imagined it would be. She wasn't really sure what she had imagined at this point in her life. She had long ago stopped romanticizing attraction and romance and sex. That was what happened when you excluded yourself from those things. And she had. Pretty ruthlessly at that.

She had excluded herself from being able to have and enjoy these things. And so she had diminished their importance in her mind. A meeting of bodies was about satisfying a physical itch, and she was modern woman enough to figure out how to do that on her own a long time ago. She had a well-developed fantasy life, and she found people difficult, so self-pleasure just seemed the way to do it. The man in her head, who did exactly what she wanted him to, and looked exactly how she wanted him to, and didn't make any demands, was enough for her. Or had been.

But the difference between a fantasy and reality was that

reality brought in another person. It stole her control. She was not in charge of this man. She couldn't tell him what to do. She couldn't force the moment to fade to black. She couldn't make this easier. His kiss was hard and dark, and when he slid his tongue against hers, it made her shiver.

Logically, she understood that people enjoyed strange and intimate things when they were aroused, but now she *understood*. On a level that had nothing to do with logic. She understood in that quiver of excitement low in her belly. Understood in that hollow place between her legs that was getting wet from that friction. And she also understood that the control would not be entirely hers.

And she had to make a decision. Right now. Either do what she did, throw up the wall and run away, or give an inch. Let a little bit of that wall crumble. Raise the white flag of surrender, even if just halfway.

Her plan had been to brazen all of this out. To offer no explanation for the scars on her body—for all he knew, she'd had them then. He'd never seen her.

To act like she was okay with them. To act like there was no story.

To act like it hadn't taken her relationship with her father from toxic to near nonexistent. To act like it hadn't made her feel like she'd ruined herself.

She was so good at walls.

She had just gotten so very good at them.

"Is there a place we can go?"

"Yeah. I was planning on parading you past my brothers and taking you upstairs to my childhood room," she said, doing a good job of keeping a straight face, because this kind of commentary was her strength.

"Great," he said. "If you're cool with that…"

"You would *not* seriously do that."

"I'm forty-two years old," he said. "I'm not going to treat you like a dirty secret."

"Oh."

"I think you're trying to push me away."

"It's the Arizona King specialty."

"I am happy to parade you through the kitchen. But are there other alternatives?"

"Yeah. There's a place. One of the cabins that's empty out at the edge of the King property. We can go there."

"I can drive," he said.

"Great."

And that was how she found herself seated in the front of his truck, her nerves growing. Tightening. Making it nearly impossible for her to breathe.

And when they pulled into the gravel lot right in front of the small cabin, Micah laughed.

"What?" she snapped. "What's funny?"

"I feel like I'm sneaking around with you. And I can't say as I've snuck around with anybody for a long time."

"Oh. Right. Well. We aren't sneaking around. We just aren't *parading*."

"I don't typically… I've never… When Daniel is with me I don't go off to have sex. But he's hanging out with the ranch hands back at the bunkhouse and I know he's good." He looked a little bit wistful. "And it's you. I'm here with you."

"You say that like it matters."

"It does. To me it does."

"Why?" She couldn't help but ask that. She shouldn't ask that. Because she felt a little bit raw and a little bit scared, and she wanted to be the Arizona that kept everybody far away from her. Wanted to be the Arizona that she had become in order to protect herself. Because it was so important. Because it had been so important.

"You know, you meet people in this life, and you forget so many of them. Time marches on, and the world changes and you change with it. And it just... It all changes. And there are certain people that stay with you. They made you feel something. They showed you something. You are one of those people for me. I always thought you were so smart and funny and I just liked being around you." No one had said anything like that to her in a long time. And she knew it was her own fault. Knew that people didn't particularly like being around her because of her own behavior. But Micah remembered her as someone who had been fun. Someone he had wanted to be around.

It was the strangest gift she hadn't known she needed.

"I'm not that person anymore," she said. "But if you still think I'm hot, then we might have something tonight."

"It's more than that," he said.

"It can't be more than that. You don't know me."

"You know me. And if you ever decide that you want me to know you... I'd like that."

"Well, I don't want to talk right now," she said. "I just want for you to get naked."

"I'm definitely on the same page."

He killed the engine truck's engine and got out and she sat for a second before following him out of the truck and heading toward the cabin. It was small, and she knew that there would've been no cooling or heat running in it for a while, but it didn't matter. The heat of the day was done, and it would be perfectly nice inside. And still she shivered.

She went ahead and pushed the door open. It was simple and small inside, a bed that was barely big enough for two shoved into the corner.

And it loomed large.

But she wasn't going to let nerves have this moment. She wasn't going to let anything but desire have it. Because hadn't she been through enough? It didn't matter that he was leaving. It didn't matter what he thought. It didn't matter that he was saying all these things about wanting to know her. None of it mattered. What mattered was this. What mattered was her finally getting what she wanted, and maybe, just maybe, it would be the thing that she needed in order to get some closure. Yeah. Maybe that was the thing. Maybe it was what she needed to be…to be her again. To be the woman that someone wanted to be around. To be the Arizona she'd been before she'd had her heart broken, and then broken herself.

So she banished all of her misgivings. Pushed them to the side. Because this was her moment. Her reclamation. Because nobody got to decide what this moment was except for her. And she decided that it was going to be liberating. That it was going to be fun, and that she wasn't going to overthink it. So she was the one to close the distance between them this time. She stretched up on her toes and wrapped her arms around his neck. And she felt… She was breathing him in. Tasting him. This man who had been her deepest, darkest fantasy all those years ago. And it wasn't even because she had wanted him. Or at least, not simply because of that. It was because she had cared. And she had always wanted to keep that part of herself protected.

Always.

It was just so damned difficult. All of this.

All of it. But this didn't feel difficult. It felt wonderful. It felt glorious.

And yeah, he would find things out about her when she took her clothes off. But she couldn't worry about it. She couldn't make it about him. She wouldn't make it about him. So she kissed him, and she luxuriated in this moment. In this moment where she was getting what she wanted. This moment where she had this victory. Because she did. This wonderful, decisive victory of this man being here after all these years. And maybe, just maybe, if she saw this moment as inevitable, it took away some of the sting of regret.

Just maybe.

They weren't meant to be. She wasn't quite that foolish. And anyway, they were strangers.

Effectively.

Her teenage love didn't matter. Not now. But her adult desire did. So she kissed him. With everything she had. With everything she was. And she luxuriated in the textures of it all. The heat of his mouth, the feel of his stubble beneath her fingertips. And she was lost in it. In him.

She kissed him like she might die if she didn't, and considering she had very nearly died when he left, it didn't feel like a totally overdramatic metaphor. No. It didn't feel overdramatic at all. His hands were rough, and suddenly she realized they were coming up beneath her shirt, and internally, she cringed. Because while most of the scars were concentrated on the lower portion of her body, there was some pretty significant scarring on her torso as well.

But she wasn't going to act like it mattered. She wouldn't. He paused, and her heart stopped beating.

"Micah…"

"Condoms," he said.

"Do you not just have them in your wallet?"

"No."

Well, shoot. She didn't have any form of birth control, because she had never needed it.

"Let me just…" She separated from him and scurried over to the nightstand next to the bed. Praying that she wasn't going to open it to find a scorpion or a mouse, she did so quickly, and breathed out a sigh of relief when she found a box of condoms. And inside there were several perfectly sealed packets.

"There's a rotation of guys who come through here. I was hoping that I could count on men to be men."

"I guess we should give thanks for the predictability of testosterone."

"No kidding," she said.

Because if she would have come this far only to be stalled out by birth control, she would've been pretty angry.

He was kissing her again, even more passionately than before, and this time, when his hands went beneath her shirt, they didn't pause. She tried to keep her breathing steady, but it became difficult. She was aroused, and she was nervous, and the cocktail of the two was pretty undeniable.

It created the swirl of adrenaline that couldn't be denied. And frankly, she had no interest in denying it.

Then he pushed her shirt up over her head, and her breath caught and held. He didn't say anything. He moved his hands over her back, around to the front. His fingers skimmed the deep, biting grooves where twisted metal from the car had tried to take a bite out of her. But he said nothing.

His eyes moved to her breasts, his gaze going hungry. But he didn't just grab her there or anything like that. He took his time. Rough hands skimming over her curves, working their way up, until his thumbs brushed her nipples through the thin fabric of her bra.

She shivered.

"Yes," she whispered.

It was a soft sound, and she almost couldn't believe something quite so pleading had come from her own mouth. She almost loved it.

Almost loved it because it reminded her of another time. Another moment. And maybe she could cast herself back and be eighteen-year-old Arizona, who had wanted all of this with so much passion that the end of it had...

And suddenly all this emotion welled up inside of her, and she understood why she wanted to run from it. Because when she'd been hurt before she had been self-destructive. In a real, serious way. Because when she had been hurt before, she had done her level best to destroy her own self.

Because when she'd been hurt before, that had been catastrophic. But not here. Not now. And it felt like justice that he was the one that had to contend with the scars. And right in that moment, she took it as justice. As her due.

"You're beautiful," he said, his voice verging on reverence and awe, and that small mean thing inside of her seemed to evaporate.

Because he didn't make her feel like a punishment. He made her feel like a gift. And that wasn't anything she was familiar with. Not now. Not anymore.

"Micah," she whispered.

He reached around and unhooked her bra, his eyes hungry as he took in the sight of her.

And she wanted to cry, but she wouldn't let herself. Because Arizona King didn't cry, not anymore.

But then his hands were on her, his palms rough and hot, and her whole body cried out for his touch. Everywhere. Even on the ruined places.

And it was like she was just so aware what she had been denied all this time.

Just so aware.

But now it was her turn. Her turn to collect a forfeit. Her turn to get a gift.

She pushed her fingers underneath his shirt and found him hot and hard.

She could feel his muscles, well-defined and glorious, and knew that they would be everything, even before she could see him.

She pushed the shirt up, and he groaned. And her internal muscles clenched tight as she slowly revealed the extent of his masculine beauty to her own hungry gaze.

His abs were sculpted and well-defined, his chest hard and muscular.

And the way that she wanted him was like a beast inside of her. Bigger and more than anything she'd ever experienced before.

Bigger, better. Everything.

She gripped his broad shoulders and continued to kiss him, hard and deep. Her bare breasts rubbed against his chest, and she gasped at the sensations.

She could feel. Everything. Not just anger. Not just fear. Everything. And it was so far beyond what she had fantasized about. So far beyond what she had ever thought she could have.

And she did feel moisture gathering in the corners of her eyes, and she did her best to ignore it.

Did her best to pretend it wasn't happening.

And she tried to focus on the feeling. The here and now. The physical aspect of it all, not the emotions that were swirling deep inside of her.

But it was hard. Because he was here. And he was Micah. And as much as she had done her best to pretend that he wasn't everything...he was.

He always had been.

She took the initiative to take the rest of his clothes off. Because she thought that maybe seeing a naked man in the flesh for the first time in her life would do something to jostle her out of this emotional space.

Because she didn't want to feel things. Not these kinds of things.

And he was beautiful all over.

She felt a slight tensing inside of her. Nerves. But she ignored them. And she wrapped her hand around his hot, hard length.

And her breath hissed through her teeth as his did the same.

"You're a very beautiful man," she said, trying to seem confident. Trying to seem like the sort of woman who absolutely knew what was going on and not like the inexperienced thirty-one-year-old virgin that she was, because that was ridiculous. And she felt sort of ridiculous.

And she did not want him to think that she was ridiculous.

And that was how she found herself being propelled backward onto the bed, her jeans and underwear removed in one fluid motion, before she had a chance to protest or process what was happening.

And she saw it. The moment he saw her. All of her. The mangled scar tissue that started at her pelvic bone and went down her thigh on the left side, curving around her calf. That whole leg had been completely mangled in the accident. Her bone had come through flesh.

And it showed.

The other side was bad off too, though the scar tissue was more a delicate webbing over different parts of her leg, rather than something wholly misshapen.

He didn't say anything. But he moved his hands over the scars, and she wanted to scream. Because nobody looked at them. Nobody touched them. She was the one who had to live with them, and she was the one who…who looked away when she saw her naked body in the mirror. Who tried never to look down at her legs. Who always wore long pants. Who would never wear a dress. She was the one who never showed her vulnerability. Not even to herself. And here he was, looking and touching like he had every right. And it made her shiver. With need, with desire, with every single thing that she hadn't wanted to feel for all these years. What if he turned away from her?

Except, then, he put his hands on her knees and spread her legs roughly, and it wasn't her scars that he was looking at now. He lowered his head, nuzzling her inner thigh, and she gasped.

"So damned beautiful," he said before burying his face in her legs and licking her deep.

A short, sharp sound escaped her lips and her hips lifted up off the bed.

She was consumed then with the everything of it all. That hot swipe of his tongue, the masculine growl of desire, the fact that he didn't seem disgusted. He simply seemed consumed. And so was she. She let her head fall back as he pleasured her. And this was so different than being by herself. His tongue created a complex web of desire inside of her, and she cupped her own breasts, rubbing her thumbs over her nipples as he continued to pleasure her that way.

It was so good. So good. She rocked her hips restlessly in time with the pulse of pleasure created by his wicked tongue. And she wanted… She needed…

He pushed a finger inside of her, and then another, and she rippled, then shattered. And while her need was still pulsing inside of her, he took one of the condom packets and tore it open, rolled it over his hardened length. And then he thrust into her. She gasped, the unexpected tearing sensation jarring her out of her haze. A raw cry was torn from her lips, and she felt tears gathering in earnest at the corner of her eyes.

"Arizona?" Her name was a harsh question, but she shook her head, biting her lip.

"Please," she said. "Just... Please?"

He nodded, then grunted, thrusting deeper into her, and this time, it didn't hurt quite so much.

This time, she could feel pleasure building even as the pain receded. She wiggled her hips, and he began to move. And it was...everything.

She clung to his shoulders, nails digging into his skin, and she looked up, her eyes meeting his. And she was seen. Utterly and completely. And there were no walls. There was nothing. Nothing but him. So close... Inside of her. And she was a fool.

Because all of her defenses crumbled. Every last one.

She shattered, and he called out her name.

And in the end, it was the two of them, sweat-slicked and clinging to one another.

And Arizona couldn't breathe.

"Arizona... Do you want to tell me about all this?"

And Arizona did what she did best. She rolled out of bed, and she got ready to run away.

CHAPTER TWELVE

HE COULD SEE IT. He could feel the withdrawal. The distance. But he wanted to know. He wanted to know what had happened. The scars, and... Why she had been a virgin. A virgin. He couldn't even handle that. How was it that after all these years...

And her skin spoke of trauma. Her behavior spoke of trauma. And she hadn't shared it with him. He hadn't known. He wanted to know.

"Don't do it," he said. "Don't run from me. You came this far. Tell me." She said nothing. She bent down to start to collect her clothes, and his eyes followed the curving, biting marks along her lower back, her ass, her side. "Arizona."

"Don't," she said. "You don't get to demand my story."

"No. I'm not demanding it. You damn silly girl, I am asking you to share yourself with me because I care. Because I care about you. Because I am the first man that you've... done this with. Because I can see that you've been hurt... And I want to know... I want to know everything."

"What good does it do? What good would it do if they all knew that this was how I looked? That this is what happened to me. That it's never gonna get any better. What good would it do. Just easier to keep people at arm's length. It's easier to keep them away. It's easier because..."

"Arizona," he said, his voice rough. "I want to know.

More. All of it. It isn't to gawk at you. It's because I want to know you. I want to know what hurts you, sweetheart. I want to know you."

"You're leaving," she said. "What fucking good does it do, Micah? What good would it ever do? You left me. You left me, and my life fell apart. I loved you," she said, her voice vibrating with conviction. "I loved you. I gave you my first kiss. I gave you everything. I loved you. And you thought that you did me a favor by not having sex with me. As if that was the thing that protected me. But you let me love you and then you left me. I told you how difficult things were with my dad. I shared with you how I felt alone sometimes, and how difficult it was for me…without my mother. Without everything. You knew that. You were the only person who ever did, and then you left. You left me," she repeated. "And it hurts. It hurts so damned badly, Micah. There was no one here to save me and I had to save myself."

"Sweetheart. I did not want to leave you. I didn't want to hurt you."

"You did. You did. I was broken. I was broken. I went driving down the highway too fast, sobbing my eyes out at night…"

"I caused you to have an accident."

"Yes," she said, the venom in her words hard and angry. "You did. You did this to me. You broke me, and then broke me even more. And I am ruined. And I keep it hidden from everybody. Because I don't want them to feel sorry for me. Because I'm pitiable. I fell apart and I got stitched back together. My body was broken. My insides were falling out of me. I… I'll never get over that. I'll never get over it. I nearly died. And I don't even know how to cry about it or feel anything about it. Because I'm just supposed to be grateful that I'm okay. And everybody thinks that I healed. But nobody knows what I look like. Nobody knows that I carry around all this stuff."

He knew enough about her family to guess that if one of them put up walls…no one would try too hard to get over them. They seemed to take emotional distance to a new level.

And that would leave Arizona alone in her pain.

"I know," he said. "And I want to know more. I'm so sorry. I'm so…"

"Don't. I didn't want to be pitied, and I didn't want to explain myself. What I wanted, all I wanted, was to rip this damned Band-Aid off. You were supposed to fuck me back then and you didn't. I would've been prettier. So now you had to fuck me messed up."

"I don't think you're messed up."

"That's where you're wrong. I'm hella messed up. And there's no fixing it. I don't want this. All these feelings. I can never give you that. I can never give you me. Not ever again. You don't deserve it. You don't deserve it." She dressed, covering her scars. But he felt them. Burned into his soul.

He felt the consequences of her knowing him all those years ago burrow beneath his skin and make him sick.

This was his fault. In so many ways, this was his fault.

"Arizona…"

"Fuck off," she said. And then she gathered all her things, and ran out of the cabin.

She didn't take his truck. She just ran.

And he was left with shattered glass were his heart used to be.

CHAPTER THIRTEEN

She did what she did. She ran. She was so good at this. At venom. At anger.

About half a mile from the cabin she collapsed. Fell onto the ground and just started to cry.

Because telling the story of her accident had opened up all those scratchy old wounds. Not the ones on her body. The worst ones. The ones in her heart. The ones in her soul.

How much she had loved him and how much it had hurt. How terrifying it had been. The way her dad had looked at her in the hospital bed.

"Stupid move. Could've gotten yourself killed. Would've been your own stupid fault."

She hadn't deserved to complain. Hadn't deserved to cry. Because it was *her fault*. And he was right. So she'd gotten angry instead. At everyone.

"Don't expect pity because you're a cripple." Her dad said that once when she was still recovering. Limping. It was why she put so much effort into never showing pain even if her old injuries did hurt her.

He wasn't cruel. That was the thing. He had always been there, he didn't hit people, not like the patriarch of the McCloud family. Hadn't abandoned them when they were kids like the father in the Sullivan clan.

No. He had been there. His words a dagger that had ground her inadequacy soul deep. She had learned to push back. To create a barrier around herself so that she wouldn't be quite so raw.

He hadn't had the decency to hit them with his fists. To leave marks on their skin. He'd just left them on their souls. Made it so they were so battered they couldn't *feel* right. Not anymore.

And then Daniel... That sweet boy. Daniel was here, and she had connected with him. And Micah was here and she... She wanted him.

It made her want to be soft. It made her want to be different. But she was afraid that it was too late. And wasn't that the most unfair thing. And it was impossible. It was all impossible. Because this was the only thing she knew how to do. She didn't know how to soften. She didn't know how to let her guard down. She didn't know how.

"Arizona."

She looked up, and he was standing there.

"What are you doing out here?"

"I made a mistake all those years ago. I left you. And I never should've left you. I was misguided. I wanted to do the right thing for my son. In the end, what I was actually trying to do was make something that looked like normal. Because I didn't have it growing up. So I thought it was what I had to do. It didn't make me happy. It didn't make him happy. I thought about calling. I thought about trying to explain myself to you. But the bottom line is, I was afraid you would be disappointed in me. I really was. I was afraid that you wouldn't want to be with a man who'd made that kind of a mistake. Had a kid with somebody else. Especially while I was here falling for you. I was ashamed. I figured you were here having a better life. I'm sorry. I'm sorry that I was one of the people that hurt you. I am sorry that everything has been hard."

"It's impossible. You have a ranch in Texas, and Daniel's mother is there and…"

"I would be happy to be here part of the year. Because I love you. Because I love you and I want to make it work. Because I never forgot you. Because I think I did love you all this time. Because when I told Daniel about this ranch and the way that it changed me, what I really meant was you. What I really meant was you all this time."

"But I'm… I'm really mean. My scars aren't even the worst of the problem at this point. I don't know how to connect with people, and sometimes I feel all this anger rising up inside of me and I…"

"I want to work on that with you. Through it with you. If you want to talk to somebody… A professional… I want to support you in that."

"Are you suggesting that I get therapy?"

"Yeah. I am. I've had it. Because I wanted to be there for Daniel in the best way that I could be, and I needed to work out some stuff. There's no shame in that."

"My dad would say that there's a lot of shame in it."

"Your dad should feel a lot of shame in the way that he's let things get with his own children. And that's the simple truth of it. He should be ashamed. Not you. Never you."

"I'm scared," she said. "Because I only know how to be alone."

"Let me teach you how to be with someone. Let me prove to you that I'll be there for you."

"I want that," she said. "I want to…heal."

"I love you," he said. "It doesn't matter that we were apart all that time. I've never loved anyone else."

"I love you too," she whispered. "I let all that love turn to acid. And I let it eat me. And it didn't do me any good. It didn't protect me from anything."

"Now I'm here to protect you. You can be soft with me. Vulnerable with me. I will never misuse that again."

And she wanted to believe it. So she did. Because she was just so desperately tired of all of this. She wanted to be different. She wanted to be new. With him.

"Okay."

WHEN HE CALLED Lacey with his proposition, she threw a tantrum. But after a mediation session with family court over video call and consultations with the lawyer, and promises of payment supports continuing, they were able to strike a deal. Daniel wanted to stay in Oregon most of the time. And they agreed that during the school year they would be here, and he would go to the one-room school, and continue to work on the ranch, and during the summer they would go back to Texas, where Micah would check in on his ranch, and Daniel and Lacey could get some visiting time. Arizona would come right with them.

It wasn't a conventional family. That was what he'd wanted. But it was happy. And he realized that he would take happy and unconventional and full of love over normal every time.

It did take a while for Arizona to let her guard down. Completely anyway.

But they moved into a house on the property, and Daniel loved her. And settled right into seeing her as a maternal figure. Finally, she agreed to marry him. And when she did, it was the happiest day of his life.

Back all those years ago, their love had seemed impossible. And now it was just their life. Their life, full of love. And there might've been a detour to get here.

But Arizona King had been worth the wait.

* * * * *